THE LOVE OF THE DARK ONES

WHAT IS IT THAT DRAWS the undead to the shores of the living? Life—the blood that sustains us. They can't resist it.

Werewolves are bad, but vampires are the worst scavengers of all. They're dead while we're still hanging on to this world, and there's that unholy attraction in between. It warps the circle, and any person with even a touch of the Gift can smell a vampire a mile away.

Even a kid like me.

Convincing regular folks that they're in danger is something else again.

NIGHT CALLS

KATHARINE ELISKA KIMBRIEL

HarperPrism
An Imprint of HarperPaperbacks

Portions of this novel have been published in slightly different form elsewhere:

"Night Calls" appeared in *Werewolves*, edited by Jane Yolen and Martin Greenberg. Anthology © 1988 by Jane Yolen and Martin Greenberg, story © 1988 by Katharine Eliska Kimbriel.

"Night Calls" was reprinted in *Amazing*, September 1992. Copyright remains with the author.

"Triad" appeared in *The Magazine of Fantasy and Science Fiction*, © 1991 by Katharine Eliska Kimbriel.

HarperPaperbacks *A Division of* HarperCollins*Publishers*
10 East 53rd Street, New York, N.Y. 10022

Cover photographs by Photonica/Steve Edson and Photonica/Michael Gesinger.

First printing: May 1996

Printed in the United States of America

HarperPrism is an imprint of HarperPaperbacks.
HarperPaperbacks, HarperPrism, and colophon are trademarks of HarperCollins*Publishers*

❖ 10 9 8 7 6 5 4 3 2 1

ONE

I WASN'T THERE WHEN Papa killed the wolf. But then girls usually aren't allowed to hunt them.

This was an ongoing argument in our household, the hunting thing, and that night was no different. As always, I lost. Promises to stay back, demonstrations of stealth, even stories of bravery while wringing chicken necks— nothing worked. Papa may boast that I'm eleven going on forty, but I'm the only daughter; that means burping babies and grinding wheat instead of fun things like tracking critters.

It was worse when Dolph and Josh came back, laughing and shouting, covered with blood, stumbling over their words as they both tried to tell Momma what had happened. I was by the fireplace stirring the soup when they came in, and I kept my back to them while they told their story.

"And then when we chased him out of Faxon's sheep pen—"

"First we had to send for the surgeon, for his little girl—"

"Boys, you're bleeding!" Momma finally said weakly, lifting a kettle of hot water from a pot hook swinging above the burning logs.

"It's just sheep's blood, Momma, don't worry," Josh said quickly, brushing at his coat and starting up the kitchen stairs. "That ol' wolf only got a few snaps off before Papa ran him through with his spear."

I couldn't resist a smile; Josh's voice always squeaked when he got excited. He might have two years on me, but I'm a *lot* older than he.

"Papa was great. Everyone else was millin' around swinging torches at it, but Papa just charged right in. Stuck that ash spear right through the wolf and pinned him to the ground." Dolph got to the heart of the story, as always. "He thrashed a long time," Dolph added thoughtfully, moving to the basin of water Momma poured for him. "Snagged a few people, but nothin' too bad. He sure chewed that little girl up early on, though."

"Never heard of a wolf going after a person," I muttered, giving the soup another swish before moving to pull Papa's wine crock from the ashes.

"Shows you haven't heard everythin', doesn't it?" Josh hollered from above.

"I haven't, either," Dolph started, taking my part like he always did.

"She's right," came Papa's voice. We all looked up, and there he was, standing tall at the wooden door, dark stains blotching his worn breeches and shirt. "Wolves don't usually bother people. That one might've been sick. You boys get some sundew infusion from your momma and pour it all over your arms and legs. I saw you touching its mouth—didn't you think? You know animals carry the foaming sickness in their spit."

"We didn't get nipped, Papa," Dolph protested. "We were careful."

"How about the cuts and scratches you got working in the field today?"

Well, Dolph didn't have an answer for that, of course, so Momma made me steep some sundew. She practically made them bathe in it, but they were acting like it was nothing, and not scrubbing very hard.

When I finally brought Papa his wine, I couldn't resist asking what he'd done with the wolf.

"Strung it up by the leg in a tree, darling," he said, sipping slowly at the warm liquid. "The coat's owed to the kill, so I'll get it tomorrow."

"Can I help?" Stupid to ask, I knew, but I wanted to help so *bad*.

Papa studied me over the rim of his cup, his sky-blue eyes gleaming in the soft light. "A lot of blood and gore, skinning a wolf," he said finally.

"I'm not afraid of a dead wolf," I declared.

"Bet a live one would'a spooked you," came Josh's scornful voice as he stomped down the oak stairs to get some dinner.

"Not Allie," Dolph said quickly, smiling at me.

I grinned back at him and then scowled at Josh. "I'm not scared of no wolf! At least not with a spear by me." Turning back to Papa, I added under my breath, "There's lots of things scarier than an old wolf."

"'Any wolf,' Allie, not 'no wolf.'" Papa's words were gentle. He didn't scold the boys much, but he always corrected me. He smiled then, and reached to tug on one of my braids. "Ripe as wheat, you are, child, and not just your long locks. You can help me skin the wolf, if you do your chores first—"

"Oh, I will! I will!" I nearly upset the wine, tossing my arms around him, but Papa just laughed and hugged me. Momma started in right away, of course, but he waved her off.

"Child's old enough to help with the pelts this winter, Garda. No sense waiting until the snow flies. She'll be fine with me, and Dolph's old enough to supervise the harvest."

I danced back to the soup pot, and when Papa told the boys he needed them in the hay fields, not *watching* him and me skin a varmint, well, I'm sure I started floating. Let Josh watch little Ben and Joe! I was gonna skin me a wolf.

The sunrise was patched like a red 'n' gold quilt, but I didn't pay it no mind. I was up in the dark, collecting eggs by feel and setting the milk out to wait the cream rising. Momma shooed me away and said she'd get it—that was her way of apologizing for last night. She doesn't like things like wolves and bears; that sort of thing scares her. But she doesn't want to make me frightened for no reason—I heard her tell a neighbor that once.

"Watch your step out there, Alfreda," she said by way of parting. "There's more between heaven and earth than any man knows, I'll tell you." I must have looked as confused as I felt, because she waved me off, her worn, pale face looking a little disgusted. "Get me some onions and garlic from the garden on your way back!"

And so I was free. There was nothing like walking through the long yellow grass, following the golden shadow that was my father. People always said Dolph and I were like him, both in looks and manner, and it was a compliment. He was the smartest man in our village. Even smarter than Father John, I thought, although Momma was always running to the priest. I don't think Papa's family ever had any use for gods. But if gods helped Momma more than the oldest ways, that was all right with Papa. "Whatever works"—that's what he always said.

"Do you think something ate the wolf, Papa?" I called as I tried to keep up.

"Hope not, child. A wolf pelt is worth a lot. We should be in time, the sun's just rising." His deep voice carried easily through the underbrush, although I'd lost sight of him.

"How much farther?" I asked, catching my cotton dress on an ash shoot.

"Not f— Alfreda, stay where you are."

I stopped tugging on my dress. His tone would have warned me that something was wrong, even if he hadn't used my full name. A bear? I waited, silent, for him to call, all the while carefully unhooking my clothes.

There was a thunk as his ax bit into wood, and the sound of something heavy falling. The grunt surprised me—had he tried to break the wolf's fall? I crept toward the clearing.

"Papa—" Before the word was out I froze, as motionless as a stone. The sweet smell of blood tickled my nose, and something queasy began churning in the depths of my stomach. Somewhere off in the distance was the sound of a beautiful birdsong, one I'd never heard before. Blood and song—it was almost more than I could bear without weeping.

He looked up from the twisted carcass before him, his face set and gray. "I told you to wait." No anger; his very lack of emotion frightened me.

"I . . . I heard you, like you needed help," I started, not sure if I should keep walking or hold my ground.

He made an abrupt gesture that drew me to his side. We both stared down at the torn and bloody lump of flesh and black fur, slashed by dog and steel.

It was a man. At least I thought it was . . . it certainly wasn't a wolf. But it was hairier than any man I'd ever seen, even the palms and soles of the feet; and the teeth seemed wrong. I was sure I'd never seen him before. For a moment I felt faint—how could my father have made such a mistake? *It was a full moon last night, you could see for miles—*

Then I understood, and I started to tremble. I'd heard tales about wolves that weren't really wolves. . . .

I felt my father reach for me, his hands tightening on my arms as he pulled me away from the thing. "This goes no further, girl. Not to your mother, and certainly not to your brothers—not even Dolph."

"But—" I started.

"We don't know whom we can trust, child. Do you see? I know someone was bitten last night—maybe more than one—but we'll never be able to find out quickly if we announce it. He might even run, like this fellow did, and plague some other community." Papa broke off then and turned from me, surveying the bloody scene. I kept my face turned toward the sunrise; the werewolf looked too much like a man, and that worried me. Finally Papa fumbled in his pocket and pulled out his pipe. Sitting down on a fallen log, he worked his flint several times before the tobacco caught fire.

We shared a long silence while the wind picked up and the sun crept through the undergrowth. I sat down beside him, grateful that we were upwind of the thing, and waited while he did his thinking. A man. That bloody mess had once been a man. Grandsir had died quietly in his bed—no blood, no pain that I could see. A man shouldn't die in a field far from home with an ash spear through his heart. . . . Shivering, grateful summer was not yet gone, I finally grew brave enough to ask a question.

"Would . . . would the church be able to help?"

Papa didn't answer at first, only chewed his pipe stem. After a while he said, "No, Allie. Exorcism's no good for werewolves. There are things both old and new that can help, though. . . ." He reached for my collar and tugged on the chain around my neck. I wore the metal cross of Momma's god, a tiny silver thing, the most valuable possession I owned. "Good. Keep it with you always, even when you sleep. Now, I need you to go get me something. Garlic. Enough to fill a hole, oh, this big." He demonstrated, making a circle with his arms. "Be quick, now, and remember—this goes no further."

Nodding, I practically flew to my mother's garden. I didn't know much about werewolves, but I did know you had to do special things when you buried them—or they didn't *stay* buried. Fortunately garlic masters night things; it both controls them and keeps them at bay. Momma devotes an entire plot to the stuff. I rooted busily in the rows, pulling up handfuls of bulbs and scooping them into my apron. Folks outside might've thought that night creatures were only bogey stories, but back here in the hills we knew better.

As I turned to start back to the clearing, I heard Momma calling me. "I'm still helping Papa!" I hollered, not stopping to hear her question. There was no way to get back to him fast enough. I sure hoped he knew how to keep the werewolf from rising again at sunset. The thought of the walking dead froze my heart.

He'd been busy while I was gone. I made sure not to look too close. The head was separate from the body, and Papa carefully stuffed some garlic in its mouth. He'd cut a piece from the ash copse, too, and driven it through the chest. Then we started to gather firewood.

It takes a long time to burn a body. We covered half our faces with scarves and stayed the course, but I will remember that smell until I die. The sun rose high above us, and still the fire raged on. I tended it carefully, watching for stray cinders, while Papa cut several thick branches from the ash copse. By the time the reeking blaze had dwindled into coals, Papa had peeled and sharpened three good stakes. The sight made me shiver, so I concentrated on locating the wolf-man's ashes.

Werewolves burn clean—there wasn't a single chip of bone left. That surprised me, since the fire hadn't been *that* hot, but Papa had left to get something, so I kept silent. Before long he returned with a wooden bucket and a shovel.

We took every speck of those wolf ashes to the crossroads by Faxon's farm. I carried the rest of the garlic in my apron and dragged the stakes. Papa dug a real deep hole right down in the center of the road. He set the entire bucket inside it, and had me dump the garlic on top. It was a shame to see that fine bucket, garlic spilling down its sides into the dirt, because I knew Papa was going to bury it, too.

"Only ash slat bucket I ever made, child. No better use for it," he remarked, as if reading my mind. After smoothing some dirt over it, we laid stones on top, and finally packed the rest of the dirt down tight, so the road looked clean once more. Papa took the stakes from me, and we started for the house.

For once I appreciated those special looks Papa and Momma could exchange, because Momma never asked to see the wolf skin, and she didn't scold when I forgot the onions. Dolph and Josh asked, of course—Dolph told me he wanted to buy it from Papa for that girl he's sparking—but Papa told them it was too tore up to save, and they believed it. I don't think I ever heard Papa lie before or since that night. He did make the older boys scrub with sundew again, and stood over them to see they did it right. Him and me too, though I never even touched the werewolf.

We were ready for supper when one of the neighbors stopped by. Papa went outside to talk, and was shaking his head when he came back into the kitchen.

"Eldon?" Momma said, and her voice quivered, as if she didn't really want him to answer.

"Faxon's little girl died," he said quietly, sitting down at our big chestnut table.

My mother gasped and put her hand to her breast. "The poor man! Both wife and child gone before the year's old."

That's when I almost messed up everything.

"It was a blessing." Like always, I was muttering; and like always, Momma heard me.

"Alfreda, whatever do you mean?" Momma was both sharp and astonished. I saw the intense look Papa was giving me and tore through my head for something to say.

"Isn't that what you always say, Momma? That God loves us; and that when bad things happen, there's a reason for it, even if we don't know it?" I feared it was awkward, but she seemed to accept my twisted reasoning. She was silent several moments before she told me not to say it in front of little Ben and Joe. Then the only sound was of Dolph drinking still another glass of water.

I didn't eat much . . . all I could taste was iron and ashes.

TWO

THE MONTH OF FRUIT wore into Vintage, and nothing happened.

But I could hear them.

Late at night the wind brought their voices to me, shrieking a nameless agony. What did it feel like to be slowly descending into madness, into terror? I had no proof that there was anything to fear, for no one else mentioned the strange calling of the wind. Deep inside I held my breath, while on the surface the harvest occupied every waking hour. Hay was followed by corn, and finally wheat, rye, barley, and oats. For an entire moon we did nothing but cut and stack grain. Last of all we sowed fallow fields with winter wheat.

Papa must've told some of the men about the body, the few he was sure of, because it seemed as if someone was stopping by every evening, "on rounds," as they would say. Momma knew things without being told; she started getting edgy and was upset whenever little Ben and Joe strayed too far from the house. Her fears were foolish, and Papa told her so . . . although I don't think he told her *why*. After all, it's at night when werewolves prowl. But that didn't help Momma.

Then the nights of the full moon came, and Andersson's baby disappeared, and everybody knew.

Momma was hysterical. I didn't get to see the tracks

until the next afternoon; she wouldn't let any of us out of her sight. But we knew more than anyone else, because they came to talk it over in our kitchen.

"At least three," said my friend Idelia's father, accepting Papa's offer of spiced wine.

"I think it's four," my father responded, shaking his head slightly. "And we all know who one of them is."

No one spoke for several moments. I couldn't believe it—Andersson's baby dead, and no one had anything to say? Papa saw the look on my face, but he didn't tell me to get back up the stairs. Josh and the babies were already up there, and Dolph was hiding in the stillroom behind the kitchen. Everyone who had gone on that hunt was afraid . . . afraid of what others were thinking.

"His father is bringing him over," Papa continued. "He's a frail lad, not made for such evil. They found him out by the well this morning, trying to slake his thirst. But no blood on him. He didn't kill the baby; the others are stronger-willed than he."

"Do you think he can tell us anything, Eldon?" someone asked.

Papa chewed on his pipe for a time, and finally shrugged. "I've heard they remember little beyond the transformation. But he may know something. Now—a skinny boy he may be, but he'll grow. So, what are we to do?"

By the time there was a knock at the door, the werewolf's fate had been decided. I had been so surprised to see little Tate and his father coming up the road that I almost missed what happened next.

They'd made a seat for him by the fire, and they had him sit down. He was practically in tears, poor Tate, and not making a lot of sense. His father looked so pale, so old, I didn't know which one I felt for most.

"We aren't going to kill you, lad," my father said

softly, and then Tate started crying. "The old Gustusson place has a barn; still solid, the doors sound. It will be your home three nights a moon. Down by the big water, in Cantev Way, they've had a werewolf some fifteen years. Has a wife and family. But they lock him up tight when need be, and so we shall with you. But we need your help, Tate. What can you tell us about last night?"

I almost fell off my stair, I leaned forward so far. But Papa's fears were right—Tate remembered almost nothing. "Tired," he kept saying. "I was so tired, but I couldn't stop running, none of us could. And the thirst, the terrible thirst . . ." He looked thirsty as he said it, and my father gave him a wooden cup full of water. Tate downed it without looking at it—he still stared at the men, as if afraid they would change their minds.

They didn't. Several of them escorted him to the barn where he would spend the night, and I knew a few would guard. The folks of Sun-Return would heed the lesson of Cantev Way. Tate was craving living flesh, fighting a thirst that would not die . . . a thirst blood could not satisfy.

I didn't creep downstairs until after Papa showed the last of them out. "Now what?" I asked quietly. After all, next to Papa, I knew more about taking care of problem werewolves than anyone else in town.

"Nothing," came my mother's brisk voice as she brought in a basket of vegetables. Her eyes settled on the lone cup among the emptied mugs of wine. Without comment she picked it up and threw it into the fireplace. "You leave werewolves to your father. I want you to keep a tight eye on Joe and Ben, day and night, and keep everyone inside all you can. We must seal the house against them, and the barn too—they'll go after stock when decent folks are abed."

Papa had a thoughtful look in his eyes, but he said

only, "I'll get mustard seed for the windows and doorways. We'll need garlic boughs as well. Help your mother,
Allie." And then he turned and went out to the barn.

Everyone in town was home by moonrise, I suppose,
although first Dolph and the others his age went to the
barn dance held by that couple wedded in the spring. No
one wanted to be, well . . . uncounted . . . between sunset
and sunrise. I went to bed in the tiny upstairs room with
a feeling of apprehension. The old oak tree scratching the
side of the house sounded like claws at the door, and the
wind seemed to carry voices to me, speaking words in a
language I did not know.

I could hear them.

Others might say it was a pack of real wolves, but real
wolves never sounded so desperate, not in the fat month
of Vintage. The werewolves were out, I was sure, their
number lessened but their strength untouched. After all,
Tate was a child, barely Josh's age, and no loss to their pack.
Though a sick wolf Tate's size could be dangerous . . .
Still, a werewolf can beguile, it is said, and that is the true
danger.

I could hear them calling.

I snuggled into the bedclothes and blew out my candle.

We found out early that Tate was dead. Died in a fall, the
men at the barn said. In a frenzy to be free, he had
climbed into the loft to try to force the hay doors, and
had fallen through an open hay chute. Papa told Momma
that he had broken his neck, and Momma said it was a
blessing, though she cried when she said it.

"How many sons will die?" she murmured as she
passed, but she did not speak to me.

There wasn't anything to say. I was wondering the
same thing.

• • •

Vintage moved into Fog, and Fog into Frost. Harvest was past; Momma brewed her solstice beer. Still a silver cross hung above our door. The men had no luck catching any of the remaining werewolves, but they discovered a chilling thing . . . the werewolves were not bound to the full moon.

"Sometimes it happens, Allie," Papa explained when I asked. "Especially when the person doesn't choose to be a werewolf."

"You can choose to be one?" I could tell by the amused expression on his face that my eyes were getting big, so I tried to squint.

"Those who deal with witchy people can," Papa answered, tapping his pipe with his finger. "Legends say that witches could use magic so a person would be a werewolf during a full moon, yet retain a grip on sanity. Only silver could kill one of those creatures. Turns out that when it's passed like a disease, there are many ways to rid yourself of werewolves—ash wood, and burning, and such."

I handed him his tobacco pouch so he'd keep talking. As he paused to relight his pipe, I whispered, "What binds them, if not their own will?"

"The phases of the moon, Allie. They start to change whenever the hunger comes upon them. The closer to the full moon, the more wolflike they become. We must be as kind as we can, daughter, even if we must kill, for this is not of their making."

We sat in silence for a time, just Papa and me. Momma doesn't sit by the fire like she used to—I think she's afraid something will come down the chimney, although I hung garlic over the mantel. She's always giving me funny looks lately. And Papa doesn't call me "child" anymore. I often wonder if they hear the wolves calling on the night breeze . . . if they hear what I hear.

I had a terrible nightmare that night. It was about Dolph's friends, the couple who got married in the spring. They were in their bed; it was dark outside, yet I could see them in their bed. Only the quilt was black, as if soaked with blood, as if someone had died a-birthing. Her throat and chest were bloody, but only his arms, I could see only his black arms—

It was Momma holding me when I woke up, trying to soothe me, but I couldn't be calmed. My heart was pounding and my breath coming quick, like when Idelia and I raced from the schoolhouse to the well. It was so real, as if I had been in the room. I kept telling her that, kept trying to tell her about the dream, but she kept putting her fingers over my mouth so I couldn't talk.

"Enough, Garda." Papa was there, by my door. "You can't keep her young forever, and you knew it might come to her."

"No! No, I won't allow it! Why do you think I had her baptized? Eldon—"

"But if it is truly a gift, woman, then God should value it as much as we do." I heard the rustle of thatch, and knew Papa was sitting on the end of my bed. "It's all right, Allie. Tell me what you saw."

So I told them. Both of them—Momma stayed for the whole thing, her body hard as wood against mine. When I finished, I heard Papa stand once more.

"I should go get Faxon."

Momma threw herself away from me, leaping to her feet. "Not until morning! The moon lit the room for her dreaming, and it's already low. Eldon, he's already killed her—"

"And he's still part wolf, Garda. Have pity. Better he die now than come to his senses over her body. I will take both ash and silver."

Something in his words must have calmed her, because Momma finally let him leave, though she clung to him a time. Then she gently tucked me in, like when I was little, and told me to sleep myself out, she'd see to the chickens. It seemed a long time before I finally heard her walk back down the narrow hall to the stairs. Sleep was forever coming, because I had lots to think about. Strange dreams, strange words, strange looks . . . For the first time I realized that Momma was afraid for me. But I didn't understand why.

I could still hear them calling.

By the time I woke the next morning, there were only two werewolves left. Something else had also changed . . . Papa wasn't going hunting anymore. None of the other men seemed upset with him or anything—he was just no longer expected to hunt werewolves. I heard one of them say, "You're needed to guard what's under your roof," but it didn't make any sense.

Nerves grew tighter as the full moon loomed near. Papa and the older boys set up the trap line, and I learned to prepare beaver skins and stretch them properly. It was hard, messy work, but Momma made it look easy, so I knew I could learn it, too, if I kept trying.

Our root cellar and egg bin were full to bursting, so we stuck close to home when the morning finally came upon us. Up before sunrise, I found the family already busy with chores. Papa was out checking traps while Josh worked by the fireplace, tightening the snowshoes. It was in the air, the snow. It would make tracking the were-wolves easier. . . .

"Take your brother some fever tea, Allie," Momma called from the front room where she was bathing the younglings before the fire. "He's out in the cold storage."

Still yawning, I filled a stone crock with whatever Momma had brewed and rushed it out to the shed. Dolph was there, all right, knee-deep in beaver and mink, covered with blood from the skinning. He looked white and pasty in the dim morning light, and suddenly I was worried. Idelia had the fever, and I couldn't bear it if Dolph had it, too.

"Here." I thrust the pot at him. "Momma says have some tea." Sometimes I'm so stupid; Momma must have noticed how he looked the night before.

He moved the lid aside and took a few gulps, and then twisted away as his stomach turned over.

"Dolph?" I knew he heard the fear in my voice.

"I'm all right!" It was almost belligerent. His eyes already had the touch of fever in them. Bad, real bad—a full moon was on the rise, and no doctor would come to the house during the full moon, maybe not even during the day.

"You should rest, you've probably got what Idelia has," I started, noticing how sloppily he was taking pelts. More like me or Josh than his usual skill. I'd have to tell Papa.

"Git, Allie. I can finish my work."

I knew that tone. I got. I took the side trek, around the house, since the path was windward, and as I shuffled through the gloom, I saw a curious thing. Green shoots peeping up from the loose dirt by the house, barely showing, already withered. I bent to examine the sprouts. Almost in response, a fantastic trill of notes floated from the woods beyond.

Garlic. *Thank you, little bird.* Frowning, I examined the entire side, the full length of the stillroom that doubled as Dolph's sleeping area. Momma would've told me if she had planted garlic over here; we would've made more of a shelter than this. I looked up, and realized

what it must be. The garlic above Dolph's window had
fallen. Some time ago, to judge by the length of the
shoots. Carefully uprooting the sprouts, I hid them under
my shawl and continued around to the door. No sense
telling Momma, she'd only get upset. Plenty of time to
hang more garlic before evening.

They got the third werewolf in the act of transformation.
I hadn't known him well—he was a widower, his children
grown, and he lived the far side of the settlement. But he
must have sensed what he was, or he wouldn't have lingered at the tavern until sundown. The men there tried to
get him into the storeroom, to lock him up, but he was
too crazy, and they had to kill him so he wouldn't bite
no— anyone. They came straight to tell Papa, and to ask
him if I'd figured out anything else.

Papa cut them off at that, and drew them away,
motioning for Momma to take me into the kitchen. We
left them in the front room and moved around to the
other side of the firewall. Josh had hidden himself
upstairs, and the little ones were asleep.

"Momma, what did they mean by—"

"Don't worry yourself, Alfreda," she said in her
mother voice. "It's nothing to fear."

"Hadn't you better tell me about it? Momma . . . am I
a werewolf or something?" I asked solemnly. After all, I
could hear the critters when no one else could.

She actually started laughing, although I could hear
hysteria behind it. "Dear God, no, daughter. Quite the
opposite."

And then she told me. Seems the folks in our family
often have what they call "the Gift"—of knowing things
no one has told them, and dreaming true dreams.
Momma's grandmother was the wizard of the village,

once, and everyone had depended on her advice. "They're hoping you're growing up the same way, what with your dream about the other night."

"But you're hoping I'm not." I wasn't sure she'd understand what I meant, but she did. Her slender face grew still, and she reached absently to tuck a long strand of dark hair behind her ear.

"I have some of it, daughter. It is a great burden. I fear the burden, which is why, I think, it comes rarely to me. I do not envy you. . . . I tried to protect you." This was very low. "I thought that if you didn't learn about the Wise Arts, they would never trouble you. I thought you'd be happier . . . not knowing." She sat studying the fire, almost unaware of me, as the voices of the men in the main room rose and fell like a bellowing trumpet of geese.

"Don't worry, Momma. I'll protect you." I said it with a smile, to try to coax one from her, but I meant it—I'm stronger than my mother, you see, in so many ways.

She sighed and reached for the kettle. "Drink some angelica tea, child. It's good for almost any ailment. I left some more next to Dolph's bed, before he threw me out." Shaking her head, she rose. "Just like his father; he has no use for nursing when he's sick. I shut the door to the still-room. We'll just leave him be, and call the doctor come morning if he's no better."

I realized I hadn't told Momma about Dolph throwing up the tea, but then Papa came in to speak to her, so I bent my head to my mug.

Somehow, somewhen, between a long draught of tea and a glance at the fire, something changed. The taste of crushed seeds lingered on my tongue, as if trying to tell me something. Tell me . . .

Angelica. The one herb that is proof against all forms of evil. Stray shards of thought came together in my mind to form a coherent whole. Angelica. Garlic. Thirst . . . My hands began to shake.

"Alfreda?" It was Papa. He hardly ever called me that; I turned slowly toward the sound of his voice, trying to see through a blur of tears. Bending one knee, he lowered himself to my level.

I waited for him to speak, but he did not. Finally my eyes cleared, and I met his steady gaze. It gave me the crawlies, that gaze, because it wasn't quite like it had ever been before. It was still my father looking out at me, but it was no longer a parent talking to a child. It was a man talking with his grown daughter.

Only a moment, and all things change forever . . .

"Alfreda, I must go with the others. To stop the last werewolf. The madness has set in, we think—he's been attacking wild animals, and that might spread the disease." Papa's eyes held mine, as if begging something from me. "I need you to take care of your momma and the little boys. Will you do that for me?"

He knew. And he knew I knew. He was so strong, I was ashamed at my weakness.

"Of course, Papa. I will take care of everything. Be careful." I reached to touch his arm, memorizing his face, afraid that something even worse might yet happen that night. "Don't let him suffer . . . anymore."

His hand was warm against my cheek as he rose. "I'll be back soon, Garda. Wait up for me, please." He reached to touch her lips lightly before turning to leave. Momma followed, to bar the door and drape the boughs of garlic securely.

I stood slowly, feeling the weight of my father's pain. Downing the rest of my tea, I set the cup aside and reached for the garlic braid I had made earlier. "Momma," I called, "I'm going to check the rest of the garlic and mustard seed."

"Thank you, Alfreda. I'll take care of the upstairs." She went past me and up the back stairs without comment, so swiftly that I wondered momentarily if she knew. But no—Momma feared the burden, so I would know for both of us now.

Checking the tightness of my weaving, I gave the braid a final tug and then reached for my father's chair. Not too heavy, fortunately, but heavy enough, so it was an effort to carry, not drag, it to the door between the kitchen and the makeshift back bedroom.

Standing on the chair, I listened a moment, scarcely breathing. But no . . . he had already left through the window.

I hung the bough of garlic over the stillroom door.

THREE

PAPA DIDN'T COME HOME till the gray light of morning was creeping through the eastern sky. I was sitting on my bed, both ears straining, but there was nothing to hear—the timbers beneath my split-oak floor were well chinked. Somehow I knew that if Dolph was still alive—if they'd been able to catch him—Momma would head for the kitchen to put a kettle on to boil. Having a werewolf for a son would take a lot of weeping and praying and sipping tea. But if the kitchen remained quiet . . .

I sat a long time, wrapped in my log-cabin quilt, waiting for a sign. I never could hear them going up the front stairs to their room, but I hadn't heard movement beneath me, either. And I'd left the door cracked, just to be sure. How long . . . ?

Too long. The silence was my answer. Slowly I unwrapped the quilt and reached for my leggings. Someone was going to have to start the oatmeal and dice the apples. That someone would have to be me.

As I crept down the hallway toward the back stairs, I could hear the outer door swing shut and the crunch of Papa's feet against the frosty grass.

I'd been wrong; not the silence but his heavy footsteps were my answer.

● ● ●

I don't like to remember the next few days. Momma crumpled like a dried oak leaf when Papa told her about Dolph. She kept to her bed and refused to see any of her friends. I kept us fed, just barely, and helped with the stock so we could keep running a trap line. Little Joseph spent most of his time crying in the hayloft or sitting at the foot of Momma's stairs. Ben surprised me—he stuck tight to my heels, one small hand clutching my long brown skirt. This made milking hard, but I didn't say anything to him. Having him close by was more of a comfort than I'd have liked to admit.

We kept busy, the five of us, in our own ways, to avoid speaking. That's probably why I didn't think anything of Papa's digging out the ink and sharpening a quill. He used up every scrap of paper we had laid by, scratching out letters. I didn't need to ask why. Family needed to be told, and my penmanship was nothing to be proud of. It was kind of him to spare Momma.

Aunt Dagmar, Momma's eldest sister, sent loaves of fresh bread and a round of sharp cheese to help tide us over, but her entire family was down with a fever, so she couldn't come in from town. She sent word that she'd written Aunt Sunhild to come help, but I wasn't sure what good that would do us—Aunt Sunhild lived a week away in *good* weather, and I had little doubt we'd already tipped into the dying time of the year.

It was a full two days into our grief before Ben finally broke his silence. He waited until he and I were alone in the kitchen before speaking.

"Allie?" His thin voice piped up from somewhere within the folds of my skirt. "When is Dolph coming back?"

Lord have mercy. Why hadn't he asked Papa, who might have had an answer for him? How did you tell a five-year-old that our brother wasn't coming home?

Would Ben believe me? *I* was having trouble believing. That was one of the problems with having no body to bury . . . something deep inside kept insisting there'd been a mistake, and Dolph would walk in any time.

But it wasn't the little voice speaking that had told me about the werewolves; this was simply a tiny whisper of anger, which popped out whenever I thought about Dolph being gone.

That wasn't special knowledge . . . that was just hope. And sometimes hope is misplaced.

I forked out the last of the pork sausages I had started for dinner and set them aside to drain. Grease into the jar, the pan wiped out to keep it seasoned . . . my mind cast round for *anything* I could use to help Ben understand. Finally my thoughts lit on something, and I took a deep breath. Wiping the cold sweat from my palms by rubbing them down my apron, I pulled up a stool and sat down. Ben curled up next to me, still wrapped in the fullness of my skirt.

I slipped an arm around him and pressed him close. "Dolph isn't coming back, Ben," I whispered. "Not ever."

"Why?"

I felt my face tighten as I winced. Here was my punishment for all those "whys" I had burdened Momma with, not so long ago.

"Because he's dead, Ben. When your body totally stops working, no breathing or anything, then you can't be alive anymore. That's the way things are supposed to be." No sense confusing him with tales of the living dead. I tried to think about what would worry him most.

"Life is a lot like a forest," I started out, glancing at Ben out of the corner of my eye. He was watching the fire, but I could almost see his ears straining my way. "There are acorns that become sapling trees, and trees in the prime of life, and finally old trees. All of them are a part of the forest—they all belong, and they all have their place in God's plan."

Here was where it got sticky. "To make sure the young trees have enough food and sunshine to keep growing, some of the older trees, especially those that have been sick a long, long time with something serious, have got to die." I moistened my lips and went on. "Well, usually only old and diseased trees die, but sometimes there will be a bad storm. And in a terrible storm, wind or lightning can destroy a strong young tree."

Ben shifted a bit, but he didn't speak. It wasn't an impatient movement, so I kept going. "Sometimes that happens in our lives. Usually it's the old or those who have been sick a long time who die—like Grandsir last year." Swallowing the sudden lump in my throat, I tried to keep my voice even. "But then there are accidents that come on folks like lightning from the sky. Young people can get hurt so badly that their bodies can't heal, no matter how much we try to help them. And when a body is hurt that badly, it finally stops working."

"Dolph's body doesn't work anymore?" The question was very quiet.

"Nope. It plumb stopped working. His soul has gone to be with God."

"What about his body?"

Good question. I felt my way through things. "Papa and some folks from town buried it, since Dolph doesn't need it anymore." Which had a lot of truth in it. Ben didn't need to know they'd burned the body first.

"Is Dolph with Grandsir in heaven?"

How could I tell him something I wasn't sure I believed in? "Wherever Grandsir is, I'm sure Dolph is with him," I said carefully.

Ben turned to face me then. "But we can't see Dolph again?"

I sighed. So much for storytelling. "Not for a long, long time, Ben. We'll probably be old before we go to heaven."

The boy's eyes filled with tears. "Will Dolph remember who we are?"

I felt myself get shaky, and a tear slipped down my cheek. "'Course he'll remember us, silly. Our souls will always recognize someone they've loved."

Ben started sobbing, clinging to my leg. I put my other arm around him and gripped him fiercely. We shared a good cry there on the kitchen hearth, and I think we were the better for it. After all, pain shared is pain halved.

That night I had a frightening dream. I was out in the woods, but it was pitch dark, except for some fitful moonlight fighting its way through the canopy. For some reason it felt like autumn to me, though I couldn't begin to tell you why. I was moving at a good clip, but staying pretty quiet for all that, dodging branches and bushes like I'd been practicing. My legs were sliding too easily, and it took a moment to figure out why. I was wearing boy's clothes! That surprised me so much I nearly woke up.

But then the fear hit. It was like the taste of blood in my mouth—sour and metallic all at once. My strength was draining into my stomach, and I was fighting to keep going, because my goal was in sight.

It was taking all my willpower not to panic, because it wasn't a big cat chasing me, or a sow bear, or even a twisty human. Whatever was chasing me held my life in its hands, and was ready to bite down. That simple.

Slick pebbles were under my feet, and I stumbled, splashing face-first into running water.

Suddenly I was bolt upright in bed, my heart slapping like a water wheel. Had I cried out? It had been so *real*!

Straining, I listened for any hint that the household had heard me. But no—the boys next door were silent, and it would have taken quite a ruckus to wake Momma or Papa.

Tugging on my feather pillow, I rearranged my bed into a warmer nest and buried myself once more within the quilts. Since I was in the dream, it couldn't be happening elsewhere . . . could it? That had been *me,* not someone whose eyes I was borrowing. Not me now, nor in the past . . . but the future?

It took a long time for me to get warm again. A long time.

The next morning, Papa announced that he had to go into town for a few things. Momma still hadn't budged, as far as I could see. Somewhere deep inside, I must have made a decision.

"May I go, too, Papa? I'll bundle up Ben and take him with me," I added quickly. "Josh and Joe can take care of things. Soup just has to simmer."

Papa gave me a long look as he tied his stack of letters together with a string. "I can ask after Idelia for you, daughter."

"It's not that." His eyebrows went up as I rushed on, "Father John should be in town today, since Mass is tomorrow. I wanted to talk to him about Momma, and about a memorial service."

I'd gotten his attention—he didn't reach for his overcoat. "Memorial service," Papa repeated.

"Yes, sir," I said with a nod. "The town needs something proper to finish this off, or it will chew at us until there's more damage done. Since Father John's only heard bits and pieces of this, I thought I'd make sure someone remembered to tell him the rest."

There was a long moment of silence, and then Papa murmured, "And a little child shall lead them." That sort of surprised me, since Papa didn't go to church, but I knew when to hold my tongue. Then he said, "That's a good thought, Allie. We'll do that. You get Ben wrapped while I hitch up Dancer." Only then did he reach for his coat.

I pulled on another sweater and my rabbit headband, and stuffed Ben into Joe's old jacket, with a knit hat on his head. I'd put on my navy wool dress, so that I'd look respectful to the dead, so all I needed was my old navy shawl. Grabbing one of the travel quilts for extra warmth, I hustled Ben out the door and up into the buggy.

We rode together in back, Ben and I, clutching each other under the quilt, and I envied Papa his heavy sheepskin coat with the wool turned inside. The ruts in the road were frozen solid, but the dark bay mare didn't put a foot wrong, flinging her hooves with her usual flair. The cloud cover weighed heavy above our heads, like rolls of dirty cotton, and the runoff ditches were lined with mirrors of ice. I could smell the snow coming, and hoped we'd beat it home.

The silence that clung to our homestead was echoed by the village of Sun-Return. A lone figure, well padded against the cold, was the only person in sight when we rolled up to Old Knut's general store. Papa pulled us both out of the quilt and quickly folded it up, like he was trying to trap some warmth in it. He nodded to Shaw Kristinsson, a slip of ice and black hair, as the boy came up to take Dancer's bridle, and the buggy moved across the street toward the big waiting area, where Shaw would throw a blanket on the mare and cool her down.

"I've got to see to these letters, Allie, and pick up some supplies," Papa told me. "You can go on ahead if you want, but it's probably warmer in Old Knut's store."

I looked down at Ben, who hadn't said much since our kitchen talk. "Do you want to stay, Ben?" I asked him.

His response was to tug at my hand. "I want to walk."

I managed a bit of a smile for Papa and said, "See you later!" Then I allowed Ben to pull me down the wooden sidewalk.

The community church was at the end of the street—not as far as it sounds, since there were only eight buildings in town, and that counted the stables. We rushed past the warm glow of the Kristinssons' boarding house and paused at the edge of the sidewalk. But there was no one coming on the cross road, so we took the street in a hurry, trying to avoid the mud softened by passing wagons. I could see lamplight at the church, so I knew someone was there.

The building we used for worship was a combination of framed wood and stone, with a real bell tower (although we couldn't afford a bell yet). There were enough Roman Catholics, Presbyterians, Lutherans, and Baptists for each congregation to have services once a month. That's because we shared our preachers with other villages. Since we were the biggest community for many miles, we got to hold our services on Sunday—not everyone was so lucky.

I pulled hard at the oak door, and it finally gave way. Ben slipped through first thing, of course, trying to help push from the other side, but I managed to keep from squeezing him in the crack. It's a pretty impressive entry, the door heavy enough that it pushed me into the vestibule as it closed behind me.

"Father John?" I said aloud, before it occurred to me he might be praying or something. And then I was pulled up short. Because it wasn't Father John up arranging things at the altar. It was a stranger.

He was fairly young, younger than Papa, though old

enough, I guess—I'd never thought about where priests got their training. A fair-skinned, blunt-featured man with a grim mouth. I'm not sure if it was shyness or instinctive caution that slowed me down, but Ben automatically grabbed for my hand. That should have told me something.

I took one step into the aisle and stopped. "Where's Father John?" I finally said, when I'd decided he was simply going to stare at me.

"Father John is very ill," the priest replied. "I am Father Andrew. I will be conducting Mass for him. Who are you, child?"

"I'm Alfreda Sorensson, and this is my brother Benjamin," I said politely. "I came to ask Father John if he would come to talk to my mother, and to find out about a memorial service."

"Memorial service?" The priest's dark eyebrows pulled together slightly, and I wondered if I was going to have to repeat myself on the subject all day.

"Yes, Father. We've been having some terrible trouble here in Sun-Return, and—"

"I heard," the man said abruptly, making a twisting motion with his hand that looked a lot like turning the evil eye. Which was odd . . . I would have figured him to cross himself or something.

"Yes, well, Sun-Return and its people need healing, and since most of the victims were Catholics, I thought that we could have the service this weekend."

I don't know what I expected him to say, but I certainly didn't expect him not to say anything. Ben was hugging my legs, like he was cold, and I wondered that the priest hadn't invited us behind the railing, where the stove was lit.

"Father John already buried the Andersson baby, and the young woman was not of our faith," the priest finally said.

"Yes, but I mean a memorial service," I said patiently. "Something to make people in town feel better, and help us set our faces toward the future. My brother and Stannes and Mr.—"

"When souls have been lost, it is better not to speak of it, lest we also fall," Father Andrew said, his tone abrupt. This time he did cross himself, his dark hair shaking with the vigor of his motion.

"Well, since we can't know for sure, can't we—"

"They died without rites." The man's voice was without inflection, and that really bothered me. "Their sins were not forgiven. There is no hope of heaven."

I purely hadn't thought of it that way, so it was my turn to stare. After a while, I said, "I'm not asking you to say anything that's untrue. All we need is a memorial service so people can get their grieving properly started. I know my momma needs something like that."

"I will be speaking tomorrow about how all true Christians may avoid the taint of hell." This was in that Sunday-go-to-meeting voice.

If I'd been thinking clearer, I would have kept my mouth shut. But Papa's words about the whole business being not of their own will came back to me, and sound just rolled past my lips. "If you've gone out to kill a sick wolf to keep it from hurting livestock and neighbors, how can you guarantee you won't be bit?"

The priest blinked—once, firmly, as if surprised I'd spoken. "If a true believer wraps himself in sanctity, his soul will be free from corruption," Father Andrew said calmly, settling into his instruction stance.

"Of course—but that won't protect your body. Doesn't the Lord expect us to take as good care of ourselves as we can? Not to tempt heaven, or some such thing?" The priest opened his mouth to speak, but I rushed on. "Well, the folks who killed that wolf took as much care as they could, but they got nipped, so they caught the sickness. It wasn't something they wanted. And I don't think God would hold it against them, or mind if we prayed for them."

By this time Father Andrew looked impatient, like someone suffering a jawing and just bursting to speak. "Child, you have no idea—"

"Father, I don't really care about how long they're going to spend in purgatory or anything like that," I told him, trying to keep my voice sounding reasonable but probably failing. "All I hoped was that you could have a service of prayer for everyone who was caught up in this, and remind folks that all the victims are in the Lord's loving hands. There isn't a rule against that, is there?" I was starting to get irritated, and I hoped he didn't notice.

A cold wind whipped under my skirt, and I heard the great door creak. Moments later a firm hand settled on my right shoulder. "How goes it, Allie?" Papa asked as he came up behind us.

"Not good," I muttered. Louder, I said, "Father Andrew, this is my father, Eldon Sorensson. Father Andrew is here because Father John is sick."

"You'll be having a memorial service for the survivors tomorrow?" Papa asked quietly. I was proud of him; I would have made the words a statement.

"I will be speaking at the Mass on how all true believers may avoid the taint of hell," the priest responded.

"That's always a good topic," Papa said in his kindest voice. "But right now people are wandering every which way, like orphaned chicks, and they need a bit of comfort, too. You'll also remind them of God's abiding love for his children, and how it's impossible to go too far for the Lord to find you, won't you?"

"Mr. Sorensson," Father Andrew said firmly, "I have

no intention of lying to the good people of Sun-Return about the location of these sinners' souls. The dead are beyond anything we can do, except pray unceasingly for them, and so I shall state in no uncertain terms. I am only grateful that the damnation or redemption of these demons is in His hands, and not mine." The priest had clasped his hands behind himself, and he reminded me a lot of the schoolmaster we'd had the year before.

"I also am grateful, Father," was Papa's response, and it took work not to gape at what he'd said. I don't think Father Andrew understood—the man looked a bit puzzled. "Come along now. Father Andrew has work to do." Papa nodded a polite farewell as he stooped to pick Ben up. Father Andrew said something about how he hoped to see us at Mass, but I wasn't listening. I was trying not to start yelling—I had a mad on I could feel right down to my cold toes.

Once we were outside, I announced, "He won't do it. I just know it." I could feel my face settling into hard lines.

"I suspect you're right, Allie," Papa said gently. "We'll give him a chance, though."

"But I'm not sure we should try to get Momma to go to Mass if Father Andrew is going to go on about hell and everything," I admitted as we started back up the street toward the center of town.

Shaw must have been watching for us, because the buggy started magically rolling back out into the street. The thought of standing out in the wind made me shiver, but Shaw didn't look cold, though he was wearing only a coat and a scarf. It just didn't make sense how a skinny, long-legged boy could be so warm and a girl so cold. *Something's not fair here,* I decided.

Papa set Ben in the back of the buggy and then gave me a hand up. I kept an eye on Shaw as I wrapped Ben and myself in the quilt. Young Shaw watched in silence—he wasn't much for casual talk—and once Papa had climbed up to the seat, Shaw handed over the reins.

Nodding his thanks, Papa slipped Shaw a coin for drying Dancer's coat and walking her, and then we were spinning our way out of Sun-Return. I could see Shaw's dark eyes in his pale face as we took the straight track south. *Yes—this is what the family of a werewolf looks like.* That might not've been fair, since I'd never heard a mean word from Shaw, but I was feeling grumpy.

Part of me wanted to talk to Papa about Father Andrew, and part of me had already made some decisions. I thought I was a pretty sound Christian, but I doubted Father Andrew would think so. Father John was always shaking his head at my reciting. I could never remember the feast days, and my theology was surely skewed. So the realization that I was setting myself up for an argument with a priest didn't upset me much. I was more concerned about the day I would finally tell Momma I didn't like her church.

"That man's God is always angry," I muttered. "Would it be such a big deal for a man of God to lead us in prayer for the victims?"

Papa heard me, of course, because we were huddled right behind him. "He seems to think so, daughter. And if he won't, I'm at a loss as to what we should do for your momma. She's not ready to talk yet."

"Maybe it shouldn't be on Sunday." Papa shifted as I spoke, so I was pretty sure he'd heard me, but I wasn't in any hurry to continue. I was still working things out. "Three of the werewolves were Catholics, and the baby. Little Tate and Stannes's wife were something different. She was Presbyterian, and Tate's family doesn't have a church—they just go to the Baptist service for the preaching."

"Which means?" Dancer had slowed a bit, because the

road was rough through the hollow, so Papa could look over his shoulder.

I was pretty sure I knew what Papa was asking. "So the Presbyterian priest—"

"Minister."

"—minister," I agreed, "comes next week, usually on Thursday. And I'm going to ask him if *he'll* do a service."

A funny sound came from the suspended seat, but Papa didn't actually say anything. I arranged the quilt over Ben's face and pulled him close. "I don't think God will mind who does the service, as long as we have a proper preacher."

"I suspect you're right," I could hear faintly from the front as Dancer's pace picked up.

I couldn't be certain, but it sounded like Papa was chuckling. Since there was nothing funny about all this, I decided my hearing was fluttering in the wind, and pulled my shawl up to guard against chill.

FOUR

YOU KNOW HOW SOMETIMES you go into something hoping you're wrong? That's how I felt when Papa and the boys and I went into town on Sunday. I didn't think that priest was going to say anything to help ease folks' fears, but I still had this kernel of hope inside. This hope required paying sharp attention, in case there was anything to report to Momma. She said she couldn't face God with all this on her soul. I suppose she meant she couldn't face the Mass itself—I mean, God knew all about what happened, and how could he blame Momma because Dolph was nipped?

Papa didn't join us, of course, but he dropped us all off and then went on to the Kristinssons' boarding house for a late breakfast. So Josh and I kept a firm grip on Ben and Joe and staked out a pew in the back of the church.

Even men of God can disappoint. Father Andrew didn't say a single word about our loss—not directly—and nothing he *did* say could count as comforting. I thought I would get mad again, but instead I found myself sad . . . I'm sure Father John would have figured out a way to help the town without the bishop being mad at him.

Practically everybody was in town for the service, even a few who weren't Catholic. Mr. Casimir's married

daughters and sons were there, and Stannes's people, too.
The Casimir girls didn't look good; the elder was pale and
wan, like my momma, and the younger red-eyed, like
she'd been crying. I envied her that, because crying was
easier than thinking. Josh wasn't really there during the
service . . . we had to keep grabbing his sleeve and pulling
him down to the bench.

I was good—I took Mass like an obedient daughter,
asked forgiveness for judging the priest by my own rules,
and didn't say anything nasty to anyone present. Other
folks weren't so kind; I heard a mutter or two about why
hadn't the priest gone to visit the Casimir girls or the
Sorenssons. Ben and Joe were both quiet during the sermon, something unheard of, so I held them tight while we
waited for the Mass to end.

Enough! Why did Aunt Marta have to be visiting family up north during all of this? Usually she was only a
day's ride away. Maybe we could have saved a few lives if
a practitioner had been here. Suddenly I was really mad
at Dolph and the others for causing all this heartache.
Something grew cold and hard deep inside me, and I
promised myself I'd speak to the minister. So what if I
didn't know him? I'd managed to talk to Father Andrew
politely, hadn't I?

Mostly politely.

Papa was waiting for us when the Mass finally ended. I
was grateful he was so prompt—the building had a dank
and lonely chill to it that day, and I couldn't wait to get
home. Even our sorrow wasn't as dark as our church.
Papa boosted the little boys and me into the back, while
Josh climbed up onto the seat. We'd brought plenty of
quilts, so there was warmth for all.

We were on the road out of town before Papa said, "I
found out from Mrs. Kristinsson that the minister's name
is Robertson. He'll arrive either Wednesday evening or in

time for Thursday dinner. You still think we should ask him?"

"Yes, sir," I answered firmly.

"Ask him what?" Josh asked.

"Allie thinks we need a memorial service for everyone who died in all this business," Papa said gently. "Father Andrew wouldn't do it, because he had some problems with the idea, so Allie is going to ask the Presbyterian minister if he'll conduct a service."

Well, I braced myself then for Josh's yelling—about my being so forward and causing talk, about how stupid the idea was—but there was silence from the front of the buggy.

Finally Josh said, "That's a real good idea, Allie. If you want me to go along, jist holler."

"'Just' holler," Papa said patiently, and suddenly I felt a lot better about everything.

Sunday was the first day I stayed glued to the kitchen. Joe was no longer waiting for Momma to get up, and helped Papa and Joshua with the chores. Ben still stuck pretty close to me, but he was willing to do kitchen stuff, like drying pans and stirring things. I made us venison stew, cutting up nice-sized chunks of meat and dicing the onions and garlic finely. I cleaned the mushrooms carefully and merely removed the stems, so we had whole buttons simmering with the venison. The carrots I'd cook separately, and season with Momma's sweet-and-sour chervil vinegar just before they finished steaming, but I had no idea what herbs and spices to use in the stew. Everyone would just have to settle for baked potatoes and butter.

I dug around in Momma's recipe book, but all it had were lists of things that went well with different meats and vegetables. Although I had eaten venison stew many times, there was no recipe. Then again, was the stew ever the same twice? After thought, I went quietly through the parlor and up the front stairs.

Since I knew Papa was in the barn, I knocked very softly and then opened the door a crack. "Momma?" I whispered.

"I'm awake, child," she said gently, and I slipped into the room. The curtains were still drawn, and Momma was bundled under several quilts. Weak afternoon light tried to creep in through cracks, but it wasn't making much headway.

There was no point in saying anything about the service or Dolph—that always set her to crying. So I kept my questions to what I needed. "What herbs do you use in the venison stew, Momma? I put in onions and garlic, but you never make it the same way twice."

Then Momma surprised me, because a touch of a smile crossed her pale face. "What herbs do you like, girl?"

"I like rosemary," I admitted, "and sweet marjoram."

"Rosemary's good with venison," she said, "with parsley and a pinch of chervil, maybe. What else are you making?"

"I put some carrots on to steam, and I was going to use the sweet vinegar on them. And potatoes and butter," I added.

Momma looked a bit dreamy a moment, like her concentration was elsewhere. Then she pushed at the quilt that was near her face. "Why don't you get out the skewers for the potatoes, and I'll get dressed. Do we have any bread left?"

"No, ma'am." That was one thing I didn't want to try without help—it was not only cold outside but humid, and I wasn't that good yet with yeast.

"Some chives for the potatoes, and some dilly bread, I think," Momma murmured as she swung her legs to the edge of the bed. I was a tad worried, since she hadn't been eating much, but she managed to stand without my help. "We can make a sweet bread for breakfast tomorrow, and the regular bread then. Go along, Allie. I can dress myself."

She still sounded as faded as little Joe's blue breeches, and her eyes were dark holes in her face. But she was moving around all right, so I simply said, "Would you like some hot water?"

"That'd be kind, child. Add a touch of cold, if you would."

I grabbed the big china pitcher out of its bowl and headed back downstairs. Ben met me at the foot.

"You didn't take me," he said, his lower lip starting to quiver.

"Hush! I think Momma's getting dressed and going to make dinner! Come on, let's show her what a good helper you are!" I took his hand and led him back into the kitchen.

Momma wasn't all right—not by a long shot—but at least she was moving again. That was something. I can't tell you how much good it did Ben and Joe, seeing her in the kitchen tossing flour every which way. Although she had let me help in the kitchen before, she had never really explained *why* she did things. That day she did.

Bruising stiff rosemary leaves between her fingers, Momma inhaled the resinous odor and carefully made a small pile on her palm. "Rosemary must be treated with respect, child," she said as she took another pinch of the powerful herb. "It's pungent, and used wrong can ruin a meal. There are few herbs you can't serve at the same table, as long as you control them." Momma tipped her hand, sprinkling the crushed leaves into the stew pot. "In a bit, we'll see how it's coming along. We may want a touch more, but first we wait. You can usually add more, but you can't take it back!"

Later, as she kneaded the bread, showing me how to keep, pulling in the corners so every bit of yeast was nudged, she told me that dill was also pungent and a touch bitter, so she just barely used it in her bread—the merest touch of dill weed, or sometimes seed, when you wanted bursts of dill flavor.

I sucked it all up like a sponge. Just a bit of greenery, and food tasted *real,* as if before it was only a mirage. "Mrs. Pederson doesn't use herbs much," I murmured aloud. "Is that why—" I stopped then, since it wasn't polite to say that my best friend's mother wasn't much in a kitchen.

"Ida Pederson is a sound cook, and she's good with onions and garlic," Momma said without pausing in her kneading. "But she didn't have your great-grandmother to teach her about seasoning things."

"Are you going to teach me?"

Momma actually looked startled, and paused in mid stroke. "Of course, girl. Who else would teach you about feeding a family, which God willing you'll someday have?"

"Can't Papa cook?" I asked, and Momma smiled and started kneading again.

"He's a better cook than most, but the mules pull better for him, so the kitchen and stillroom are my province." Glancing over and seeing my expression, she said, "Oh, yes, I used to help with the plowing, before your brothers were old enough to work the fields." She faltered a bit, the dough stilling under her hands, and I could have kicked myself.

"We may need to help Papa come spring," I murmured, offering her a cloth to drape over the dough.

"Or one of the town boys," she said in turn, slapping the dough and flicking the towel over the bread board. "You have a lot to learn, daughter, if you want a stillroom

and root cellar bursting with good things to eat."
Glancing up at the only kitchen window, which looked
west, she said briskly, "Have I ever shown you how to
make mulled juniper pears? Juniper is how gin is fla-
vored, and three or four crushed berries with brown
sugar, pears, a squeezed orange, and a splash of wine
makes a lovely finish to dinner."

We didn't mention plowing again.

Monday was baking day, so we were pretty busy, and
Tuesday Momma pulled the spinning wheel closer to the
fire and tackled the big box of fluffy wool. I ended up
combing wool that had been carefully stored from summer shearing. Sometimes I think all I ever did during winter was comb wool. But my hands always ended up soft,
so I didn't complain. It was good thinking time. I had a
lot of thinking to do—remembering things about Dolph,
planning what I would say to the Reverend Jon
Robertson, and wondering about the extra bed Papa
asked me to make up.

"Folks are coming for next rest day," was all he said.
"Most will stay with your Aunt Dagmar, but a few will
come here, and at least one prefers a bed." But *who*, he
wouldn't say. I suspected he meant Aunt Marta—really
Papa's second cousin, but we called her aunt—since she
was the only one I know of who insisted on a bed when
she could get it. She also didn't care for Momma's sister
Dagmar. But Papa didn't volunteer who, so I didn't ask.

It was no problem ... this time no one even had to
give their bed up. But distant kin coming to pay their
respects when a youngling died? When old folks passed
on, yes, but people lost children too often to send more
than sympathy. I wasn't sure Momma wanted—or
needed—a full-blown wake. Still, Grandsir always used to
tell me to watch and learn, so I waited to see what would
happen next.

I'd decided to go back into Sun-Return on Thursday, after our big noon meal. With any luck the minister would have arrived the night before—or at least in time for his dinner. I wanted him warm and full to the brim before I broached the subject of a memorial service. Papa said I could ride Snowshoe in by myself if the weather stayed above freezing, so I kept a weather eye out and combed a lot of wool.

In the end, I had an escort into town I hadn't expected. The wind was calm and the sky clear as a bell when I started out to the barn to get Snowshoe. As I looked out over the stubble of the closest cornfield, I could see a rider coming in the western gate. A white horse? Those were almost as rare as white mules like Snowshoe. A few steps more and I realized it was Shaw Kristinsson on his father's stallion.

Well, I was knocked galley-west, that's for sure. I mean, Bjorn Kristinsson never let anybody ride that stallion—not even his *eldest* son. It was too valuable, for starters, having a lot of A-rab blood. But "Bear" Kristinsson always said Frostfire was gentle enough to carry a child. So instead of getting Snowshoe, I stood there like an addled turkey and watched that beautiful horse move up our dirt path.

Long strides eat up a lot of ground, and after a bit Shaw was pulling up at our front door. The stallion was still fresh, playing with the bit as he pranced, showing off a shiny new set of shoes.

I couldn't resist. "Does your father know you've got him?" I asked, even as my fingers itched to stroke that silky white mane.

"Pater told me to take him," Shaw replied, his voice quiet as always. "Mr. Robertson came in last night. Mater said to bring you into town."

So I'm the speaker, eh? That wasn't exactly comforting.

Mrs. Kristinsson was an impressive woman, friendly but full of dignity. If she preferred for me to talk to this minister . . . "I'll get Snowshoe."

Shaw extended an arm, and I saw that the palms of his wool gloves had leather stitched to them. "Two ride warmer than one."

I thought about it for a long minute. He was right, of course—and I was dying to ride that stallion. Perhaps more important, Shaw had nudged me into some crazy things before, but he'd never put me into danger. Reaching behind me with my right hand, I pushed the heavy door open a crack.

"Shaw's here, Momma. Mrs. Kristinsson sent him to get me. He'll bring me home before dark." I looked sideways at Shaw as I spoke, and he nodded once in agreement. Before anyone could come up with an objection, I pulled on the knotted rope, sealing the doorway. Then I offered Shaw my left hand.

I was up behind him in that big saddle and trotting off down the path before I remembered that Momma would have no idea why I was leaving or where I was going. But Joshua knew, and Papa—and I wasn't going to take the chance of ending up on Snowshoe!

Before we were out of sight of the house, I didn't care if I got switched for not asking. This ride was worth a switching. We were scarcely trotting, but the stallion's liquid stride made it feel like we were cushioned by a down comforter.

"He doesn't mind carrying people?" I said in Shaw's ear.

Shaw turned his head slightly and said, "His ancestors carried people across the Sahara desert. He hardly notices us at all. But the ground's still frozen hard, so we can't go fast today. Might hit a hole."

And that was why Bear Kristinsson trusted Shaw with

this horse—some boys couldn't resist showing off. But then, just being on this animal was like heaven ... speed was too much to hope for. I found myself dearly hoping that Papa had enough extra money in early spring to introduce Dancer to Frostfire. What a foal that would be!

The ride was over all too soon. Shaw took me straight to his mother's boarding house, and even dismounted to help me get down. "Mr. Robertson won't go out visiting people until after dinner," Shaw said as he pulled the reins over Frostfire's head. "Go warm up by the fireplace, and when you're ready Mater will introduce you." With a nod, he led the stallion off toward the stable.

Straightening my petticoat and dress over the pair of pants Josh had loaned me, I rearranged my shawl and set my hand to the cold brass doorknob. The wooden entranceway had a beautiful leaded glass oval in it for light, one of the prettiest things in Sun-Return, and I touched the lead channels gently as I opened the door.

Mrs. Kristinsson's house was divided, like many frame homes of the time. The door led into a hallway, which ran straight back and also held a big staircase with a wonderful banister. Shaw and I had slid down it a few times, back when we were Ben's age. To the left was the parlor, for paying guests, and to the right the room with two big drop-leaf tables, which was for both guests and any people who just wanted to buy a good meal. The tables were set for a heap of folks, clean down to cover cloths, so I knew dinner was yet to come. A fire was burning brightly in the fireplace on the east wall, so I sat down on one of the benches and loosened my shawl.

Mrs. Kristinsson came through the swinging door just then—I guess she must have heard the door open—and gave me one of her warm smiles. She was a big woman, as tall as her husband, and rangy, with beautiful black hair piled high on her head. There were touches of white above

her ears, like the brush of a bird's wing, and they comple-
mented her deep gray eyes and pale skin. Some said her
face was too strong for a woman's—those high cheekbones
and that strong chin left no room for nonsense—but I
thought she grew more lovely with every passing year.

"Alfreda," she said in her warm voice, and already I
felt welcome. It was like meeting a queen. "I'm so glad
you could come today. Would you like to stay for dinner?
It's just a vegetable beef barley stew and biscuits, with a
trifle for dessert, but there's plenty if you're hungry."

"It sounds wonderful, but I think I'd better see if my
stomach calms down," I admitted. Well, she laughed, of
course, but it was a kind laugh, and not for the first time
I envied Shaw his mother. I knew Momma loved me, but
she never showed her feelings—not like Mrs. Kris could.

"The Reverend Jon Robertson is very easy to talk to,"
she assured me. "He has been welcome here for many
years. I think you'll like him." That made me feel a bit
better, because Mrs. Kris didn't say people were welcome
unless they *were*. She never lied, but she had ways of
speaking. I knew for a fact she didn't care for the Baptist
minister, although she was as polite as could be to him.
And he stayed in her house, too, since his congregation
paid his board.

"Why don't you give me your shawl and gloves, and
I'll keep them warm," Mrs. Kris suggested, taking my
outer things. "If you'll go into the parlor, I'll call Pastor
Jon and bring something warm to drink."

"Mrs. Kris?" I said quickly before she could vanish in
a swish of skirt. "Have you said anything to him about a
service?"

That wonderful smile again. "No, dear. I just told him
you had something important to speak with him about."
The door shifted, and with a flicker of deep green wool
she disappeared into the depths of the kitchen.

Well, the queen had spoken, so I got myself over to the parlor door and carefully turned the handle. There was a small fire burning in there, too, with an ornate screen to protect the Oriental rug from stray cinders. There wasn't much furniture in the room—just a couch, a rocker, and two parlor chairs for sitting—but everything was *interesting*. I sometimes wondered where Mrs. Kris had come from, because her things didn't have any of the extra carving and frills that were so popular. It was all clean and simple, from the cedar chest to the armoire.

I settled myself in one of the high-backed chairs, which was a woven mesh from some foreign clime, and waited for the minister to show up. It was then I realized I was being watched. Someone was sitting in the rocker by the north window.

It was a man, as old as Papa or older, maybe, and substantial . . . at least his clothing was fine wool and real silk. He had been reading when I entered the parlor, but now he was studying me. I figured this gave me license, so I studied him back.

Then the man smiled, his long face crinkling along miles of laugh lines. No one would call this fellow good-looking, but there was kindness in his tanned face, and good humor, and I felt myself warm to him. He had the most vivid green eyes I'd ever seen, like fresh maple leaves.

"Are you a fellow tenant of this fine establishment?" He had a deep voice, not bass but almost, and resonant, like he was a big one for singing hymns.

"No, sir," I said gravely. "I'm here to see the minister." I was practicing my formal manners, so I stressed the last two words.

"Will any minister do?"

This was extremely sensible, coming from an adult, so I was a bit surprised. But after thought I said, "Yes and no. The priest who came in place of Father John wanted nothing to do with the idea, so I thought I'd trot it past the Presbyterian minister and see what he thought."

Nodding once, the man murmured, "Indeed." He said it like he was really listening, though, so I didn't mind. "So this is an appointment?"

I grimaced, and saw his eyes crinkle up in response. "I didn't actually leave a note, but I planned on catching up with him today. Mrs. Kris sent Shaw out for me, though, so my timing's a bit off. I wanted the pastor fed before I talked with him."

"Well, he has his coffee late in the morning, you see, so you won't catch him on an empty stomach," the man said with a smile.

"Good," I muttered, giving the fellow a long eye. He had thick dark hair, his hairline high but not patchy. For some reason he seemed to find me very interesting, but I had no idea why.

Then he suddenly said, "You're one of Emma Schell's great-granddaughters, aren't you?"

Blinking at him once, I managed to say, "Yes, sir," since I didn't know if he was one of those adults who don't like kids nodding at them. "I'm Alfreda Sorensson, daughter of Garda Schell and Eldon Sorensson."

Closing his book and setting it on the blanket chest beneath the window, the man stood slowly to a great height and said, "Then I should introduce myself. I am Jonathan Lee Robertson, Presbyterian minister for the congregations of this region. My hostess said you have something you'd like to discuss with me?" His eyes twinkling, he added: "I am eager to find out what a priest had no interest in that a minister might!"

My embarrassment was swallowed up in those laughing eyes. However this turned out, I had a feeling I was going to like Pastor Jon.

FIVE

PARENTS CAN SURPRISE YOU. Momma had yet to weep for her firstborn son, at least in my presence, but her eyes filled with tears when I told her what I'd done. She didn't say anything, not right then, but she reached out and pulled me close. We stayed that way a long time, teary and half hidden in the shadows of the flickering kitchen fire, and neither of us said anything.

"Ripe as wheat," Momma finally whispered, which sounded familiar, but I couldn't place it. "Thank you, girl. He'll rest easier with the proper words said." Her grip was fierce, pressing me so close you could scarcely tell where Momma left off and I began.

All along Papa had been in the kitchen, though he had let me tell the bulk of the tale. Now he was rattling around over by the sink—I could hear fired clay clinking—and then his firm footsteps moved across the smooth kitchen floor.

"Here, Garda," he said gently, offering her something just out of my sight. Momma didn't move at first . . . then she slowly loosened her hold on me. I felt his warm hand between my shoulder blades. "Why don't you go see if Joshua needs you in the barn, Allie? I'll help your momma with dinner."

That meant he wanted to talk to her alone, so I grabbed my shawl and scooted out the doorway. This would give me time to tell Josh what was going on, without Momma hearing it. Pastor Jon had suggested we have the memorial service before church on Sunday, to put everyone in a more hopeful mood. He'd also asked me about the huge oak grove that was in the big area between the tavern and the doctor's office. Why he cared about the common where people rested their teams, I didn't know, but I had told him to check with Idelia's papa, who kept track of the county records.

Josh had finished with the two cows in milk and was now feeding Thistle, the cow that was currently dry, so I let the geese back into the barn and took care of the nanny goats. My brother was full of questions about Pastor Jon, and not completely happy with my answers.

"But you don't know what he's going to say?" Josh kept asking.

"Not exactly," I repeated for about the eighth time. "He told me he was going to come up with something simple, and that he needed to talk to a few folks about an idea he had."

"Allie, sometimes you're too trusting! He could say jist about anything! How are we going to know if we should take Momma?" Josh was scowling fit to break his face, his eyes fixed on me. I was glad for the dimness of the barn, since those gray-green peepers look too much like glass for my taste.

"I already told Momma," I announced, patting Clover reassuringly. Our goats are pretty steady ladies, but Josh was almost yelling, and they clearly didn't care for it.

"Allie!"

"I have a good feeling about Pastor Jon," I went on. "I think you'll like him, Josh. He felt right to me. It's not likely he's going to get up there and tell everyone that Dolph is an angel or something, but I bet people will feel better after it's over. Talking about things helps."

Straightening up, I pointed at the bucket and said, "Will you lift it, please?"

Good move on my part. Josh was developing a fine set of muscles, and was still dumb enough to want to show off about it. Although he was still muttering to himself (I'm not the only one in the family with the habit), he lifted the oak pail with little effort and carried it to the attached cheese hut, where he was straining milk.

I heard some of what Josh said, but I decided not to rise to the occasion.

Sunday morning matched our moods as we drove into town in our funeral best. It was overcast and snowing lightly, the kind of tiny, early flakes that don't stick long and form wavy lines in the corn and hay stubble. Still, there was a clear light beyond the cloud cover—none of that heavy gray feeling.

There was already a crowd at the church when we arrived, although the boys were taking the wagons down to the common and blanketing the horses. The stove had been fired up hours earlier, and the church was toasty warm. I was still glad for the wrapped bricks we'd brought for our feet, though. Then Pastor Jon invited us all to join him by the blasted oak.

Well, I had suspected he was thinking about an outdoor ceremony in the grove, but the blasted oak? It was a big old stump about as tall as Papa, the top jagged and seared from the lightning bolt that had split the tree. Most of the wood had been used already in the church stove, but the stump remained, free from insects and the bark completely gone. I had wondered aloud why no one cut it down lower, but Momma told me some people had a thing about lightning-struck wood.

We were bundled up against the cold, and I could

wait for an explanation, so we trooped off down the
street, the majority of the folks in the region coming
along behind us.

All the boys who had taken their family wagons to the
common had remained in the grove. As I approached the
huge old stump, as wide as I was tall, I realized that
someone had sanded and waxed a big section of the side
facing the street. And burned words into the wood. At
the top was the year, in big Roman numerals. Below it . . .

"'In memory of our loss in the months of Fruit,
Vintage, Fog, and Frost,'" I read in a whisper. Beneath
the words were the names of everyone who had died,
from Faxon's little girl through my brother . . . even "one
known only to God." It took me a moment to realize this
meant the werewolf Papa had killed, back when all this
began. At the very bottom it said simply: Psalms 139,
7–12. That's when my eyes filled with tears.

Strong arms swathed in black wool wrapped around
me from behind and pulled me close. I could smell lavender and bergamot, and knew it was my mother. A small
fist tightened in my skirt, and I knew Ben was clinging to
us both. Through a haze of mist I saw Papa and little Joe
move over near Joshua, who was standing with his friends
Shaw and Wylie. Then the tears got thicker, and I could
no longer make out faces in the crowd.

Pastor Jon didn't speak long—not so much from the
cold, I thought, but as if he felt he had said enough. He
thanked Bjorn Kristinsson and his three sons for preparing the "monument," and thanked all of us for coming to
this "memorial service for our pain."

"Make no mistake," Pastor Jon continued, "this service
is for those who survived the evil times that fell upon
Sun-Return. Our Lord instructed us to comfort our
brethren when they have need. We must not worry about
those who fell in battle against the dark, for they are in

God's loving hands. Instead we must remember that we too are embraced by the eternal light, which will ease our sorrow and lead us into the future."

I don't remember much more about the service, except that Pastor Jon said more about love than he did about pain. There was no way to gauge how the community was receiving his words, except for the muted sobbing I could hear off to one side. All I knew for sure was that Momma no longer felt so . . . rigid. Something in her arms seemed to relax around me, and it was the best thing that had happened in a long, long time.

There were a few minutes of silence after Pastor Jon gave a benediction, and then people started slowly moving away. A few folks stopped to give the Casimir girls a hug, or to squeeze my momma's arm, but no one said anything. I didn't mind the quiet—it was the first time in many days a gathering wasn't tinged with tension.

I turned in Momma's arms, and we walked, arms linked, back toward the street, Ben firmly attached to Momma's other hand. As we grew closer to the entrance I glanced up from my feet and saw that several people were waiting in the falling snow. One of them looked very familiar. . . .

As tall as a mountain, and moon-faced, although he didn't carry any extra fat, the man had dark hair and eyes, tanned skin, and a neatly trimmed beard tracing his jaw. Covering him was the most audacious fur coat I've ever seen, made of thick, shiny black fur, the hood lined with what looked like wolverine. Nothing had a coat like that . . . except a wood pussy. And no one that big had a skunk coat except—

A run of liquid notes seemed to come from the west, in the trees behind the tavern.

"Cousin Cory?" I said carefully, giving the figure a doubtful look. Surely not; he lived a good ten days away.

My mother halted in her tracks and looked wildly around, finally focusing on the hulking form. Jutting cheekbones and a prow of a nose rose above lips that split apart in a tremendous flash of fine white teeth as the big man strolled toward us.

"Garda, darlin'!" His voice was as big as he was.

"No!" Momma clutched me like I was her hope of heaven. "No! I won't allow it! You're wasting your time, Corrado!"

Well, I knew Momma was mad, because she only used his real name when she was really annoyed with him, but something else was in her words. If I hadn't known better, I'd have said Momma was scared of Cory. And that was silly—he was a terrible prankster, but he'd never harmed anybody that I heard of.

Still smiling, Cory stopped in front of us and tipped the huge, shapeless felt hat he wore on his head. "Now, Garda, you know better than that," he said gently, giving me a smile. "Let's not be foolish. I'm so sorry for your loss, darlin'."

"Don't you understand?" This was barely a whisper. It was as if no one else was around, and it's true that everyone else was giving us a wide berth. "I've already lost one child to the dark. I won't risk her, too!"

Cory cocked his head and gave Momma a long look. He was still smiling, but his smile was sad. "I could feel her a se'nnight past and more, woman. That is not a Gift to ignore." And then, his voice much softer: "Can you protect her, Garda?"

Suddenly I wasn't sure I was glad Cousin Cory had come to visit, because Momma was rigid again . . . and then her tears were falling on my shoulder. Where was Papa?

Cory reached over and put an arm around Momma's shoulders, giving her a big hug. I was amazed to see she didn't argue with him. "It's not your fault, woman. Stop blaming yourself. It's not your fault!" Hunching his shoulders a bit, Cory started to pull us down the boardwalk. "Let's go hear the good reverend's sermon, cousin, and then we'll have dinner with Dagmar. Nothing's been decided yet—you know we wouldn't do that without talking to you."

I could smell Papa's tobacco, and knew he was close by, but he didn't try to take Momma away from Cousin Cory. The only sounds on that crisp morning were the hollow thud of many feet on wooden steps and the soft burr of Cory's voice as he continued to speak to my mother.

Cousin Cory, all the way from the orchard country, in the river bottom! That was quite a distance. Whatever had possessed him to come visit? I could only remember seeing him twice in my life, though he wasn't a person you forget. Cory's wild daddy had gone south in his youth, following the biggest river to the sea, and brought back home a foreign bride from New Orleans. Aunt Dagmar always thought the wife looked Spanish, but Aunt Sofia claimed she was from Italy, and she had no reason to lie. So Cory had always been different.

He was also a practitioner, like Aunt Marta . . . what normal folks called a wizard. Considering how tightly Momma was clutching me, I couldn't help but wonder if Cousin Cory's visit had something to do with my hearing the werewolves, and those dreams. But that was silly. If it was a ten-day trip to Cousin Cory's, then there was no way he could be here only eight days after Papa sent those letters.

Was there?

I'm ashamed to say I didn't hear much of Pastor Jon's sermon. My mind was whirling like an eddy as I worked my way through Cousin Cory's presence—and his words. Protection, and *feeling* someone . . . me? How? I was sitting between Momma and Papa, and I kept a tight grip on both of them. This entire business was making me uneasy, and the sooner explained the better.

Now I understood why Momma hadn't put dinner on to simmer before we came to town. If Aunt Dagmar expected us, then we were going to Sunday supper in Granny's house—there was no arguing with Aunt Dagmar.

Momma was the youngest of six children, and the third daughter. Aunt Dagmar was the eldest—she had inherited the family home, as was the custom in our part of the world. Her husband, Uncle Lars, was the only college-trained lawyer for a week's ride in any direction, so they made out real well. Good thing, considering the size of both the house and their family.

My cousins were a little too well-behaved for me, but I didn't mind seeing them on special occasions, like weddings and funerals. I supposed this was as close to a funeral for Dolph as we were going to get. Stella, who was Dolph's age, usually met us at the door, so I braced myself for her unrelieved cheerfulness. How she could act that way at a funeral, I didn't know, but I'd seen her do it twice before, so I had no hope of reprieve. You'd have thought she was Irish or something.

This time Aunt Dagmar greeted us in the entranceway, stately in black silk. I thought it was nice of her to dress up, and I decided to be on my best behavior. I always managed to say something Aunt Dagmar thought unladylike, even when I didn't plan to rile her. Maybe if I simply did what Stella did . . .

Momma and her sisters looked a lot alike—slender, delicate, and dark-haired, with big eyes and high cheekbones. All three of them had married and had children, but you wouldn't know it to look at them. Aunt Dagmar was so thin she reminded me of a heron—elegant and feathery. Aunt Sunhild, on the other hand, was truly the swan girl; she was grace incarnate.

As if thinking of her conjured her out of thin air, Aunt Sunhild suddenly appeared at the archway leading into the drawing room. She was also dressed in black, a fine wool dress with freshwater pearls on the bodice, and looked like the professor's wife that she was. I'd always wanted deep blue eyes like hers, but I knew it wasn't likely mine'd darken any more at my age.

"Sunhild?" my mother said, as if questioning her presence. My aunt responded by moving straight to Momma and embracing her.

"Surely you didn't think we'd let you go through this alone, Garda," Sunhild said in her sweet voice. There was something a bit innocent about Aunt Sunhild—as if someone forgot to tell her that people are often nasty to one another. Her husband was a dour Scot, however, so they balanced out.

"And how are you, child?" It took me a moment to realize that Aunt Dagmar was talking to me.

"As good as can be expected," I said gravely, remembering something I'd heard at the last funeral I'd been to. Aunt Dagmar blinked at me in a decided sort of way, but she didn't seem offended or anything, so I figured I'd passed the first test of the day.

"Come in and greet the family," Aunt Dagmar said as she helped the boys out of their coats. I moved into her formal living room to take off my shawl and wet shoes, and found a lot more people than I'd expected. Uncle Karl, the eldest brother, turned away from the fireplace and gave me a sharp look through his Franklin spectacles. Two other dark heads lifted, and I was amazed to see Uncle Stefan in his rector's collar and Uncle Henrik as well! All of Momma's siblings?

"Yes, the whole kit and caboodle," came a familiar voice, and I started to smile before I could control myself. Papa's cousin Marta! Then I remembered she'd been gone when we needed her, and my smile faded.

Aunt Marta, as we called her, was to one side of the fireplace, her familiar needlework in her lap. Her angular face, striking rather than pretty, tilted so she could see me, and her cornflower-blue eyes held all the peace in her heart.

"I know," she said calmly. "It's not fair, is it? There are never enough practitioners, Allie—not good ones. And a practitioner must go at the first call. Two babies and a good woman are alive because I went north, and there's no cure for the werewolf curse." Her expression grew remote as she added, "I might have been able to identify them before that young woman died, though. That is something I'll always wonder about."

"Why didn't you come as soon as you got back?" I heard myself say. Indrawn breath back near the entrance told me I'd already managed to upset Aunt Dagmar.

"I did," was the answer. "I came here straight from Willow Run."

Well, I just stared. Willow Run was two days beyond Cousin Cory's! Meeting my look evenly, Aunt Marta said, "By the time I could leave, Allie, the folks of Sun-Return had things under control. No more humans were in danger. I came straight here because of you."

"How did you know about my dream?" Now, I don't know why I said that, but I did.

Setting aside her stitching, Aunt Marta rose to her full height of six feet and came over to me. Taking my shoes from my hands, she said, "Stockings, too. Your momma brought extra, I'm sure."

As I sat down on the polished wood floor to take off my wet stockings, Aunt Marta added, "Your dream was just the beginning. When you read truth in angelica, I knew there was no time to waste."

At first I kept my eyes on my wet stockings. If she knew about *that,* then there was no more to be said. I hadn't had the time or the desire to tell anyone about that. Finally I looked up, but Aunt Marta wasn't looking at me—she was looking over at the entrance.

"No time to waste, Garda." Marta spoke firmly, as if there was no possible argument to her words, and I readied myself for the storm.

"Food first, business later," came Aunt Dagmar's brisk voice, and the way that everyone started moving toward the dining room told me that I wasn't the only one grateful for the interruption. I rolled to my feet and headed back toward Momma, who was pulling dry socks out of the big pockets inside her coat. Her hazel eyes were as big as saucers, but she didn't say a word.

Aunt Dagmar's cook stuffed us with ham, sweet potatoes, green beans, and fluffy biscuits. There was trifle for dessert, which surprised me, but I figured it was in honor of the Sabbath, not the service. We kids all ate in the kitchen, so we got to watch those beautiful glass jars be filled to the brim with sponge cake, fruit compote, and whipped cream.

Full plates didn't stop my cousins from looking at me out of the corners of their eyes. Stella was old enough to eat with the adults, but her brother Lars didn't hesitate to speak his mind.

"I say they're all here because of you," he announced between dinner and dessert. "Uncle Stefan's not too happy about it, either, and Uncle Henrik got pulled away from his warehouses right when a big order was expected."

Lars was always too smug for words. "And I say your opinion isn't worth a fig," I said calmly, pouring Ben some more milk. Of course, I was pretty sure Lars was right, but I wasn't going to give him the satisfaction of knowing it. "If it was me, why would the uncles care, anyway? If I really have the Gift, they won't have anything to do with the teaching of it."

There. I'd said it—before witnesses, if little ones count. Josh was across from me, and he gave me a long look. That's when I remembered that he hadn't heard Momma and me talking.

I was proud of my elder brother—right then no one would have thought he and Lars were the same age. Joshua went right on with the conversation, and saved arguing for later. "You mean like Granny had?" Josh actually sat up straight in his chair. "You're kidding! No one's had it since Granny!"

"That's why everyone came," Lars said around a mouthful of trifle. "Lotta prestige in having a practitioner in the family, and all ours are distant kin."

"Aunt Marta is Papa's second cousin," Josh said quickly, and was rewarded by a scowl from Lars.

"That's your pa's side. Ma's side goes back to the old country, and it's famous. Folks were starting to say our blood was thinning out." This sounded like gospel from someone or another—probably Aunt Dagmar—so I wasn't too interested. "Ma always hoped one of us would show the talent. She still thinks we might."

I could see where this was going. Aunt Dagmar was mad that it wasn't her child with the Gift, so she was going to try to run the show. But the only practitioners I'd seen in the house were Aunt Marta, who disliked Dagmar and wasn't kin to her, and Cousin Cory, who always went his own way. I didn't think Aunt Dagmar would get far with either of them.

"Maybe Allie doesn't have it," Josh suggested, keeping an eye on me. "It flares sometimes when things are hard on a family, doesn't it?"

Now, I appreciated that—Josh wasn't sure if I liked the idea, so he was trying to drag a red herring past Lars to see if it would foul the track. Truth to tell, I hadn't decided if I liked the idea or not. Learning about herbs and stuff could be interesting, and a good herbalist was always in demand. Momma sold herbs (though not the really strong or dangerous ones) to people who didn't want to make the day's ride to Aunt Marta's, and she was a good midwife to boot.

Powerful practitioners could do more, it was said— track an animal (even a human!) on a trail days old, draw water from the air, and speak to the dead. Many folks said a wizard could take on the shape of a beast. A few people thought wizards had familiars, but I knew better—only those who trafficked with the dark ones needed a keeper.

Swallowing a slab of trifle, Lars shook his head. "Cousin Cory said he saw Allie's dream, that she threw it all the way to the big lake. That's more than a flare!" He gave me a glance of pity. "You think we got a lot of lessons now? Wait until they put the extra stuff on you!"

I gave him a superior smile. What Lars didn't know was that I had just completed the last reader. All I had left to do was finish up my ciphers. There was plenty of time for me to start studying something else, and being a practitioner might be interesting. After all, wizards could be as eccentric as they wanted, and folks didn't mind. Maybe I was born to it . . . that might explain how upset people got around me.

First, though, I wanted to know what it took to be a practitioner. No Sorensson ever bought a pig in a poke, and I wouldn't be the first.

I expected a long afternoon of keeping the little ones occupied, but I got a surprise—Stella came into the kitchen after the adults were served their port and told me to go on in. She looked a bit paler than usual as she spoke, so I figured the hollering had already started.

Smoothing my skirt to brush away stray crumbs, I pushed open the swinging door and went into the dining room. A quick look around the candlelit table told me that no one was yelling yet, although a few folks looked about at daggers drawing. Uncle Karl had his doctor look on his face, and Uncle Henrik was looking at me as if I was an especially big problem to him. Like a bundle of expensive furs that hadn't been tanned properly, maybe . . .

Cousin Cory was down by Momma, and was speaking to her in a low voice. I heard something about "what choice do we have?" but it was only a scrap of conversation. Momma's face was frozen again, and her lips thinned, so she surely didn't like what she was hearing. Aunt Marta was sitting below the salt, but she seemed unaware of the insult (or wasn't giving Aunt Dagmar the satisfaction, I suppose). She motioned for me to come over by her, so I walked to the foot of the table and to her side.

"Well, girl, have you figured out why we're all here?" Aunt Marta asked me. It was sort of a private question, since she looked right at me and didn't raise her voice. But I could see that the others were listening as hard as they could.

"You think I have Granny's Gift," I said in turn, my face as serious as I could make it.

"I know you do, Allie," she told me. "People don't flare a fortnight away as if they were in the next room. You have a strong talent, Alfreda, and we think it should be trained. How do you feel about it?"

I'll admit—privately—that I hadn't expected to be asked about it. I mean, no one asks girls *anything*.

'Course, if I learned the Wise Arts, I'd have status. No one could dismiss me as "just" a woman . . . not if they knew what was good for them.

"Do I have a choice?" I looked her in the eyes when I said it, so she'd know I wasn't being coy. Momma feared the Gift; I doubted she feared without a reason.

Aunt Marta is a dear; she knew I was serious, and did me the courtesy of a real answer. "Yes and no," she said bluntly. "If you're as powerful as I think, you *must* have certain kinds of training. You have to know how to protect yourself. There are creatures that live in the dark on the other side, things that seek power. Why they seek it varies, but few are friendly to us, and several are dangerous." Aunt Marta paused, as if weighing something behind her eyes. Then she said, "The truth is, Allie, we can teach you to protect yourself, as your momma was taught. But only to a certain level—some protections you can't learn without learning everything else that goes with the Wise Arts. I think you're going to attract things that will badly want your power, so you need the strongest protections possible."

Silence. I let my eyes drift and considered the past few months. "If I don't learn the strong ones, can I protect friends and kin?" I decided to ask.

"Very little—only on the lowest level of threat," was her answer, even as Momma drew a shaky breath.

"Then Momma shouldn't blame herself about Dolph, because she never learned the Wise Arts, did she?" A murmuring broke out at my words, and Uncle Stefan reached across the table to cover Momma's hand with his own. Perhaps that question shouldn't have been asked. . . .

"No, Allie, she couldn't have saved him from becoming a werewolf," Aunt Marta said firmly. But she added, "Even if she'd known the Arts, all she could have done was subdue him. No one knows how to free a person from the wer curse."

"He would be alive!" Momma said fiercely.

Aunt Marta looked over at Momma, who was sitting at Aunt Dagmar's right hand. "Perhaps," she said in a kind voice. "But you caught the first lad, didn't you? And you couldn't keep him safe. Even as I couldn't save my daughter's firstborn." The private buzz of conversation muted a bit, and Aunt Marta said, "Maybe the twins make up for that, a little. Maybe Allie is meant to make up for that."

"She could enter the church," Garda said quickly.

That didn't make much sense, so I looked to Aunt Marta for an explanation. A faint smile touched her lips. "Your momma means you could take vows and become a nun."

"Me?" It took a lot to strangle the laugh that wanted to escape. "I'll be lucky if Father Andrew doesn't try to get me tossed out." I hadn't planned on telling Momma about that, but I didn't want to give her false hopes. I turned so I could see her and said, "Father John told me once that I was a good person, Momma, but I wasn't much of a Catholic. I don't think a nunnery would take me." I saw only Papa's profile, since he was on the same side of the table as I was, but I could tell by his smile that he didn't think much of the idea, either.

It was plain I needed a lot more information. It was also plain that Momma was getting very upset. So I stuck with the topic and felt my way through it. "If I had known simple protections, would I have heard the were-wolves calling like I did?" I asked.

Silence. Aunt Marta turned away from me then, toward Cousin Cory and Momma. I looked, too, for lack of a better place to set my gaze, and saw that Momma was even whiter than before. Cousin Cory's thick eyebrows were raised in surprise, but he didn't say anything. Then Marta turned back to me.

Was it a candle guttering, or was she a bit paler than usual? "Yes, Allie," she said softly. "If you could hear the werewolves as they roamed, you would still hear them, even with lesser guards."

That's when I started thinking about what Aunt Marta hadn't said . . . but had implied. Somehow she had known about my dream . . . about my finding Dolph's name in the angelica. Cousin Cory had said something about "hearing" me, too. There was a lot about this that no one was telling me.

But I had heard the wolves calling . . . and I didn't think Momma had. I was sure she had learned nothing from the angelica. Which sort of hinted that whatever protected her wasn't going to work for me.

No night critter was going to et me if I could help it— and something in me itched to understand the how and why of those dreams. "I think I'd better," I said slowly, watching Aunt Marta's face for clues. "As much as I can learn." There was a sob from the other end of the table, but I carefully didn't look that way.

My favorite aunt broke into a radiant smile, and for a moment she looked like a Valkyrie to me, as glorious and strong as the morning. "You'll never stop learning, Alfreda," Aunt Marta said earnestly. "Unless you choose to."

Small chance of that. If you're not growing, you're dying.

SIX

WELL, THAT WASN'T THE END OF IT, of course. I was on tenterhooks the entire afternoon while the battle raged on. Momma had her back to the wall in more ways than one, but she was going to go down fighting. Having me admit that I thought learning the craft was a good idea seemed to fire up something in her. The family could blather on all they wanted about my "training" and such, but my parents were still my parents—and they *would* have their say about the business.

Momma was all fiery and indignant, showing more spunk than I'd seen in years, constantly in motion, walking around the formal dining room. On the other hand, Papa was very quiet. He was tilting in his straight-backed chair with his long legs stretched out in front of him, his gaze on the dregs of his port in the fragile crystal glass he was holding. The two of them seemed to alternate in the discussion. First Momma would go her length, and when she tired, Papa would step into the breach. The major bone of contention concerned *where* I was going to be taught.

After an hour or two of this, Aunt Dagmar suggested that everyone adjourn to the parlor for tea or coffee. She also suggested that I might like to go back with my cousins, but I just gave her a speaking look. Go up to the playroom when it was my future they were deciding? Not likely!

Cousin Cory seemed amused by my aunt's remark, and put a proprietary arm around my shoulders as we all moved toward the parlor. "Alfreda's not one of your meek misses, Dag," Cousin Cory said with a chuckle. "You're not going to leave her out of this!"

I waited for Aunt Dagmar to freeze up—she hates to be called Dag, since it's a boy's name.

Sure enough, Aunt Dagmar drew herself up even taller, if possible, and actually sniffed her disdain. "The discussion is likely to be tedious," she said severely. "In my day, children let their parents choose what was best for them."

Cory just gave me a quick look with his bright black eyes, that genuine smile flashing quickly across his face. He lifted both his eyebrows quickly, so fast I doubt anyone else saw him do it, and then his face relaxed into its usual good humor.

I about had a spasm trying not to laugh, but somehow I held it in. No need to say what we were both thinking— if my momma had her way, there'd be no training! And I could just imagine the row that would cause. As I wove through the maze of heavy furniture to the corner, I saw Momma trying to catch my eye. She had her special look on her face, the one she seemed to get only for me—that "I saw what you did, don't do it again" look. Knowing Momma meant I wasn't to make fun of Aunt Dagmar in her own house, I dropped down on the planed oak floor and laced my arms around my knees. Not out of mind, maybe, but out of sight. We didn't need a diviner to know it was going to be a long afternoon.

I won't bore you with all the details, but the gist of it was that I was eleven years old already and had no training whatsoever. That meant a lot of catch-up, and Aunt Dagmar and my uncles were worried about it. Papa politely begged to differ, pointing out that I was quite a

scholar and already finished with all the readers, except
for the math.

"Plus she has been learning her chores right along, and
sews a straighter seam than you do, Dagmar," Momma
added firmly. "I've just started teaching her how to cook
with herbs." There was no mention of when I'd started
learning about herbs, of course, but that was fine. I paid
attention to my teachers, and I'll bet I tucked away more
information in one afternoon than any of my cousins
could have managed in a month.

"Alfreda will not spend her life sewing seams," Aunt
Dagmar said severely.

"You'd be amazed what a practitioner needs to know,"
was Aunt Marta's gentle response, a touch of humor in
her voice.

That's when I realized that Aunt Marta and Cousin
Cory were just plumb pulling the wool over the eyes of
everyone present. They already knew what had to be
done—they were just waiting for the right time to speak.

And the right person to do it. "She's too young," my
momma said once again, wheeling and taking a turn
around the crowded parlor, the swirl of her skirt just
missing a Chinese vase. "I have lost my eldest son, and I
will not have my only daughter snatched from me as well!
There is nothing she needs to learn in the next three years
that I can't teach her myself."

"Nothing, Garda?" Aunt Marta said, her gaze on the
teacup in her hands. "Will you teach her the ways of the
woods? How to build fires without flint and feed herself
in an emergency? How to trail an animal, or keep from
being tracked herself?"

Tracking animals? Fire without a flint? Whoa, there—
what did I need with stuff like that? I mean, taking pelts
for the family was one thing, but tracking animals like an
Indian?

Momma's face was so bewildered I had to look away. I let my gaze rest on Aunt Marta, and saw she looked relaxed . . . kindly, even. However kind, though, I knew Momma wasn't going to like what came next.

Then Papa spoke up. "I can teach her, Marta."

That was all he said. But those simple words caused everyone to sit up straighter. I twisted my head to look over at my father, who was sitting near the door to the entranceway. Did Papa know enough about all those things to teach me? Of course I knew he ran trap lines, but . . . *The farming will be harder without Dolph.*

"Can you devote enough time to it, Eldon?" Cousin Cory said seriously. It was as if we were thinking the same thoughts.

Papa actually shrugged, not looking at either Momma or me. "I will do what is necessary. Allie must be trained, but I agree with Garda that she's too young to leave home. Of course, in a year or so, she could go spend a few weeks here and there with Marta. But none of you can deny that Garda knows the Base Lessons as well as any child of the line. And I make more money from the woods than any man—or woman—for five days' riding. With the exception of Marta," he added with a smile. "Someone in the family will have to take over the wood-craft. Allie can learn it as well as Josh."

I was watching Momma again, and I'll swear she actually bloomed. Her entire expression changed, her slender face blushing with color, her full lips pursing slightly. I admit I was bewildered—you see, I'd never realized until that moment that my momma was a very pretty woman. Always she'd looked so much older than her sisters.

"And you already have a student," Momma pointed out. "A student in her last training. You need to concentrate on her, Marta. I can start Allie out as well as you, and help her finish up the other things she needs to know before coming to you."

"It's truc I don't want to slight any student," Aunt Marta said calmly as she reached for the hot-water pot. "I'd rather devote myself full-time to Alfreda when she finally comes to me. And I have no doubt that you're capable of teaching your daughter in double time everything an acolyte learns in the first five years."

I watched as Aunt Marta diluted her tea down to nothing. Her phrasing had been curious: "capable," not "can" . . . In that moment I decided that Aunt Marta wanted Momma to teach me—but wanted it to be Momma's idea. So I flicked my gaze to the logs glowing in the fireplace and waited for the game to play itself out.

"Good solution," Uncle Karl said abruptly. I could see him out of the corner of my eye as he nodded once in his brisk way and peered at me through his Franklin spectacles. I'd never thought much one way or another about Uncle Karl; he didn't care for children, except his own, and had ignored me most of my life. This time, though, his look was as searching as any Aunt Marta had ever given me, and I thought I saw a gleam of approval in his eyes.

"Garda and Eldon will divide the teaching of Alfreda the next few years, then?" Aunt Marta asked the group at large. "She will come to me for First Lessons after that? When?"

"When would be best?" Momma said, sounding suddenly unsure of herself.

"Immediately," muttered one of the uncles, but I couldn't tell who from my vantage point.

Marta smiled and said, "I suggest that she come to me no later than the autumn after her fourteenth birthday. If she's not quite ready, I can fill in the cracks after she comes to Cat Track Hollow."

"One thing," my momma said softly, her gaze moving to the glowing logs burning merrily in the fireplace. "Only family is to teach her. No one else. And no eighth cousins twice removed, either!" This was said intensely, and I peeked over my folded arms and gave Momma a sharp look. There was something behind this, I was sure, but no more was forthcoming.

With a rustle of petticoats, Aunt Marta turned slightly to face Cousin Cory. "Well, Cory? Will you uphold the honor of the other side of the family?"

"Esme could also teach her," Aunt Dagmar said abruptly.

Esme? There was the sound of movement, and a rustle or two, along with a snort that sounded like Uncle Karl in a disgusted mood.

"I confess I didn't think to send her a letter," Papa admitted ruefully, "what with her having to come so far."

"With Esme, Alfreda would be one of several apprentices, Dagmar," Marta pointed out, "while she would have my exclusive attention. Also, Esme's custom is huge. It would extend Alfreda's apprenticeship several years, because of her work for Esme. Then there's the risk we'd take, sending her East." Aunt Marta gave my eldest aunt a long look, and Aunt Dagmar's color heightened as everyone in the room looked accusingly at her.

Well, I was all at sea. Then I noticed Cousin Cory trying to catch my gaze. He gave me a broad wink (out of Aunt Dagmar's sight, of course). I lifted my eyebrows in turn, trying to let him see the question in me. He nodded slightly, and I knew he'd explain later on.

"But my major objection would be that we could not fulfill Garda's requirement if Esme taught her. You forget that the Second Lessons must be from a practitioner of the opposite sex."

Oh, must they? Aunt Marta was continuing: "Will you

then have her shipped back to Cory, with days of train travel as well as rough roads between her two instructors? Her mental talents may not be strong enough for that strain. Do we want her on the road, most likely alone, during her late adolescence?"

"Isn't it better that one instructor come from each side of the family?" Uncle Karl asked thoughtfully, shooting Cousin Cory a sharp glance. "Esme and Cory are both from our side."

"Marta and Cory will teach her," Papa said quietly, the underlying steel in his voice surprising all of us. "If Esme offers to give her a bit of town polish afterward, that's between Esme and Alfreda."

I thought I was starting to get the drift of the discussion. It had something to do with a practitioner the family didn't want me involved with, but wouldn't name, and with Aunt Dagmar's way of putting on airs. So, she wanted a niece taught by a town practitioner, did she? I vaguely remembered a distant cousin of my mother's named Esme. A wealthy, successful wizard in an East Coast city . . . If Esme taught me, that meant a man from Papa's family. I didn't know of any male practitioners on his side.

"Does that meet with your approval, Alfreda?" Aunt Marta said suddenly, calling me back to the moment. "You will study basic herb lore with your mother and woodcraft with your father until Vintage of your fifteenth year. Then you will come to me for women's arts, and finally to your cousin Cory for the male attributes. We'll talk about your cousin Esme later," she added.

I managed a smile for my momma and said simply: "I'd like that." Anything else I might have said would have sounded too matter-of-fact or excited.

It seemed to be just the right tone. The room relaxed suddenly as the people within stirred from their rigid pos-

tures. Momma finally reached for a teacup, and Aunt
Sunhild got up to pass around a plate of cookies. It
hadn't been simple, but it was accomplished.

I was going to be a practitioner!

You will be a wizard, child. I have no doubts about it.

Fortunately I wasn't holding a teacup, or I would have
dropped it. This was worse than the wolves—I was hearing *people* speak inside my head. It had to be in my head,
because it sounded like Cousin Cory, and he was all the
way across the room. Slowly I raised my face and twisted
my body toward him.

Sure enough, he was looking at me, and gave me
another one of those big winks. I caught myself wondering if I could learn to do that, and Cousin Cory's smile
grew broader.

It's not nice to eavesdrop, I thought distinctly, since I
knew he'd plucked that thought from me, and had to
smother a laugh as Cory stiffened up like a schoolboy
caught whispering in church. Although I couldn't feel his
presence within, I figured I should ask while it was on my
mind, and thought: *But real practitioners aren't called
wizards by any but the foolish, are they?*

*Don't strain like that, darlin', just think in real sen-
tences,* was the reply as Cory relaxed again. *There are* real
*wizards, great ones of power. But not all practitioners
reach that level.*

Are you and Aunt Marta—? This was interesting, but
sort of tiring.

There was an audible chuckle from Cory as his
thoughts came back at me. *You're not doing it right yet.
You're pushing too hard. I'll teach you this before you
come to me, so don't worry. No, we're very good, but not
quite wizards. It has to do with instincts, believe it or not.*
He rose from his seat on the horsehair couch and moved
over to sit in the polished maple rocker in my corner.

"Tea, Corrado?" Aunt Dagmar asked as she saw him move.

"Coffee, please, Dagmar," was his reply, using her full name, so I could tell he was done teasing her. Quietly he said to me, "It's exhausting at first to pass thoughts, but I'm staying for the holidays, since I'm already here, and I'll teach you 'fore I go. I don't think you'll have any trouble learning it, and I think you're adult enough not to abuse it."

I thought about that a moment. "Like dipping into people's heads?" I asked, giving him a hard look.

"Exactly." He gave me a hard look back. "Trust me—you don't want to know what people are really thinking. Not most of them. And there's no need to tell your momma. She doesn't need to know yet that I trusted you with the knowledge."

I thought on this a while as cups of tea and coffee floated past and Aunt Sunhild pressed a fresh macaroon on me. That "yet" reassured me. We'd tell Momma eventually . . . and I'd really have to be on my best behavior. After nibbling on the cookie a while I said, "What was that business about Esme? Isn't she a cousin of Momma's?"

Cory's rumbling chuckle vibrated behind my ears. "The last time a fledgling practitioner was sent East, the Northwest Territory lost him. The lure of the city was too much. Now he's got such expensive tastes, I don't think he can come back—he can't afford the cut in income."

"You're afraid I'll like the city too much?" I said, surprised. Sure, I liked new clothes as much as anyone, and a hair ribbon for a barn-raising, but I couldn't even imagine the threat of the city. I mean, once you'd seen the parks and the great homes, there were only the lending libraries left, weren't there? And girls had to ride sidesaddle there, which was no way to control a restless horse.

Cory smiled faintly. "Your cousin Esme is a good practitioner, and very successful. She married a doctor, so their work melds well together, and they have a fine living between them. But although her children all have the talent, especially the girls, none of them have learned more than the herb lore."

"Why?"

The simplicity of my question seemed to surprise him. A half-smile touched his face, and it wasn't nice at all. "People can be cruel, Allie, especially the young. If you don't fit in, I mean."

"Amen to that," I whispered. At least now I had a real reason for people to think me odd.

"Well, most young men are fools." I looked up, startled, but Cory's face was serious. "I was one myself. They listen to the worst of the talk from their fathers and brothers, and value the wrong things in a woman." He gave me one of his corner-of-the-eye looks and said, "Esme's daughters didn't want to chase away their fancy city suitors. So they played dumb . . . and stopped learning. A bit further along, not knowing a spell properly can be dangerous."

"They must not have wanted to learn," I murmured.

"Not the craft. The boys wanted good money as fast as possible, and it takes a long time for a practitioner to become established. One son is an excellent herbalist, but on the sly, since he's a doctor. The other two boys are in trade and law and, I expect, will do well."

"And the girls?" For some reason, it seemed important.

"Oh, some would say they've done very well," Cory said with a barking laugh. "One married a visiting nobleman and went overseas. One married into one of the wealthiest banking families in Boston, and one married a budding politician. But none of them practices. There's one granddaughter who has shown talent and interest . . . by current standards, she's not pretty, you see."

I blinked at him. Whatever did that have to do with it? Hadn't the chance to learn to communicate with animals or spirits excited them? Hadn't they even been afraid *not* to learn?

That last was heartfelt, and Cory must have caught it. "If you decide not to believe, there's nothing to fear," he said quietly, the rocker beginning to move slightly. "When one of them finally gets swallowed by the other side, the family will probably really believe that it was a stroke or a fall that killed or incapacitated their sibling." My cousin shook his head slightly. "Risking life in an asylum for the riches of the world." He looked at me again and added, "I think you'd find them fools, Allie, but if you wait to visit till you're grown, you can enjoy the good and ignore the bad." Then that sudden smile flashed out. "'Sides, I'm selfish enough myself. I want to go down in history as one of your teachers!"

That made me laugh. "I hope there's not a lot of math in practice, or this could be a long apprenticeship!" I admitted softly.

"You'll do fine, darlin'," he said quickly. "You're interested, and wanting the knowledge keeps you going through the hard parts. You'll like my momma when you come. She keeps house for me, and she's an incredible cook. You can learn to make pasta!"

Well, I didn't know what pasta was, but I smiled at his enthusiasm, which he seemed to appreciate. Then one of the uncles asked Cory a question, and I was left with my thoughts. Such as why a man would not want the prestige of a wife who was a practitioner, and why Cousin Cory called himself a fool about women. This ran on to other thoughts, and before I could help myself I had blurted out, "Can you show me how you trapped skunk without ruining the pelt with stink?"

Well, Uncle Henrik doesn't approve of children's talking

around adults, and gave me a quashing look, but Cousin Cory only chuckled. Holding up a finger so I would hold the thought, he finished his conversation with Uncle Henrik while I sat quashed. Then he turned back to me.

"It's a gorgeous pelt, isn't it? Strong and warm, too. But black isn't your color, darlin'. You need a blond or golden brown color, or a creamy beaver belly. Your papa will teach you the tricks on tracking, don't you worry. Before you're done, you can even learn live trapping, so you get only the animal you really need."

Well, that was Cory's wealth talking, since he made his living as a practitioner. We depended on trapping for half our living, and ate everything we caught. That's how it was when you were money-poor and land-rich. If I actually learned how to trap, maybe we could save enough pelts for me to have my own coat. . . .

"Be sure to have him teach you about duck blinds." Cory's chuckle was wicked. "You and Josh will like that. It's not easy, but the ducks have a real sporting chance. Much better than going hunting with a duck gun."

As if we could afford a gun Papa would trust us with! But I won't deny Cory had me curious, which I'd never been about the woodcraft part of a practitioner's work. I liked the forest much better than the plowed fields . . . maybe that part wouldn't be so bad after all.

All this led me to wondering if duck blinds were like deer blinds, and what kind of animal had a golden pelt, and what my friend Idelia was going to think of all this fuss. The room was very warm, the fire was friendly, and another cookie or two just filled in the edges.

Next thing I knew, Josh was shaking my arm. "Wake up, Allie! We've got to get home and milk!" He already had his coat on, and was holding my shawl and stuff.

The real world is never far away, if you know how to look for it. I reached up to take my shoes, and started thinking about whether I could talk Josh into shoveling all the manure, and what kind of bribe would work.

The last time it'd cost me three nights' dessert. Maybe if I made cookies . . .

I started lacing up my shoes.

SEVEN

AUNT MARTA CAME HOME with us in the wagon, wedged between Papa and Momma on the seat. She placed her carpetbag on the bed back in the stillroom and settled in like she'd lived with us for years. By the time Josh and I finished the milking and Papa had all the stock fed, Momma and Aunt Marta had a wonderful light supper laid out and waiting for us.

We ate hot bread, chilled milk, and ham 'n' beans for supper, and Aunt Marta made a mean corn muffin! They whipped up something secret for dessert, which was a surprise, after the wonderful dinner we'd had. It was an apple compote, and I knew I could taste a hint of licorice in it.

"Do we have licorice?" I asked, trying not to make it sound like a demand. I'm very fond of licorice, I must admit.

"No, but your momma had plenty of aniseed," Aunt Marta replied, giving Momma a quick smile.

You might have thought that things would be awkward between my momma and Aunt Marta, but they weren't at all. They talked about Aunt Marta's new grandchildren, like nothing had happened that afternoon. In fact, Momma seemed, well, *warm* toward Aunt Marta, if you follow me. Afterward we all sat in the kitchen with the light of a blazing fire on our faces, and sipped hot tea with mint leaves floating on the top.

Bedtime comes early in the winter; mostly we go to sleep not long after the sun. Soon both Ben and Joe were nodding by the fireplace, and Josh was yawning over his reader.

"Time to close down," Papa announced, leaning his rocker forward to knock his pipe clean on the edge of the firewall. "We've got a big day tomorrow."

Papa always seemed to say that, but this time it was true. Not just that Christmas was coming, and I had to get my gifts finished, but all the new things I was going to learn! Thinking about it almost woke me up again.

I think Aunt Marta must have seen my eyes get brighter, because she said, "Come help me with the bed, Allie," as she stood to say good night. I stuck as close to her heels as the dog star to the hunter, and we moved back into the cool silence of the stillroom.

For those of you who have different customs, the stillroom was where Momma preserved her herbs and made her beer. We stored the eggs in there, too, and one pair of doors to the root cellar was set beneath the window. I hadn't been in the stillroom much since Dolph died, except to get eggs or make the bed for Aunt Marta, so it felt strange to be going in there. But I knew I had to get used to it, because that was where most of the herb work got done.

Aunt Marta was already rummaging in her enormous carpetbag, and a familiar odor wafted out at me. I remembered bees, and honey. She pulled out what looked like a tree branch, and then something circular in . . . pieced wood? It was hard to see in the faint light from the fireplace, and we hadn't brought a candle. The tree branch attached to the circle, and she set the contraption on the table against the north wall. Then she moved back into the kitchen. In a moment she was back, a lit spill in her hand, and in its tiny light I could see that the tree branch was some sort of weird candle holder! It held six—no, seven candles, and I could smell the beeswax from where I stood by the bed.

Gracefully she lit the tapers, starting at the top and working down and out. Soon there was more true light in the stillroom than in the kitchen.

Smiling at my surprise, Aunt Marta said, "It's called a candelabra when it has so many branches. My husband made it for me, long ago." Gently she touched a twisted, polished branch of the glowing red wood.

Slowly I moved over to the table and peered at the candles. The holder itself was twisted like flame, and there was no pattern I could see to where the branches popped out. "I've never seen wood like that," I said aloud, and immediately felt foolish. As if I'd lived long enough to see all the wood there is! But I used to haunt the carpenter's shop, and I had seen a lot of types of wood—even ebony, from Asia, far away.

"I'd be surprised if you knew this wood," Aunt Marta told me. "It's from the far south of this country, down where my husband had kin. He had a big family, you know," she added, and I realized that sometimes she still needed to talk about my dead uncle. "Folks call it *bois d'arc,* but its real name is osage orange. Your uncle Jon peeled and polished this branch many a night, the first winter we lived in Cat Track Hollow. I had complained that people were always calling me away and then stuffing me in a dark corner for sleeping. That's when he made me this, so I wouldn't have to dress by feel."

"What does the tree look like? Are the flowers pretty?" I said impulsively, and was rewarded by one of her glowing smiles.

"I've always said you ask the right questions," she said in turn, which made me blink at her. "The flower's nothing

special, and hard to describe until we teach you the terms
to describe leaves and stems."

"How much can you say about a leaf? It's round or
long, pointy or smooth, big or small—" I started.

She held up a finger in warning, and I immediately
stopped speaking. "It has ovate-lanceolate deciduous
leaves, three to five inches long and up to three inches
wide—"

"Are you going to teach me what that means?" I inter-
rupted.

"Your momma will," she said calmly, turning back
toward the table. "*Bois d'arc* has huge multiple fruit, like
a pomegranate, only ugly and inedible." She demonstrated, holding her hands to indicate a ball bigger than a
baby's head. "One falling on you could knock you out, if
it hit you right! The plant can be hedge or a fine, straight
tree, and the wood is dense and hard. It has rounded,
scaly bark, but the inside is blood red and beautiful. I
think that's why Jon chose this wood . . . because the
inside is so different from the outside. To remind me not
to judge things only by what I see." She moved the candelabra toward the back of the table, bending with interest
over what I realized were tiny living plants.

"I didn't know those were here!" I blurted out.

"Didn't you smell the fresh mint?" she asked, pointing
out the lush leaves spilling over the sides of the container.

"It always smells like herbs in here; I just thought it
was the last mint Momma harvested," I admitted.

"Basil, fringed lavender, balm of Gilead," Aunt Marta
murmured to herself as she examined the pots. "Even two
hop plants . . . she must be worried about her garden
plants freezing. Winter savory, thyme, sage—I didn't
know your mother had oregano!" She brushed her fingers
against the sprawling dark green plant and held them up
so I could catch the scent.

No problem—the bruised leaves filled the air with a pungent aroma. It was a spicy-sweet odor I remembered from a cheese dish Momma sometimes made. "I think she traded with Aunt Sofia for that," I said, glad Aunt Marta wasn't one of those people to stick her hand right under your nose. I have an excellent sense of smell, thank you very much.

"I hope she'll give me some when she has enough to trade," was Aunt Marta's response. "Help me remember to ask her about seed. Ah, she forced some chives!"

There were more herbs in pots on the open shelf beneath the table, and the lack of stray dirt made me think that Momma rotated them to get the light from the window. I gave the window a sharp look and said, "Could we build her a shelf for her winter herbs?"

Shaking her head, Aunt Marta lifted the candelabra and moved west down the narrow room toward the floor-to-ceiling shelves. "Too cold, Allie. That window is only one pane of glass thick. She needs a table that can go over the root cellar doors and be moved easily. I'll ask your father about it."

We were quiet for a while after that as Aunt Marta examined Momma's stores. Rows and rows of dark glass and ceramic jars stared back at us, some with engraved pottery labels and some with tiny metal name tags on chains around their necks. I knew the tall, thin bottles contained herbal oils and vinegars, as well as the tinctures made from the alcohol Momma's still produced (and you wondered why it was called a stillroom!). But most of those jars were a mystery to me.

That didn't seem to stop Aunt Marta from talking to me about them. "A good friend of my mother-in-law brought me several hot-pepper plants two years ago, up from the Deep South. I didn't know your momma liked exotics. I'll offer her a few plants for next spring." Setting the candelabra down on the other edge of the table, Aunt Marta took a jar of lady's mantle off the shelf and carefully pulled the stopper. She inhaled the fragrance, and then quickly replaced the stopper, setting the jar back on the shelf.

When she finally turned toward me, my aunt was smiling. "Your momma hasn't lost a bit of her talents," Aunt Marta announced. "She still loves the art as much as she ever did. You'll do fine under her instruction, Allie. Just don't be afraid to ask questions. If she gets short-tempered about something, you know how to write a letter. Ask me! But only if you can't find the answer in her books." After that pronouncement, the woman reached up to unbutton her collar.

I was still thinking about the jars of herbs. "Why . . ." I thought about it, and tried again. "Why did you pick that jar to sniff?"

"You think there's a special reason?" was her response. She had that secret smile on again.

"There usually is," I pointed out, and my aunt chuckled.

"Lady's mantle is a hard herb to keep," she said as she dug in her bag for something. "It absorbs moisture from the air, so it can deteriorate or grow moldy. Good herbalists replace their supply every year . . . and your momma is a good herbalist. She'll teach you as well as I could about the craft—except for the dangerous herbs. Garda wants no part of the responsibility. Not that I blame her," Aunt Marta added.

A flannel nightgown of brilliant yellow flew up into the air and settled across the pillow of the bed. "I've been traveling forever, it seems, Allie," the woman said softly. "We'll talk more tomorrow. I don't need to leave for a day or two yet."

"One more question?" I asked.

She gave me a stern look. "A hard question or an easy question?"

I grimaced and admitted I wasn't sure. At her nod, I said, "Why doesn't Cousin Cory want Momma to know that I can hear him talk in my head?"

My aunt grew so still, I wasn't certain she knew what I meant. She said, "You mean you can understand his words without hearing him speak?" I nodded, and she put her hand on the stillroom door and pushed it shut. Then she reached out and pulled me into her arms.

"You going to believe me when I tell you something?" she whispered into my hair.

"I don't think you've lied to me yet," was my response as I turned my head sideways so I could breathe easier.

Some adults wouldn't have liked the way that came out, but Aunt Marta just chuckled. "There is nothing wrong with a practitioner having that talent, Allie. Nothing!" She was a bit fierce, and I think she knew it, since her voice grew gentler. "It's something people usually don't learn until they're further along in their studies, that's all. Normally Cory would have taught you when you came to live in his village. Your momma was always afraid of that gift, and since it takes time and will to learn it, she didn't. I don't think she fully understands the talent—it's not what most folks think." She pushed me back a step and lifted my chin so she could see my face. "Have you been hearing other people's thoughts floating around?"

"No, ma'am," I said, since shaking my head was awkward at the moment.

"You need strength to speak without words, and more strength to dip into people's thoughts. It's not a casual thing for most—and it's a foolish thing to do, hearing folks' private thoughts," she added with some of that fierceness.

"Can you do it?" I asked.

"Of course." As if it was as common as sewing a straight seam!

"But you won't teach me? Cory will?"

Smiling, Marta shook her head. "You'll learn some things better than others, depending on who teaches them to you. Leave it at that for now. Cory must have heard you toss out a thought, and decided to see if you could hear yet." Her gaze grew unfocused for a moment, and she added, "I think I know why he decided to do it, but that's his story to tell, not mine.

"Now"—her deep voice dropped a notch or two more—"I have got to get some sleep! No more startling revelations until morning!"

"Yes, ma'am." I gave her a quick hug, so she knew I wasn't still smoldering about her being gone from the area so long, and then I grabbed the soft leather loop that was the door handle to the stillroom. "Sweet dreams!"

"And you, girl. And you too."

Papa had banked the fire for the night, so I walked carefully in case the boys had left something on the floor. I could feel my aunt's gaze between my shoulder blades until I made the turn at the back staircase. It wasn't an anxious stare, but it was definitely thoughtful.

I wondered what she was thinking.

Momma didn't lose any time with my new lessons. By the time Josh and I had finished our chores and come in for breakfast, she was already up to something. While we ate gruel with honey and cream, she was over fussing in the hutch that held everything from the family Bible to Momma's tiny china teacups.

I tried to watch out of the corner of an eye, but Aunt Marta was asking Josh and me about our lessons, and about what we were making for Papa and the little boys for Christ's birthday, so there was no chance to see what Momma was up to. Believe it or not, I was trying to be least in sight. When we finished our gruel and tea, Aunt Marta popped up like a jumping jack and hustled our bowls off the table.

"No problem, Allie," she said cheerfully as she moved the kettle off the hob and poured hot water into the sink. "I think your momma has something she wants to show you. Dishes are always something a guest can do."

"I could dry," I offered, giving the towel a last wipe across the table and carrying it back to the sideboard.

"We'll see," was all Marta would say as she handed Josh some bread and cheese to take with him.

"No peeking," Josh warned as he disappeared outside into the early glow of Indian light, so I turned back toward the kitchen and saw that Momma was over at the big table doing something. When I started toward my chair, she held up her hand to stop me. Then I saw that she was setting out sheets of paper. They looked thick, like expensive drawing paper—at least the ones on top. I thought I could see the corner of a second sheet beneath one of them.

"Come, child," Momma said, reinforcing her command with a rolling curl of slender fingers. Turning her hand over, she pointed to my usual chair. I quickly sat back down.

There were four drawings spread out on the table. And what drawings! Even by firelight I could tell that the drawings were done in color. They were of plants—herbs, to be pre–cise—and looked so real that for a moment I thought they were dried flowers.

"Now, daughter," Momma began softly, "I want you to look closely at these and tell me what they are."

"Queen Anne's lace," I said promptly. Was she starting with the easy ones to get my confidence up?

Momma gave me a long look. "Are you sure?"

I started to say of course I was sure . . . and nothing came out of my mouth. *There's a point here,* I suggested to myself, and looked again. After a moment I realized that the leaves on each plant were different. One was lacy, still another looked like parsley, one had sort of a milkweed pod skin attached to it, and the fourth was delicate, each finger of its leaflets finely divided.

Drat. I was willing to wager my desserts for a week that I had four different plants in front of me! And I was so addled I couldn't for the life of me guess which was the Queen. Then inspiration struck.

"Aunt Marta, may I borrow your candel–abra?" I asked. The light wasn't what I'd call good for fancy work—and trying to pick one plant out of a crowd by only a drawing was harder than any embroidery I'd ever tried.

"Of course, Allie," she said as she pulled a bowl out of the hot water. "Help yourself."

So I went back into the stillroom and brought out the funny candle holder. I set it back from the pictures; beeswax may burn cleaner, but I wasn't taking any chances. Then I fetched a spill and carefully lit the tapers in the same order Aunt Marta had the night before.

All that soft light made a world of difference. Between the candles and the fireplace, I was able to recognize how the Queen Anne's lace got its name. There's a tiny dot of color—sometimes red, sometimes purple—that is in the center of each white clump of flowers. Legend says the first plant was stained by a single drop of Queen Anne's blood. I found the mark in the second drawing.

"This is the Queen," I announced, touching the edge of the drawing carefully.

Momma relaxed, her shoulders easing. Until that moment I hadn't realized she was tense. "Do you know any of the others?"

I shook my head. "This one looks a little bit like parsley, but the flowers should be yellow-green, and I doubt the artist would make that kind of mistake. I don't know the others."

"You will," she said in turn, and sounded a bit grim. "No, your great-grandmother didn't make a mistake. That herb with white flowers is called fool's parsley." There was a pause, and then she added, "Its other name is dog poison. The leaves and roots can kill you if you eat them."

I blinked in my surprise. Kill? Something that looked like faithful Queen Anne's lace, the wild and woolly carrot, was poisonous? I gave the herb another hard look, noticing the beardlike tiny leaves right under the flower cluster, and how Granny had turned over a leaf in the drawing to show its shiny yellow-green underside.

"The back side of parsley leaves has no shine—that's the major clue," Momma went on. "And its smooth stems. There are medicinal uses for fool's parsley, but you'll learn about them from your aunt later."

"What's this one?" I asked, touching the drawing with the fuzzy sheaths that looked a little like milkweed pods.

"Kin to the Queen," Momma said promptly. "That's usually called cow parsnip. You can't miss the white, woolly undersides of those leaves—a bit like maple leaves, they look. The flower heads can get huge, sometimes a foot across, and I've seen them with a lavender tint. Some folks get a rash from touching the leaves."

I just stared at her. She kept all that in her head about just one plant? And that was just to help you find it— she'd said nothing about what it was used for. Looking down at the drawings again, I pointed to the last in the row.

"Ah." The word sounded flat. "That's the other reason you have to be so careful. That's poison hemlock. All of it is poisonous, especially the seeds and roots. People have died, thinking they were eating young Queen roots. Those grooved stems with the purple spots are the best warning, those and the lacy leaves. They look too much like Queen leaves for my taste—that's why I never let you children help me harvest herbs. You've got to reach a certain age to be right every time."

"There's still another plant that has those tiny white flowers clumped together," came Aunt Marta's voice as she moved up behind me. "Water hemlock. The umbels— the clusters of flowers—are flat, and the leaves look a bit like angelica. But you can't miss the yellow sap that flows from its cut stem; it smells like parsnips."

Suddenly I was scared—real scared. I could feel myself break out in a sweat. How was I going to remember all this? This was just the surface of a couple of herbs, and I knew that there were dozens—hundreds, even.

Light that aided me could help my momma as well. My face must have showed what I was thinking, because she curled the back of her fingers across my cheek, the way she does when she's pleased with me.

"I didn't expect you to get these right, daughter," Momma said gently. "Or even memorize all we're telling you. I just wanted to know how far you had to go in the most important thing of all."

There was a long pause; the women were tall and shadowed above me. I suspected it was my turn to talk. There were only two things this lesson had taught me, and I didn't think Momma was talking about recognizing the Queen. So I volunteered the other thing I'd learned. "Knowing how much I don't know?" I suggested.

"There's hope for her, Marta," she said conversationally. "That's one way of putting it, I suppose. Respect, Allie. Respecting the power of what you're going to learn. Even the least of it can cure or kill. If you misspell a word, it usually doesn't hurt anything. If you get a recipe for an infusion wrong, someone could end up even sicker than before—or dead."

"We don't mean to scare you, child," came Aunt Marta's voice as she bent over and squeezed my shoulders. "But in the Wise Arts, it's better to err on the cautious side. If you can't tell wild carrot from fool's parsley, you'd better go hungry!"

"No doubt about that," I agreed fervently. "Do you want me to start studying these plants?" I touched the corner of one of the pictures.

"Not yet." Momma started to pick up the heavy paper. Beneath the drawing were sheets with a great deal of writing on them, and I spotted the name *poison hemlock* on one. Good—there was lots of information about each herb. "We have fresh herbs growing in the stillroom, so you might as well start there. You can compare the living plant to your granny's drawings."

"How many mints do you have, Garda?" Aunt Marta asked as she hung the dishtowels near the fireplace to dry.

"Only a dozen this winter," Momma replied as she carried her drawings over to the sideboard.

Only a dozen? "How many kinds of mint are there?" I asked carefully as I got up from my chair.

"Oh, a few hundred or so," my aunt said as she lifted the candelabra and carried it back into the stillroom.

I was almost certain she was kidding. Almost.

Cousin Cory arrived as a pale winter sun was trying to cast shadows in the front yard. I'd divided my day between a mess of mint and embroidering one of the shirts I was making for Christmas presents. Turns out there *are* hundreds of kinds of mints—and they're about as choosy when prop–o–gating as a queen cat in heat. But

there are families of mints, and that's the important thing
to know. Folks choose mints by nose, not by name.

It was kind of fun, actually. First I had to get my nose
working, and then recognize the different leaves one from
another. I learned that mints tended to have opposite
leaves, which means that they grow out of the same node
on opposite sides of the stem, and that the flowers are
generally but not always lavender. Momma said she had
yet to meet a mint that didn't smell minty-spicy, which
was a comfort. A couple of mints grow weird—"sessile,"
which means they have no stalk, or "petioled," which
means the leaves have stalks, or even both on the same
plant!

In honor of my studies, we made a boiled chicken
using mint as one of the ingredients. I'd never thought of
mint for cooking, except for teas and desserts, but mixed
with chives, parsley, coriander, and orange rind, along
with basics like onion and salt and pepper, it smelled like
pretty tasty stuff. Since it was so cold outside, we used
some precious white sugar and lemon juice and made a
spearmint sorbet (*sorbet*'s a fancy word for a frozen
drink). Little Ben helped me with that, although he kept
wanting to go outside and peek while it was freezing.

Despite the sun, Cory was covered with a dusting of
snow, which he shook off before coming in the house. I
took advantage of the confusion to get my hands on that
wonderful coat of his, and wrapped myself from nose to
ankles in what the fur folks call anything except skunk.
Lord, it was warm and silky! And smelled the same as
any properly tanned pelt. Someone—Cory, maybe?—had
lined it with black satin, and I swear I felt like royalty.

"Don't grow too attached to that, darlin'," came
Cory's voice, and I looked up to see he was watching me.
"I'll need it on the trip home!"

"Now what have you got in that sack, Corrado?" my

mother said in that mock-severe voice she sometimes uses with Papa.

Cory shook his head mysteriously. "I promised Joe I wouldn't open any bags until he got my horse settled." Then he gave Momma a beseeching look. "But I would like to know if you've got enough of whatever smells so good for me to stay for dinner!"

"Since I imagine you're staying through Christmas, I should hope I have enough for dinner!"

"Two chickens in all kinds of things!" I burst out. "I didn't know mint could be used with meat!"

Cory gave my mother and aunt a long look. "Have you deprived your children of spring lamb with mint sauce? Shame on you, Garda!"

Momma shrugged and turned back to the biscuits she was cutting out. "Our sheep are for wool, Cory. Next year we just might have enough births for a few meals, but we'll have to wait and see."

"We eat a lot of chicken, and different kinds of beans," I told Cory as I pushed him back toward one of the rockers. "And venison! Papa gets at least a deer a month."

"Then I'll look forward to venison stew," was Cory's reply. "And Mediterranean chicken tonight!"

"Mediterranean?" I said, glancing over at Momma and Aunt Marta.

"One of the places coriander was first found," my cousin began. Before Cory could continue, Joe and Joshua threw open the front door. I quickly tossed Cory's coat over the shirt I was working on.

"What's in the sack?" Joe hollered, charging into the kitchen.

Momma reached for the bundle, which Cory had set in the middle of the table. "Let's open it and see. It's pretty heavy."

What with Ben and Joe pulling at the cloth, it took

twice as long as it should have for Momma to open the present. When she did, you might have thought we were a church choir.

"Cocoa!" my brothers crowed along with me. The tin was *huge*—I didn't know they could make cocoa tins that large.

Aunt Marta gave Cory a wry glance. "I hope you haven't stashed something else in there." The man was already shaking his head, but Momma had pried open the lid, and the aroma rose to compete with the chicken.

"Hot cocoa for breakfast," Momma announced to general groans of protest. "The sorbet is enough treat for tonight. Is your father almost done in the barn, Josh?"

"He's not— Yes, Momma," Josh said quickly. I wondered what they were up to, but it *was* the month of Snow. It's best not to ask too many questions that close to Christmas.

"Then set the table, boys. Allie, why don't you go hang up Cory's coat in the front room?" She gave me a long look as she spoke, so I knew she was giving me a chance to smuggle my sewing away. Around birthdays and Christmas, we always had fires big enough to warm the entire downstairs. That way folks could keep warm while they worked on presents, Momma supervising in one room and Papa in the other.

I'd been smart that year—I'd already finished both Momma's and Papa's gifts, so I could float from room to room. I hustled both the coat and the shirt I'd just finished into the parlor and hung Cory's coat up on the beautiful wooden rack that stuck out from the back wall.

Quickly I opened the cedar chest I'd been hiding my presents in, folding the linen shirt to shove it inside. As I was digging under the top blanket, my hand grabbed hold of another shirt.

It was the unbleached one I had made for Dolph. The collar and cuffs were covered with vines and wheat sheaves and gourds, the embroidery all in white instead of colors . . . a man's shirt, like Papa's.

It was the unexpectedness of it that brought the tears, you see. I had completely forgotten about presents and the holiday while I was looking for a priest for the service. And now I had a beautiful shirt that no one would ever wear.

"We can't even bury you in it," I whispered, rubbing the back of my index finger against the soft linen cloth.

So. Would I just keep the shirt? Or would I give it to someone? Save it for a sweetheart, maybe . . . No, I bet I'd want to make something special just for him. I had made this for my eldest brother, not a man I could call my own.

Sitting down on my heels, I considered the words my thoughts had formed.

I still had an eldest brother . . . Joshua. I'd made the shirt I was holding for him, full of deep green pine boughs and black acorns and a pair of bright cardinals that had turned out pretty good. The colors were for someone pale, like Momma, and with dark hair and light eyes. Someone like Josh.

But little Joe had the same coloring as Joshua. And I was making the shirts big enough to grow into, anyway. I hadn't even cut out Ben's shirt, which saved the fabric . . . and in this part of the country, you had to be of a saving disposition. I could put the same designs on Ben's shirt as on Dol—Joshua's, only in color. Ben worshipped Josh, and would be thrilled.

And like it or not, Josh had to be almost a man now, be he only thirteen. I tucked the colorful shirt into the pile and closed the chest. The idea of Josh enjoying the shirt sat better with me than leaving the fabric to yellow

and rot. *I bet you'd approve,* I said silently to my
brother's shade.

"Trip over a piece of your past?" came Cousin Cory's
voice.

I considered his words as I turned, and realized that
I'd prevented Dolph's shirt from becoming just that—a
piece of my past stashed in cedar. "Actually, I just dis-
posed of a piece—a potential piece," I replied, pulling my
sleeve across my cheek to wipe away the tears that had
escaped.

"Ruthless when necessary," was Cory's comment, even
as he gave an approving nod. "Travel light in life, darlin'.
Dolph knows you have to get on with things."

"But I miss him," was my protest, even as another tear
escaped my lashes. "Why did he have to mess with that
wolf's mouth?" I was surprised at how angry I suddenly
felt.

Cory just shook his head. "Young folks sometimes do
reckless things to try to impress each other. But what's
done is done. We can love his memory, and be angry that
he left us so soon, but we gotta go on."

I thought about it a bit, settling on top of the cedar
chest. Cory had mentioned something I'd wondered
about. "Is it okay sometimes to be angry about it?"

"You mean mad that he died? Or mad at him for
dying?" Cory shooed me to one side and sat down on
the other end of the big chest. "'Course it's okay. We
can't always know why people have to leave us, darlin'.
Sometimes they're old or too sick to heal, but sometimes
it just seems like Death has pointed a finger and said,
'Today I think I'll take you.' I was mad at God for
longer than I can remember, back when my daddy died.
But Daddy's time had come, and finally I realized that
even a practitioner can't save someone who's been
called."

After some silence, I whispered, "Were you ever mad at your daddy for leaving you behind?"

Cory chortled. "Sure was. I went out in the orchards in the dead of winter, where no one else could hear me, and yelled at him." He winked at me. "Don't know for sure if I reached heaven, but I suspect I woke a few apple trees!" His face grew somber as he gazed off at nothing, and he went on, "You know, Allie, I'm not sure folks are ever ready to lose someone they love. Even though we know that everyone dies in the end, young or old, we rail against fate." Shaking his head again, Cory whispered, "I knew my daddy well enough to know that if he'd had a choice, he'd never have left me and Momma behind without saying good-bye. So I didn't waste too much time blaming him for dying."

Looking over at me again, Cory said, "It's okay to be mad—that's natural. But try to work your way through the mad. Dying is not too hard on the dead, you know— it's hard on those left behind."

The truth of that really got my attention, and we were quiet together for what seemed a long time.

Somewhere in there, my tears finally stopped flowing.

Cory stood up and stretched his huge frame. "Are you ready to learn about mind talkin'?"

"Now?" The abruptness of it startled me.

"Tonight, maybe. If you think you can sew and learn at the same time," he added with a big smile. "Being busy helps when you're hurting, and I promise you, you'll be busy!"

"Alfreda! Wash up for dinner!" came Momma's voice from the kitchen, cutting off any reply I might have made.

"Maybe if we're lucky, your momma will be supervising present-making and we can hide in here," Cory said as he caught sight of my disappointment. "We'll get to it, Allie. I won't leave until you've got down the shell."

I knew better. My brothers would be so excited about Cory's being here, I'd never get him to myself. At least not that night. The important thing was, Cory hadn't forgotten. And I was going to learn how to pull people's thoughts from the air.

I wondered if I could learn what a cardinal was thinking. What would Dolph have thought of that? Probably would've yanked on a braid and pretended not to believe me, until I was so red in the face I looked about to pop. Then he would've asked what it was like.

Would anyone else ever ask me what it was like?

EIGHT

THERE'S AN INTERESTING THING about learning to know people's thoughts. The hard part isn't knowing what they're thinking—it's avoiding knowing what they're thinking, if you catch my drift. But I'm getting ahead of myself.

I'd been right about getting Cory alone. It took three or four days for the newness to wear off and the boys to leave him be. A real snowfall helped me catch his attention. The flakes fell steady and deep, the air biting and cold enough to freeze the hairs in your nose. My cousin was a sly one; he knew just how to tire the little folks out. After a morning bout of lying on their backs making flailing angels, Cory, Joe, and Ben trooped to the north field, where they packed blocks of snow and built a fort. Then they made snow soldiers creeping up on their position, and *then* Cory showed the boys how to make snowballs that didn't fall apart yet couldn't hurt anyone.

You'd think they'd done enough to exhaust a dozen children, but Ben and Joe spent at least another hour targeting those soldiers from different angles. Finally Momma hauled them in, to a chorus of protest, Cory shaking snow like a big black bear. In truth, I think she called them to save them from falling flat on their faces. I'd never seen such tired children! Josh and his friends inherited the fort, so that took care of stray family, since

Papa was helping a neighbor with some repairs to a barn.

The frost-nipped pair of boys managed to down some soup and bread before drowsing before the roaring kitchen fire. Momma and Aunt Marta had been sitting in the rockers cleaning cotton bolls, and returned to it while I washed up the dishes. I was scalding the washcloth when I heard Cory say:

"I'm staking out the front room, ladies, so you can gossip with a clean heart." He had gathered up the rest of the bread and another bowl of soup. Of course, this left him no way to carry his mug of beer. You getting the drift?

"Gossip isn't kind, Corrado," was my mother's reply as she glanced his way. "We're merely catching up. It's been a long time since Marta and I could talk to our heart's content."

Cory just grinned, his white teeth flashing above the indigo of his flannel shirt. "Bring that mug along, will you, Allie? That's my girl." And that was it—he wandered off into the front without another look back, and if anyone noticed I didn't return, no one said anything. Not for the first time, I wondered who was in which conspiracy.

My cousin settled in the big maple rocker that came from all the way overseas. I carried over one of the stacking tables Papa had made, and set it by his side. Thanking me with a stately nod, Cory arranged his dinner and gave me a wink.

"Patience is usually rewarded," he began, taking a sip of the beer. This was followed by a big smile and a sigh of contentment. "Lord, your momma makes fine beer! If I'd known she could make beer this good, I'd have courted her myself. See that you have the learning of it," he added, gesturing toward the big old cushions piled in the corner and covered with a quilt. "Now, make yourself comfortable, girl, and we'll start on the mysteries."

"Mysteries?" I prompted, smoothing the bear paw quilt back into place and dragging the largest of the cushions over next to his chair.

"Anything that is directly related to our own inborn talent for straddling the worlds is called a mystery when we refer to it in front of those who aren't practitioners," Cory began quietly. "That's to remind us that there are things we don't yield to those of different gifts."

"Different gifts?" I almost didn't ask, but I didn't want the entire discussion to be Greek to me.

"Just because folks don't have the gift of straddling the worlds doesn't mean they have no talent." He cast an amused glance my way. "Can you shoe a horse properly that needs its gait corrected, or build a china hutch with tight, clean joints?"

"Oh." Remembering the bird house Papa had let me build, I knew the local carpenter had nothing to fear from me.

Cory's expression was very serious. "So you see my point. Practitioners need to beware the deadly sin of pride, Allie, for the safety of both our souls and our bodies. There's enough envy and misunderstanding about us as it is. Fuel the flames of discontent by arrogant behavior, and folks start talking about the devil and familiars. Next thing you know, your house has been burned down!"

I nodded to let him know I was paying attention. I hadn't thought about it in quite that way, but envy and misunderstanding were something I knew about.

"Back to the mysteries. Folks don't understand them and are more than a bit frightened by them. It's better not to say anything than to say only a little bit. So instead of arguing constantly with our patients and clients, we allude to the mysteries."

I adjusted my skirt over my knees and clasped my hands in my lap. "So where do we begin?"

"At the very beginning, child. We begin with the elements." Cory lifted an eyebrow then, and gave me a long look. "Some of this may be harder than it needs to be, because of lessons you haven't had yet. But you heard me, Allie, when I spoke silently to you. That means you can learn this lesson now. We'll just skip over a few steps and fill them in later."

"How can we skip if everything builds on the last lesson?"

Cory's smile returned. "I'm glad to know you remember chance conversation. We can skip because you know how to believe in people. I'm going to tell you some things, and you're going to take them on faith. Later on, you'll learn the whys and wherefores from Marta and me, but for now, you'll simply *do,* and let *why* remain a mystery."

I felt myself slip into a frown. "Isn't it dangerous to do something without knowing how it works?"

"Not this time. You'll understand the basics, and trust they work. I'll warn you about any dangers. There are other things you could do with this learning, but not yet—not yet." He paused for a spoonful of soup. "For now, you will learn how to protect yourself from many dangers."

Protection was always valuable. I sat still as a mouse 'neath the wings of a hawk and waited to begin. My cousin did not continue, however; he applied himself to his soup and bread, and quickly finished his meal. Only after he had pushed aside his bowl and retrieved his mug did Cousin Cory continue.

"We will begin with earth," he said quietly. "Can you guess why?"

I thought about the earth for a moment, and said, "Folks always speak of the earth as our mother. Does it have something to do with that?"

Cory smiled and sipped his beer. "Not bad. Close, but it's even simpler than that. Earth is our mother because we come from earth and return to earth. We begin this lesson with earth because earth is one of the major powers of a woman. You're going to be a woman, so you need to base your shields in women's magic."

"What are the other major powers?" I realized I had whispered, and felt foolish that he'd cowed me so easily. But my cousin didn't smile.

"Earth and water are the source of creation, and the strength of women," was his answer. "Air and fire are the heart of transformation, and the strength of men. A good practitioner can learn to use all the elements, but it's always easiest to use those that are kin to you. If we were in a boat on a lake, we'd start with water. Since there's solid ground beneath this cabin, we'll start with earth."

With a quick jerk, Cory lifted his mug and drained it in one long gulp. Setting the empty container next to his bowl, he said, "You need to get comfortable. Choose a place to sit and lean, 'cause you'll probably need some backing before we're through." He gave the room a quick sweep with his gaze, and pointed to the stone wall surrounding the fireplace. "Would that be too warm for you?"

"As long as you don't build the fire up too much, it should be fine," I agreed, standing and dragging my pillow over to the cooler end of the stone lip. Cory followed me and made sure the fire screen was tight against the open mouth.

"Sit and lean, Allie. Let's do as much as we can this afternoon. Your momma has Marta to help her pluck seeds from those bolls." Hooking another cushion with his long arm, Cory pulled it over and sprawled across it. "Stone warm enough for leaning?" he asked as I positioned myself against the smooth granite blocks.

"Just fine. Now what?"

"I suggest you close your eyes, so nothing distracts you. You won't have to do that once you learn the trick, but it helps at first." Cory's voice had become softer, almost blending into the snap and pop of the fire. "Just try to relax. Let your arms and legs get heavy, like you're going to fall asleep, but don't nod off. Stick with the sound of my voice."

While he talked on, I let myself get real loose and quiet, like when I was sitting out before dawn trying to see the deer feed in the pasture. He hadn't said anything about concentrating on something, so I held in my mind the image of his round, strong face, light and shadow in the reflection of the fire, the room sharply illuminated beyond.

"You're getting very heavy, Allie. So heavy the floor can't hold you anymore. You're going to sink right into the floor, but don't worry about breathing or anything, 'cause it's your inner self that the floor can't support, not your body. Feel the weight of your old soul, girl, and let it sink into the bones of our mother."

For a long time, it seemed, we sat there, me feeling heavier and heavier, Cory's voice murmuring from in front of the fireplace, and I waited for some kind of change. "How long does it take?" I muttered after a while.

"As long as it takes. The first time is often hard."

Even as he spoke, I felt a bit cooler, and wondered if I'd made it. Papa told me once that some people dig down into the soil for their homes, and have walls of earth, because if you dig deep enough the ground stays the same temperature all year round. Then I realized I could no longer picture Cory's face ... all was dark and motionless. I was inside something that was dead—no, not totally dead, but what life existed was below and beyond, not where I was hidden.

"What do you see?" Cory said softly.

"Darkness."

"What do you feel?" he asked.

"It's cooler, and mostly dead. I can feel life below and beyond me, but not where I'm hiding."

"Not where you are? Huh. I'm going to touch your arm, Allie. You'll feel a tickle in the back of your mind. I'm going to see what you see inside and feel what your old soul feels." I felt Cory's warm fingers, full of smooth calluses, lightly settle on my left arm, and then something like a tiny itch at the back of my head.

"I'll be damned," came Cory's voice, which startled me, since he was careful of his mouth around us children. "Well, it's one thing or another. Let's find out." His hand moved away from my arm. "Can you move, darlin'? Try to lift your fingers. It's all right if you break the trance, you're not deep enough for the snap to bother you."

Well, the next thing was purely weird. I tried lifting my thumbs, since they were on top of my clasped hands, and they wouldn't move. I pushed at the sensation a bit, but my fingers ignored me. That scared me, so I shoved hard, willing my body to respond. Finally I gave a twitch, like a chill from a spooky story, and then my flesh belonged to me again.

I could hear chuckling over my racing heart, and opened my eyes. Cory looked amused, and pleased in a funny way. "'Fraid the pillow is gonna have to go, child. Your dress should keep any chill from you. Move a bit to your right, so you're sitting on the wood floor, not the flagstones."

"Where was I?" This sounded a bit demanding, but he didn't get mad. Cory just chuckled and tugged at the pillow. I rolled over on my elbow, letting the cool air of the corner caress my face, and felt the pillow disappear.

"I think you were inside the chimney rock," he finally answered, as if that was a normal place to be.

"But that's not earth!"

"Sure it is—there's tiny grains of rock in dirt, along with the dead matter that makes soil rich. Most people take the path of least resistance, Allie, and soil is easier to slide into than rock." He held up the cushion and punched it. "But the pillow is cotton and feathers, and that confused your old soul. It doesn't know it can drop through all kinds of things—it just has to learn to adapt to the changes."

I decided to be honest. "I got a little scared there. I couldn't move at all."

A Cory grin erupted. "That's why I suspect the chimney. A rock in the ground wouldn't be large enough to hold you—your hand would have slowly started to move. There's a trick to moving through rock, hon, but let's aim for dirt first!"

I managed a ghost of a smile for him, and tried to calm my blood. I'd expected to be scared a few times during our lessons, but not learning to block thoughts! Wherever we were going, this talent was nothing like I'd imagined.

Suddenly Cory was all business again. "Straighten up again, Allie. Close your eyes and feel your arms grow heavy."

After the chimney, packed, frozen dirt was easy. I let a tendril of thought wiggle its way down, down into the ground, past rocks and bright hard bits Cory said were minerals, past hibernating animals and decaying leaves. The animals seemed to have a pale glow of their own, as if radiating the life that fueled them, but everything else carried only echoes of spirit.

"We're looking for two things, honey," Cory was saying. "Flowing water and bedrock. If we hit rock first, we want to creep along it looking for a crack. The water always finds a way up and down, so there's always an opening in the bedrock if you go far enough."

"I thought the earth was solid," I murmured, not sure if the thought was aloud.

"Practitioners believe it is," was Cory's response. "But before the solid core there's shifting layers of stone, the rock that becomes mountains or volcanoes, or makes crevices in the ground. And below that, it's so hot even the rock burns."

"Burning stone?" *That* was an image!

"Melting rock, at any rate. The guts of a volcano, my first instructor told me. Well-traveled, that man—he'd been across the water, and seen a real volcano spewing fire and molten rock." Cory chuckled at some memory, but I was busy with other thoughts and didn't ask about the joke.

"Cory? Can we go all the way to hell?"

There was silence a while. Then Cory whispered to me, "Darlin', I don't believe hell is under the earth. I think the ancients feared wildfire, so it came to represent the fear and loneliness and pain of hell. I think hell is separation from God, the light of the universe. Some say otherwise, including your momma's priest." He continued, but silently, the change as smooth as water pouring from a pump. *But I will tell you this . . . many practitioners have searched for hell in the fire below. And no one has ever found it.* "Make of that what you will."

"So either it's not there, or it's there but we can't find it for some reason— Cory, I found damp soil!" In my excitement, my voice got louder, but no one spoke from the other room to interrupt our search.

"Good! You've found the water table. A bit farther, and you'll find an underground stream—maybe a river. Can you taste the difference in the ground?"

Taste? Without a mouth or tongue? I thought about it

a bit, and decided that something was more metallic than it had been. "As if someone left a piece of iron in a well?"

"It's that way for some people," he agreed. "Now I'm going to shift into our thoughts, Allie." *See how much simpler it is when we let go our tight grip on our bodies?*

He was right, of course. It was no effort at all to listen to his thoughts—not like before.

Now we've reached the part where if we try to come out of our trances too quickly, we'll get dizzy. Some folks even get sick to their stomachs. There was a faint rustle of cotton cloth, scarcely audible over the hushed roar of the flames. Someone must have tossed on another log from the kitchen side. *I'm going to touch your arm again, darlin'.*

When he did, there was a feeling of something . . . expanding, like bread dough after kneading. Suddenly I felt larger than I'd been. It took a moment longer to realize that Cory and I were somehow linked, deep inside ourselves.

What we're going to do now is learn about hiding places. That's the secret of a practitioner's defenses. If you know the real world the way you should, from the tops of the clouds to the core of the world, then you can "become" a drop of dew, or a patch of light on a dead leaf, or a tiny pebble inside a mountain.

All of you? I asked, fascinated. *Or just your old soul?*

Would you believe that Cory's chuckle still sounds like him inside? A bit louder and deeper, maybe, but still Cousin Cory. *Your old soul is you, Allie. The more you learn, the more you'll see that your body is merely a shell. The things that might track and hurt you on the other side often can't see or hear your body, but they can smell your soul. So you must hide it so well that they can't find it.*

And if they can see your body? It was of more than

passing interest, you see. Those werewolves had had eyes, after all.

There are spells to hide the body, to hide tracks, to brush out a trail. You'll learn them. But first you have to learn how to root yourself, and to hide.

And then he did something I wasn't expecting. Cory pulled me through darkness lit by a pale, moonlight glow, and suddenly I was in the mind of a sleeping reptile! I had time to realize that the water table wasn't as deep as I had thought, and then I found myself tucked behind a turtle dream.

Slow, very slow, and deeply relaxed. I think that turtle took a breath maybe once a minute, if that much. There was even a vapor of water droplets covering him, but he didn't mind at all. He was so cold he had no interest in anything except sleeping.

Now, Cory whispered from somewhere beyond me, *we put on his dreams like a suit of clothes. If you had snuck in here to hide, you'd just feel like a sleeping turtle to something scanning for a practitioner.*

Why would something be looking for me?

Silence. And then Cory said, *Think, child. Think of the circle of life. Everything is either predator or prey—a few things are both. Either something wants to eat the power of your soul, or it thinks you're a danger. If you're a danger, that creature will either fight back or try to get you first.*

Quickly I thought turtle. After a while, I let a question trickle out of me. *How would they know I have the power if I don't use it?*

There was sorrow in the mind voice that answered me. *That's what your momma thinks—if she doesn't use the Gift, it won't trouble her. But all living things have an energy that glows from them—did you see it as we entered the turtle?*

There were furry things hibernating as we came down, and they had a glow. I was becoming awfully sleepy, sitting in this turtle's mind.

Exactly. Well, you and I are like a bonfire to a candle, the way we glow to those with other sight. And I suspect you're gonna blaze like a volcano once you're a woman grown. Cory seemed to stir next to me, and then he said, *Notice how we're getting drowsy?*

You too? I think this turtle is catching, if you get my drift. I wondered if it was safe to sneak back into the dirt.

He is catching, darlin'. That's the danger of hiding in living things. Stay there too long, and your thoughts are made over into theirs. Same in transformation, although it's not quite so bad then. Time to leave. And we drifted away, as easily as a wisp of cloud on a summer day.

I have wards—protections—all around the property, Allie, right down to the water table. You've got plenty of time to learn how to hide. Now, let's ease back up and practice diving. His mind was filled with an image of a small boy diving into a duck pond, only the lake was mud!

Diving into dirt? I asked, feeling him pull away like a drop of milk sliding down my finger. Now I felt like I was following somebody with a lantern on a moonless night.

Let's see how fast you can sink a tap root and build a root network of soul.

It's a good thing I'm not supposed to talk about these things to anyone outside the trade. They'd think I was three sheets in the wind.

We actually had a lot of fun that afternoon. Cory wasn't kidding about sinking tap roots. Remember how I was wiggling down toward water? Well, I learned how to do it fast, a summer's growth in a blink of an eye, sizzling like lightning. I branched like lightning, too, touching rock a half a dozen places at once, then zipping into the water table.

The funny thing is, no matter how many pieces you break down into, your soul knows how to suck them all back up. It's easier to do in pure element, like water or fire, but you can do it anywhere, any time. I learned to hide in a scale on the side of a root, or in a half-gnawed acorn a squirrel had buried. I floated like a leaf on an underground stream, stashed in a piece of water so small the eye couldn't see it. Tucked into the mind of a slimy creature at home in the deep, I learned to swim the length and breadth of a cavern.

As long as a fragment of you is safe, all of you is safe. Make sense? Something might be able to hurt you, but it can't get you or kill you—a comfort, considering all that's out there lying in wait. Hiding in all four elements at once is best, but I sure learned a million places in earth and water.

"Can I try the fire?" I asked after we'd worked our way back to the surface again.

Smiling, my cousin shook his shaggy head. "You're more tired than you think, darlin'. Let's not push too hard. There are still some important things for you to learn about finding water and earth."

"Like what?" How could there be more? I suspected I had touched every living thing within five miles that had a toe in dirt or frozen pool.

"Like can you shield when you're walking?"

I blinked at him and felt my jaw loosen. Moving?

"Can you cover yourself with an element when you're on the second story of the house? And can you hide while you're sleeping?"

"While I'm sleeping? You mean, not wake up and still shield with elements?" I started stretching my fingers, trying to wake them back up. They weren't tingling, they were just very far away—and not interested in moving. "How would I know? If I can do it, I mean?"

"Because I'll sneak into your dreams and pretend to be a demon or something," Cory said, giving such a big stretch I heard joints popping. "When you've got the lesson down, your mind will seek shelter like a rabbit fleeing a wolf. No questions, no time to think—just do."

Suddenly the rest of my body woke up, and my stomach announced it was hungry! I swear, Momma must have heard it growl. I tried to keep from blushing, but I've never been much for controlling that.

Grinning, Cory said, "Takes energy to do all these things. That's why your Aunt Marta and I have such healthy appetites. You'll never see a fat practitioner—not if they're any good at all." Leaning on one hand, he pulled his feet up and tipped over onto his soles. Only then did he straighten. Offering me a hand up, he added, "Let's go talk your momma into red meat and biscuits tonight, eh? Tomorrow you can start with your daddy. You need some fresh air, girl!"

NINE

PRACTITIONERS START TALKING about power at the wrong time. It's not when you reach lessons of creation and transformation that you need a guide—it's when you're starting out. You see, from the moment folks know you're going to be a practitioner, they start treating you differently. And it all has to do with power. Not strength, not authority . . . power.

Of course the family decision spread through Sun-Return like wildfire. Who starts talking about these things? I can't imagine any of my aunts doing it. Maybe my cousin Lars, or Aunt Dagmar's cook . . . or maybe rumors started because Cousin Cory and Aunt Marta stayed in town.

Anyway, the damage was done, so to speak, and word was out. Before I knew it, every eye was upon me, and I'm not exaggerating by much. Suddenly every adult in the region was greeting me by name when we went into town. And their tone was . . . respectful-like. Father Andrew surely heard all the news his next Sunday, since Father John was still feeling poorly, but he never said a thing to me—about anything. He only watched whenever I passed by. I never caught him making the sign to avert evil, but he must have said or done *something*.

I say that because Josh borrowed Skinny Joe's pet skunk and put it in the back room of the church. We'll just skip that story, but I'm sure you can imagine what happened when a nervous skunk was surprised by a stranger. Father Andrew was with Sun-Return for six services total before our own priest returned to us, and I could still catch a whiff of skunk off him that last Mass he celebrated. I still can't believe Josh did that to a priest. . . .

And then there were the other kids in the area. One and all, they seemed to take a giant step backward. Judith and Abbie both started avoiding me, unless there was a mess of people around, and even Idelia seemed watchful. The boys were bolder, asking all sorts of strange questions about my studies, like if I could brew love potions and did I know the devil's name.

That last question caused a ruckus. I was too surprised to say anything at first, and by the time I got my wits together Idelia was roaring like a cougar protecting a cub. "Have your wits gone begging, Rick?" she shouted at the boy who'd mentioned the devil. "Allie's got no use for the devil, nor he for her. You're just jealous 'cus the Schell family is going to have another practitioner!" Idelia was a pretty little thing, small and neat and creamy with dark hair and eyes. But she walked right up and slapped Rick across the ear—and he a head taller! Rick knew better than to hit back, but he let out a yell and headed for home.

I'm pleased to say that after hearing the story, Rick's daddy whopped him, too. 'Course, that could have been because Rick let a girl hit him in public, but still . . .

Some folks might think Idelia's nature meek, but none of the kids who saw that slap ever made that mistake again. Whatever the time or distance between us, Idelia may always call me friend.

A few folks had a different response. One girl, Gweneth Eriksson, had never taken much interest in me before. She was pretty and popular, and had no trouble making friends. But she spent some time trying to get close to me. I wasn't too comfortable with the whole idea. You see, Gwen was real curious about what a practitioner learned. That's harmless enough, I suppose, but she wasn't content to hear about herbs and trapping—she wanted to know about magic. Since I had no intention of telling her anything about the mysteries, I simply told the truth—that no one was teaching me any magic yet. After all, there was nothing magical about learning to stretch your mind, now was there?

Well, Gwen was real disappointed, I could tell, but she seemed to accept it. Although she stopped shadowing me, she was still friendly when we ran into each other.

It was Gwen who made me realize just how much people thought things had changed. When my family was leaving church on Christmas Day, after the town had gathered to pray and sing carols, Gwen handed me a present as we left the vestibule. It was a tiny oval of linen in a metal frame, with a wild rose branch carefully stitched upon it.

I managed to thank her for being so thoughtful, but inside I was purely confused. It's not like we were on a gift standing, you see. Then I heard murmuring, and realized Abbie had said something to Gwen as the girl smiled at me and moved on.

Gweneth's hissed retort was swift and sure. "I am not half-cocked! You are! She's going to be a *wizard,* Abbie. If you want to be on the wrong side of her, fine, but I don't!"

I didn't say a word the entire way home. If any of the family had heard Gwen's voice, they chose not to speak of it.

Two days later, I began to understand what Gwen meant. I discovered just how much things had *really* changed.

The day was cold, but not bitterly so, and the snow

sifted down like fine flour. Momma had given permission for Idelia to come spend a few days with me, which was a fine treat. First thing we did was mix up some hermit cookies, since we had both buttermilk and dried apricots on hand. We even experimented, adding a couple table-spoons of powdered cocoa to the dough. They turned out fine, but hermits improve with age, so we put them away in tins until the next day earliest.

Then we moved on to use our Christmas presents. Idelia had given me a bunch of gray netting she'd made, which I was anxious to turn into real church gloves. I'd found her an unusual piece of seasoned oak, long and thin and delicate, and drilled holes in it. Long hours of polishing with oil had given it a beautiful satin feel. It was for holding silks and threads, and she'd already started stocking it.

So we staked out the front room as our own and spent a few hours with our needles. I was pleased to find that I could maintain what Cory called my "block" without a lot of effort. The problem with practicing how to hide from other minds is that your ability to listen gets sharper. The better you are at hearing, the more likely you are to hear. So you had to be just as good at blocking. I was in a nice little ball of silence of my own constructing, and very pleased with myself.

"Alfreda? Were you two going to card that wool today?" It was Momma, simply raising her voice from the kitchen.

"I hadn't forgotten, Momma," I replied, gathering up my netting. And I *hadn't*—but I must admit I hadn't real-ized how late it was getting. It was as good a time as any, so I put away the glove I was working on and went to get the breaking cards and the dyed fleece.

Momma and Aunt Marta were busy putting bread in the oven, so I grabbed a sack of bright yellow-gold fleece we'd dyed with dyer's chamomile a few months back. The breaking cards, which are used to make wool batting, were in their usual place on the pantry shelves, so I grabbed two sets and carefully made my way around the firewall.

Idelia had set aside her embroidery and was waiting for me by the fireplace, reaching to take the breaking cards out of my hands. She was standing in the usual path, so I swung out, handing her the big rough-toothed cards before I dropped the whole mess.

And then suddenly I wasn't there anymore. I know that's crazy, but I can't describe it any other way. It was like I'd stepped into a pit of darkness. Up, down, and sideways had no meaning, and I couldn't feel my body anymore. All I was aware of was darkness, cold, and damp—and it was pleasant to me.

Well, I realized I had somehow stumbled into an animal's mind—how, I didn't know—but I had to get back out fast. A swirl of wonder and a spark of fright was with me, and then suddenly I was back in my own body, down on one knee in the front room of our house, my hands gripping Idelia's.

I must have stumbled when my head went south; it was all I could think of. As I tried to get my fear under control and work my way through what Idelia saw, I glanced up at her face. It was very white, and her black eyes were both surprised and wary.

Then I realized that all the scared I was carrying around wasn't just my own . . . part of it was Idelia's. She'd gone along with me to wherever we'd been.

For a moment we were still linked—maybe through our hands. I felt *her* surprise, not my own, and how startled she'd been . . . and I felt a tiny blossom of fear unfurl in the depths of her mind. Not of what had happened, exactly.

Of me.

I'd had more than enough of my dip into another mind. I managed to force a giggle and pulled myself back to my feet, dropping her hands just as soon as it was seemly.

"I said, what are you two doing in there, Alfreda?" came my mother's voice. "All that crashing around." Her brisk step announced her imminent arrival.

Glancing quickly at Idelia, I said, "It's all right, Momma. I stumbled and dropped the cards. They look all right, though—no broken teeth." I bent to pick up the big paddles and handed my friend a set. "Wait until you see this yellow, girl," I said, pulling at the neck of the sack. "You'll be at your momma for some of your own."

By this time my mother had reached the corridor between the rooms, next to the firewall. She stood there a moment, wiping her hands on the big flour-sack apron she'd tied around her dark dress, and then nodded once to the both of us. "Be careful with those, child. I don't want to have to ask your father to make us a new set." And then she was back in the kitchen, leaving a haze of flour in her wake.

Idelia had already returned to her seat, a bunch of wool clenched in one hand. "This did turn out nicely, Allie. I like the colors you get when you dye the raw wool, but my momma likes to dye spun threads. The color's real bright that way, but heavy, you know? Like that skirt my little sister's wearing now. This will be bright yellow, but soft."

"We're going to do some cotton and linen with this dye next year," I offered, setting the bag between us. "But Momma says the dyeing is more work. I guess the color doesn't set as easily in plant fiber." If Idelia wasn't gonna say anything, I wasn't—at least not until I'd figured out what to say. And I'd made sure my block was intact once more. I couldn't tell her what had really happened, and yet . . .

Papa always said that if you tell the truth every time, you don't have to keep track of your story—it never changes. Somehow I could bring truth out of this, and satisfy everyone . . . if I had time to think. I didn't know what I'd do if Idelia was too scared to ask what had happened.

We were making bats, the first step toward preparing washed wool for spinning. The soft mats of separated fibers started taking shape, as wide as the breaking cards and slightly more than half as long. Carding requires strong wrists and enough concentration to count strokes, if you haven't learned to tell when the bat is ready just by look or feel, so neither of us spoke for a time.

Finally Idelia shifted in the rocker, more than she'd need to before reaching for a handful of yellow balls or setting a bat aside. "Was that supposed to happen?" she said conversationally, as if confident I'd know what she was talking about.

So, I was being given a choice—yes or no. *Tell the truth until it will do damage.* . . . "No," I replied.

A firm forward stroke, and then two light backward strokes . . . the finished bat was on her top card, which Idelia turned over so she could peel off the wool rectangle. "Will it happen again?" It was pure question, without any trace of fear or curiosity.

"It shouldn't." Now, if she would leave it at that . . .

"Why did it happen?"

I prayed for guidance on this one—not to lie, frighten, or tell her too much. "All practitioners learn to protect themselves from all the busy minds, human and animal, that are around them. My protection weakened, so I was open to all the minds around me." True enough, and a good start.

Idelia looked over at me. "Even the cows and goats in the barn?"

"Could have happened," I said offhandedly. "The closest minds first, of course. It felt like the thoughts of something hibernating in a burrow under the house." Also true, as it happened.

"And I heard the echo," she murmured, loading her top card with more raw wool.

I didn't say a word. Although I was careful to stay away from her mind, I could tell by how Idelia was sitting and the tone of her voice that she was relaxing. No point in telling her that I thought I'd been tossed into an animal mind and had hauled her in with me. I was confident Cousin Cory could teach me how to keep it from happening again. It wasn't necessary for her to know the hows and whys.

While I was thinking this, Idelia gave me a sidelong glance. "I can see why you need all those special lessons, if that can happen to you any old time," was her comment. "I'm not sure I'd like having everyone's mind pressing at me, like a crowd on First Saturday." She was talking about the big food and crafts market we had just outside of Sun-Return once a month from snowmelt to snowfall. Lord, what a racket on market day!

The rhythm of Idelia's cards clashed merrily with mine, breaking fibers every which way. "I noticed Wylie Adamsson giving you the long eye while we were singing Christmas morning," she said casually. "Do you like him?"

I love Idelia. Nothing has to be complicated when she's around—we only have to let be.

As it happened, I *did* sort of like Wylie Adamsson. But I tried not to think about it too much, because boys like

Wylie trail after the popular girls. They don't notice tall, gangly things like me.

I'd underestimated the lure of power.

The business with tossing myself into that animal was fairly easy to solve—it was the last thing Cousin Cory showed me before he left. What happened was, I had tripped over the underground stream beneath our house! Have you ever heard of such a crazy thing? In a way, I'd been too well grounded in soil, so when I suddenly sidestepped over water, my anchor didn't flow with me. Cory showed me the difference between a firm grip and a tight grip, and I haven't had that problem since.

Aunt Marta left after the New Year, and we were sorry to see her go. Before she left, she called me into the cool stillroom and over to her big carpetbag.

"I have something I want to loan you, Alfreda," she said seriously as she dug into her things. Finally she pulled out an old book. It was as tall as my forearm was long, and about two-thirds as wide as it was tall. The binding was dark tooled leather with a gilded design in it. No title or author on the front, though. She handed it to me.

Carefully I opened the cover and turned back the beautiful Italian endleaf. The first page had written on it in large, beautiful script *Denizens of the Night*. I looked up at her.

"My great-great-grandmother began this book," Marta said seriously. "Others of us have added to it as our knowledge has grown. The paper is better than my own personal copy, so I'm loaning it to you. Eventually you'll want to make your own workbook and note things that are important to your studies. For now, you just need to read and remember as much as you can." Her Valkyrie smile flashed out. "Besides, her handwriting is better than mine!"

I closed the cover *very* carefully. It was an incredibly precious gift—so much so, I was nervous. "Are you sure you want to loan me this?" I began slowly. "I mean, I have a pack of brothers roaming around here—"

"And your parents will skin them alive if they so much as look cross-eyed at it," Marta finished. "I know you're careful, Allie. Just don't eat or drink around it, and you'll be fine. Oh, and I'd advise against taking it outdoors." Her smile was gentle as she went on. "I know it's tempting to read out under a tree on a fine spring morning, but books like this have a habit of walking off . . . and sometimes the things that help them wander are not human. Just keep it close at hand."

Well, that was not exactly comforting, if you catch my drift. But I managed to give her a hug and thank her without signaling just how disturbing the book might be.

I spent the next few nights submerged in *Denizens*. It was full of fascinating stuff, like "Ghosts are the souls of humans who have departed this life yet not found peace in the next. In their struggle for corporeal form, they take on the guise of living bodies. Often a ghost does not understand that it has died, and must be helped to realization. With a benign spirit, that is usually enough to nudge it into paradise."

Yup, it's just as you're thinking. *Denizens* is more than a reference book; it's an instruction book for dealing with the dark on the other side. Everything from what we call fox fire, the *ignis fatuus* of legend, to the screaming skulls of many English manor houses was included. It covered poltergeists, plague maidens, and musical instruments that named murderers. The many guises of the Reaper were named, and how to guard yourself against him and his minions. Until I saw this book, I had no idea how many ways there were to deal with ghosts, both friendly and full of malice. Exorcism isn't the half of it!

It's interesting that the ghosts of most lands are not dangerous—pathetic, startling, or full of warning, maybe, but not menacing. But the ghosts of the northern lands, which most folks call Scandinavia—they're different. Nasty, and powerful.

Banshees, black dogs, and things that masqueraded as "other"—fetches, navky, pookas—the world was crawling with them! And they followed the people who first discovered them. There were Irish, Scandinavian, and British in our region, with a few from the Germanic kingdoms. All of them had their own creatures of the night . . . all of them had been followed to the New World. And I might deal with all these things, eventually.

I didn't expect to have my first encounter before snowmelt.

It was still the month of Ice, but well past the first of the year (whether you used the new calendar, the old, or the oldest), when I discovered that courage was no bad defense against a call from the night side.

A pale winter sun gave me a faint shadow companion as I walked along the frozen dirt road. It was cold, but not too bad, 'cus I was wearing an old pair of Josh's wool pants. As soon as Papa finished with the harness he was working on, he was going to show Josh and me how to make a woven leaf shelter, just like squirrels do. I'd made sure he wouldn't have to wait on me shedding skirts.

Momma had asked me to return Mrs. Heidreksson's pudding mold to her, with some cinnamon bread for thanks. Mrs. Heid had been home, and happy to get her mold back. She'd fed me hot cider and fresh applesauce donuts, and then sent me on my way back. Good donuts, those—Momma didn't make them often. I'd have to see if Mrs. Heid would spare the recipe. . . .

My thoughts were full of making donuts and seasoning cider, so it took me a while to notice that there was a figure standing out in the middle of the Heidrekssons' north field. At first I thought it was the eldest son, so I didn't pay any heed . . . and then I recognized the dark green sweater peeping out of the wool jacket. Caked snow lined one side of him, like he'd fallen into a drift, but other than that he looked the same as always. It was Wylie Adamsson!

I actually stopped walking, I was so surprised. It wasn't like he was good enough friends with the family to pause in their fields, even during the fallow season. Sure, that field was a shortcut to his father's meadows, but . . .

It was *cold* outside. Why was Wylie just standing?

Curiosity is truly my besetting sin. I sidled over to the fence separating the road and the field, and peered over at him. Let's be honest, now—Wylie was always easy to look at, fair and smooth-faced and going on tall.

And sharp-eyed. "Allie? Is that you? Praise God who answers prayer!" His voice seemed higher than usual, but it carried just fine to where I stood. "Come here, quick!"

Huh. Wylie wasn't what I'd call real religious. Grateful for my leggings, I climbed the split-rail fence with ease. All that tromping in the woods was doing wonders for my wind.

Wylie hadn't budged from where he was standing, not even to face toward me, which was purely strange. In fact, he was standing so quiet and still I was starting to get nervous. I mean, the snakes were all sleeping. What was he afraid of rousing?

I approached slowly, coming up from his back side, so I didn't see what he was doing until I was right next to him. One cold, white hand was clutching the top of a single, unmarked wooden post. The sides of the marker were planed, so it wasn't an old tree stump. I looked around quickly, but there were no other posts in sight. Not part of an old fence, then . . .

A trill of notes echoed across the field, and I startled. That was an alarm call, or I didn't know much of anything.

Maybe your folks never warned you about this, but you never, *ever* disturb a solitary post in a field. Because it may not be just a marker . . . it may be holding something down. And from the color of Wylie's face, I was real suspicious.

"Wylie, you idjit, what've you done?" I hissed at him, keeping my distance. If he'd freed something nasty, we might have to run for help, and I wanted to be far enough away not to attract any attention, if you catch my drift.

"I didn't pull it out!" It was a strangled whisper, as if something was listening, which made me look around again.

There was nothing to sense. Even my bird was silent. That was a comfort; whatever was frightening Wylie, he probably hadn't freed it from its restraints. Unless it was so powerful it could cover its tracks, in which case we were both dead already. "Then what's the problem?" I asked, matching his tone of voice.

"I grabbed the pole to pull myself out of a drift," came his tortured reply. "That's when I heard the voice. I'm afraid to let go, and I sure ain't gonna do what it told me!"

"What did it say?" I asked promptly.

I could hear him swallow, it was so quiet—not even the whisper of wind over snow. "It said, 'You pull, and I will push.'"

The pale shadow from the post seemed to waver a bit, as if seen from a distance on a hot day, and I shuddered. "In English?"

"Of course in English!" This was furious.

"Not of course, Wylie. You're not thinking straight," I said swiftly, digging through my memories for instructions on what to do in such a case. "It might have been Swedish or Norwegian or German, just to name a few possibilities."

"Do you know what to do?"

I'd never had a boy plead with me before. It was rather invigorating.

"Maybe," was my response. There were two possibilities. One, the thing under that post had once been human, and a Christian. That gave us one possible solution. The second possibility was grimmer—that it hadn't been Christian while alive, and not necessarily human. "Did the post loosen when you pulled yourself up?"

"I don't think so. It felt real solid. There was this tingling, and that awful voice . . ." Wylie sounded real high-strung, like his little brother after the big boys have been teasing too much.

Tingling was not good. At least the body of the thing was still tamped down tight, but if Wylie could feel the energy of the soul, then he could take an echo of it along home. That meant the spirit might be able to use Wylie to finally work its way free.

And I didn't have any dried St.-John's-wort in my pocket. *See if I ever go outside again without it.* Doing the chant to hold down an unbaptized spirit is no fun, even with the herb to help. I prayed that the evil held below Wylie's hand was a fallen Christian, and tensed my muscles for what was next.

"I'm gonna set my hand on yours, Wylie," I warned him. "After I speak, if I jerk on you, let go of the post fast. If I pull away without jerking on you, then keep hanging on, 'cus I'll need to do something else." *Please let it be a fallen soul*—otherwise I'd have to run for some St.-John's-wort and pray that Wylie didn't panic and bolt.

Taking a deep breath, I stripped off my left glove and dropped my hand over Wylie's cold one.

As he'd promised, there was a tingling numbness rising up through the post. A muffled, eager voice immediately whispered, "Good. *Good.* Pull, pull! I will push if you pull!" The rankness of the spirit almost gagged me. There was no repentance here, only watchful intent. This thing was so eager to get out, it didn't even try to offer us something to free it. Maybe it felt my sensitivity. . . .

I'd been taught that words contained power—why else call a book of spells a gramarye, like *grammar*? Knowledge for eyes to see that can. Some say that words can even kill. If you believe a curse can kill, the curse will get you. It's that simple.

If you believe in the power of a spell, words can also save you.

"In the name of our Lord Jesus Christ, son of the living God, begone!" I both said and sang it, the way Momma had taught me long before, because words need both memory and belief to have potency. And I felt a . . . a quailing within the post, as if I'd touched the spirit with a living brand.

Hallelujah! It was a fallen soul!

The presence within the wood drained back into the cold soil, fleeing the strength of my words. As soon as the wood felt dead, I snatched Wylie's hand away.

"You owe a lot of prayers, mister," I said severely. "And you were lucky—it was a fallen soul. If it'd been pagan, you could have been there the rest of the afternoon while I went to get the stuff I'd have needed to free you." Quickly I stuffed my hand back into my glove.

"I knew you could do it, Allie," he said, reaching over and hugging me. "I was praying that God would send you to me, because I didn't know what else to hope for."

"Didn't your momma ever tell you how to banish a

night demon if one ever came after you?" I was curious, I admit—I'd thought everyone learned that chant.

"I learned the words, but not that weird little melody," he replied, taking several steps back from the post. "I kept saying the words, but I could tell it was still there, and I was afraid it would follow me."

You were right, little bird—there was *danger.* "You had good reason to be afraid," I offered, starting for the road. "It was strong, and I don't think it regrets its wickedness one bit."

Wylie followed in my footsteps. Apparently shortcuts had palled, but I didn't tease him about it. "Would that melody work for me?"

"If you believed it would." I hoped he'd leave it at that, because I didn't need to be announcing my crazy theology all over the region.

"What do you mean?"

With a sigh, I said, "When you say those words, Wylie, you're doing two things—you're acknowledging the power of the light, through its emissary Jesus Christ, and you're putting yourself *completely* in the palm of God's hand. For good or ill."

Wylie thought about that. "You mean even if you believe, it might not work?"

"Yup. But your belief will save your soul, even if your body dies."

He stopped walking. "But I don't want my body to die!"

I turned and gave him a disgusted look—I couldn't help it. "Not many of us do, but that's a possibility every day of our lives. And even more likely when you run into dark things like that." I hooked a thumb in the direction of the post. "We need to remember to tell Mr. Heidreksson what's in his field. He may suspect, but not know." Turning back around, I kept walking.

"You knew we might die, yet you believed God would save us?"

This time I held on to my sigh. "Yes." It wasn't something I was comfortable talking about, but it was something my talks with Cory and Aunt Marta had skirted . . . death was literally the flip side of life. And I was tossing a coin every step I took into the mysteries.

Finally we heard some noise—it sounded like wild geese were passing overhead. I hunched my shoulders at that and recited an avert charm in my head, 'cus it was too late in the season for geese. Would Wylie notice that the Wild Hunt had just passed over our heads?

We'd finally reached the fence. Wylie came up next to me and offered me a hand up. "Thanks, Allie. It's surely good to know you can count on someone." He actually avoided looking at me as he boosted me over the rails. "Would you mind if I walked you home?"

Well, maybe he hadn't noticed the hunter of souls and his pack of hounds, the Gabriel Rachets, but it seemed he had finally noticed me. I decided to be content with that!

TEN

IN BARELY A FORTNIGHT, Josh and I were in charge of the trap line. Josh already knew a lot about running lines, but I paid better attention to the little things—like rubbing your hands in charcoal to keep your scent to yourself, and weaving ash and sinew together so your snares smelled like something natural. In a family land-rich and coin-poor, trapping earned the most hard gold, so Papa had placed a lot of trust in us.

We did our best not to fail him.

Papa trapped for weasels, like mink, skunk, martin, and wolverine. Minks are one of the few animals that would kill just for the love of killing. I didn't have much sympathy for minks. He tried not to get otter, for which I was grateful—otters are just too friendly, and not nearly good enough eating. I'd rather watch otters play than wear them.

The line was also set for muskrat and beaver, the most valuable skins. Only a few—if you took too many in one place, you'd trap out an area. We were pretty careful about protecting what lived on our land.

Folks sometimes say that everything is dead in winter, but that's showing how little they know the forest. Our lessons took place in a cathedral of red juniper, cedar, pine, and hemlock, the blue juniper berries and green needles a sharp contrast to sleeping oaks and ash. Once you've seen a tree full of chirping chickadees hanging every which way, and followed the tracks of everything from a field mouse to a cougar, you'll know you're not alone.

We had even more company. Papa was teaching Wylie and Shaw about trapping and survival, too. I can't tell you how much fun we had, building tools and snares, and figuring out how old a track might be. There were a lot of lessons to be learned about living from the land—even a silly squirrel slept warm and dry at night. Papa taught us all those lessons—or the animals did.

Oh, yeah—come summer Papa did teach us about the duck blinds Cory had mentioned. You see, you tie reeds to your neck and head, and then wait in the water still as a reflection, until the ducks—

But I didn't enjoy it, though I'm good at it. So I think I'll skip that story. I wouldn't want you to think that tale was a boast, not with duck death at the end of it.

There was another unseen visitor who dogged our tracks from snow right through a muddy spring. That strange bird call still sounded when I least expected it. But Josh and Wylie didn't seem to hear it, and I'd learned that Shaw was too shy to answer many questions.

I didn't ask Papa.

My bird sang even into the month of Sun, when most eggs had hatched and babies were fledging. It found me in town, on the trap line, and over at the little lake.

I heard it in my dreams.

Sun slid into Fruit, which then wore into Vintage. Hay was scythed and stacked on layers of rocks and fresh bracken to protect it from ground damp and rats; first corn, then wheat, and finally oats, rye, and barley were brought in. Momma brewed her rich, dark beer for the cool nights of the approaching equinox. I brought herbs inside by the score, tucked them into pots, and lined them up in snug rows. The stillroom reeked of fermenting ale and growing things—it was my favorite place in the house.

I'd sit back in there on the cot sometimes, stitching together a tiny buckskin pouch I was making. The heady odors made me a bit light-headed, but I'd somehow gotten the idea that Cousin Marta's entire house was like this, so I wanted to get used to it.

I'd taken time to stain the pouch a rich middling brown, but I wasn't sure I had time to decorate it in any way. Because someday, when we least expected it, Papa was going to turn to one of us in the woods and say, "You stay here until I come for you." And then he was gonna walk off. Momma had been acting a bit nervous, see, and I'd nudged her about it.

I'd decided that there was no point in ever having to start from scratch if I didn't have to. So I was making a pouch to carry a bunch of sinew cord, my flint and steel, a fat candle, and a compass, if I could ever afford one. The pouch had its own belt, slender and strong, and a place to hang my knife sheath. But Momma got upset when I wore the knife all the time, so I knew I'd have to do without it and hope for the best.

If I made the pouch pretty enough, it would look like a reticule, a lady's little bag. Then no one would question why I wore it all the time. I was wondering if the tiny wood cup Josh had carved for me would fit inside. . . .

Maybe Momma was trying to forget I had to spend the night (or nights) in the forest alone, but Aunt Dagmar hadn't. More than once as we worked through the month of Vintage, she'd managed to catch my father in the village, or even when folks were helping harvest our corn, and ask him if he'd given up that "foolishness" of having a young girl alone in the woods at night. What with cougars and bears and wolves and trappers about, how could he think of such a thing? She wasn't worried about Indians, of course, because of the protective spell that covered the region.

I didn't hear all the conversation—I was binding shocks of corn, along with other women and children, and I had to keep to the rhythm or I'd slow my row. But Papa hadn't really answered her, not any of those times, which was why I was sure my time was coming.

The dying time of the year was one of the best, because that's when we all worked together. Hard work, harvesting the fields, but everyone who owned land, and a few townies, too, would be out there. We'd start wherever the crop was ripest, and move out like locusts, from field to field, struggling to beat cold nights and early winter rain.

The corn shuckings were the most fun. Every few days we'd have another one, going from farm to farm and setting up in the barn. The men and children would shuck up a storm, while the women cooked a fine supper. At our farm, Momma had hidden a huge jug of her bock somewhere in the pile, for whoever could shuck down to it. Some folks gave prizes for whoever found the first red ear—choice of partner for the first dance, if there was time for dancing, or baked goods, or even a kiss from the person of your choice!

Momma didn't approve of folks kissing in public, though, so when Wylie's older brother found the first red ear, he got one of Momma's rum cakes. You could tell how Momma's reputation as a cook had spread, since he was the center of a general envy.

Found out something very interesting at our corn shuck. I was sitting next to Mrs. Kris while we stripped ears. Though I didn't ask, I figured that she cooked enough at her rooming house—she probably welcomed the change. Papa was nearby, shucking like wildfire as he and Josh each tried to get the biggest pile of corn ears. Aunt Dagmar had come in with a pitcher of ale and was refilling glasses as she walked the room. Of course she stopped next to Papa and took her time filling his mug.

"Eldon, have you thought about what I said?"

Strong fingers ripped down a section of husk, slid under silk to get a firm grip, and then whipped off the rest of the dried leaves. "Which time was that, Dagmar?"

Aunt Dagmar kept her expression calm, but I'm sure it took work. "You know very well what I mean, Eldon. This business of Alfreda in the woods alone. Surely this part of the country is tame enough that the training is unnecessary?"

Uh-huh, not a bit of danger—as long as I didn't set one toe beyond the "Indian border" set up by the practitioners of the region.

Papa tilted his head toward her while he reached for another ear. "If the country is so tame, why are you concerned about her being out there?"

I watched Aunt Dagmar's lips tighten, and waited for the explosion. But suddenly, from beside me, Shaw's mother spoke. Without even looking up from the corn ear she was stripping, Mrs. Kris said, "My husband will be watching after the boys, Mrs. Nels, and I will be chaperoning Allie. You need not concern yourself."

Then the interesting thing happened. My aunt's face ran a gauntlet of expression—surprise, interest, objection—and finally she looked what I could only call peculiar. I supposed she was wondering what I was wondering—how I could spend a night alone in the woods if Mrs. Kris was there—but she didn't say so.

Finally Aunt Dagmar said: "That would be good of you, Mrs. Kris. We would all appreciate it."

Smiling her warmest smile, Mrs. Kris held up her mug for some of the bock. "Not at all. Sorensson has done my family a service, including Shaw in his classes. We owe him great thanks for allowing us to keep Shaw at home a few extra years."

And that was it. I knew I couldn't have any beer at a big gathering like this, so I didn't bother to try to weasel a mug out of my aunt. After thought, I also decided not to question that last sentence. It probably had to do with whatever Shaw's apprenticeship would be. Not black-smithing—his parents would never have encouraged him to play a fiddle if he was meant for the smithy. But some skill he had to leave town to learn. Shaw didn't talk about his plans much.

I glanced around Papa and Josh to where Wylie and Shaw were sitting, having their own husking race. Quite a contrast, those two, and an unlikely pair to be friends, what with Wylie's easygoing noise and Shaw's thoughtful silence. Wylie looked just like what he was, a strong, healthy young man, while Shaw . . . Shaw reminded me of a well-tended knife.

Odd, that. But Shaw held secrets, while Wylie wore his life on his sleeve.

Shaw never spoke much to me, but shyness wasn't a crime. I decided I'd miss him when he went. Good thing Wylie was going to be a farmer. I couldn't bear it if Wylie got sent away, too.

Funny I should think that. Because the next day, Wylie got snatched right out of a field by my papa and carted off to who knew where. And as soon as Papa retrieved Wylie, Shaw disappeared for three whole days.

We saved our talking for when we were together again, gathering in the yard out back of Bear Kristinsson's blacksmith shop. Wylie was full of himself, playing to the gallery. He swore he'd heard a bear sniffing around his shelter. Shaw, on the other hand, reminded us to break down any snares we'd laid, once Papa came for us.

"Wonder how long we'll be out," Josh finally murmured, and was rewarded by a look from Wylie.

"Whatever your pa thinks you need, I s'pose. *You* can always go back out—my ma ain't so sure any longer about all this. I bet she'll start arguing now 'bout me going to the woods with you." Wylie looked glum. His ma *was* one to get riled about things—even worse than Momma.

"You never know when you might need this stuff," Shaw said mildly. "Your pa will bring her around."

Then Shaw's wiry father came out from the dark shop and gave one of his clipped yells for assistance. Not a big man, Mr. Kristinsson—Shaw was already his height—but there was something about his pale blue eyes that warned you not to mess with him. Folks treaded carefully around Bear Kristinsson; he wasn't a man to pick a fight with.

We waited while Shaw helped his father, but Papa showed up with the wagon long before the metal was ready to be quenched. Good-byes were said, and Josh and I piled in behind Papa. I didn't get to hear the rest of Shaw's story—not for quite a while. Because Papa dumped me in the woods that very afternoon, while taking the long way home.

I ended up in a mixed forest, with both old growth and shrubby young trees. The logging road disappeared into long bleached grass and a few faded flowers. It was still early afternoon, so I didn't need to get worried about nightfall. I just sat down where I was, since it was a patch of sunlight, and paid attention.

It didn't take me long to be sure of my directions, to

locate the prevailing wind, and to hear a mess of rustles
that had nothing to do with the breeze. First, I needed
shelter . . . then water. If there was time, I'd think about
eating.

There was nothing to stop me from harvesting as I
walked, of course. I was still wearing my apron, so I had
something convenient to stash supper in. I found some
fresh pine cones that the squirrels hadn't worked on
(much) as well as ripe acorns. I should add that they were
white oak family and pin oak acorns —all acorns can be
eaten, but only white and pin can be eaten raw.

I had my tiny wooden cup, but I didn't know yet if I'd
have an area to boil things, so I didn't plan on it. That's
why I didn't take pine needles—boiled, they make a tea
that's as good for you as a fresh-squeezed orange. But
pine needles are easier to find than ungnawed pine cones.

It was late in the season for berries, but in the mile or
so I walked I found a few on each bush I passed—blue-
berries, huckleberries, and currants, which I could eat
fresh, and a few bunches of barberries, for maybe cooking.

Unless I had trouble, I planned on a fire, so I broke off
a strong dead oak branch and used it to dig up some
clover and comfrey roots. Found a few dandelions and
took the whole plant—dandelion and comfrey root, dried,
roasted over the fire, and ground up, would improve the
flavor of my pine needle drink, plus if I was here long
enough, I could make a hollowed area for boiling and
cook the old leaves.

Seeded flower heads from goldenrod to add to my tin-
der, groundnuts and Jerusalem artichoke for eating raw
or like potatoes, young maple seeds for munching, wild
peppermint to add to any tea I could make— How could
people say there's nothing to eat in the woods?

A mile or so west of the road, I came on a patch of

evergreens, their lower branches forming a nice wind-break. I wormed my way under some firs and white spruce, and found that if I wanted to make a shelter I could stand in, it was possible. Years and years' worth of dried leaves had blown under the canopy of branches.

I pinned the tips of a few living branches with a log, and then wove branches of a recent fallen giant in through the lowest branches of the living firs. The weaving gave me something to stack green brush against. I'd have to tear it down before leaving, but this looked to be the fastest and easiest shelter. I'd have solid wood and woven branches on two sides of the fir, a fire on the third, and a mess of trees with drifts of dead leaves on the last side.

It took a few hours to get the little hut warm enough, but I filled it right up to the top with fresh fall leaves. No wind could push them away with all those breaks, and the thick upper branches would slow down most rain before it reached my dome. The soft, fresh leaves made a fine bed.

Next I started looking for firewood. I found a trickle of sweet water coming out of stone just west of my hut, which was another need satisfied. Then I moved away from where the spring sank underground and started looking for dry, fist-sized rocks. There was plenty of light left, and I was gonna make a cooking pit.

By nightfall I had a nice small fire burning, a pit dug and full of my peeled roots, and a tiny pile of roasted comfrey and dandelion root mixed with diced pine needles and peppermint leaves. I also had a rock twice the size of my head with an indentation the size of Papa's fist in it. The depression was full of fresh water—I'd been sure that cup would come in handy! I'd found a bunch of tiny rocks and was busily heating them in my fire. When they were sizzling, I'd use two sticks to pick them up and drop them in the water. In a little bit I could scoop out peppermint-and-other tea with my cup.

I hadn't forgotten to say my thanks—that it wasn't raining, that the temperature was cold but not freezing, that a cougar wasn't out there coughing my name. Having my knife would have been useful, but so far I'd done all right.

You know, it was a lot easier when it was only me. No boys to argue with, nobody frightening off game or spoiling tracks. . . . Josh was getting the hang of things, and Shaw was a natural, but privately I'd admit that it was a good thing Wylie had a rich farmer papa—he was gonna need help getting launched in life. That was okay. I could be the trapper in the family. Everyone should do what they do best.

I'd just decided that things were pretty cozy when I heard a familiar rising run of notes. Sweet Lord, not here too! How many of those birds were there?

Then the water in my rock started boiling, and I was busy dipping with my wooden cup. By the time I'd set a pinch of my mixture to brew, the forest held the silence of twilight.

For a long time I sat there, thinking about that trill, and about stumbling around in an unfamiliar, darkening forest. "Foolishness, Allie," I muttered to myself, and set my mind toward sipping that tisane. The stuff was okay in an emergency, maybe, but it was never gonna be one of my favorites.

And then I saw the wolf. She was standing between two of the neighboring firs, half hidden in the hanging boughs. When the wolf realized she had been spotted, she promptly sat down on her haunches, her eerie light gaze upon me.

Well, my heart started crawling back down my throat

toward my chest. I'd checked the area carefully for cat or bear tracks, and had seen no sign of a wolf pack. But here was a brindle wolf, big as life. Bigger than life—she was as big as the male someone had trapped a few years back.

I realized I was clutching a good-sized rock, one of the ones I'd decided was too damp to go into my cooking pit. Its smooth, cold weight reassured me. If I needed to argue with this wolf, I was holding an argument.

The important thing was not to lose eye contact. You can hold off a predator by standing and making eye contact, but the moment you glance away for a stick or rock, or stoop to grab something, the animal will spring.

At this point, the wolf dropped her head down to her paws, still watching me intently, and wagged her tail.

It is a strange thing for a wolf to wag her tail at you. I mean, I knew wolves were playful, at least with their packmates, but I'd never had one come up and imply I should throw a stick for her. The image made me smile, which brought the wolf's head up, although she continued to wag her tail. The brushy fur pushed aside dry leaves and needles, raising a bit of dust. After this display of enthusiasm, the wolf grew still, her tongue lolling out in a wolfy smile.

Huh. So I got to make the next move. I'd let my senses float, looking for threat of any kind. But the closest big cat was miles away, and the only hostility I could feel was a great horned owl single-mindedly pursuing a terrified mouse. In fact, the wolf was going out of her way to appear friendly. It was as if she knew me. . . .

I thought about that a bit, considering the idea. How could a wolf know me? Had my brother run with a real pack for a while? Or . . .

"Are you a . . . friend . . . of Mrs. Kris?" I asked softly, aware I sounded timid. Well, wouldn't you be careful, talking to a wolf as big as you were?

The wolf's response was to slowly close her eyes and then open them.

"Just dropped by to pay your respects, eh?"

Sure enough, the wolf gave me another pronounced blink. I didn't know a wolf could do that!

"Well, you're welcome to stay, if you'd like, but I'll bank the fire before I go to sleep." I had some funny, squirmy thoughts about this wolf, but I wasn't ready to volunteer them aloud. So this was my guard for the night, in case anything went wrong. . . .

The she-wolf stood with a stretch and gave me another toothy grin. Then she slipped noiselessly back into the fir trees. I watched where she'd disappeared, but there was neither sight nor sound of her.

There'd been a few passages in Aunt Marta's book, at the bottom of the section on werewolves, that had mentioned shape-changers.

I remembered something about ancient family lines that went back to the great spirits of the land, who'd been personified in both human and animal form. Some of those creatures took humans as mates—and passed on many of their gifts. In fact, some people think you can't be a practitioner without a bit of the oldest blood. You can't learn to become "other" without it.

But there are a few around who aren't necessarily practitioners, yet have another physical form. Folks around here simply call them shifters. I've heard of wolves, bears, great cats, huge birds—even folks becoming seals that swim in the seas. Nothing's really said about it—I mean, lots of folks go fishing in their spare time. It's no one else's business if they do it as a bear.

Could we have . . . here in Sun-Return?

Would Papa satisfy my curiosity, or was it one of those things people never talked about?

This would certainly explain Aunt Dagmar's strange expression. . . .

I set the thought aside. There would be a time and place to ask. In the end, I'd know the answer. For now, I'd just have to bide.

ELEVEN

I SURVIVED MY OUTING JUST FINE, thank you. In fact, I'd just snuck up on a ruffed grouse and whopped it with a throwing stick when Papa appeared out of the bushes. So we broke down my leaf hut, setting free the living branches, and then went home to a grouse dinner.

Josh held his own, too. He found shelter and food during his sojourn in the woods, and reported a mess of bear tracks in the area. Big tracks.

"See any wolves?" I asked conversationally.

"Nah, no wolves. Heard some howling, but it wasn't close by," was his response.

Papa didn't volunteer anything, but he gave me one of his clear-eyed looks. I decided not to ask my question . . . in a sense, I'd had my answer in that stare.

As Wylie had predicted, his ma was up in the trees over his stay in the woods. Finally, to keep peace in the family, his pa said no more overnight trips. Josh and I felt for him, but we spent half the winter alone in the forest. I don't know that Josh ever cared for camping alone, but we had a good time together.

We sure missed Shaw. He'd been packed off right after the Yule, heading for the orchard country. He hadn't volunteered what he was going to study, so I hadn't asked, but folks wondered. I overheard his mother dismiss someone's prying by saying, "Shaw doesn't want to talk about it until he's sure he wants to take up the trade. It's a calling, and a tough one."

That set me thinking it might be law or medicine—both tough professions. But then why had Shaw stayed in Sun-Return and learned trapping and such from Papa?

Life's a mystery.

Winter rolled in, blanketed us in dazzling snow, and then withered away, leaving a barren patch of living until spring tiptoed up. I memorized herbs and learned to find them first in spring and then summer. Josh, Wylie, and I spent a lot of time stalking each other and trying to hide from each other. The green maze of the forest was paradise for us. Even Momma didn't scold us about ducking chores, as long as we'd been in the woods.

We never talked about bears or wolves.

Then came a time of testing I hadn't expected. I found out why some folks tell you not to be good at boy's things.

Papa's words about life being a cycle often sent my thoughts back in time, back to things my grandfather and great-grandmother had taught me. I'd lost all my elder kin by my eleventh year, and I always felt closest to Grandsir, but it was Granny who gave me the words I carried wrapped around my heart.

I'd asked her about the dark on the other side, you see. Gran told me that life was one pillar of the great triad, and the only other things that counted were love and death. In the midst of life, we look for love and hide from death. In love, we chase life and flee death, while in death, we have love at our back as an anchor as the next life beckons to us.

Of course she meant that life calls from several places—the past, the present, and the lives to come. I know that, now.

Some people never learn these things; some learn only one or two of them. People like Gran and me, well, we see them over and over again. Gran liked that word *triad,* but I always think of life as a circle. Though I'm getting older and bolder, the image holds true—we end up where we started. Only the lucky ones ever truly recognize the place.

What does this have to do with the dark on the other side? Now think about it; what draws the undead to the shores of the living? Life—the blood that sustains us. Vampires are the worst scavengers of all. They're dead (or undead, to be pre-cise) while we're still hanging on to this world, and there's that unholy attraction in between. It warps the circle, and any person with a touch of the Gift can smell a vampire half a day away.

Convincing regular folks is something else again.

I was into my thirteenth year of life when a vampire was found in Sun-Return, and my youth was nearly our downfall. Folks believed I was strong with the Gift, after that business with the werewolves, but elders won't listen to a youngling to save their lives—not until the wolf's at the door. Although Aunt Marta said I was a woman grown, and was learning my lessons as fast as hops, I might as well have tried to whistle down the wind—it paid more attention to me. As far as Momma was concerned, I was merely a long-legged child eaten up with a deadly sin.

Even people who dream true dreams hope for love.

Of course I was jealous of her—her face, I mean. As fair as a spring day, with dark, dark hair and eyes, Livana looked like a Celtic queen, and every boy for ten miles in any direction knew it. Me, I was nearly as tall as Papa and flat as a board, while she was tiny and curved like the course of the Wabash River. Long blond braids can't compete with that.

They came out of nowhere, the Hutchensons did. One day the Gustusson place was abandoned, red barn missing its doors and log cabin open to the sky, and the next morning they had started the repairs. Just the three of them, an older couple and their granddaughter, with a coop of chickens and a Jersey cow in tow. "From Cantev Way, by the sea," was all the history I ever got about them. Usually we're a bit slow welcoming newcomers; you can never be sure about strangers. But a daughter of near-marriageable age made folks offer the Hutchensons open arms.

Old Hutchenson was a hard worker, and paid a fair day's wage, so he had no lack of help. I accused my brother Josh of hoping to see Livana, and he didn't bother to deny it. *That* I could live with, but when Wylie started sniffing around her the night of the Jakobssons' barn-raising, well . . . I let my tongue get the better of me.

Why didn't I notice that the Hutchensons were never seen except at night? Instead of helping with the baking, Mrs. Hutch arrived with crisscrossed apple pies still warm from the oven. 'Course, Mr. Hutchenson was a bit bent for raising a barn, but he played a good fiddle, and he was in time to lead the dancing. Perfectly simple reasons for things, or so Momma told me in no uncertain terms.

"Something different about those folks," I muttered under my breath, grabbing another loaf of warm bread and slicing it up. I was always mumbling—and Momma never missed a word.

"Good, hard-working people," Momma said calmly, giving the big crock of vegetable soup over the open fire a good stirring. "And their granddaughter has a lot of snap and color. It's no wonder the boys think she's pretty."

"That's not what I mean." My words stopped my movement, and I waited, listening to the silence. "Ever notice how Livana avoids all the womenfolk? I don't think she's said more than three words to any of us."

"No wonder, Alfreda." Momma's tone made me wince. "You're smoldering like a poker, girl. Show a little kindness. As if she could help having the face of an angel! Do you think any of those boys value a word from her lips or the work of her hands? Not likely."

It's not that Momma was right—it was the way she said it that kept me on edge. "I thought Wylie had more sense," I blurted out.

The reward for envy is misunderstanding. "Well, Miss Green Eyes, if he has, he'll be back, and if not, you're better off without him." With a last swish of the spoon, Momma called over her shoulder, "Soup's tender, Mary!" As she paused to dry her hands, Momma added, "Likely she'll settle on one of them soon, and then things will get back to normal."

"Why doesn't she want friends?" I whispered in turn, only half listening. Yearning for black curls or no, I knew I was right in this: Livana avoided me, and something about the Hutchensons made my palms itch. My gaze grew blurred and my hands slowed as I considered the problem. Was I right, or was the rest of the town right? And *what* was I right about? As my thoughts followed my sight, I realized I was staring in Shaw's direction . . . which meant we were staring at each other.

Things had been different since Shaw had come home on a visit. Where we once had had the habit of easy silence, now something waited in that silence. Shaw had taken to watching me when he thought I wasn't looking. Gave me the crawlies, it did, and this gathering was no different from any other. If only he'd speak, and tell me what was on his mind, but no—he never spoke, he never interfered, he never so much as twitched an eyebrow concerning me . . . he just watched.

Shaw could have been Livana's brother, as fair and dark-haired as he was, but now he had less meat on his bones than I did. Where Wylie was carved of round muscle, Shaw was nothing but cords, and while Wylie was blessed with rose and gold coloring, Shaw was black and white. My eyes had always been drawn to color, but now I was unsettled. Why was it Wylie who blew hot and cold about me, and Shaw who always watched me?

Maybe Momma was right; at the least, I could offer Livana some fresh bread. A quick glance around the dark clearing told me Wylie currently had the attention of the prize. They were seated over near the pump, Wylie perched on the edge of the trough, balancing with his usual flair. Tossing the last two loaves into a handbasket, I smoothed my soft blue cotton skirt with taut fingers and moved toward the pair.

Wylie's high-pitched laughter caught me by surprise, and I hesitated by the center fire. No, he was laughing at something Livana had said, not at me (at least not to my face), so I kept walking. He didn't seem at all surprised to see me, but Livana jumped visibly at my arrival.

"Thought I'd bring you some of Mrs. Jakobsson's finest," I announced, placing the basket on my hip and facing the both of them.

"Lord bless, Allie, that's good of you! Nothin' tastes better than fresh bread still steaming from the oven." Reaching under the cloth, he pulled out several slices of the cracked wheat. "You gotta try it, Livana—Mrs. Jaks makes the best cracked wheat bread in the region!"

Smiling faintly, Livana accepted the piece of bread from Wylie, but she didn't take a bite. Catching my gaze, she immediately lifted the food to her lips.

Well, staring wasn't the way to convince her I was

harmless. I let my eyes shift slightly, turning so I was looking between them instead of at either of them, and let Wylie do the talking. He was full of funny stories about the barn-raising, things I had either missed 'cus I was cooking or hadn't seen the humor of, and he was amusing more than just Livana. A way with words, my Wylie; even folks who had been there since sunup were enjoying the tale.

During a chuckle, my gaze dropped to the faint wavering of the trough water . . . and my stomach knotted tighter than a piece of crocheted lace. There was the black shadow of Wylie, golden in the firelight, and me a tall candle flickering a few paces farther on . . . but no Livana. She simply wasn't there.

Bewildered, I hazarded a quick glance to my left. No—she still sat on the hogshead next to the pump, her red and white striped dress black with the evening. But there was no matching dark outline rippling beyond her.

To this day I have no idea what I said or did. Dipping into Livana's mind didn't even occur to me. I only know I left a good chunk of bread with Wylie, and mumbled something to them about enjoying the dancing. Then I hurried back to those tables groaning with food.

"Isn't she sweet?" said a familiar voice, and I turned to see Idelia. She was sawing away at a haunch of venison, the slices toppling like wood slats peeled from a log.

"Who?" I blurted out.

"Livana, silly. She's real nice. I saw you over with her and Wylie." Did I imagine it, or did Idelia's big brown eyes momentarily flick in my direction? "Wylie seems real taken with her."

"You've talked to her?" I asked, ignoring the hint.

"Sure. Early on, when we were unpacking her mother's pies. Livana always does the seasoning—she's good with desserts. Best apple pie filling I've ever bumped a thumb into." This last was said with a giggle.

"And you've bumped a few," I agreed. "Was that all you talked about?"

"Not much time for anything else. How could you get close to her, the way the boys sit in rings at her feet?" Sighing, Idelia tossed the big bone to one of the Jakobssons' dogs. "I could scratch her eyes out if she wasn't so nice." Idelia had a few months on me, and was already starting to "blossom," as folks put it. Wylie's older brother had taken notice, as had Josh and several other fellows—until Livana came along.

"She didn't speak to me at all—just Wylie." I wasn't sure what to say. Idelia was usually pretty observant, but if she hadn't noticed anything strange about the Hutchensons . . .

"'Course not. Everyone knows that you and Wylie have been stepping out. If a boy liked you better than his old girl, how would you act around her?" Idelia was both amused and concerned, her face intent.

Sympathy can surely reduce hostility. "Polite, I hope."

"She was polite to me," Idelia offered. "You're pretty imposing when you want to be, Allie. Maybe you make her nervous."

"She makes *me* nervous," I retorted.

"Fair is fair," Idelia said in a placid, infuriating way.

My urge to pick a fight was nipped in the bud by the whine of a fiddle. Or was it? It sounded more like a frightened dog. A few more notes . . . no, it was a fiddle. Then came the moment I grudged Livana the most, 'cus Wylie was a powerful good dancer. He didn't hesitate to take her hand and escort her to the circle. As they walked toward the bonfire centered on hard dirt, one of Jakobsson's mutts trotted near. Almost by instinct, Wylie snapped his fingers invitingly at the big yellow animal.

Then something happened that I couldn't explain away. Animals loved Wylie; he just had a way with them.

But for the first time I saw a dog refuse to go to him—not just ignore him, but stop dead in its tracks and refuse to budge.

Wylie looked bewildered, but his face smoothed as Livana shrank against his side. "Don't be afraid," I heard him say to her. "Bo's as gentle as they come. See, he can smell your fear!"

As he spoke, old Bo turned tail and fled the firelight. I caught a good look at the dog as he tore past, and saw my impression confirmed—that animal was *scared*. Hadn't Wylie always told me that an animal that sensed fear was likely to *attack*? Didn't he remember his own words? Couldn't he see Bo's fear?

Suddenly it was very cold; I didn't feel like dancing anymore. Hugging my arms to my body, I considered whether the walk back to our place would be too far. The moon was young, shedding little light, and would set early. . . .

"Allie?" Papa's deep voice startled me out of my thoughts. "Your mother has faded with the sun, and the little boys are tired. Josh is hitching with Faxon as far as our gate, and they'll have room for you—"

"I'd rather leave now, Papa," I said quickly, my gaze still fixed on the whirling figures circling the bonfire. "I'm . . . I'm a bit tired myself."

Finally I glanced in his direction, to see his sky-blue eyes catch the light and briefly flare red. *Well, he's surely not fooled . . . .*

"All right," Papa said gently, removing his pipe from his mouth and tapping debris from the bowl. "I'll tell Faxon you're coming with us. Say your good-byes and meet us by the big oak."

Somehow I didn't care for his choice of words; it sounded too *final* for my taste. But I went to say good night to Idelia.

• • •

After a sleepless night tossing and turning, I spent the next few days convincing myself that my overactive imagination had finally pushed me into foolishness. Livana might be dangerously pretty, and her grandparents standoffish, but neither of those things was a crime. It didn't soothe the unease burning in my breast, but it calmed the tiny voice within that kept carping at me.

Still, I wasn't sleeping. My dreams were haunted by tree branches rattling in the winds of Vintage, and days of helping Momma harvest willow rods were wearing me away like stones beneath a stream.

I don't think Momma noticed; she'd been a bit distant since the werewolf business. After Dolph was killed, she'd withdrawn from us, as if she didn't want to pin her hopes on anything as fragile as a child. Lately she'd had a dreamy glow about her that made me hope there was another little brother or sister on the way. I thought it might do her good.

Papa knew—about me, at least. We always knew about each other, he and I, which was funny, when you realized the Gift came mainly from Momma's side. I'd asked Gran about that knowing once, and she said something about male-female flow and sympathy, but I was still not sure about it. Since I had to study with both Aunt Marta and Cousin Cory, I was sure it had to do with learning some things from women and others from men. There was more to this than "women's" or "men's" magic, but there was time and more to figure it out.

In the meantime, I was tired and irritable, Momma thought I was sulking, and Papa looked worried.

All this worked to my advantage about a week after the barn-raising. Papa was going to Sun-Return, after a long day sowing winter rye, and Momma decided I could get the things she needed. That was her way of telling me I wasn't being too useful with the basket-weaving. Knowing she was dead to rights, I climbed up into the wagon without protest, and soon we were well on our way to the village.

We talked of simple things on the trip in—the new rocker Papa was making Momma for Christmas, the smokehouse we'd left Josh building, and what kind of design I wanted on my quilting frame when Papa finally got around to working on it. What else could I have said? I had a lot of bad feelings, but nothing concrete. I'd almost convinced myself I'd imagined that Livana had no reflection.

All that changed when we arrived in town. There was a sizable crowd at the general store, where Joseph Halvdan was negotiating with Old Knut, the shopkeeper, for the loan of his digging hound. Big Joseph spotted me slipping in through the swinging door, and waved for me to come over. I pushed my way gently through faded calico and chambray as the majority of customers pretended they weren't listening to Knut and Big Joseph.

"Allie, girl! I was just wishing for you!" He put an arm around my shoulders and pulled me close. The odor of oiled leather clung to him. "Tell me, is there anything you can give Knut's dog to protect him from snakebite?"

I felt a frown cross my face. "A preventative? Well, people can put tanned leather between them and a snake. I don't know if—"

"An herb or something, darling. We already discussed a chest pad for him."

"I wish. No, Big Joseph, there are plenty of things to reduce swelling and draw venom, like blazing star and the snakeroots, but I've yet to hear of a preventative." Wanting to be helpful, I added, "You might ask my cousin Marta over in Cat Track Hollow."

Both Big Joseph and Knut shook their heads. "No time for that. I think I've got snakes nesting in a burrow under the house," Joseph said. "All these warm days and cold nights have them riled up, and they're crawling up through the floorboards, looking for a nice place to sleep. My boy's been bit two nights running."

"Poisonous?" I asked quickly.

"He's still alive, so I'd say not, but it's not comfortable for him, poor tyke. Bit on the crook of the arm and the neck. A bit feverish and tired, but still breathing." Joseph tried to keep his expression cheerful, but I knew better. Little Joe was an only son, and his parents doted on him. After five daughters, he had been long hoped and prayed for.

"Tell Mrs. Joseph to boil a heaping teaspoon of blazing star root in a cup of milk, divide it into four doses, and give him the decoction four times a day," I suggested. "It'll make him pass water faster, and get any venom out of his system. Just to be sure. And then more water, so he doesn't dry out."

"I'll tell her," Big Joseph said, nodding his blond head in thanks. "Hope I can give it to Knut's Blue Boy, too!"

"If necessary," I said seriously as several men chuckled. Sending a dog after snakes wasn't funny—Knut certainly didn't look amused. But better a dog than a man. Surely they had tried smoke already. . . .

Big Joseph and Knut drifted back to their talk, which was filled with the merits of a leather pad as opposed to wrapping thin tin around the poor dog, while Mrs. Knut measured spices for my momma. Papa had hinted on the way in that Momma was indeed going to present me with another brother or sister, so I used a piece of my precious horde of copper and bought several flower bulbs. Annuals for color and perennials for longevity . . . thinking of her huge garden, I had to smile.

Lost in thought as I was, I didn't hear Wylie come in the store. He was right up next to me before I noticed him in one of Mrs. Knut's mirrors, and what I saw froze my mind.

He looked exhausted, as if after a hard day harvesting. Only the crops were mostly in now. Usually golden from the sun, Wylie seemed faded, as if his skin had turned overnight to bleached parchment. Never before had I seen circles under his eyes; now the skin between his lids and cheekbones looked bruised, as if someone had punched him. The faint smile he managed upon seeing me was familiar, but that was about it.

"Wylie?" I must have looked as shocked as I felt, because immediately his lips pulled tight. "Are you feeling all right?"

"I'm fine," he said loudly. "Just staying up too late, that's all."

"You're sure?" I heard myself ask . . . the words were faint.

"Quit playing doctor, Allie," Wylie snapped, moving past me in a hurry. "If I start feeling poorly, I'll go see Doc Wilson."

"I'm not playing doctor," I told his back as he disappeared into the depths of the store. "But I see what I see." As the words left my lips I was aware of a silence that hadn't been present before. Glancing at the mirror hung to one side of the double doors, I saw that folks were watching me out of the corners of their eyes. *Stupid. So this is how people act when your man cheats on you.* But he wasn't really my man, so he wasn't cheating anyone—except himself, if he really was sick. I was in the back of the store before I realized I'd started walking.

"Wylie—" I touched his shoulder to get his attention, and felt the tension threading his muscles. As he turned toward me, I saw the bite . . . and couldn't pull my gaze from it.

Bit on the crook of the arm and the neck. Big Joseph's words echoed in my head, making it suddenly ache. Something had definitely nibbled on Wylie . . . more than once.

"What happened?" I gestured toward his neck as I spoke.

Wylie rubbed at the spot in response. "Bugs have been bad this fall," was his answer. "I told you I've been out late nights."

"What do you talk about, Wylie?" *Now why did you ask that, fool?*

"Huh?" The change in the conversation confused him.

"Livana never says hardly anything. What do you talk about?" I repeated the words slowly, as if talking to a youngling. Something in me had to know if it was merely physical, or if she had other strengths as well.

"Only you would ask that." Wylie shook his head slightly. "Any other girl would scream, or cry, or throw something at me—and there's plenty in here to throw— but not you. You always question. Can't you ever just let be and enjoy something?"

He sounded resigned, almost pitying, and I found I had some anger after all. "I don't know why I waste time worrying about you! No matter what I say or do, it's wrong; why does it matter what I choose?" Drawing myself up straight as an ash tree, I said, "So go get gnawed in the dark! The least she could do is invite you in the house!"

A bit weak for a parting shot, but it was the best I could manage. Spinning on the ball of my foot, I stomped back over to the counter and picked up my purchases. Nodding my thanks to Mrs. Knut, I walked out of the store without looking back, trying to be dignified without looking prim.

Sweet Lord, that hurt! I don't think I knew what Wylie was to me until I knew he was thinking about somebody else. My misery just about blinded me—I almost walked flat into Shaw Kristinsson, who was leaning up against the frame wall of Mrs. Kristinsson's boarding house.

"I know you won't believe this, but he's not worth it," Shaw said. His voice was quiet, as always; I didn't think I'd ever heard him shout, in anger or in joy.

"He's not himself," I retorted, stiffening, tilting back my head to keep any tears from escaping.

"No," Shaw agreed, shaking his head slightly.

We eyed each other for a time, as I wondered what Shaw suspected . . . or knew. But old habits die hard, and that new-found shyness had hold of me, so I kept my thoughts to myself.

"Ready to head back, Allie?" I heard my father say. "It'll be dark before we're home as it is."

"Coming, Papa," I answered him, nodding once to Shaw and moving past him to where our wagon waited.

Too much too quickly . . . it made it hard for me to sort things out. I was quiet the trip back, listening to the new gelding's firm tread—not like Dancer's merry pace, but she was carrying a foal, and wouldn't be pulling any cart for some time to come. Papa respected the silence. We were less than a mile from home when Papa's voice finally came out of the twilight at me.

"Are you thinking about a trip to your Aunt Marta's?" As calm as always, as if a whim to take one of the mules and ride a day to Cat Track Hollow was a common occurrence.

"I don't know what else to do, Papa," I admitted. "Something feels very wrong, but I don't know what it is."

"So take all you know to Marta," Papa said, letting out the reins a bit to give Juniper his head over some rough road. "If you go over it together, you'll be able to sort coincidence from catastrophe."

"Do you think I'm moonstruck or something?" I asked suddenly.

"Depends on what you mean," was the response. "If you mean feeling romantic, maybe a bit. No harm in that—one way or another, you'll survive it. I'm not so sure Wylie is the right fellow for you, but there's no harm in liking him." This was matter-of-fact, as if he was talking about someone who wasn't there. "But the other— whether you're unbalanced? No, Alfreda, you're not moonstruck. You see, Livana *does* avoid you; she avoids your mother, too. She even avoids me, and I wasn't born with your sight, although I've trained myself a fair piece." Although it was fairly dark, I knew Papa was looking at me. "Alfreda" was only for serious times.

"Then I'm not imagining it." I made a statement out of the words.

"I just said that, daughter." There was humor in his voice. Papa does so love to tease me. "Talk to Marta— that's what a good teacher is for, to set your feet on the path of knowledge."

"It's a long walk," I muttered, but Papa either didn't hear or chose not to speak.

TWELVE

THAT WAS HOW I ENDED UP perched on Snowshoe's broad
back, facing into a crisp morning breeze. Crimson clouds
tore across the sky like bloody rags; streams of early
golden light made the clouds' undersides glow. I'd packed
bread, cheese, and apples for the trip, and was riding in
Josh's—now my—canvas pants.

Aunt Marta lived leeward of Cat Track Hollow, on the
banks of Wild Rose Run. I still thought of her as "Aunt,"
as I had learned in childhood, despite her being Papa's
cousin. As I considered it, maybe it made sense that Papa
should be so sensitive to the dark on the other side. But
Momma's siblings showed no signs of the blood . . . perhaps the Gift didn't breed true.

I had yet to learn the names of Marta's teachers, and
had plumbed only the shallows of her knowledge, but I
was confident she'd have some answers. My aunt Marta
was a formidable woman; I figured that few ghouls could
stand up to her.

It was a long, long ride. I stopped two or three times to
let Snowshoe rest, and to grab a cold drink. My lunch I
munched down on the way, chewing in rhythm to my companion's gait. A mule was rarely as smooth-gaited as a
horse, but it was steady enough for a long day's work.
Compared to her usual duties, toting me to Cat Track
Hollow was child's play, so I had no trouble with Snowshoe.

Old Sol was westering when we finally reached the run. Water called to us through the yellowing peach leaves and black willows, gurgling through an intricate path of stones. Climbing stiffly down from Snowshoe's back, I led her through the drooping arms of the rare weeping willows and up to the chinked log house Aunt Marta called home. Basket willows competed with sassafras, witch hazel, sweet crabapple, and black apple and plum trees, while the familiar arching canes of the prairie rose covered the front wall. Smoke rose from the chimney—praise God she was home. Now that I'd arrived, my anxiety had returned.

I took my time with Snowshoe, checking her feet for stones or cuts and then brushing her coat until it was smooth. We'd moved slowly enough that she was already cooled down by the time I tied her up in the lean-to—fresh water and hay was more than enough to tempt her. The Tennessee walker that was my aunt's pride and joy was missing; either pastured out or on loan, I'd bet. Would I find . . . ? Yes; there was a bucket of bran mash cooling on a shelf. Shaking my head, I poured the meal into a trough for the mule.

How did Marta always know when I was coming? And would I be able to know that type of thing someday?

Now *that* thought gave me shivers.

The leather latch was out, so I knocked three times and swung open the tongue-and-groove wood door. Wonderful odors greeted me as I stepped over the sill—Marta's famous split pea and ham soup, and her cornmeal bread with real kernels mixed in the batter and cheese melted on top. Before I'd even seen her face, I felt welcome.

Marta was opposite the kitchen fireplace, working at

her small quilting frame. Her striking, angular face tilted in my direction, and those sky-blue eyes of my father's family mirrored mine.

"Took you long enough, woman," she said dryly. "Set yourself down and have some mulled cider, I pressed it this morning."

Huh. Maybe this would be easier to explain than I thought—once she was through scolding me. I pulled the cork set loosely in the fired ceramic crock and, using several quilted pads to protect my hands, poured myself a mug of hot cider.

"So. Tell me everything. How are Eldon and Garda and the boys? Have you been keeping up with your reading? And tell me about your vampire."

I just stared at her.

Marta tossed back her sleek pale head and laughed, the wings of white hair at her temples flashing like flags. "Sweet Jesus, woman, anyone with the Gift as strong as ours could smell that creature from three days away! But you weren't sure what you had until yesterday, were you?"

So I told her everything, from the arrival of the Hutchensons to Wylie's "bug bite." Marta didn't interrupt me, except for a nod now and then. Her fingers flew over the pattern we called Canada Geese, finishing the block in her frame even as I wrapped up my tale.

"You see the signs now?" she finally asked, loosening her frame and removing the completed block.

"But none of them *looks* right," I responded, hating the whine edging my voice. "They look, well, normal!"

"No one's ever seen the granddaughter by day," Marta said calmly.

"She's my number one candidate," I admitted. "Her granddad works his fields, and Mrs. Hutch has been seen in town, but I've never seen Livana except at night."

"The older the vampire, the more light they can bear—some say they can even move around during the day if they line their shoes with their native soil," Marta reminded me. "They can't stand direct sunlight, though. That'll fry them to a cinder quicker than anything. But I doubt the old folks are nightflyers. Most likely they're kin of hers—parents, or even children . . . Livana may have had a family before she was stricken. But she's old enough in her power to have a considerable aura—that's why everyone else is so taken with her. She can smell that you're different, too. Why do you think she avoids you and Garda? You're the only ones who might penetrate her disguise. They made a mistake, settling here, but with a little luck, they could last a year or more before having to move on."

"Momma doesn't seem to notice anything," I said hesitantly. "Although Papa agrees with me."

"Your father is an exceptional man," Marta replied, pulling another quilt square from her basket. "If we hadn't been so closely related, I'd have set my cap for him myself. But don't blame your momma for spinelessness. Ever since that werewolf bit Dolph, she's been only half a person, and she never was that strong. She's a good woman, and she's done her duty, passing on the power. Some haven't the strength to face it, that's all."

"Momma's increasing, though she hasn't announced it yet," I said quickly, because I knew Marta would want to know.

"Boy or girl?" she demanded.

"Girl," I started, and then stopped, confused. *Now, where—?*

Marta smiled. "You try too hard, Allie. There's a special little voice inside of you that tells you things. You just need to recognize when it's talking to you. Now—" Clamping the new quilt block into the frame, she moved it aside and stretched into her great height, wiping her damp fingers on her flour-sack apron. "Let's have some of this soup and plan our attack. Can't have a vampire running around chewing on our good villagers, much less the boy you're sweet on."

It wasn't until later that I realized Aunt Marta kept referring to Wylie as "the boy." Not so remarkable, except that she'd started calling me "woman" . . .

Well, Livana might not alternate between gaunt pallor and the bloated, mottled red that the old writings warned us about, but a vampire was a vampire, and certain things would cow her right quick.

"Catching her in her coffin would be best," Aunt Marta said as she finished up her share of the corn bread. "But we can't count on it. If her family is keeping her secret, they may be willing to fight for her—if only because they fear her. I doubt she's more than a hundred years old, if those folks bear her any resemblance at all, which is to our advantage. If she's still young, she probably hasn't much talent yet for shape-shifting. Becoming mist or a bat takes a lot of work. If she hasn't needed to learn, she'll be clumsy."

"They definitely look alike," I assured her.

"That's a point for our side—but we don't count on it. Chances are she *does* have the dog shape, which is part of the reason Jakobsson's animal was so afraid of her. But mist and flying are more dangerous for our purposes."

"I wonder how she became a vampire," I whispered, reaching for another piece of corn bread.

"First we get rid of her," Marta said firmly. "Then you can question her folks."

"But you don't think we should get help." This had been what we'd been arguing about ever since we started our little council of war.

"Remember how long it took to find all the were-wolves?" Marta had her shrewd look on her face. "We don't need a mob for this, Allie. Odds are we'd lose her in the confusion. No, this has to be done quickly and quietly, by as few people as possible. I think that you, your father, and I can take care of the situation. But we need a plan. And protection."

Rising from her favorite rocker, Marta moved over to the beautiful cherry keepsake box Uncle Jon had made her as her wedding present. Opening it, she pulled out several polished chains of silver and brought them over to my side. "Give me your hand," she said.

I extended my left arm. Deftly Marta fastened a flat bracelet of woven silver strands around my wrist. She'd set another one in my lap, and soon I was wearing it as well. There was no time to protest the matching close-fitting necklace, for she brushed my words aside.

"Your silver chain and cross are useful, but you need more silver at your neck," Marta said seriously. "We don't want any chance at all that she might brave a tiny silver burn for a chance to attack you. The cross is double protection, and you may need it elsewhere."

"But what about you?"

Chuckling, Marta tugged down the high neckline of her peach-colored dress, revealing an identical necklace. "When you reach my level of seeing, woman, it will never leave your body, except for an occasional quick polish. The more you see, the more things come to visit."

That wasn't encouraging. "Where did all these come from?"

"They're very old, Allie. This set belonged to my teacher, Dame Emma. She left it to me to give to my successor."

"Gran?" Had she known about me even then?

"Indeed. She suspected you had the power, but she knew how your momma would react, so she kept her peace." I opened my mouth to ask another question, but

Marta anticipated it. "Your father has a similar set, though he don't talk about it. He'll be fine. Now—let's get down to details."

We hammered out our plan as the fire burned low and the candles guttered. Marta's Sweet William was pastured, as I suspected, but we'd bring him in early and be back in Sun-Return by dusk. Whether we'd mount our attack that same night depended on how strong we felt, but Marta expected us to need a full night and day of rest before we made the attempt.

In the end it was mostly moot. The trip was simplicity itself, and Papa was keen to aid us in our need, but Marta woke that fateful morning with swollen eyelids and a hacking cough, and I knew we weren't destined to hunt vampires together. Not this time.

What do you prescribe for the foremost apothecary in a week's riding? "Comfrey and slippery elm with a pinch of ginseng?" I suggested, settling next to her cot.

"Just what I was about to request," she said hoarsely, and I jumped up to prepare the decoction. Just getting the water to boil would take a few minutes, as Momma had already emptied the pot, so I rattled about shaving roots and bark, my thoughts filled with vampires.

"We can't wait long," I heard myself say aloud.

"No," Marta agreed, and started coughing. I brought her a glass of cool well water to ease her throat, and when she had control again, she said, "You can't wait for me. You'll have to go ahead tonight."

"But . . . but how can we do it with only two of us?" Originally the plan had called for Marta and me to scope out the Hutchenson place during the day. If we could find the coffin, we'd get there before dusk and do the deed then, with Papa acting as our rear guard should the

Hutchensons—or anyone else—care to interfere. If we failed to find the coffin, we'd have to watch the place until Livana returned toward morning, and follow her down into her lair. Still, there was no room for error once we'd begun, which was why two were necessary. Livana wasn't going to lunge up when that stake hit her chest if someone was pinning her across the throat with a garlic braid threaded by a silver chain.

The idea of trying to stake a vampire without that control made my hands shake. Although the undead preferred to feed over several nights, in order to drain every scrap of soul and vitality, they were perfectly capable of draining a body in moments. . . .

My hands weren't the only thing shaking.

"It's harder, but possible," Marta whispered, recalling my attention. "And I might be able to find you a third, although it will take me some time, feeling like this." Another sip of water, and Marta continued, "Instead of guarding the coffin, your papa will have to destroy it."

"*Destroy* it?" I was appalled. "But—but how can I get the drop on her—"

"You can't." This was weary. "It's too dangerous. In the coffin, she's on her native soil; even before sunset she'll have enough energy stored to spring out at you, if no one chokes her off. And you *must* have a guard to attack a coffin. What if old Hutchenson came up behind you with a pitchfork?"

Shuddering, I moved back into the kitchen and poured boiling water into an enamel bowl that already held diced bark and shaved comfrey and ginseng root. "So what am I doing while he's smashing up the coffin?"

"Depends on where it is. If it's close to the house and the old ones will hear, you'll have to guard for your papa. Then you both wait until she comes back at Indian light, and drive her into an enclosed area until the sun is up.

Without her soil to give her strength, she'll be weak enough that you can run her through at a distance, with a long stake. Once she stops struggling, the rest is the same."

Have you ever felt your face freeze? That's how I felt, listening to Marta speak—like my face was made of frozen stone. Even so, I moved back into the stillroom to give her my attention.

Something of what I was feeling must have shone through, because Marta said gently, "I know. I hoped we could do it the other way. It's hard enough to hammer a stake into a girl without all that. But before it's over, you'll know what you're dealing with isn't human anymore."

"And if the coffin is in the barn, or something?" I asked, my gaze lifting to the window and the woods beyond.

"You'll track her while your papa burns or smashes the coffin and scorches the soil. When you find her, frighten her off from any victims if you can, and keep her away long enough for him to finish destroying her box. Then—" Marta went into another coughing jag, and I reached to hold her until it passed. "Then you either follow her or lead her back to the Hutchensons' farm. Eldon will be waiting."

"Sweet Jesus," I whispered without a trace of irreverence, easing Marta back down. Following Livana was bad enough, but leading her! If she saw me, the game was up—it was kill or be killed, since she would know there was little chance her glamour would work on me. And if she *could* change to mist—

Something occurred to me then. I remembered my companion the night I'd spent alone in the woods. . . .

"There are one or two others in the area with some—talent," I started, keeping my voice calm. "Could they be any help?"

Marta blinked quickly, as if I'd surprised her, and then said, "If we were trying to keep Livana from breaking out of an area, maybe. But those folks have specialized talents, with the strength of their forms. There's not necessarily any other power associated with that gift." Marta paused, swallowing carefully to control her cough. "One of them can help, if I can reach him—he's got the Gift, and just happens to have family with active shaping. But I've got to find him first. You can't help with that."

So. Just Papa and me, at the last. I had no doubt that Papa would pull his share, but to be honest, I wasn't sure *I* was ready to tangle with a vampire.

"You can do it, Allie," came Marta's weak voice. "I wouldn't let you try unless I thought you could handle it. The important thing is not to panic, and I don't think you will. Just remember that Big Joseph's child and your boy are doomed unless we stop her tonight.

"In the meantime, we need to get you ready. We need a powerful amount of garlic, woman!"

"Garlic is one thing we're never short of, cousin," I finally said as I rose to strain the decoction and add cold water to it. "You just relax and drink some of this while I fetch some bulbs, and we'll braid the day away!"

I tried to keep my tone light, but Marta wasn't fooled. She pressed my hand as I brought her the medicine. "You can stop her," Marta said again.

"I have to." It was that simple.

Come sundown I found myself squatting in a brush pile behind the Hutchensons' barn, waiting for Livana to head out on her nightly round. I was wearing a flannel work smock and a pair of Dolph's old wool pants. Momma was never happy about the pants, especially at night . . . but this time she didn't know I'd gone out with Papa. Cousin Marta had said she'd tell my mother what was needful.

I didn't envy her the job.

Along with my silver, I was wearing a huge garlic braid. It looped my neck and then crossed between my breasts (what there was of them), ending up tied around my waist. Since I could barely stand the smell myself, I doubted that Livana would choose to get close to me.

Papa was similarly bound in bulbs. He sat right next to me, wrapped in stillness and darkness, and I was grateful for his presence. It was up to us now—Marta hadn't despaired of finding help, but the person she had in mind was apparently farther than Sun-Return, and he might not make it here in time. At any rate, we weren't waiting for him.

Shoving my hands into my pockets, I fingered one of the many cloves of garlic nestled within. With luck, I wouldn't have to defend myself with anything except a stake, but my side pouches were stuffed with garlic, just in case. Just in case—

Then we saw her leave the barn. She was wearing white, which made her a lot easier to spot. The waxing moon had yet to clear the trees, but when it did, it would give us light for over half the night. Praise be that Papa had come by earlier and scouted out the place. Clever of them to put her coffin in the old tack room. It seemed there was more than one reason why the Hutchensons had no mule. No visitors would ever think to go in there—even if they were in the barn. That isolation was one less thing to worry about.

My job, besides braiding garlic, had been to see to Big Joseph Halvdan's son. After a great deal of thought, we decided to tell the family what was going on. It took some fast talking on my part to keep Big Joseph from going

after the Hutchensons with his ax, but once I explained
the plan, he was game. The hardest thing was convincing
Mrs. Hal that the boy had to remain in his room. Livana
would know something was wrong if the room was empty
or had another person in it.

I had spent the afternoon reinforcing the room: hanging garlic braids around the doorways and windows,
pouring mustard seed in cracks, painting runes and
crosses at every possible opening. Last of all, I gave Mrs.
Hal a tisane of bee balm, chamomile, marjoram, hops,
and peppermint to make sure the child slept. All the
wards on earth couldn't keep out a vampire if the victim
invited it in—and what with Livana's hypnotic manner,
the boy had undoubtedly done just that several nights
previously, although he had no memory of it.

My mind kept returning to those wards. Would they
hold? The slightest opening was enough, for Livana had
already been invited into that house. Only if my efforts
succeeded would she need another invitation to get past
those crosses.

Even as I worried about my precautions, I watched
Livana disappear into the woods. Touching my father's
shoulder briefly for strength, I crept after her.

Livana was moving fast. A slip of long dress was all I
had to follow; it flitted in and out of the trees, weaving
like a shuttle among the trunks. My heart was racing
faster than my feet; she was heading straight to the
Halvdans' farm. It was no mean distance to the place—
we would spend the best part of an hour getting there.
Why couldn't she use the road? I knew better than that;
there was a chance, no matter how remote, that someone
might spot her on it. And of course she couldn't get hurt
tromping through the darkness. *I* was the one who

would trip over logs, get scratched by branches, and have night critters startle me.

If she's hungry, she can't change shape, Marta had told me. Thank heaven for small favors, because Livana was moving fast enough as it was—I'd never keep her in sight if she shifted. I had the short stake with me, and had to keep it hugged across my chest to keep from tripping. Holding the thing was going to tire my arms, but I couldn't sling it over my shoulder, 'cus it would catch on branches. I just had to make do.

It seemed like forever, slogging through those woods, but finally we reached Halvdan's north field. Corn-husk teepees loomed tall in the growing moonlight, and a flapping noise made me seize the cross dangling from my neck.

An owl? No—worse than that, the scarecrow, catching a stray gust of wind. Feeling foolish, I looked around for Livana.

Halfway across the field! Climbing between two rails of the fence, I hurried after her. Grateful for my sturdy boots, I did my best to make up my losses, but Livana arrived at the house long before I did.

I could hear her gasp and hiss of dismay quite clearly in a lull of the wind. So—first check. *Something* in my protections had slowed her down. Did she suspect my handiwork, or did she think her glamour had failed with the parents? What would she do next, seek another victim?

No; not yet.

As I grew in knowledge, I would learn that getting a potential victim to accept the vampire was more than half the battle. Although I didn't know it then, Livana was not about to give up so easily. She paced every step of that wall, seeking an unguarded crack . . . examined that house so carefully my body cramped from lack of movement. All those hours spent pouring mustard seed had been worth it.

Fighting off sleep, I stretched my neck from side to side, trying to prevent the muscles from tightening. At that moment Livana froze in midstep.

Did she hear something—cloth rubbing against the garlic braid, the wood stake catching on a thread? Or did she *smell* me . . . smell living blood that was too large for night vermin and not confined by wards? Whatever the reason, she knew she wasn't alone.

My pulse was racing like a coursing deer as a lump rose in my throat. Keep her busy, that was my job. I had walked this property from one end to the other, and it was time to lead my quarry a merry chase. Slowly I slipped away from the house and toward the southern boundary of the farm.

Livana followed.

There was no haste to this walk; I kept a healthy lead, and she did not lose my trail. With effort, I could move almost soundlessly—almost. If you want speed, you must make a bit of noise. But I wasn't sure if Livana was tracking me by nose or ear, so I had to leave her something to go by.

Then I heard the dog.

It sounded big—I heard large sticks snapping as it moved through the underbrush—and it was getting closer. There was no reason to fear a dog, especially since they didn't like vampires. . . .

A trill of notes burst from the silence around me, riding the octaves, frantic in its speed. I was so startled I nearly jumped out of my clothes. There was my blasted bird, screaming to the moon—

To me. Now I could hear the haste in its voice, the warning. Not about the moon . . .

The dog.

Nothing to fear, *unless it was Livana*. Suddenly I had wings at my feet. If she was shifting, I had lost all advantage, and I had to get as far away as possible. Stepping onto the path that led to the creek, I started running.

THIRTEEN

THERE WAS NOTHING OF GRACE or subtlety to that run—I knew it was my life that was being weighed, and at the moment it wasn't worth much. Fear swept through me like a gust of wind, the sour, metallic tang of blood in my mouth. Basic teachings rose from my inner consciousness, and I increased my speed. The creek; I had to cross the creek, or I was doomed.

My strength was draining into my stomach, and I fought to keep going, because I could hear my goal, the blessed gurgle of a broad, shallow creek. Behind me was the dog, still snuffling, seeking my trail, tracking my passage—

The creature belled, giving voice to its find, and it was all I could do to run.

Fortunately my feet had more sense than I had; they kept moving. Boots touched slimed rock, and I fell facedown into the shallows of the narrow stream. Scrambling for purchase, my toes found pebble-packed mud, and I churned to my feet. Hallelujah! I'd found the ford!

A moonbeam pricked out the stepping stones, but it was a little late to think about preventing pneumonia. Grateful that garlic kept things at bay whether wet or dry, I waded over to the other side and up the bank. Finding a friendly tree, I threw myself into its shadow. To my surprise, I found I was still hanging onto the stake with a death grip.

Would her new shape protect her from running water?

The beast reached the ford and immediately halted, weaving from side to side as it checked its scent trail. A gust of wind stirred a flurry of leaves, and when they had settled, Livana stood next to the creek. It was that simple. . . .

She stood listening a while, her head cocked to one side, her fingers flexing like talons. Then she backed away from the water and started down the trail toward the farmhouse. Only a few steps; she was difficult to see, but I could just make out her shape as she moved off the trail and into the undergrowth.

Silence.

I didn't need a signpost to show me the way things were going. She was waiting for me; I had no doubt of it. *You're going to wait a long time,* I vowed, shaking, as I knelt in the mulch layering the forest floor. *I don't need to eat, and I think you do. Thank you, thank you, little bird!* Shifting must have taken something out of her. The question was, how long would she wait until she decided I wasn't going to panic and bolt?

Because I wasn't. I knew my teachings, and there was running water between me and that vampire. The only way Livana could cross it was in her coffin, and then only at greatest risk. And although she didn't know it, her coffin would be crumbling into ash about now. Praise the powers that be that there wasn't some special link between a vampire and its coffin!

Moonlight crept through the trees to pour down upon us like molten silver, and still we sat, Livana and I. The waiting was harder than I thought it would be—terror alternated with stupor, as long moments of inactivity dulled my instincts. A trick of the shivery light brought memory back, and I was stunned to realize that I had just lived one of my dreams. Right after Dolph died, but before the service . . . I remembered I had run in terror, then stumbled and fallen into running water.

It had been the first time I'd really understood I could dream the future. The memory sobered me and stiffened my backbone. There were things in this life left for me to do; I wasn't going to become a meal for a vampire.

I was just beginning to wonder if she planned to wait out the night when I saw the white spot detach itself and start back toward the Halvdans' buildings.

It was a long moment before I crossed that creek.

I moved a bit faster than I should have, trekking up that trail, but there was no danger—not there. Livana was still prowling around Big Joseph's house, looking for an opening. She even entered through the front door, and I heartily prayed that Big Joseph and his lady were in their own bedroom. They were safe, never having invited her in, unless they surprised her—then the rules might change. Would the garlic and crosses at the inner door deter her?

In moments she returned to the porch. A tiny sigh of relief threaded through me, and I tightened my grip on the stake. The moon was past the roof of the sky and heading west . . . should I wait, or force the issue?

Livana decided for us. Without hesitation she started back toward the Hutchensons' farm. There was enough haste in her manner that I felt mildly alarmed. Did she suspect something? Had she started thinking about the coincidence of all that garlic, plus someone spying her out? Papa was alone. . . . I increased my speed.

The wind had picked up, and the temperature dropped; we were edging up on a storm. Occasionally I grabbed a handful of fresh-fallen leaves and stuffed it in my shirt for extra insulation. Branches creaked and rubbed against each other, echoing the quaking boughs of my dreams. I was a bit turned around in the trees, but it seemed the gusts were from the north, and I was grateful, for that meant the wind was now in Livana's face. *Carry me away,* I prayed. *Carry my scent far, far away.*

A front meant clouds, and clouds meant fitful moonlight—the going was harder heading back. I used the stake as a staff, making sure Livana wasn't leading me back by way of any pits or anything. In the meantime, I kept my eyes fixed on her. If she had the strength to shift again, I'd lose her for sure.

We reached the Hutchensons' clearing just as night rolled over into Indian light, that hazy gray before the dawn that warns the darkness will soon end. Entering the tack room proper required moving around to the east side, so we swung to the right, over barren fields. Try as I might, I couldn't smell any trace of burning. I hoped that meant Papa had covered his tracks well.

Livana was nearing the doorway; shifting my grip on the stake, so I could get a running lunge if necessary, I lengthened my stride. *Freeze up and she'll kill you both, it's as simple as that,* I told myself, trying to draw oak into my backbone. She'd be fighting for her life, and that meant she'd be more dangerous than anything I'd ever faced . . . or could hope to face.

Powers that be, lend me your aid! It was light that repulsed the strength of darkness . . . light. Whatever else I might someday be, I'd admit to being in the service of the Light. Now it was time to prove it.

We'd agreed on a signal. Papa had a lantern with a night shield on it, and he'd brought it along. When I saw a flicker of light, I was to move up to the door and block it, trying to keep her penned inside. If she shifted, I was to move—we didn't want to fight a ravening dog in close quarters, and we couldn't contain mist. As for a bat, Papa had even brought a net with several silver threads, something Aunt Marta had pulled out of a trunk—

Suddenly I could see light, and I thought my heart would stop. But I kept moving, now at a run, right up to the doorway—

Praise be that "short" stake was more than three feet English, and that I'd kept it pointed before me! Livana popped up at the door frame so fast I nearly impaled her then and there. Her face was distorted, furious, and as she backed up and turned halfway toward the lantern, I could see that her canines were visibly longer than usual. There was nothing ladylike about her dainty form now . . . her hands *were* talons.

With a snarl she leapt back into the tack room, reaching with long arms toward the lantern. Beyond the bright beam the tip of a stake appeared, poking right back at her. Flinching, she tried to keep away from the wood even as she groped for my father. As my eyes adjusted to the glare, I could see him; cool as an autumn breeze, his face betraying no anxiety, Papa was methodically pushing Livana back into a corner.

His actions gave me time to snatch up the longer stake I'd left waiting there. I tucked it under my left arm, pulling my strength behind it, even as I switched the shorter stake to the right hand.

Then Livana shifted, and the nightmare began.

In the narrow beam of light I could occasionally see what had been tracking me though the woods, and if I'd eaten dinner, I'd have tossed it. A more misbegotten-looking creature you have never seen, scarcely dog at all—and strong. It had shoulders like a mastiff's, and jaws like a pit bull's. If it got hold of one of us, we didn't have a prayer.

There was a lot of snarling and barking as the Livana beast grabbed hold of Papa's stake and started chewing on it. The sound echoed, as if another animal answered somewhere outside, but I didn't have time to figure it out. I kept poking at her to see if I could force her to change back (it takes strength to stay in another form, and she hadn't fed that night), but I also moved away from the open doorway. Papa had taken the precaution of bolting the double doors that led to the barn proper. Although their timbers shook like birch leaves in a high wind as Livana threw herself against them, the bar holding the doors could be moved only by human hands.

Finally the dog charged past me out the door. I whirled, just in case she planned to return immediately and make mincemeat of me, but it sounded like she was too busy. A horrible noise broke out, one I had never heard before—it sounded like a dogfight, only a hundred times worse than any I'd ever imagined. Even as Papa set fire to a second lantern and carefully placed it to give us more light, I peered around the doorjamb.

It *was* a dogfight. Livana was wrestling with something fully as big as she was. Swallowing what little spit I had left, I contemplated leaving the tack room, and then decided against it. Whatever Livana was fighting, it seemed determined to keep her from getting much farther, which was all to the good for our cause. There was only one place for her to run—back into the tack room. So I looked for someplace to stand. My back to the wall, with a bit of height . . . The fight drew closer, and I quickly chose my spot.

Not a moment too soon, either. The dogs crashed into the doorjamb, Livana dragging the other almost into the tack room before the new creature let go and ran out of the barn. I heard it slide to a stop, though, just beyond the lantern glare, and knew it was still there. Someone else was nearby, too; I could hear stones crunching against each other underfoot.

Even as the sounds registered, Livana changed back into a woman . . . or the semblance of a woman. Her arm was torn where jaws had gripped her, but no blood poured forth—it was like slicing a corpse. It might have been a real bug bite, the way she ignored it. She was too busy watching the two of us.

Then the crowning glory of the night burst forth. Walking right into the tack room as if he owned the farm was Wylie. Even by lantern light, he looked worse than when I'd last seen him, and I knew instantly that we had trouble. The expression on his face was horrified . . . but he was staring at my father.

"Have you lost your mind, sir?" Wylie asked, walking right up to Livana. "Why are you in here waving that around when there's that big monster of a dog out there? Part wolf, by the look of him, and—"

"Wylie, help me!" Livana shrieked, throwing her arms around his neck. "They're going to hurt me!"

"What?" He looked at her in concern, and my blood froze.

Glamour. What kind of a fog was he in?

"I . . . I waited for you, Livana, a long time, and when you didn't come—" Wylie started slowly, reaching to loosen her tight grip on his shoulders.

"I couldn't get away to see you tonight, not until just a few minutes ago, but they won't let me leave! I don't understand!" This last was a wail, as she gripped his hands.

Returning her grasp, Wylie turned to Papa and said, "Is this true? Why are you frightening her?"

Papa slowly gestured at the pair of them with his long ash stake. "Move away from her, Wylie. She's very dangerous."

"Dangerous?" His voice was thick with disbelief.

"She's a vampire, Wylie," I piped up, unable to keep silent. "We've got to stop her before she kills someone. She's been draining Little Joe Halvdan—and you."

Wylie just stared at Livana, which was *not* what we wanted. The more he met her eyes, the stronger the spell between them. "Have you been chewing loco weed, Allie?" he finally asked. "Or are you jealous after all?"

"Wylie, she's a—"

"Where's her coffin?" Wylie said sarcastically.

"What's left of it is smoldering out in the midden," Papa said conversationally.

Livana let out a scream framed with terror and fury and lunged for Wylie's throat. Papa swung his stake like a quarterstaff and slammed it across her back. With a squall she fell to her knees, moaning in pain, and I was shocked to see a weal begin to form, even where her dress had taken the blow.

It was the chance I'd waited for, and I grabbed Wylie's arm, tugging him back toward the door. "Run!" I hissed. "You don't have any protection, and we do! Run!" Wylie just stared at me. It was obvious that this scene had shaken the glamour, but he was still partially entranced.

Livana was back on her feet and reaching for Wylie, but I got my stake across us both, shaking it in her face even as Papa prepared to shove his into her back. Sensing danger, Livana whirled and started stalking him—and he didn't back away.

Sweet Lord, could folk wearing silver be entranced? "Eldon!" I screamed, naming my father and beating at Livana with my ash stake.

Someone flitted past me like a shadow and started throwing necklaces of garlic all over the place. One settled over Livana's neck, and it snapped the trance like a blow across the face. Gasping for air, she clawed ineffectively at the braid even as another settled over her form. It was Shaw Kristinsson, lit by the first golden shaft of morning. Livana slashed at him, her talons shredding his sleeve to tatters.

I acted without conscious thought. Shoving Wylie hard, I pushed him back into the darkness of the tack room. Diving like a child at play, I slammed into Shaw and we both collapsed against the far wall.

A woman was screaming. No . . . not a woman. Something that had once been a woman, maybe, but that voice had nothing human in it. The smell of burning filled the air; first the smell of torched cotton, then singed garlic, and finally sun-kissed, rotted meat. Rolling over, I saw a sight I will never forget—framed in a rectangle of golden light, Livana was lit like a torch, smoke rising from her like ground fog.

Desperately she tried to walk, but her strength was gone. Crumpling into a heap, she even tried crawling out of the sunlight. There was time for one last, pitiful attempt to dig her talons into dirt and pull herself along, then her flesh caved in on itself and the flames died as if doused by water. All that was left was a blackened skeleton.

It happened so quickly I had no time to be either frightened or sickened. Finally I understood what Marta had meant: *You'll know what you're dealing with isn't human.* Nothing human could have burned like that, so quickly, crumbling into ash—

Wylie's croak of anguish broke off my thoughts. He was creeping over to the skeleton even as I heard familiar coughing just outside the door.

"Sweet Lord, Allie! How will you answer for this? What did you do to her?" Wylie was so appalled he didn't know what to do.

I started getting mad. I knew he was still bespelled a

bit, and I knew I should be patient, but I'd had a long night, and I didn't need to be where this was going.

"I'll take him, Alfreda," came Marta's voice. She was leaning against the doorjamb, a smile on her thin face.

"Aunt Marta!" Suddenly I realized I was all tangled up with Shaw, and Momma would *not* approve. I struggled to get my foot out from under Shaw's long legs. "You shouldn't be up—"

"No coddling, woman," Marta ordered, holding up one hand. "I'm not at my best, but I'm not at death's door, either. Everyone needs a test before they are brought into the mysteries . . . a vampire was as good as anything." She paused to pull her wool shawl tighter around her shoulders, eyeing my soaked and leaf-stuffed form with dry amusement. "But I found out after you'd left that these folks came from Cantev Way. The vampire they drove out of Cantev Way wasn't more than a hundred, but she had a reputation for cunning and glamour that I didn't like. I was afraid she might prove too strong for two of you, so I went out myself to find Shaw."

"I was off digging roots for Cory," came Shaw's quiet voice from behind me. "Since no one else knew where to look, no one had found me. Of course Marta couldn't tell them why it was so important."

"The other dog?" I asked, turning around and wringing the rest of the water out of my braid.

"Wolf," Shaw said without a flicker of expression. "A friend of mine."

Uh-huh. I studied him a moment, waiting to see if my power responded to him. It did, and yet . . .

No. Not a werewolf. Whatever had happened, there was nothing evil in it. So the family talent had passed to the next generation, unless his mother was skulking outside somewhere. Digging roots for Cousin Cory, eh?

While taking a break from his studies . . . *Exactly what are you studying, Shaw?*

Everyone needed a test before learning the mysteries . . . what had *his* test been? I was suddenly very curious about those wizardly secrets, but for the time being I set my attention on my father.

Papa was getting stiffly to his feet, but his tired face wore a smile. "Getting too old for this sort of thing," he said, rubbing the back of his neck. "Good thing you screamed my name, daughter. That gaze was as deadly as a snake's when she chose to use it!"

"Deadly is the word," Marta agreed, nudging the pile of charred garlic and bone. "We'll need to separate the head from the neck, and run an ash stake through the heart area before we finish burning the corpse. For safety's sake, we probably ought to put her with what's left of the coffin and burn everything together." Sighing, Marta glanced at Papa. "Can you find us a crossroads with nothing at the heart of it? If you'll take care of that, I'll break the news to the Hutchensons."

We *did* seem to need a lot of crossroads in Sun-Return—we'd buried four werewolves in my lifetime alone!

"And you," she went on, turning to me. "You did well, woman. It's dangerous, killing a vampire, but you made it look easy."

I gave what I now recognize as my equivalent of a shrug, lifting my eyebrows as I rolled my eyes and tilted my head. "Took three of us, plus a wolf." I'd play dumb on that secret until I was invited in. "And it didn't feel easy at the time."

Marta's smile was genuine. "The second test was whether you know your own limitations. You'll do, cousin, you'll do." Marta nodded once to Shaw before leading the dazed Wylie out of the tack room. "Thank you again, friend. Go get yourself a big breakfast!"

"I had a stake in it, too," he reminded her, nodding in turn.

Watching his thin face, a pattern of planes and shadows, I said, "What stake?"

For the first time I saw Shaw look startled. "I mean . . . if you'd failed, Marta and I would have had to go after Livana again, and she'd have been warned."

He wouldn't meet my eyes. Feeling a smile pulling at my lips, I said, "Try again."

"Well . . ." He hazarded a glance in my direction, and I caught his gaze with my own.

Maybe that was a mistake. Dark, those eyes, like a well. So dark you could fall in and forget to climb back out . . .

"Sometimes your eyes are like fog, and sometimes they are full of the sun," Shaw said suddenly.

I was getting an inkling of something. The thought wasn't fully formed yet, which was just as well—I still had a soft spot for Wylie, foolish and beglamoured or not. But now I had some other things to think about . . . and the thinking might prove interesting.

"Come on," I said, gesturing with a crooked finger and pulling a stray leaf out of my hair. "It takes a lot of brush to burn a coffin down."

FOURTEEN

IT'S A HEADY BREW, triumphing over something as evil—
and tangible—as a vampire. I was feeling a bit giddy
about the whole business, and I think Shaw was, too. He
was walking a bit taller than usual, anyway. Papa and
Aunt Marta had no censure for us. She was wearing her
Valkyrie smile, and Papa actually got out his pipe when
we hitched up the wagon to head home.

Funny how fast something good can go sour.

We crept through Sun-Return long before the dawn
cleared the hills, dropping Shaw off at his mother's
boarding house. Mist shrouded everything round us, hiding familiar landmarks and making our white mule
ghostly. The euphoria of success was slowly wearing off.
. . . I curled up in the back of the wagon, filled with a
sleepy satisfaction.

"You spoke to Garda?" I heard my father ask Marta.

"I told her there was business to be done, and that
Allie was ready for her test," was Marta's response. "It
didn't please her, but Garda knows what's at stake. She
wanted to come, but I asked her if she wanted the little
ones alone at such a time. 'Course she stayed with the
boys."

"Were you really worried about it all springing back in
our face?" A puff of Papa's mellow tobacco whipped
back, so I knew he'd exhaled before speaking.

Marta gave an unladylike snort. "Only if it turned out Livana had the bat shape. Didn't seem likely, but it's best to assume the worst."

It slowly came to me what they were talking about . . . that Livana might have slipped our trap and attacked Momma and the boys. Surely Momma had warded the house! I shivered, and pulled one of the travel quilts over my legs. Always leave your loved ones guarded behind you, so you can do the deed at hand. . . .

That thought led back to the Hutchensons. We'd been right about a connection—we simply hadn't gone far enough. Mr. Hutchenson was Livana's grandson, his spouse in tow. Seems the eldest survivors of the family always took her in, to keep her away from the bulk of her descendants. Their constant relocation had succeeded in protecting their own kin, but her grandson never could bring himself to stake her—and the wife hadn't had the courage to try alone.

There had been both sorrow and relief on their faces when Marta had told them Livana was finally dead. I wondered if they'd try to stay, or if they'd move closer to their children's children.

I wondered if I would have tried to hold on to life like Livana had. . . .

I heard the slam of the barn door as we pulled into the clearing before our house, and Josh appeared out of the fog, damp enough that I was pretty sure the chores were done.

He gave us all a long look, and then said, "I don't think Momma ever went to bed. Just what were you up to, anyway?" He reached for the mule's harness as he spoke.

"Taking care of a predator," Papa said briefly as he hopped down from the seat. Lifting Marta down as if she was dressed in her Sunday best, Papa extended a hand to me for balance so I could crawl over the side of the wagon.

"You might want to take your time with the mule, though," Aunt Marta added with a smile.

"Yes'm," Josh said quickly, nodding politely to her as he led Snowshoe toward the barn. He'd very carefully avoided looking at me . . . seemed I looked worse than I'd thought.

Momma hadn't gone to sleep, eh? Suddenly I had the feeling that this was going to be unpleasant. Still, I'd survived Momma's lectures before, and I'd survive this one. A friendly beam of sunlight broke through the eastern trees, shimmering through the veil of ground fog. It seemed to reassure me about the day to come.

I sure hoped a catnap would be part of the deal.

Fresh bread, hot oatmeal, and a whiff of cinnamon greeted us as we opened the wood door to the house. The kitchen and living room seemed filled with darkness after the floating light of the fog. It hovered, that darkness, leaning over Momma and the little boys as they finished up their breakfast. My mother was just rising to her feet as we walked through the entryway and into the kitchen.

"Sweet Mary!" Momma nearly flew around the chestnut table and scooped me into a fierce grip. I was bewildered for a moment before I realized she was thanking the mother of Jesus.

"All is well, Garda," my cousin said from behind me. "The vampire is dead, and none of us was touched."

"How can you be sure?" Both my mother's voice and gaze were fierce as she rounded on Marta. "How do you know it didn't succeed in shrouding her spirit?"

Aunt Marta's smile was momentarily wintry. "You can trust my inner sight, woman. Allie blazes like a bonfire at winter solstice. As long as she's my student, even in name only, she'll carry my mark. She's not going to do anything—or have anything done to her—without my knowledge."

Momma turned those haunted eyes back toward me, taking in my damp and disheveled appearance. "Dear Lord, child, you look like you spent the night in a swamp! Get out of those clothes while I boil water!"

Papa was already dishing up some breakfast for us. "Might as well let her sit by the fire and eat while you heat the bath. Allie needs warming both inside and out." He handed Marta and me big bowls of oatmeal as he shot Momma a narrow glance. "Don't forget some sweetening."

I sidled over to the honey pot, avoiding Momma's eye. "I'm fine, Momma. Just slipped at the creek, that's all."

"And what were you doing near a creek last night? I thought you were destroying her coffin." With a familiar twitch of her flour-sack apron, Momma picked up the boys' dishes and carried them to the sink.

"You fellows get moving," Papa murmured to Ben and Joe as they gathered up their slates and readers. "Don't want you late for school."

I gave Ben and Joe a hug in passing and worked my way into the shadows by the fireplace. Briefly I wished I was still attending school—an excuse to leave the room would have been nice—but there wasn't anything left for the schoolmaster to teach me. Maybe I *should* have gone upstairs to peel off.

"Well, Alfreda?"

Oops. I'd hoped Momma was just asking the air, but it seemed she really wanted an answer. Telling her I had been running from a vampire beast was *not* gonna be a popular answer.

Always *let the truth serve.* . . . "We had to keep an eye on Livana, Momma. I did the tracking while Papa broke up her coffin and scorched her earth."

Fists on hips, Momma whirled back to Papa and Aunt Marta. "You let her follow a vampire? *Alone?*" The last came out as almost a squeak.

Well, the idea had made me a bit squeaky, too.

"She's still a child, Marta! You had no right to test her this early," Momma went on.

"The testing comes at a certain emotional age, Garda," Marta said with a cough. "Allie was more than ready. She did just fine—"

Momma ran right over Marta's words. "You could have waited until she knew more, was more confident— "

"Overconfidence can be dangerous," Marta broke back in. "Better to master fear and work through it."

"Work *through* fear?" Momma sounded incredulous.

"Some people are made weak by fear, and some become strong through it," Papa murmured, taking another bite of oatmeal. "Good cereal this morning, Garda. You have a touch with it."

"You could have waited until you were stronger and then dealt with the situation." The words were flat, more accusing than any I'd ever heard from my mother.

"And what if the Adamsson boy and the Halvdan child had died in the meantime?" Marta's voice was scarcely a whisper.

Momma threw up her hands in disgust and then seized the bread board, slamming it down on the cabinet. "You can't play God, Marta! Do you think you're the territorial governor as well? No one can be everywhere at once, and people owe their allegiance to family first!"

Well, that might be true, but there was still the community to consider. I opened my mouth to speak, and then thought better of it. Right now this was Marta's battle.

"Part of the training is acknowledging consequences, Garda," Marta murmured, breaking off to cough. I set

aside my bowl and went to pour her some hot water for a
soothing tea. "The biggest consequence of all is choosing
to learn the mysteries. Once that choice is made, a practitioner doesn't have the option to stay home—not if
there're deeds to be done."

"My child had no business out there!"

This was loud enough that I winced. I cast a quick
glance over at Papa, but he was finishing his oatmeal,
seemingly oblivious to the argument.

"She's not a child anymore, Garda. She could run this
household if she had to, and keep the entire family
healthy through forest gleanings alone. You forget that
you were engaged at sixteen—and if you'd been one of
your friends, and not a Schell, you'd have been married
by that solstice!" This time Aunt Marta's voice was sharp.
She accepted the cup of tea with a nod of thanks.

"We're not talking about marrying, Marta, we're talking about horrors from the dark on the other side."
Momma's breathing seemed labored, and I gave her a
sharp look. She was really getting worked up. "None of
your own daughters is a practitioner. You don't know
what it is to lie awake at night, wondering if your child is
still alive or has had her soul eaten by some undead
thing! You don't know about the nightmares that she
has—you haven't watched her cast a suspicious eye on
everyone and everything she crosses paths with, checking
to be sure they're human!"

"But Alfreda never did look at others in quite the same
way you do, Garda," Marta said, her voice a bit calmer.
"We're not depriving her of anything she ever knew."

"We've deprived her of choice!" Momma's voice broke
on the last word. "What about a home of her own? What
about a family? At least you were riveted to Jon before
you started laying ghosts and stalking demons!" Momma
turned toward the fireplace and held out her hands

beseechingly to Papa. "Who will have the courage to ask for a woman who spits in the eye of a vampire?"

That startled me, the last bit. "Dear Lord, Momma, I wouldn't do that! They're tricky enough without aggravating them!"

Momma whirled in a fine flash of temper toward me. "Don't tell me you haven't noticed how careful folks have been around you! Are you ready to be an old maid?"

I flushed at that. Well, sure, I'm tall, but I'm not ugly. The werewolf business hadn't stopped Wylie from coming around. Then I remembered his anger and confusion the night before. I pushed the thought aside. "You saying there isn't a single man in the valley who'd want a healthy woman from good stock with herb lore as a dowry? It hasn't scared off Wylie so far!"

"So far," Momma repeated softly. "Child, you've scarcely begun. Right now all you're doing is knowing snips of the future, dangers to folks nearby. But once the moon touches you, you'll be able to tell when a woman will carry to term, what sex the child is, and whether it will live to its majority! You'll be able to sing down moonlight and wear another animal's skin! How do you think he'll handle *that*?"

I'd never seen Momma look so intense, so I took my time answering. "I don't know," I admitted, thinking about the possibilities. "He took subduing that unrepentant soul in stride," I added in a mutter.

"Wylie Adamsson is a good lad, and I hope to God he asks for you, but it takes a strong man to cleave to a practitioner—and a strong woman as well," Momma added softly. "It's no easier for a wife. But I'm afraid that this thing flaring so early has robbed you of choice, girl." Suddenly tears sprang into her eyes. "I wanted you to have your pick of those boys, not take the one so hungry for power he'll face any nightmare for it!"

Well, I don't handle seeing my mother cry any better than the next person, so I rushed over to fold her into my arms. "Please don't, Momma! Tears won't make this any easier."

I found myself clutched in turn. "The only thing that would make this easier would be for the talent to sleep until you're grown," Momma whispered into my dirty hair.

"Then I'd just have to learn how to protect myself when I'm grown and have a family to worry about," I pointed out. "Easier to learn when I'm the only one at risk, isn't it?"

Momma pulled back and just stared at me. Slowly I stumbled on. "What if Aunt Marta had been away when I got there, Momma? What if Wylie had died, and Little Joe, and others, because I wasn't sure what to do and there was no one to stop Livana? No one to see through her glamour?"

"Would you have a town of the dead and undead, Garda? Deserted and open to the elements?" Marta's words were soft and sad.

"I have to do this because it *has* to be done, Momma," I said firmly. "There aren't very many folks who have this talent. You keep hinting I've got it pretty strong, and God must have given it to me for a reason."

"To protect your family," Momma said firmly.

"I will . . . but a practitioner's family is a bit larger than most. All Sun-Return is my family when trouble's brewing. And—" I paused there, because I wasn't happy with what was about to come out of my mouth. "If the only men who want to marry me are men I don't want, then I won't marry. It's not like I can't support myself, if I must."

"You'd give up the only thing we leave behind us in this world for the Gift?" Momma truly sounded amazed.

"I *have* to know things, Momma ... and foolish and beglamoured or not, I can't leave people to be eaten by vampires when I might be able to stop it." I shrugged, feeling helpless in the clutches of the desire that rode me. "Just call me a busybody and have done with it."

Momma gently touched my cheek with the back of her fingers. "My changeling child," she murmured. "I never had a daughter, only sons. You're stronger than any of us, aren't you?" She sighed and let her hands drop to her sides, her gaze wandering toward the fire. "Are you ready to take her home, Marta?"

I stared at my mother. A sinking feeling of heat and nausea fluttered in my stomach. But I was supposed to spend another year at home before joining Aunt Marta!

"If you're ready to part with her," Marta said steadily.

"I'll never be ready," was my momma's whisper as she turned back to the bread board and reached for a fresh loaf. "But it's worse every time she goes on one of these jaunts. I don't think I can take much more of it. We'll start fighting, Marta, I know it ... she might end up hating me. Spare me that, at least."

"Momma, I'll never hate you," I started, stepping toward her.

"If I kept you from vanishing into the woods for a few days?" Momma said abruptly, not turning. "Or if I told you I didn't want you to learn about exorcising demons?"

Not ever? Just trust to the local priest ... if he happened to be in town?

Momma turned back toward me and gave me a steady look. "If I said no more studies until you were married?"

"But that could be years!" I blurted out. *Sweet Lord, I hope she doesn't mean for me to take up crocheting! What would I do with my* mind *all that time?*

Momma managed a faint smile. "You're right, Allie. Seems you were born for this. Otherwise you'd be grateful

to work only at your chores and your hope chest."
Glancing at Aunt Marta, she added, "Has enough energy
for ten women."

"That she has," Marta agreed.

"We'd come to it, daughter," Momma said gently,
turning back to the board and starting to slice the bread.
"Just because you love people doesn't mean you like
everything they do. For all I know, I might put you in
danger by trying to slow you down."

"Yes," Marta murmured, sipping at her tea and rocking steadily.

I suddenly thought of my night alone in the woods . . .
or almost alone. What if I hadn't read about night creatures? I might actually have attacked that wolf—or shivered in my hut until morning. Momma hadn't liked that
book—I could tell by her distaste when she moved it
from side to side on the sideboard when she cleaned—but
she hadn't kept me from reading it . . . not then.

What if I hadn't known that a vampire can't cross
water?

"So you go on with Marta, girl, and study your craft.
Write and tell me how you are, and how your bread and
beer are coming along. I'll try not to imagine your lessons
. . . and you keep your adventures to yourself. Better for
both of us."

Her voice grew husky at the last, but she kept her gaze
firmly on the bread board, so I held my ground.

There didn't seem to be anything else to say.

Well, exhaustion waits for neither questions nor answers.
I got my catnap, and by the time I was awake, Momma
had already started packing her grandmother's blanket
chest for me.

To get down to brass tacks (much as I hated to do it),

there wasn't really a choice. I could try to back and fill all I wanted, but Momma had taken the wind from my sails. Giving up my studies now—even for a few years—would be an agony. I'd end up spending more time in the woods, I knew I would; that would set Momma worrying more, and keeping a sharper eye on me, which would keep me in the woods longer—

Well, you get the idea.

Momma had seen all the way through to the other side. I didn't like it, not one bit, but if leaving now meant avoiding fights with Momma, then I was for it.

Didn't mean I wasn't gonna cry about it.

How did folks find out things? It was like there was an invisible river of thought flowing around the shores of Sun-Return, and all you needed to do was dip into the water to find out every bit of news for ten miles in any direction.

Idelia came by with something she'd been working on for me—the most beautiful doll I'd ever seen. It had a real china head that had entered her family through marriage a while back, and Idelia had attached a new stuffed body with tiny hands and feet carved of white maple. She'd made a cotton batiste chemise and other delicate unmentionables trimmed with real lace, and had used a scrap of silk, from China far away, to make a dress in the latest fashion. There was even a reticule to match.

"I haven't finished the hat, or even started the boots," she admitted. "I thought I'd have time before you left town." Gently touching the horsehair curls, Idelia added, "She's special, 'cus she has dark hair and eyes, like me. You don't see that often. This way, even in a strange place, you can tell her the things you'd tell me . . . and you won't feel alone."

Keeping my eyes on the doll, I said, "I'll call her Ruth, then, and think of you." A lovely smile crossed Idelia's face, because the name *Ruth* means "beautiful friend."

"I didn't know I was going so soon, and I don't have anything for you," I started slowly, but Idelia gestured for me to hush.

"My life has been one big adventure ever since we first played together," she said quickly. "Each morning I'd wake up wondering what new thing you'd think up for us to do that day. You've given me more than I can name. All I ask is that you try to get back for my wedding!"

I gave her a look out of the corner of my eye. "That on the schedule?"

She smiled faintly. "Not yet, but if I have my way, it will be by Christmas!"

Well, at least she'd picked the Adamsson boy with sure prospects—if I'd been reading the signs correctly. Hugging her, I said, "I'll surely do my best. Thank you again for bringing me Ruth . . . and for being my friend."

"Have a safe trip—and write once in a while! I'll send the hat along by Pastor Jon when I finish it." Giving a friendly nod to Marta, who was bringing in a basket of eggs, Idelia headed back down the trail toward the main track.

"That was kindly of her," Momma said from behind me. "That doll is worth more than pure gold."

I was still watching Idelia as she made the turn onto the road. Holding the doll tightly to my chest, I said, "I'll never sell her."

"Of course not. That girl has been a good friend to you. Come now, child. I need to do some measuring." Momma touched my shoulder as she headed back inside the house.

• • •

Wylie didn't come by at all. I just tried not to think about
it. Later . . . I'd think about it later.

The evening was spent in the front room, turning two of
Momma's old dresses for me and selecting yard goods from
Momma's horde. There was white cotton so fine it should
have been ladies' handkerchiefs, and the long dress that had
been woven from that bright golden wool we'd dyed the
year before. It was so elegant I'd thought Momma had
made it for Sunday meeting, but she only shook her head.

"You're growing like a weed, girl. Come winter you'll
need a new skirt for special occasions, and this will look
grand with this fine pale green wool for a stole. A few
more months and you'll look foolish in short skirts."
Giving me a hard eye, she added the rest of the white cotton to the chest. "You'll need all of this come spring, for
new drawers and a petticoat and chemise."

"Why are you putting all of Allie's clothes in that
chest?" Ben asked suddenly. He had been quietly reading
his lesson near the screened fireplace, and now lifted his
dark head to stare in our direction. Joe, however, seemed
to pay us no mind, and kept his pale blue eyes focused on
his ciphers.

Yes, when *was* Momma (or Papa, for that matter)
going to tell the others? Dinner had been so silent I'd
been afraid to bring the matter up. I surely didn't intend
to leave without saying good-bye. That was too close to
how Dolph had left. . . .

"Allie is going back tomorrow with your Aunt Marta,"
Momma said without preamble. "She's going to learn to
be a practitioner."

"Tomorrow?" Ben's thick eyebrows rose in surprise.
"What about All Hallows', and Thanksgiving, and
Solstice, and Christmas?"

"Allie might be back for Christmas," came Marta's voice as she came down the front stairs. In her arms was a waterfall of violet cloth. "Was this the dress, Garda?"

"Yes, that's it." Momma rose from her rocking chair and reached for the gown. "It's a good twenty years old, but silk can last forever. It took a great deal of material for a dress back then. You should be able to make something pretty for Allie out of it."

The rich violet shimmered like ground water at dusk. I was almost mesmerized by the shifting shades of color. For me? What would I do with something so grand? Had Momma gone to parties in dresses like this?

Momma chuckled at my expression. "I was courted by the man who will probably be territorial governor before you're old enough to put your hair up! There's more where this came from, up in those trunks, but you won't need most of them right now. In truth, this color is a tad strong for someone who's not 'out,' but pastels will fade you away." Glancing over her shoulder at Marta, she added, "Don't ever put this girl in white." Momma held up the violet against me as she spoke.

"Not I," Marta said, nodding her satisfaction at the color. "We'll think of something to use it for, this year or next."

"But not for sure?" Ben said, and we all looked over at him. I'd purely forgotten what Marta had said to him. He was all of seven years old now, and always careful never to be seen crying, but this was testing him. There was a quiver in his voice.

"She's got lots to learn if she's going to come back and practice in Sun-Return," Joe broke in. "Good thing there's nothing on your quilt frame, Allie. Want us to go take it down?"

We all looked over at Aunt Marta, who smiled and nodded. "Quilting can be a comfort on cold winter nights," she said calmly. "That's a good idea, Joe."

"Come on!" Joe bounced to his feet, Ben right behind him, and they charged out into the light of the rising moon.

"Get Josh to help you!" Momma called after them as she stepped to the doorway.

You'd think I'd have been crying for sleep, but I wasn't. Everything had happened so quickly, I was feeling a bit overwhelmed. We got the trunk completely packed, even down to Granny's book of herbs. Momma was lending it to me for my studies. By then Marta was ready for tea and cookies, and said so.

Momma frowned when she saw how late it was, but gave in with good grace. Papa and Josh joined us, after tossing the boys in bed, and we had a little party of sorts. Papa told a funny story about when he and Uncle Jon were younger, and Momma told about the mysterious cousin Esme, who was also a practitioner. Esme's wedding should have been the loveliest of the season, but it had turned into a comedy of errors, with the groom locked in a water closet, a bridesmaid passing out at the service, and the musicians so inebriated the fiddler fell into the cake!

It was a good evening, the best in a very long time. It was the first time I remember that Momma treated both me and Josh like we might make responsible adults someday. At the end of things, Momma calmly announced that, come the month of Flowers, we would have another addition to the family. We offered our congratulations with as much dignity as we could—and Marta never said a word about discovering the baby's sex.

Guess just because you *can* do something doesn't mean you should.

That night it took me forever to fall asleep, but I finally did. It was a time for vivid dreaming, the kind that told me things. My first vision was simple, although it was exciting in its way. I saw our trip the next day, Papa driving us in the wagon, with Sweet William tied up to the sideboard on a longe line. Marta was trying to take my mind off a tearful parting from Momma—she was telling me about some of the things I would learn before the snow flew. Things like pulling water vapor from the air to turn moisture into a refreshing drink, and how to purify a poisoned well. I would learn how to tell the time of day or night by the angle of the sun or the wheel of the stars. There were dozens of books at Marta's house, and I'd get to read every one of them.

Then, when my moon time finally started, I could begin to learn true women's magic. Can you imagine knowing when a seed is fertile, and how to stir it into swift growth? How to tell the sex of an unborn babe—and how to rush the birthing by days, weeks . . . even months, when lives depended on it? And once learned, the knowledge would be mine, even when the moon gave up its hold over me.

I remember her saying something about pulling lightning from the skies, and riding a mare's tail, but it didn't make much sense at all.

And then I was standing in the middle of a forest, the cool chill of autumn breathing down my neck. It took me a few moments to realize that I was in a meadow graveyard. Not my choice of a place to visit, and especially not after dark . . .

Night was falling fast. There were others around me, muted figures in the growing twilight. I could see Marta; the other folks I didn't recognize, but they all seemed to know me.

The stench of fear was so great I almost gagged from it. All of us, every person present, was fighting to control terror. I could feel a circle of magic around us, but it wasn't coming from me. We were all looking toward a slender man in spectacles, but the fellow refused to look anyone in the eye. He was looking beyond us, at something we couldn't see. Anxiety was growing inside of me, a trembling I could not control. We were running out of time. Why didn't he speak? We were running out of time. . . .

The next day, when Marta was telling me about condensing water vapor, I tried to act like I hadn't heard it before. After all, something new can always happen, can't it? And then I heard that trilling voice, a dancing call of notes rising toward the sun.

Marta stopped speaking, her head tilted, as if listening, her eyes unfocused. Then she contemplated me for a minute or two.

Finally! Someone else had heard that song!

But my cousin kept right on talking about gathering water from the air, and I decided not to ask.

FIFTEEN

WE DIDN'T EVEN HAVE the first night to ourselves.

The horses scarcely had been cooled and fed, and the big fire built back up, when there was a scratching at the wooden door.

"Hello the house!" came a gravelly voice. These words were followed around the tongue-and-groove door by an elderly, stooped man, his thinning gray hair neatly combed over to one side of his head.

"Is that you, Mr. Winston?" Marta asked from where she knelt before the fire.

"It is indeed, Miz Marta," the low voice continued. I watched as the wizened gnome took an uncertain step across the threshold. "I'm sorry to bother you when you're scarcely home, but a letter arrived yesterday for you, and someone wrote 'important' across the back."

"Indeed," Marta said easily, rising to her feet. "Then I appreciate your bringing it out here."

A smile creased Mr. Winston's face—looking much like a slice in a dried apple looks. "'Tis my duty as postmaster to make sure every letter is delivered as addressed." Slowly the gnome reached into a side pocket of his trousers and retrieved a pair of Franklin spectacles. After balancing these on the tip of his nose, Mr. Winston fished a bent piece of heavy paper from his seat pocket and held it up to the blood-red rays of the sun. "Mrs.

Marta Donaltsson, Wild Rose Run, Cat Track Hollow,"
he said carefully.

"I'm the only Marta Donaltsson in this region," my
cousin said seriously. "Let me take a look while you say
hello to my cousin Alfreda Sorensson. That was her
father Eldon out with the horses."

The gnome startled, and quickly looked around. "Bless
me, child, I didn't even see you!"

I gave the fellow a smile and offered him my hand. He
seemed marginally surprised, but took it between his own
and beamed at me. I'd decided to put my hair in one big
French braid down my back—not up yet, but no longer a
pair of braids—so Mr. Winston was probably trying to
gauge how old I was.

"Here for a visit, then?" he said in his low voice.

"A long visit," I agreed. Maybe a good two years,
depending on how fast I learned things.

Fuzzy eyebrows lifted, and the man gave me a sharper
look. "Studying with your cousin, eh? She's very good,
one of the best. You couldn't hope for a better teacher."

I'd learned by then that such a comment wasn't an
invitation for a child to discuss an adult's qualifications
for anything, so I just nodded and smiled some more.

Marta was angling the letter to catch the last of the
daylight. Her slender face seemed harsher now than it
had when we first stepped down from the wagon, and she
was reading swiftly.

"Someone's left you a sack of pumpkins, Marta," came
Papa's voice from outside the front door.

"Bright golden orange, a bit longish?" she asked as she
finished the letter.

There was a pause, and Papa said, "The very same."

"Hector must have brought them over. First samples
of the new crop, I'd guess. I always trade with him—he
gets the sweetest meat in his squash and gourds! We'll

bake one tonight and make a few pies for the road."
Marta turned toward Mr. Winston as she finished speaking. "Will you stay to supper? Nothing fancy, but the company will be good."

Smiling faintly, Mr. Winston finally let go of my hand. "I'll pass this time, Miz Marta, though I thank you for the invite. A letter like that usually means you're heading for the road, and I don't want to rush your preparations." Slowly the man turned to go back out the doorway.

"I'm afraid you're right, Mr. Winston," Marta agreed as she followed him outside. "We'll leave in the morning, if we can get ourselves together. But tell me first if there's anything that needs my attention."

"I'm pleased to say that everyone's health has been good . . ." Mr. Winston's voice faded off as they moved toward the old man's buggy. Papa's coming distracted me; he had another armful of seasoned wood.

"Let's get that stove fired up, Allie," he said as he set the wood into the huge tin prepared for it. "Maybe Marta will make us some of her wonderful corn bread."

We're leaving tomorrow, and that's all you can say? But I didn't speak aloud. I thought "we" because Marta would never leave me there alone. It was bad enough she lived there by herself, much less leaving children in charge. And you know my momma still thought of me as a child. So unless there was bad illness involved, I was going wherever she was going.

Still, there was no point in sleeping cold and hungry, so I went to fill the copper kettle with water. I should mention, if I haven't before, that Aunt Marta's cottage was built in an older style. It was all one story, with wings at either side. The family room and kitchen were one huge room, with the big chimney directly across from the outside doorway. The bedrooms were to the right, and the stillroom to the left. The house had three chimneys!

But then I've heard Uncle Jon was good with mortar, which explains a lot. Everything was whitewashed and neat as a pin, of course. I don't know where Marta got the time to do all the things she did.

Aunt Marta came back from seeing off the postmaster, toting a copper pot full of soaking beans Momma had given her. "Let's heat these up and toss in some seasoning," she said briskly. "We'll need to store your bolts of cloth and bundle things for my pack mule."

"Will you need my escort, Marta?" Papa asked as he laid wood in the stove.

Aunt Marta didn't answer right away, which meant she was actually thinking about the offer. That surprised me—where were we going that we needed an escort? She'd gone all the way to her daughter's house alone, and that was, what, ten days?

"Thank you, Eldon, but I think we'll be fine," she said at last. "Jon had family in Twisted Pines—a cousin still lives there. Her man will meet us a day's ride from the village, and the last stretch is all I'm concerned about." Marta's gaze grew unfocused for a few moments, and then she added, "You could post a letter for me, though. I want to send word to Cory about this."

Cousin Cory? Since when did practitioners keep in touch about what they were working on? "Twisted Pines?" I said, fishing for information. "Where is that?"

"Know that mountain you can see in the distance?" Marta gestured off to the northeast. "It's at the peak. Used to be called Cloudcatcher when I was a girl. They have some sort of trouble up there, something they're not willing to talk about in a letter." Marta frowned as she said it. "Normally I'd write back for specifics, but Elizabeth mentioned two practitioners who have already tried to deal with the problem. Neither succeeded."

Neither Papa nor I said anything. Then Marta added, "They've both lit off home."

Uh-oh. Practitioners didn't give up easily—it was the nature of the people born to serve. Not one but two routed . . . that was more than a bit uncomfortable.

"How far?" Papa finally asked.

"Almost four days," she said briefly. "If we start a bit late because of the baking, it won't matter much. We'll stay at my crossroads camp the first night, then the DuBois place, and finally the inn at Castle Rock. We'll have our escort from there."

"You're sure?" His tone was easy, but I knew Papa wasn't comfortable by the way he was sidling around the subject.

"Oh, yes," was her thin-lipped reply. "If two practitioners have given up, the folks of Twisted Pines won't risk offending me. Or something happening to me," she added as she started cutting up rounds of carrot. "We'll be safe enough until we get there. It's when we get there that concerns me." Glancing over at me, Marta paused in her chopping and said, "Pick up that letter, Allie, and see if you notice anything."

I reached for the folded piece of rag paper. As my nails curled under the edge to lift it, I was suddenly shivering and yet drenched with sweat. Something queasy was flopping in my stomach, and it was all I could do to keep from going into hysterics. Fighting the sensation, I gripped the table with my other hand to steady myself and lifted the letter.

"You feel it, too." It was more statement than question. Numbly I nodded my head.

Marta started chopping again. "Worse than me, seems like. Interesting. Wonder what's so strong it's tainted everything that passes through the village. If you'll take over here, Allie, I'll start pulling supplies for the trip."

Seasoning beans didn't require thinking, at least by me, so I told my stomach to behave and took over making dinner. In the meantime, Aunt Marta prepared a huge bag full of herbs and spices and strange pouches labeled with the names of minerals and I don't know what else. Several books went into the packs, and Marta told me to bring both the book she'd loaned me and Granny's herbal.

"You brought the silver I gave you?" she asked at one point, and I assured her the jewelry was in my trunk. "We may need it. You have some warm clothing?"

"My blue shawl, and wool petticoats." At her frown I added, "Also two pairs of wool pants and a new coat Papa and I made this summer, from a sheepskin." I hadn't needed that big, warm jacket yet, but I was itching to wear it. My own sheepskin coat, woolly side in, the skin oiled and waterproofed against snow and whatever.

"Good." She nodded absently as she sliced a small sweet squash in half crosswise and removed the seeds and strings. "We'll think about other things over dinner. Put your feet up, Eldon, you've done enough today. I won't have you going home tired." She paused long enough to make sure Papa was through fiddling with the logs in the fireplace, and then set the pumpkin in a pan, shell side up, for baking. "Pies tonight, and bread in the morning . . . cinnamon and Concord raisin, I think. Don't forget an onion, Allie."

Onions and no more information . . . how could that letter affect me like that? I diced with extra vigor, but managed not to cut off a finger. Whatever was going on in Twisted Pines, it was something Momma *definitely* didn't want to know about.

The pies and bread got baked, a slew of them, as well as spiced apples for a dessert. I made my first batch of Aunt Marta's special corn bread while she wrote a letter to Cousin Cory. We didn't talk a great deal about our coming trips, except for Aunt Marta planning to send a pie and loaf of bread home with Papa. Marta not only had Sweet William and her own mule, she had a friend who owed her a big favor. That meant there'd be a horse for me, too.

She talked lightly about the trip, which was a "rougher road than most" (meaning there was no road to speak of) and the DuBois family, a large, gregarious bunch of French folks she'd made friends with years ago. It was a safe, clean stopping place, as was the Washington Inn, where we would spend the last night. But whatever she was thinking about in the back of her mind—and I knew her too well by then to think she was brushing those thoughts off—she wasn't speaking of it.

I didn't say much, but I was definitely thinking.

It was my first long trip on horseback, and I loved it, even though my legs ached from being in the saddle so long. The days still had a flicker of warmth, and the color in the woods was vivid. Such a road may you never see—it was miserable, sloping and full of deep ruts and rocks. We had to walk often, to keep the horses from twisting their legs.

My mount was a steady old gelding, an undistinguished bay with a rocking-horse gait. Nothing bothered him—wolves howling that first night, rabbits and pheasants exploding out of stubble, gurgling stream beds. Old Ned took it all in stride. He wasn't quite as comfortable a ride as Sweet William, but I bet I would have been safe on him even in a sidesaddle.

Cousin Marta used the time we spent traveling to ask me questions about my studies. For the most part, she seemed satisfied with my answers, but she didn't comment

much on things. I kept waiting for her to talk about that
letter, but she never said a word. At least she didn't offer
me a chance to read it for myself—I had no interest in
handling that scrap of paper again.

The night we spent at the inn, a big, rambling old
place with its upstairs divided into two low-beamed sleeping rooms, was cold enough that I went out to check on
the animals. The mule was fine, of course, and I swear I
could see the hair growing on Ned and Sweet William.
They'd become friends and were keeping close company
for warmth. I'd started thinking about Wylie on our ride,
and was feeling a bit melancholy, so the presence of the
animals was a comfort.

I saw something strange as I walked back across the
courtyard. Off to the east, in the woods beyond the corn
stubble, I saw a pale, drifting form. That stopped me in
my tracks. *What in the name of heaven . . . ?* I looked
sharp, to make sure a barn owl hadn't flashed its face at
me. No, that bird was white.

"I saw a snowy owl in the woods east of here," I
announced to my cousin as I started to take off my split
traveling skirt. We were the only women guests that
night, so we had a quarter of the upstairs to ourselves,
since there were only two sleeping lofts.

Marta looked up abruptly. "A snowy owl? Are you
sure?"

I nodded solemnly. "I was so surprised, I looked close.
It definitely wasn't a barn owl. Awfully early for a snowy,
isn't it?" They were birds of the far north, and were seen
here only rarely, and in the dead of winter at that.

"Very early," Marta murmured as she tucked her hair
into her flannel cap. "There's another possibility, Allie.
Sometimes demons and ghosts are known to take on the
guise of snowy owls."

A cold, creepy feeling walked up my back. I didn't

need that thought, thank you, no—I was nervous enough because Gavin Tregellas hadn't shown up yet. We studied each other a moment.

If I hadn't been blocking, I'd have sworn Marta was reading my mind. "Tomorrow we'll go on till noon," she said slowly. "If Tregellas hasn't appeared by then, we'll come back to the inn."

The breath trickled out of me slowly, so Marta didn't notice how relieved I was . . . I think. Whatever was waiting for us at Twisted Pines, I wanted a bit more information before meeting up with it.

Come morning we shook out our traveling clothes and borrowed a hot flatiron to press a few wrinkles. Marta dug in her carpetbag and pulled out a necklace I'd never seen before. It was long and intricate, strung with polished amber and tiger eye and crystal, among other things. There were teeth from bear and cougar for sure, and other things as well. She settled it on her breast, outside on her shirtfront. Then she felt around in the bag and pulled out a thin strand of metal.

God love me, it looked like gold. There was one lovely amber bead on it, a tiny winged creature frozen forever in its depths. On either side was polished, irregular tiger eye, the most golden I'd ever seen. She opened the clasp and gestured for me to come near.

"Gold for the Gift, amber for immortality defeated, tiger eye for creatures of air and darkness," she murmured like a chant. "Shaw made this for you. It's good to get your talisman from someone who cares."

"What is it?" I looked down at the huge bead in wonder, and then transferred my gaze to Marta's magnificent, almost savage chain.

"Each item has a meaning—something from my career," she said simply. "You'll learn what each piece can mean. Practitioners have taken to wearing them outside when we want to be known for what we are. Can you feel the hum of power in this?"

Extending my hand, I held it out toward her necklace. There *was* a palpable energy about it, like waves of heat from glowing coals. The three rocks around my neck had warmth that was their own, but they didn't radiate.

"Give it time," Marta said with a smile. "Now they have only my warding and your two triumphs in them. When you reach my age, that chain will be a relic of power in its own right."

I didn't know what to say. Finally I murmured, "That was kind of Shaw, to do this."

Marta nodded as she placed her hairbrush in her bag and closed the clasp. "He wanted you to remember him."

As if I'd forget the man who bought us time to kill a vampire. That he'd put together this thing for me . . .

You never saw such amazement on a man's face when we went downstairs to pay our reckoning. The innkeeper's cheeks went several shades lighter, I would swear it's true, despite the dim light of the tallow candles.

Nodding his head respectfully, the man said, "You bring us great honor, wizard. Is there anything else we can do to ease your travels?"

Smiling, Marta shook her head and extended several silver coins. "Our beds were clean and comfortable, and your ale and bread well made. What more can a weary traveler ask for?"

A stirring from the kitchen beyond, which jutted back into the courtyard, announced the arrival of the innkeeper's fair, plump wife. She was carrying a cloth sack. "I hope you will take this with you for your midday meal, lady," the alewife said shyly. "I wish we could send ale with you, but here is fresh cheese, black bread, apples, and venison jerky."

Marta responded with a graceful nod. "That is kind of you, goodwife. If there is any service I might be able to do for you in return, I'd like you to tell me about it."

The woman's cheeks flushed like a wild rose, but all she said was, "Any blessings you can spare, lady, are always welcome. Safe trip to you."

Nodding again, Marta led the way into the courtyard, where one of the tavern keeper's innumerable children had saddled up our horses and loaded the mule. I tied our night bundles to our saddles while Marta strolled thoughtfully around the garden. Finally she stopped at the well and extended her right hand over the opening. Lacing the fingers of her left hand through her necklace, Marta closed her eyes and stood motionless. I wasn't sure what she was up to, but I could see a sharpness about her, not quite a luminescence—especially about her right hand.

Suddenly dropping her hand and releasing her necklace, Marta walked briskly to Sweet William's side. The shaggy boy holding the reins offered her a hand up.

"Thank you," Marta said in her usual gracious manner. "Best tell your father to see to a cover for that well. And it wouldn't hurt to chain one of your dogs near it." She gave him a sharp eye as she spoke. "Foul weather's coming."

The boy looked startled for a moment; then a look of understanding crept across his face, and he nodded vigorously even as he took a careful step backward.

As we sauntered off down the sunrise trail, I heard the boy's clear voice shouting, "Pa! Pa! The wizard knows about Clem and his boys!"

"Clem?" I asked as the path widened into a narrow road.

"All the uneasiness we've been feeling isn't totally from Twisted Pines—or our worries," Marta said simply. "There was a smell of wariness about the place, although the owner didn't show that face to us. Someone wants his spot at the crossroads and has been trying to push him out. There was malice floating about. The well felt especially fragile, so I laid a good word on it. Nothing short of a dead calf is going to poison that water."

"But it would be even better if he put a cover on and left a dog to guard it," I finished.

"God helps those who help themselves," my cousin said placidly. "The alewife could have simply brought us a slice of bread for breakfast, a kindly courtesy. But she went to the trouble and expense of packing a considerable lunch."

"She thought you'd do something to help?" This was interesting. "Or she was afraid of us, and wanted to make sure we'd do no harm?"

Marta smiled faintly. "Most practitioners don't announce themselves if they're either too tired to work or not interested in trade work—like lunch for a spell. The necklace told them I felt fairly fresh and had liked their inn. I put it on because I caught a whiff of evil intent when we arrived last night. And because the alewife was worried. 'Course," she went on, glancing over at me, "it could have been a sick child needing a doctor, or something that would take some time and more strength than I can spare, not knowing what we're heading into. . . ."

As her words trailed off, I considered what she'd said and hadn't said. "What would you have done if it'd been more than you could handle with a simple slow-release spell?"

Marta blinked once at me. "Now where did you hear about slow-release spells?"

"I heard Mrs. Kelly tell Papa on the sly that she'd paid

for such a thing for their tavern," I answered with a grin. "To help keep tempers under control and cut down on the fighting. Expensive, she said, but no one had gotten hurt badly since the spell was laid. Did you do it for her?"

"I did indeed, O mouse at the keyhole. A complicated and time-consuming spell, which is why it's expensive." She smiled and turned her face back to the rising sun. "The spell on the well was much simpler. I encouraged movement in the water, so any herb dumped in it will be purged quickly. And I tied the innkeeper's awareness to it. If anyone other than family messes with the lip or bucket, he'll get uneasy and head for the courtyard. Those two things should get them through this threat."

"What if that hadn't been enough?" I persisted.

"Then I'd have told him his weak points, and suggested he send west to the great lake for a practitioner who could ward his place." Without a change in voice or expression, she added, "Since I wouldn't have offered myself in hire, he would have known I was already busy on something big."

"Would a practitioner ever pretend it was worse than it seemed?" Not that I'd ever seen such a thing, but people talk all the time about "playing the practitioner."

Marta cast me a sidelong glance. "If you mean pretend the problem was something it wasn't, not an honest practitioner. If you mean pretend to mumble fancy words, and make the spelling look harder than it was, just for a touch of sympathy and to impress folks more, a few might. I don't think a good practitioner needs to bother with such foolishness."

I mulled on this a bit as we traveled up into the foothills of Cloudcatcher Mountain. Although the road was too pitted for a wagon, it was easily wide enough for two horses to ride abreast. For this I was grateful, since the mule (who answered to the name Donnybrook when he had a mind) was becoming increasingly unreasonable about the trip. Nothing I could threaten him over, of course, but he was definitely dragging his feet.

Marta noticed, of course. A faint smile crossed her face before she leaned over and smacked him once on the rump. Startled, the mule took several fast steps before settling into a parody of Sweet William's flowing walk.

"Mules are sensitive to atmosphere," she said briefly. "He knows there's something odd about the direction we're heading, and he doesn't like it."

"Whatever could cast such a wide net?" I asked seriously, taking a tighter grip on the longe line.

"Soon, Allie," was all Marta would say. "We'll know soon."

We ate lunch beside a bubbling stream before the sun reached its zenith. The water looked all right, but looks can be deceiving, so we drank only from our gourds, which we had filled back at the inn. The venison was fairly soft and not too salty, while the apples were some of the best I'd ever had. I collected all the seeds, in hopes of a tree.

My aunt was steadily growing tense—it was like watching someone wind a clock too tightly. Any minute the spring was going to pop loose. Where was Gavin Tregellas?

As if thinking his name summoned him from thin air, suddenly we could hear the steady thud of hooves on the packed earth beyond. Finally a bay mule with white stockings came through the trees, a man in a battered tri-cornered hat upon its back.

The newcomer was small, spare, and weathered, his features dark and delicate under his tan. Not a rider—he sat in that saddle like a sack of potatoes. It was his eyes that were the most interesting, though . . . they were thoughtful, and the deepest green I'd ever imagined.

"Marta Helgisdottir Donaltsson?" he said in a surprisingly deep voice as he pulled up his mule.

Marta nodded, her composure intact, though to my eyes she was still tense.

"Praise God you've come," was the man's fervent murmur. "I'm Gavin Tregellas. Have you finished your meal?"

"Finishing," Marta said wryly. "What proof have you that you're Tregellas?"

In response the man reached for the collar of his shirt and pulled out a thin silvery chain. On it was strung a ring. Looking hard at the trinket, Marta nodded approval and started to stand up.

"You realize we need to talk before we go any farther," Marta said smoothly. As the man's face darkened, she added, "I'm not taking a new apprentice into the unknown. It will do you no good if I get killed before I reach the mountaintop."

Tregellas's color returned to normal and even paled a little. Clearly he hadn't thought of that possibility. There was silence while he thought through her ultimatum.

"Can we talk on the trail?" he asked finally. "I purely do not want to risk being out after dark."

"We can," Marta agreed, tying her gourd back to her saddle and tightening William's cinch. "Can you mount, Allie?"

Well, I'm not so graceful getting into a saddle, but I do all right. I even remembered to tighten my own cinch, so the whole kit and caboodle didn't slide off when I tried to climb on board. Old Ned just kept eating—you'd think the animal had never been properly fed. Lord knows what Mr. Tregellas was thinking.

As we started up the winding trail there wasn't any

sound except the creek itself, gurgling its farewell. I understood the animals being startled by our arrival, but surely the birds would have started up by now. . . .

"Do you have wards, Miz Donaltsson?" the man said suddenly.

"Yes, I do," Marta answered.

"Good. That will help us get home." He was kicking his mule into a lively trot, and wonders of wonders, it wasn't arguing. "Have you ever been up on Cloudcatcher?"

"In my youth," Marta said, nodding at me to pull Donnybrook up ahead of Sweet William.

"It was a beautiful little village once, glittering in the fresh sunlight," Tregellas said softly. "Folks took pride in their homes, and everyone had enough to eat. We let no one go hungry in Cloudcatcher."

"But traders call you Twisted Pines now," Marta said gently, leading the man on.

"We are twisted," Tregellas said with emphasis. "Something stalks by night on the mountain, wizard. It wails louder than the wind, and wanders between homes and farms. We hear scratching at doors and windows, and more than one home has been violated by this thing."

No one spoke for a time, so I took it upon myself to ask the unasked question. "What is it?"

"That, little lady, we hope you can tell us. And tell us how to get rid of it." There was a slight tremor in the man's voice as he spoke.

I realized what I was hearing was fear.

Sixteen

WHAT CAN I SAY ABOUT a town that was dying? We knew there was trouble even before we walked down the only street. As we climbed the last hill into Twisted Pines, we had to lead the animals to protect their legs from deep ruts in the road.

The sun was getting low by the time we reached the peak. Slanting rays of gold picked up glints from the water that pooled in deep gouges along the trail. My first impression of Twisted Pines was that it smelled really bad. I wouldn't let a pigsty get that way, much less my own home.

After a twitch of her nose, Marta said, "Don't touch the water, Allie. Someone's privy has overflowed."

Dear Lord, I'd never heard of letting a privy fill up high enough to run over. I was careful to keep my feet on dry tussocks, and promised myself I would boil any drinking water.

I'm not sure what I expected to find in Twisted Pines, but the reality was very odd. These were not elderly buildings dozing in the last light—they were warped and faded shadows of what had once been a nice little town. Roof lines were ragged, and there wasn't a sign of paint or whitewash. No brick or stone buildings, either.

The place stank of evil. I'm not sure I can explain that to someone who doesn't have the Gift, but I'll try. Ever visit a place that simply gave you the crawlies? A place you couldn't wait to leave? Where you felt like you were being watched by unseen eyes, and behind those eyes was something angry? The stink of evil is a lot like that, only worse—much worse.

Aunt Marta surveyed the dirt road ahead and seemed to make a decision. She mounted and indicated that I should, too. We kept the horses to a slow walk, in case there were hidden dangers, and avoided pools of water. I noticed that Mr. Tregellas didn't offer up a single word . . . he just let things speak for themselves.

Some of the eyes watching us could be seen. Children with pinched faces peered around water barrels and broken wagons, and one man came out to stand in the doorway of what looked to be a general store. There was scarcely any merchandise in his window, though.

Mr. Tregellas pushed on through the village, looking neither right nor left. After we made a curve in the road, the houses were farther apart. Stubble beyond peeled rail fences hinted at gardens fallow for the winter. Windows empty of oiled parchment or precious glass hinted at families who had given up and moved on.

At the end of Twisted Pines proper, before another bend carried the road away, stood a house that did not look quite as bad as the others. It had neither paint nor whitewash, but the roof and wooden porch were in fine repair and the fences sound. A tall, fair-haired woman with thick braids coiled around her head rushed out the front doorway and straight to Mr. Tregellas's mule.

"When the sun started going down, I was afraid—" The woman cut off her words, swallowing obvious fear. I could almost see the lady visibly calm herself. "Supper's ready." Then she turned toward Aunt Marta.

"Praise all the gods there be, Marta. I knew you wouldn't fail us." There was no real excitement in her voice—just a dreadful intensity, like Aunt Marta was a rope tossed to a drowning swimmer.

Marta looked rueful. "I wish you had given me a few hints, Elizabeth," Marta said as she dismounted. "I hope I have the right supplies with me."

"If you can just solve this, we can wait on supplies," Mr. Tregellas broke in. "Sometimes just knowing can ease fears." He dismounted and handed his reins to a tall youngster who had appeared from around back. "Gavin the third," he added, briefly setting a hand on the boy's shoulder. "Elizabeth calls him Trey."

Other small, dark heads leaned over to peek out the doorway at us. Smiling, Tregellas opened his arms and received an avalanche of boys.

Her tight face momentarily softened by genuine affection, Mrs. Tregellas pointed as she called off names. "This is Evan, Carey, Thomas, and the little one is Dylan," she announced as the smallest child tossed his arms around her knees. "Is this your latest apprentice?"

"My cousin's eldest daughter, Alfreda Eldonsdottir Sorensson," Aunt Marta said, using the old Nordic form that indicated my branch of the family. "She is indeed my latest apprentice, and a great help to me. It's a joy to work with such talent."

"We're so grateful you're here, my dear," Mrs. Tregellas whispered to me. "Maybe some of the women will feel better coming out during the day if they see you moving about."

"Why shouldn't they come out?" I decided to ask, trying to maintain a smile.

"No reason we know of," Tregellas said shortly. "But fear doesn't know reason." Looking down at the youngster trying to wrestle his arms, he said, "Time to wash up."

Although the boys looked disappointed, they rushed

off around the house with a minimum of grumbling or slapping at each other. Tregellas was already pulling off my lunch sack.

"Trey and I'll take care of your animals. You go on inside and get comfortable. Are there any of these I shouldn't handle, Miz Donaltsson?" His hand paused above my clothes bag.

"There's no problem as long as you don't drop or open any of them," was my cousin's response. I noticed, however, that she pulled off the bag of herbs and potions herself. "Do I smell sweet potatoes, Elizabeth?"

"You do indeed, and a fresh baked ham. Come along and get settled!" Mrs. Tregellas turned and led the way into her home.

You had to be paying attention to notice the quick glance she gave to the west, gauging when the sun would set.

I swallowed my impatience and hoped Elizabeth Donaltsson Tregellas was a good cook. If I knew my cousin, we were gonna have some answers that night—or at least a few explanations. Long talk went down better on top of dinner.

"Cousin" Elizabeth, as Mrs. Tregellas asked me to call her, was a very good cook, if not the equal of Momma or Aunt Marta. Her mix of salt and seasoning on a ham was one of the best I'd ever tasted.

The boys ate in a hurry and were excused from the table to do their lessons. I stayed put, and was rewarded by everyone carefully talking about various connections I didn't know. Balked at asking questions, I kept my eyes open.

The Tregellas home was like many houses in our part of the world, with an all-purpose table and chairs, two rockers by the fire, and stacked beds in one corner that looked to hold no less than three children. Things were serviceable, but not really finished—I'd never realized how good a fine carpenter my father was, or how unusual our foreign furniture must have appeared to my friends. I'd never before thought of myself as from a rich branch of the family, although I knew my father owned outright over a hundred thousand acres of prime forest and farm-land.

Cousin Elizabeth wasn't much of a quilter; the cover-lets were mostly string and crazy quilts, made to use up the last scrap of material. There were a few unusual things, like a painted portrait locket hanging on the wall, a folding screen, and a violin case set on top of the hutch. There was also an oven set into brick next to the fire-place, with another oven or maybe a wood hatch beneath it. I'd never seen anything quite like it before.

Then there were the really unusual things. Garlic and mustard were strung at every window, and over the door and fireplace. Also fresh holly, interestingly enough, and the first of the mistletoe, the berries pale and gleaming. The family hadn't missed a trick; when I stood up to help clear the plates, I could see that someone had carved a cross within a circle on the nearest windowsill.

A piping-hot apple-and-raisin pie was served with pale white cheese, and I felt rewarded for a hard trip up that mountain. I confess I would have enjoyed it more if Cousin Elizabeth hadn't kept one eye on the growing darkness. Even the boys glanced up from their book occa-sionally, as if waiting for something. There was nothing to see, not even moonlight—but I could hear the wind starting to rise. Funny how nervy a gust of air can make you. . . .

Could be that Elizabeth's fidgeting got to Marta, or maybe my teacher was just ready to go to work. At any rate, Marta left her pie and went to the wood and leather door, her fingers laced through that necklace she was still wearing. I couldn't see the motions she made, or hear any words, but she stood still for several moments before moving to the two windows and the fireplace.

"Is there a window upstairs on the back side?" she asked after looking up from the fire.

"No," Elizabeth said quickly. "Too much wind from that side for a window."

"Good," Marta pronounced, returning to her chair. "That will hold most things until I can set wards on the house."

"Can you ward the barn?" Mr. Tregellas asked slowly, as if embarrassed to be making any requests.

"I could," Marta replied, giving him a sharp eye. "Has this thing been bothering the stock?"

"Not so far," the man admitted, poking at the rim of his piecrust.

"In that case, let's not waste any strength warding animals. We may need that power later." Marta then applied herself to her pie, and I didn't think we were going to get anything else out of her until the last crumb was gone.

As I was sneaking a finger up to chase a flake of crust around my platter, I heard the patter of footsteps outside on the road. It seemed a tad loud for packed dirt, but every new place has its own echoes.

The sound might as well have been a signal. Trey closed the book he and his brother were reading and placed it on the pile of slates. His face was set and his lips drawn thin.

"Time for bed," he said abruptly to his siblings, and they didn't offer a peep of protest. Quickly stripping down to their long johns, the three little boys crawled into their trundle beds and snuggled beneath the coverlets. Trey and the second eldest—Evan?—nodded in passing and hurried up the narrow pegged steps to their room. Marta and I would share the other one, while Mr. and Mrs. Tregellas slept in the bed hidden behind the folding screen.

Wind pushed hard at the little house, thrumming the top of the chimney. Somewhere in the midst of that prolonged gust of wind, I thought I heard a voice. No words . . . just sniffling. It began as a few broken sobs, like a child that's been cuffed by a parent, and slowly crescendoed into full-scale crying.

The weeping faded a bit, as if something had moved away from the house, and I realized that the hair on the back of my neck had risen. I'd heard creepy wind before, but this was in a class all its own.

Then the wailing began. For a moment I thought there was an injured child or animal outside, and I rose to my feet in response. It was a quick look at Cousin Elizabeth that stopped me in my place.

She sat quietly, hands folded in the flour-sack apron protecting her dress, her eyes staring off over the table toward the fireplace. It was such a relaxed pose, until you looked at her neck muscles and realized they stood out like cordwood. Sitting down again, I caught a glimpse of her eyes—and wished I hadn't. If it was possible to witness a flicker of hell through an untended window, then I'd seen way too much already. Elizabeth's eyes were haunted; there's no other word for it.

"How long have you been hearing it?" Marta said softly, her voice threading into the pitiful sobbing.

"The first time I distinctly remember hearing it was six years ago come Yule," Elizabeth replied, her voice just barely steady. "I thought there was an injured animal out there somewhere, or that S—a neighbor had tossed out one of his children."

"I couldn't hear it," Tregellas added. "Eliza had me out looking under every bush within a quarter-mile, and all for naught. I didn't start hearing it until the following spring . . . but every woman in town knew it well before then."

He stopped abruptly at the sound of scratching against wood.

It's at the door. Suddenly I was terrified; I knew if I didn't move I'd jump out of my skin. Standing, I reached for several empty platters and moved with them to the sink.

The window over the basin rattled suddenly, as if someone had thrown a wadded-up coat at it. I jumped, losing my grip on a platter. The wooden plate slid into the sink. And they'd lived with this six years?

"This happens almost every night," Tregellas went on. "Occasionally we have a fairly quiet evening, but in some ways silence is worse—it means the thing is stalking. Folks out after dark are followed by it . . . we can hear heavy footsteps, but there's nothing to be seen. It doesn't tire like an animal might."

"Just following?" Marta threw in, rising from her seat to carry her platter to the counter.

"At first." Tregellas seemed to swallow carefully. "When you start to tire, that's when this cold band tightens around your chest, making it hard to breathe."

"And then?"

Tregellas looked down at his hands. "I've never seen what happens next. I may be alive because I stumbled into Little Cloud Creek. That's why I think it's some sort of demon. Why else did it leave me in peace?"

"What about others?" I managed to get out.

"Joe Goldsmith, he was paced from Castle Rock all the way to the river," Tregellas said, his intense eyes looking up to meet mine. "About ran himself into heart failure. Was so punch-drunk for lack of air he pulled his knife on the thing—and wonder of wonders, the creature vanished!"

"But Joe never saw anything?" Marta asked slowly, pushing for details.

Elizabeth shook her head. Her eyes closed as she murmured, "Not like poor old Nate the Needle Man. Folks knew him from Old Dad Knob to Green Hollow. He hadn't been by for a long time when folks found what was left of him at the foot of our hill." Opening her eyes, the woman said flatly, "No panter could have done that much damage, Marta. A cat couldn't keep up that fury, not long enough to rip a man into small pieces. Every bone was broken . . . even the tiny ones in the hands and feet. Every bone!" The last was whispered as she once more closed her eyes.

"So it likes its victims alone and far from the village," Marta said, moving to the fireplace and pouring herself a cup of black coffee from the pot near the flames.

"It's branching out," Tregellas continued, his voice now clipped. "It's managed to get into several houses. Two women have been attacked in their beds—scratched till they bled. I think the wards the last practitioner left us are fading."

"Some types of wards need tending," Marta agreed. "Few spells can be launched to spin on their own."

Tregellas got up and fetched two mugs, pouring coffee for his wife and himself. "It may have nothing to do with this, but there's been reports of snowy owls in the woods already, months too soon. And Joe told me about a big black dog that's been seen on the main road." Glancing across the pot at us where we stood by the sink, he added, "No one in these parts has a shaggy black dog."

"Dog and owl, yet never truly seen," Marta murmured, sipping at her coffee. She gave me a hard look as she drank, so I didn't mention the owl back at the Washington Inn. "And running water and iron seem to turn it." She looked up, her keen glance falling on Cousin

Elizabeth. "Has everyone hung cold iron in their windows and doorways?"

The woman blinked, seeming to come out of her thoughts. "It doesn't have to be held to be effective?"

Marta gave one of her snorts. "You know your teachings better than that! The Good Neighbors never bother anything locked up by cold iron. It's worth a try."

I immediately bounced out of my chair, looking around for iron. There was a big, long fork, the kind you pierce a roast with to see if the juices run clear, and also an iron skillet. Mr. Tregellas had made—or had had someone else make—two pretty twists of black iron to hang towels and aprons upon. I lifted the forged metal from the wall and laid one each on the windowsills.

"Just set the pan against the door for now," Marta said, laying the fork across the thin mantel. Turning back around, she told them, "This thing definitely has demon traits. Has anyone tried an exorcism?"

Tregellas leapt from his chair as if stung by a bee. "Dear God, not that again!" Fear was so sharply etched on his features I looked away—it's not right for a youngling to see that in a stranger's face. Quietly I started stacking the platters next to the sink.

My cousin remained calm, lifting her eyebrows in inquiry.

"The first practitioner, from Old Fort St. Joseph way, she tried an exorcism," Tregellas began haltingly. "Whole business came right back in her face! The creature was ten times as bad after that—Nate was found dead before the week was out."

"That was the last time a practitioner tried anything with an audience," Elizabeth added softly. "The last fellow was heading to Fort Chicago, coming from Traverse Bay. He didn't trust the first practitioner, I guess—he tried an exorcism, too. The thing went after him. Tore up the outer rim of his circle, and spun a whirlwind of sticks and such around him. He was scratched up plenty good from it, and grateful his own wards held." She looked over at us both as she added, "I reckon the wards had to have held, or he would have died like Nate. It's stronger now, Marta. It gets louder, and stronger, every night. Some folks are starting to crack."

My cousin moved slowly back to the heavy table, settling in one of the open chairs. After a sip of black coffee, Marta said, "I think what I've already done will hold for tonight, because the new moon'll pop up just before sunrise. Alfreda and I will set proper wards then. Probably in your courtyard . . . it will give some protection to your livestock, if they stay close by the house." She seemed to be adding up something in her head. "I brought some powerful aids, out of habit—I'll use a few of them tomorrow. One thing I won't do is underestimate the problem."

"Do we need to prepare anything now?" I thought to ask.

Marta shook her head. "I brought enough of everything that we can set the wards without any more mortar work. Later we'll need to replace materials—then I'll need your strong arm." Marta smiled at me. "For now, I'll need your concentration and strength."

Setting down her cup, Marta's face grew smooth and chill. "I do not suggest anyone attempt to watch our work," she said clearly, in a voice loud enough to travel upstairs. "Painful things happen to unwelcome visitors."

"Those boys wouldn't dare interfere with you, Marta," Elizabeth protested. "They know all too well what's at stake—Evan was one of those who found Nate."

"Children are born curious," was Marta's smiling reply. "I don't want to have to spare any strength to protect them if the ceremony draws your demon."

In the silence that followed, Tregellas asked haltingly, "Could your warding draw trouble?"

Marta gave the tiniest of shrugs. "Possibly, but not likely. What it *will* do is let the creature know a practitioner has come to challenge it. Alfreda and I should move to an unoccupied house tomorrow—it will be safer for everyone. Can you arrange that, Gavin?"

Pulling at his lip, the man gave a slow nod. "The Donovans' place is empty now—it's nearby, and the roof's sound. I can get someone to clean it for you come first light."

"That will be a help. I'll need to cast at least two circles tomorrow, and I won't have much strength left for scrubbing." Looking over at me, Marta said, "The more sleep we get, the better. Come along, cousin. Let's get a few coals for our bedsheets."

Elizabeth was already lifting the copper bed warmer from the hook where it hung. We left her to load it with coals, as a good hostess would, and took our bags upstairs. All the bags—Marta said quietly that we'd dress for work before leaving the house.

Even with Elizabeth warming our sheets, I didn't see how we were going to sleep with all that racket going on. It hadn't bothered me so much when Marta was talking . . . I guess her voice could always pull me in. But once she was through speaking, I became aware of that crying just beyond normal hearing. The sound seemed to push at the walls of the house, like a toddler trying to open a door. Tore at the heart, it did . . .

My cousin had her familiar candelabra lit by the time I got all the bags upstairs. Light revealed it was a small room, the floor studded with raised knots from feet wearing down the pine planks. Two low bunks were made up, heaped with quilts I was sure we'd need.

Marta had also made two small cups of chamomile tea.

Sipping one, I could taste other things within, and was certain she was giving us the best chance possible for a real rest.

As Marta blew out the candles, I couldn't help but wonder if sleeping here was safe.

Let it be said that I can sleep through almost anything. The next thing I remember was Marta's soft tread near my cot. She had on an old work dress; I could just make it out by the one candle branch she'd lit.

Gently she laid fingers upon my forehead. "You can sleep a while longer, Allie," Marta murmured. "I'm just going to the outhouse and to scout for a good ceremonial spot." The light faded—Marta had taken the candelabra with her. I slipped back into strange dreams, where my aunt danced beneath a full moon with her hair hanging down to her hips. I guess I was there, too, much to my surprise—I couldn't be sure, what with tree shadows interfering, but I don't think we had on a stitch of clothes. I wasn't cold, though—I remember that clearly. Cold couldn't touch me.

A cool finger against my cheek popped my eyelids open.

"Good," Marta whispered. "Sleeping too soundly has its dangers. Put on this dress, and don't braid your hair. You'll need your sheepskin coat." She'd set her candelabra on the only flat surface, a broad trunk covered with an embroidered counterpane, and was taking several small pouches out of her saddlebag. *Small* can mean a lot of things, of course—one of the bags was easily as long as my forearm.

The dress was pale and simple, with long sleeves and no waistline. I lifted it up, and found no petticoats beneath it. *And she said she wouldn't dress me in white,* I thought, amused despite my foggy head.

"You're not a practitioner yet," Marta said simply, not turning. "Nor an initiate. So you'll wear white until your status changes."

Blinking several times, I peered in her direction. It seemed as if she was wearing something . . . purple? Long and full, bound at the waist with a glittering belt . . . Marta turned, and I realized that her hair was down, something I'd never seen before.

Really seen, that is—outside of dreams.

My cousin rustled softly as she walked, and I could tell she had no petticoats on under her dress . . . if it was a dress. Marta was gathering up the drawstrings of the small pouches she'd pulled from her work bag. Looping them over one wrist, she turned back toward me.

"Hurry! We need to have the circle in place before the moon rises. There's hot water in the basin by the candle," she added, turning back to her heavy leather saddlebag.

I didn't need to be told twice. Might as well get it over with all at once. Whipping back the quilts, I swung my legs around and reached for the loose dress. An icy cold draft crept by my legs, but I ignored it and dug for my stockings.

"Just the dress, Alfreda," Marta said without turning around. "You'll be warm enough once we start."

Silently I pulled the garment over my head, since there were no buttons or hooks. It fell to my feet, full and soft like fine cotton. No stockings, eh? . . . I didn't even try to put on my drawers. I did put on my new necklace, however, since Marta was wearing hers. Right then I admit I was more interested in the full-sleeved garment Marta was wearing. It looked like . . .

"Is that silk?" I said suddenly.

"Yes, it is," was her calm answer. "Are you ready to go?"

My cousin was barefoot. *Oh, no,* I thought. I hate cold

feet. "Almost." I stepped carefully over to the trunk and splashed warm water on my face, flicking my eyes and rubbing soda on my teeth. A quick rinse, and I dried off on a scrap of blanket. It only took a moment to unbraid my hair. "Now." I turned and found Marta holding what looked like a wooden tray with folded legs of some type. Sitting on top of it were two boxes, each a large, flat square.

"Think you can carry these things down the stairs without falling or dropping them?" When I nodded, Marta offered the tray to me.

"Follow along," she said calmly. "We need to fetch a lantern. Don't set down the tray."

Maneuvering the narrow stairs in semidarkness wasn't much fun, but I managed not to drop everything she'd handed me. Marta paused in the kitchen, fetching a lantern off a shelf and lighting it with a spill from the crock by the fireplace. Only then did she blow out the candelabra, leaving it in the center of the dining table. Turning, she took the tray from me.

"Put on your coat."

And so I did. I wondered if she was going to do the same, but Marta merely handed back the wooden tray. Picking up the lantern, she headed for the door.

In the back of my mind, I'd noticed that the wailing had died down sometime during the night. There was still a lot of wind, but now it was only a brisk breeze . . . the strangeness was gone.

For how long?

Marta paused on the threshold, one hand on the lantern, the other, looped in bags, clutching her necklace. She paused for a long moment, and then stepped to one side, ushering me out and shutting the door behind us.

"Can you do what I ask for now, without my stopping to explain every step?" Marta asked quietly. "What we're about to do doesn't always need all these trimmings, but we're using them now to help my concentration. Concentration is crucial—our lives may depend on it. And ritual helps focus the mind. Make sense?"

I nodded slightly. She must have seen the motion, because she smiled and turned to lead the way around the back of the house.

The place my cousin had chosen for the warding was treeless and fairly flat, without wagon ruts or muddy hollows. There was still grass, despite all the animals that crossed the area daily, but I could see no telltale signs of manure. Probably Marta had taken care of that on her first trip outside.

"Here," she said simply, stopping and setting the lantern down. "Just stand there and hold the altar." Pulling at the mouth of one of the pouches, Marta drew forth something and began tossing it with the traditional arm sweep for sowing seed. She was murmuring softly under her breath—it sounded like Latin. Occasionally I caught a few words I recognized, like *purify* and *blessing.*

When she had covered the immediate area, Marta reached into a different pouch and pulled out a polished silver cup. There were images carved on the outside, but lantern light was no good for seeing detail. Running her index finger continuously around the rim of the cup, Marta continued to circle the area, whispering in Latin. After a bit, she stopped messing with the rim and put her right hand into the cup. Pulling the hand out, she flicked it over the circular area, and I saw water droplets fly free.

This went on for a while, until the water was all gone. Only then did she gesture for me to bring her the tray.

As I stepped into the area she was treating, I suddenly felt funny, as if I'd been sniffing church incense too long. It was a giddy sensation, like a sip of applejack. Marta reached for the tray, but did not take it. Instead she folded down the legs on either side, snapping them into place. Only then did she take the oak tray from me and set it down in the center of the area she'd been circling.

"Sit—there," Marta instructed, pointing to a place diagonal to the standing tray. She started laying her bags on the oak table. From one of them she drew a black-handed knife. With it she proceeded to draw a large circle around us, starting in the east and continuing around without pausing or breaking the line. When she reached her starting point, enclosing us completely, she seemed to relax slightly. Facing back to the north and the table, she held the knife aloft and firmly said something (still in Latin, but strange to me). This was followed by facing each cardinal direction in turn and holding up her blade.

Of course, you must realize by now that although I didn't know what any of this meant at the time, I do now. But it's not needful for you to know details about the mysteries. It's not to keep control of the business, so to speak, that makes practitioners so careful—it's what people might do with partial or misunderstood information. Talk about dangerous! Trust me—if you need to know this sort of thing, a practitioner will seek you out as an apprentice.

While I was wool-gathering, Marta was drawing another circle, about a foot inside the first one. Then she took two of the pouches and began sprinkling powder and crushed herbs into the space between the circles, all the while whispering a chant and writing something with her knife. She continued around the entire circle in this manner.

After the double circle was full of runes and powders, Marta moved over to the, well, altar, I guess, and began opening bags. Two short, fat beeswax candles appeared, as well as a long, slender black rod, and a disk of polished metal with a star etched on it. Finally the black-handled knife joined the assortment upon the oak tray. Last of all, she took out a tiny censer. The bags vanished over the side, into darkness, for Marta leaned over and blew out the lantern.

Oh, boy, was it dark. There wasn't so much as a slip of moon, and the stars had begun to fade. Marta seemed unconcerned; I heard rustling, and then there was a tiny flare. Both candles were lit and burning.

Now, how did she do that? I hadn't heard a flint strike, nor any wood whirling. The odor of incense reached my nostrils—spicy and barely sweet, but not at all like church incense.

Marta opened the first small box. From where I sat I could see a glitter. Not metal—crystals of some type. My cousin scooped up the tiny, faceted round stones and held them up in the air. The Latin continued, almost like a chant, for several minutes. Although the wind occasionally lifted a strand of Marta's hair, the candles scarcely flickered. I could feel something gathering around us, like the heaviness before a summer storm.

And then, as if we'd called her, a sliver of moon appeared in the east. For the first time, Marta spoke in English:

"By all the powers of land and sea,
As I do say, so shall it be.
By all the strength of Moon and Sun,
As I do will, it shall be done."

And so help me, those stones began to glow with a light of their own! I watched, unable to look away, as the tiny balls gathered strength. As they glowed I felt a tugging at myself, but I ignored it. Surely nothing could happen in this circle that Marta didn't know about.

"Alfreda, come here, please," Marta said quietly. "Leave your coat back there."

I bounced to my feet and let the coat drop off. As Marta had promised, I scarcely noticed the cold at all. Even my feet had blood in them.

"Stand on the other side of the altar." I hastened to do as she asked. Once I was in place, she fixed me with a firm eye. "Are you a virgin?"

I just stared at her. Whatever did *that* have to do with *this*? "Yes," I admitted slowly.

"I don't care either way right at this moment, but your condition changes how I'll do this," Marta went on.

"Well, I kissed Wylie a couple of times, but that was it," I clarified. "I thought you were a virgin until you tried to make babies."

Marta actually dimpled. "Something like that," she agreed. "If all you did was kiss, then you're still a virgin." The glow from the crystal balls had continued to grow while we spoke; it was getting hard to look at Marta's hands. I noticed she was wearing strange rings I'd never seen before, one on each middle finger.

"We will complete this spell together. That ensures the wards will still hold if something happens to one of us. As I speak, you will take one ward at a time from my hands and place it back in the box. Do you see the compartments?" Looking down, I realized that there was a ring of half-moons in the velvet lining, with another dip in the center.

"I see them."

Marta closed her eyes against the light. "As I speak each word, place one ward in the box, starting with the east, which is on your left. Go in a circle, always sunward, but as if you're standing where I am. Do the compass points first. That means the second will be closest to you—north—and then the third to your right, or west. It seems backward, but it's correct for the person doing the chanting. Do you understand?"

I worked my way quickly through her words, and then

said, "I think I have it. After the first four, I go back to the east closest to me and continue?"

Marta smiled faintly, that proud smile Momma gets occasionally. "Very good. Then let us ward by the power of the growing moon. *Primus!*" Her voice grew commanding on the last word, which I recognized as Latin for "first," so I reached and took the topmost ball from my cousin's cupped hands. She hadn't said anything about the balls being different, so I silently named them to myself, giving them their places.

"Secundus!"

There were nine balls in all, counting the solitary one in the center. It turned out to be larger than the others, as I could see when the pile grew smaller. At that time I didn't know that the large ball was the capstone, which carried the weight of the spell. But common sense told me to place it in the center.

"Well done." Picking up the second box, she opened it to reveal another set of crystal balls, similar to the first. "And again." She slipped back into Latin, holding up the handful of stones first to the altar and then the new moon. Once again the glow poured from her hands like starlight; once again we placed them snugly back in their boxes, naming them as we worked.

The glow diminished but did not fade beyond a pinprick of fire at the center of each stone. As I studied the two open boxes, Marta picked up the black-handled knife and held it up first to the altar and then to the east. She bent her right knee and let her left foot slide back as she extended the knife above and before herself.

A Latin whisper began once again as she repeated the gesture and the words at each of the four major compass points. Finally she returned to the east and said something briefly, the knife held high. Then she brought her arm down in a slashing motion.

At that moment, the first true ray of sunlight shot up from the distant horizon.

Suddenly the giddy feeling was gone, and I blinked, expecting to find I hadn't slept the night before. The weariness in my limbs was surprising, since I hadn't done much.

My aunt returned to the altar and put each item back in its own sack. The glowing crystals were closed up in their boxes, and the candles extinguished. When everything was to her satisfaction, she lifted the altar and folded it, offering the tray to me.

"I'll get your coat, child." Marta purposefully wiped away the circle with her right foot, starting in the east and moving sunward. I waited until she was finished before I stepped beyond the scuffed ring.

"We have warded the Tregellases' home and immediate land," Marta explained as we started back to the house. "We also made a traveling ward that will follow us wherever we go, and extend far enough to cover the house we move to and its privy. Beyond that, the power of the wards will fade rapidly." Looking sharply at me, Marta added, "I think you could use breakfast. We'll see what Elizabeth has in her larder."

When we went back into the kitchen, we found Elizabeth Tregellas stirring up the fire and setting platters on one of the chairs. She was carefully avoiding even looking at the candelabra on the table, much less moving it.

After the past half-hour, I could scarcely blame her.

SEVENTEEN

IN TRUTH, I FELT FUNNY the next few days, wandering around as if I was a normal person. Well, wouldn't you? I'd taken part in a ritual, for heaven's sake, and by the light of a new moon, no less. I'd known some folks planted according to the phases of the moon, but I'd never had a lot of faith in that. Now I'd seen magic; real magic, that I could feel.

I'd been a part of it.

But God hadn't struck me down for the doing, so I'd just go on as I'd started. Something was out there killing this town bit by bit, and I feared that Marta and I were the only hope for Twisted Pines.

The first thing we did, after storing Marta's tools and those outlandish clothes, was go over to inspect the Donovan cabin. It was about the same size as Cousin Elizabeth's, only the loft was one open room. Bats were roosting upstairs, but Aunt Marta wasn't concerned.

"They're only flying mice, Allie," she pointed out as she moved back down the ladder. "They're welcome to the loft, if they want it."

Well, I'd never minded bats—although I didn't remember ever sharing a house with them. So we went to tell Mr. Tregellas that the house would be fine, and that the ladies needed only to clean the downstairs. Then we dived into a hearty meal of buttermilk pancakes with maple syrup. At least the sap still ran in the spring. But would anyone last long enough to collect the next crop?

After breakfast we met Mrs. Thompson, a tiny, plump woman with a gray streak in her hair. We exchanged the usual courtesies and then left her to clean in peace. Aunt Marta had stressed that Mrs. Thompson shouldn't bother with the loft, which I thought foolish—might as well put a sign up saying Mysteries Stored Here—but I held my tongue. Wouldn't Mrs. T. be surprised if she braved that ladder . . . I hoped she wouldn't fall off.

Both Marta and I were wearing our necklaces as we walked slowly into town. There were branches down from the previous night's wind, and a shack had blown over. Most of the mud had dried up, although the bad smell lingered. I suspected that Marta was getting a feel for Twisted Pines, and even checking for an aura of "rottenness," if you will. I contented myself with smiling at children and keeping a careful grip on my own protections. I could feel the traveling ward like a mist about us . . . it was a bit of comfort.

Imposing in her green wool dress, the color deep and bright like leaves in summer, Marta seemed to head straight to the town well. I'd been relieved the night before to see that Cousin Elizabeth boiled her water—it was an old family trick for driving badness from fluids. Now Marta purposefully moved aside the wooden lid from the lip of the stone.

A fetid odor rose from the depths. Placing a good word on this wasn't going to be enough.

"Do you smell it?" she asked me calmly.

"How could you not?" I replied, taking a step backward. "Can we do anything about it?"

"I think so." Marta slid the reinforced circle of wood back over the opening. Glancing wryly at me from the corner of one eye, she added, "Most folks couldn't smell that. The death in the well is from malice to living things, not from large corpses."

"What can we do?"

"Herb magic, I think," she murmured, continuing on down the rutted road. "We'll see. First I want to survey the entire town."

Smoothing my golden brown dress, I touched the lace collar at my throat reassuringly and followed in her wake. I sure hoped I looked dignified enough to inspire confidence. But although Marta hesitated before several homes, she stopped at none of them. Right now her major interest seemed to be the well.

Returning to the Donovan cabin, we found Mrs. Thompson finishing up, actually scrubbing the covered porch attached to the front of the house. "Good heavens, Mrs. Thompson, that wasn't necessary!" my cousin exclaimed. "We only needed the house swept and aired, and the heavy dirt taken care of."

Rising slowly to her feet, Mrs. Thompson wiped her bare forearm across her brow. "Ah, but it was necessary for me, my dear," she said softly. "I feel safer in a wizard's house than in my own." She took her bucket of dirty water off to one side and dumped it, and then began rolling her wool sleeves back down to her wrists.

"You will be safest when you're with us," Marta admitted. "However safe that might be."

Shrugging, the woman patted the heavy bun at the base of her neck. There was an air of defeat about her— as if she was afraid to hope that we could turn away the evil plaguing her community. "What will be, will be. Mrs. Tregellas has spoken to you about the church quilting?"

"We haven't been back to their home since first light," Marta said smoothly. "I'm sure Mrs. Tregellas will tell us all about it as soon as we go in to dinner."

Now, if we could just find our appetites after smelling
Twisted Pines all morning . . .

Sure enough, Cousin Elizabeth mentioned the church
quilting as soon as we sat down to the main meal of the
day.

"You said you wanted to meet as many people as possible," Elizabeth started as she passed us fresh biscuits
and syrup. "Once a month the small groups from our
community—we call them 'stars'—get together to assem-
ble and quilt up the month's work. The quilts go to needy
families in town, or the surrounding area." Elizabeth faltered at the last words. "I suppose that sounds silly now.
It's been a long time since we've sent quilts off for mis-
sions. Folks right here need them."

"See to your own people first, Elizabeth, at least the
basics," Marta agreed with a nod. "No sense in warming
the savages and having your own children sleep cold."

"That's God's own truth," Gavin Tregellas muttered as
he took a serving of beans and salt pork. "No sense in
worrying what others think of us—we're at the lip of the
abyss as it is."

Marta fixed the man with a stern eye. "Not true, Mr.
Tregellas," she said firmly. "If you were, we've hauled you
back from the edge. Have faith."

The two youngest boys were very quiet during this
conversation, packing the food away like it was their last
meal. The other three were still at the schoolhouse. So far
there hadn't been any known threat to children, so Marta
wasn't worried about that building . . . not yet.

Prying apart a fluffy biscuit, Cousin Elizabeth said, "The
quilting will be tomorrow at the Gunnarsson home. I
thought Alfreda could sit with the girls, and you with our
dames." She paused to spread fresh butter on the biscuit.

"Not that you'd find out anything during the quilting, but the sooner folks get used to you, the more likely they'll be to trust you with secrets."

Good thinking, to my mind.

I spent some time musing about it after the meal, when I wrote a letter to Shaw. It was a strange feeling, writing to someone. I don't think I'd ever sent word to anyone except family. There wasn't a lot to tell, except to thank him for the necklace and to say I was sorry we hadn't got to say good-bye. Somehow I filled the page twice, turning the paper sideways so the lines crossed properly. How folks rattle on when they're far away . . . it was easier to write to him than to talk with him.

At least that time.

I wasn't ready to try writing Wylie.

My leisure was over for a while. I spent the balance of the day at the Donovan house grinding various herbs into powder. Marta had a wonderful mortar and pestle, made from polished marble. The job had never seemed easier. I felt happier than I had in a long time, because a man in town was going to Castle Rock at the crack of dawn and he'd agreed to carry my letter west.

People who complained about the cost of spells—or medicine—had no idea how much time and effort all that studying, growing, harvesting, and grinding took. Dill, vervain, ginseng root, mullein, rosemary, larch, laurel leaves, mugwort, milfoil, rue, St.-John's-wort—I felt like we were tossing half the satchel into the smooth wooden bowl Marta was filling! The only thing I missed was angelica.

"We'll save that one," was Marta's comment when I asked about it. "Angelica is very powerful; we could overwhelm the benefit of the others. Start out gently, woman. You can always add force, but it's hard to take it away."

I thought on that a while as I ground things. Although

I couldn't guarantee the first was always true, the second surely was . . . another thing to remember.

The ceremony for the well was surprisingly simple. Marta recited a charm of purification over us and the bowl, and then included the well. We sprinkled the mixture of ground herbs in a circle around the well, starting at the east, and then scattered the rest inside the well itself. No special time or anything—we just made sure we were finished before dark.

Cousin Elizabeth had an extra teapot, so we had our own tea at the Donovan house, but we ate a light supper with the Tregellas family. Hastily. Before night rose. And then got ourselves back to the other cabin, where Trey and Mr. Tregellas had carried our bags, beds, and a table and chairs.

Even a fire couldn't warm me that night . . . because there were footsteps outside that did not cease pacing until sunrise. I was beginning to understand those circles under Cousin Elizabeth's eyes. Very grateful I was that Marta started explaining about her ceremonial tools. It kept my mind focused.

But morning came all too soon. We were still alive, so the wards had held. Cousin Elizabeth had poached eggs and fresh bread waiting for us when we'd finished with our sponge baths, and I felt like a queen to be eating so well. Not fancy, but Elizabeth seemed to know that practitioners needed a lot of food.

"The wards," Marta remarked as we dug out our thimbles and got ready to accompany Elizabeth to the Gunnarsson house. "The wards draw partly on us for their strength—it's the only way to put up a ward that powerful—so we have to keep feeding the spell."

"Can't you set wards and not tend them?" I was sure Cousin Cory had done that while visiting last Christmas.

Marta nodded as she closed the door to our temporary

home. "Wards of that nature are simpler. A circle isn't even necessary, unless for some reason you're tired. Those wards keep out most things, and trigger alarm in you if something nasty is prowling the perimeters." Casting one of her sidelong glances at me, she added, "If something bad has been stalking you, you can rig a ward to explode in the face of a demon. You'll learn that spell from Cory—it's a spell of air."

While we spoke, we'd reached the Tregellas house, where Elizabeth was giving instructions to one of Tregellas's nieces, who would watch the younger boys. There was an edge to the woman's voice I hadn't heard before, and the girl looked a bit wide-eyed.

It might not have been my place to speak to an elder, but I wanted to reassure that gangling child.

"Just keep them close to the house," I told her simply. "The ward is strongest there. The farther out they go, the less protection." Glancing at Cousin Elizabeth, I said the last for her as well, "Remember, there's been no trouble during the day. You should be fine."

I guess it was what both needed to hear, for Elizabeth's face cleared, and the girl—getting tall but with no form yet—visibly relaxed. She looked old enough to handle two rambunctious boys.

In fact, from the way her voice carried as we walked on down the road, I'd say that she must have had brothers of her own.

"If you're going to worry, Elizabeth—" Marta started as we rounded the turn into the village proper.

"No, no," the woman said quickly. "Mary's a good girl, and always keeps a tight eye on them. Nothing has happened during the day. I'm being as foolish as Mrs. Gunnarsson." Smoothing the dress of fine brown wool she'd donned, Cousin Elizabeth kept her face toward the town square. "I need a day of talk and sewing."

"Is Mrs. Gunnarsson all right?" I asked casually, letting my steps lag behind the others by maybe half a body. Could this have to do with the weeping?

"She's very frightened," our cousin said simply. "If her husband didn't own so much land in this region, I think they would have left long ago. Gunnarsson hired the two practitioners who agreed to come," she added. "He'll want to negotiate a contract with you. He likes things in writing."

"Interesting," was all Marta said. I looked over at her and saw that secret half-smile. Guess she got the same feeling about Gunnarsson that I did—in our communities, if you needed a written contract, it meant you didn't trust someone else's word.

So, either Mr. Gunnarsson had been cheated once, or his own word wasn't good. Which was true remained to be seen.

We discovered we hadn't noticed the Gunnarssons' house from the main road—our oversight would have wounded Mr. Gunnarsson, I'm sure. The big home was set back on its own broad roadway, which was carefully tended by loving hands. No ruts or privy water was visible there, just smooth river stones.

The house was made of red-brown brick, in the style folks called Georgian, with painted wood columns and landscaped gardens to one side of the entrance drive. Cousin Elizabeth knocked on the front door, and was received by a fair young woman with huge gray eyes. She was pretty, if a bit peaked, and dressed with simple elegance in a fine muslin dress with no waist that was gathered under her small breasts.

"Welcome to Lone Oak Farm, Mrs. Tregellas," she said softly. "My mother is with our other guests. Would you like to go back to the Yellow Room? The frames are set up there."

Cousin Elizabeth swiftly introduced us to this gracious
woman-child, and Jesse's eyes as she looked upon me
were both friendly and relieved.

I relaxed just a bit. Pretty, tiny girls with fancy dresses
and hair that's never fought wind always look like trouble
to me. But if Jesse thought my clothing old-fashioned, she
didn't say a word. Soundlessly she gestured toward the
back of the house, and we walked with her down a polished wood floor to the sitting room of the lady of the
house.

It was hard not to gawk. There were high, carved ceil-
ings and shining oak floors covered by huge Persian car-
pets. Dainty furniture that had traveled a long way graced
the mansion (anything with two stories and that many
rooms had to be a mansion), and there was a massive
mahogany table in the dining area. A lace tablecloth
adorned the many leaves, with real English china and silver flatware.

True, it was magnificent, but it was also cold—cold in
a way I'd never imagined before. I felt an itching between
my shoulder blades, as if someone was standing behind
me and watching everything I did.

When we reached the sitting room, I met Mrs.
Gunnarsson, and I felt a lot better about the house. As
tiny as her daughter, Mrs. Gunnar was dressed in the
older style, with a snowy white wrap draped around her
shoulders and pinned with a brooch above her breasts.
Her skirt was as full as mine, and . . . yes! Her hair was
powdered beneath her cap! I didn't think *anyone* still
powdered their hair.

It was when I looked closely at Mrs. Gunnar that I
remembered why we were in Twisted Pines. If Cousin
Elizabeth looked haunted, Mrs. Gunnar had aged beyond
her time. Beneath her facial powder, the circles under
her eyes were so sunken I wondered if she had fading

consumption. This woman did not even have the bright cheeks of some wasting folks.

Mrs. Gunnar was not alone in the sitting room; numerous ladies of the village were seated around her, several examining a quilt top and another group rolling top, cotton batting, and bottom onto one arm of a quilting frame. Most of the ladies were attired more or less like Marta, in severe, tasteful dresses trimmed in lace, but a few wore the country frocks of my grandparents' time.

Unfortunately, the women reminded me of a gaggle of geese. The noise level in the house was quite high, the conversation animated. It was all a sham, of course—one had only to listen and look closely to see the guarded expressions, the open fear. But no one spoke of "it."

Except Jesse. She had moved over to a set of lovely doors that opened out onto a covered verandah. Gazing out the pieced glass, she seemed removed from us, part of the fading beauty of the autumn garden.

"We've always held the quilting out there," she said softly, almost to herself. "And then came inside to eat. Even on a windy day, the trees protected the back porch. I wanted to quilt outside again, but Mother wouldn't hear of it. She'd never last the morning, much less the day. Mother doesn't go outside anymore. . . ." Glancing over her shoulder, she asked, "Do you enjoy quilting, Miss Sorensson? Or are you a victim of guest courtesy?"

It was a surprise to hear myself called Miss Sorensson—it meant Jesse Gunnarsson thought I was as old as she, sixteen, at least. Well . . . I was here to establish ties, and there was no harm in encouraging that belief.

"I enjoy it more than I did," I started slowly. "My mother only made up a half-dozen coverlet styles, and I would become terribly bored after a while. My cousin rarely repeats a design. I will like that challenge."

Nodding her understanding, or her courtesy, Miss Gunnarsson gestured at one of the frames. "We younger people will work on the Crossroads quilt, probably in slanted lines. Mother wants to finish that Irish Chain, but the group has yet to pick a quilting pattern."

"Zig-zag," I suggested, turning a sharp eye on the cream and greens of the Irish Chain, its tiny squares laboriously stitched together.

"I bet you're right," Miss Gunnarsson said, and then several other young women arrived, and our rapport vanished.

I am pleased to tell you that I was a very good quilter, young as I was then. Mending clothes had always bored me, and my housekeeping was acceptable, no more, but give me a needle and a challenge, and I could make something beautiful. Quilts were best—beautiful and useful.

Since Marta was an excellent quilter, we slid almost seamlessly into the local church group. Neither of us talked much, accept when asked about our own villages, but there was a lot to hear. Babies born and family fights predominated at the Irish Chain, while at the Crossroads, who was stepping out with whom seemed to generate the most interest.

Jesse was probably the prettiest and best-dressed of the group, but all the girls looked fairly healthy, their families prosperous enough that their clothes were like mine, only a few years behind the fashion. For that's what Jesse's new dress turned out to be—the latest fashion, sent by her aunt all the way from Philadelphia. "Empire waist," it was called.

It was their eyes that gave away family secrets . . . some of these families were living on their savings.

Fashion wasn't the only topic of conversation. The girls were also curious about what I had to do as an apprentice. I told them some of it—recognizing several hundred herbs in any season, for example—but I could usually steer the conversation back to local romances.

How does one sift the life of a town? I swear I felt my ears growing, I listened so hard. Through a morning of quilting, a lovely sit-down dinner with soup and roast fowl and creamed peas, and into the afternoon, I kept hold of my tongue. By the time we returned to the quilt frame, I could tell you who the most popular girls were, who their best friends were, and how many others each pair influenced. I knew who was a flirt, who was a blue-stocking, and who was probably seeing a boy on the side.

Jesse could have been a born leader, between her looks and her parents' wealth, but she was quiet most of the time, sharing few comments and laughing seldom. I wondered if she was coming down with something, and hoped not—this town did not need fever on top of everything else.

At the least, these girls needed to know people wouldn't shun them because of the grief their town bore. If all I could do was make friends with some folks, I would accomplish something.

We closed up shop well before sunset, so the women who drove in from local farms could get safely home. Two more quilts were finished for the church stores, and a well-cooked meal had been presented in a lovely setting. It should have been a triumph for Mrs. Gunnarsson.

It was like watching a garment unravel. The woman started abruptly looking out the windows early in the afternoon, and by the time we were finished, she was visibly agitated. I'd never seen a person look so torn—she was desperate for us to stay, and terrified that we wouldn't leave in time.

I didn't hear what Marta said as she and Cousin Elizabeth thanked Mrs. Gunnarsson for her hospitality, but the woman seemed less terrified, more simply frightened. I'd helped Jesse stack the quilt frames to go back to the church, and was saying my good-byes myself.

"I hope you'll be able to come again," Jesse said suddenly, and sounded like she meant it.

"I will if I can," I told her, straightening my skirt for the walk back. "Pray that our efforts go well."

"I pray unceasingly," Jesse whispered, her face suddenly pale.

Impulsively I reached out to take her hand. "It will be all right, Miss Gunnarsson. Truly it will."

Jesse's grip was spasmodic. "I hope so." She seemed distant again, as if her thoughts were elsewhere, so I said good-bye and added my thanks to my cousins'. Mrs. Gunnarsson nodded tightly, her eyes begging for something.

I think she wanted us to take her fear away with us. But that was something Marta hadn't taught me, if such a thing could be taught,

That night I prayed for Mrs. Gunnar.

One of Marta's many talents was the ability to make paper. Usually she used the scented results to line drawers and trunks, or for drawing, since it was partially from herb fiber, but this time we used bunches of it to make lists and genealogies.

Every family within a two-hour drive was included in our scribbling. Marta was interested in my thoughts about the way the girls treated each other, and had me write that up, too. Best as we could, we added in the young men who still remained in Twisted Pines. Somewhere in this mess of words there might be a clue. Had someone done what I'd kept Wylie from doing, and pulled a stake from a field? Had someone disturbed an old grave with new building or plowing? Had someone even dabbled in magic?

Trying to answer those questions was an agonizingly slow process. Around us the folks of Twisted Pines tended their sheep and cows, harvested their grain, and hung on to their wits by their fingernails. The noise in the night wasn't gone, not by a long shot—and it was getting stronger.

We knew something had changed when we were rousted from our house at dawn by a distraught man. He was usually a quiet, unassuming fellow, who raised milk cows and apples down in a hollow near Twisted Pines.

His need could be gauged by the fact that he must have left his home before sunrise to get to us so early. I'm not sure there was another man in a day's riding brave enough to do that.

"It came inside," he kept saying over and over, still shaking in the strength of his fear. "It came inside, and it wanted Annie."

I do mean before dawn—we were both still in our nightgowns when we heard pounding and yelling at our door. While Marta spoke to the fellow in a soothing voice, trying to settle him in the porch rocker, I pulled on my clothing and went to fetch Mr. Tregellas. This fellow might become violent, and we'd need help to deal with him. I suspected Marta could save our lives, if necessary, but I wouldn't count on the farmer surviving it.

Even warded, even with both houses warded, I was nervous crossing to Cousin Elizabeth's. Things were just too quiet, if you can understand that.

Tregellas was having his breakfast, after taking care of the first chores, but he dropped his biscuit and charged over to the Donovan house as soon as I gasped out what was up.

"You don't understand! It wanted Annie!" I could

hear as we reached the porch of the house. "It scratched her up something terrible, trying to get to her eyes. I couldn't stop it, my hand passed right through it!" The farmer, whose name was Miller, had backed Marta up against the firewall. I don't think he'd touched her, but he was extending his hands, pleading with her. Marta had wrapped her hand around the poker and was clearly gauging whether it was time to go on the offensive.

"Franklin! Let be, man! You'll have us all thinking you're possessed!" Mr. Tregellas's words were harsh, but he'd gotten through to his neighbor. The man stopped yelling, looking both surprised and bewildered, like someone coming out of a dream.

"I'm not," he said faintly, lowering his hands. "I swear by my Lord I'm not!"

"Did it reach her eyes?" Marta said coolly, her gaze never leaving the man's face.

Miller shook his head vigorously. "She'd taken to sleeping with her scissors under her pillow, though she hadn't told me. She thrust at the creature, and it backed off, wailing up a storm."

"So she has cuts to be tended, but otherwise she's all right?"

"All right! She's cut up on her arms and neck, and—"

"But she's not blind, and she's not dead," Marta broke in, and Miller grew silent. I guess their good fortune had finally sunk in. "You can be proud of your wife, Mr. Miller. She'd been given instructions by Mrs. Tregellas, and she followed them. You had cold iron at the windows and door?" When Miller dumbly nodded, Marta went on, "Clearly cold iron at the entrances is no longer enough. Everyone will have to sleep with iron—man, woman, and child."

Turning to me, she said, "Rouse up Trey and Evan. They'll need to help you check in the village." Looking over at Tregellas, she asked, "Is there a doctor in Twisted Pines? A surgeon?" When the man shook his head, Marta continued, "Then I'm for it. As soon as I'm dressed, we'll go to the Miller place to see about Mrs. Miller. Others must check all the neighboring farms, to make sure no one else was hurt. Tell Elizabeth to pack me some food; I'll need fuel for this work."

Nodding his agreement, Mr. Tregellas stepped forward and took hold of Mr. Miller's arm. "Come along, Franklin. We'll pour some coffee into you and then get back to your good wife."

As soon as the men had passed the threshold, I pushed shut the door and asked, "Does this mean more warding?"

Marta looked grim as she answered, "It does. We'd lose too much strength trying to ward the entire mountain. We'll have to ward sleeping areas in every home. And Allie—we need to make some headway with this. We're running out of time."

Swallowing in a dry throat, I nodded once and then went to get Trey and Evan.

Mrs. Miller hadn't been the only one under siege. Another young woman had been attacked during the night, but her husband had defended her with his hunting knife.

A third woman hadn't been so lucky. She lived alone, on the other side of the hill, widowed ten years and her children grown and gone. I was glad I hadn't found her— the thing had slashed her up something terrible, and gouged her eyes out. The poor widow was dead when she was found, whether from blood loss or fright, we couldn't tell.

The older Tregellas boys and I had checked maybe half the houses on the row when a young woman, as dark-skinned as the night, came running up to me.

"Oh, miss! Please come! Miz Gunnarsson is in a terrible way!"

"Was she attacked?" I asked quickly. The girl was brought up short, her eyes frightened. "Was she cut up?"

"No! No! I didn't see no blood, but she's shrieking something awful, and Miss Jesse and her father can't do nothing wit' the lady!"

Hysterics. That I could deal with, if Mrs. Gunnar didn't have any other serious health problems.

"I'll need my bag," I told the woman. "Tell them I'm coming."

I hadn't yet seen Mr. Gunnarsson. He'd asked Marta to come up a few days back, so he could discuss payment with her. I wondered how Marta was going to react to the insult of a written contract, but I should have known she already had plans.

"Money, Allie," she'd said simply. "It's all people like that understand. I double my fee for people who want it in writing, and the price goes up from there, depending on how much trouble they turn out to be. And danger pay in advance, in this case."

The young black woman opened the door for me, but Gunnarsson almost ran her down. He was a big, fleshy man, dressed in the frock coat and knee leggings of a country squire, his hair powdered like King Washington's had been.

"Hurry! Did you bring laudanum?" He stopped abruptly, his eyes fixing upon me in a way I didn't like at all. "Where is your teacher?"

"Helping a woman who was slashed up last night," I said quickly. "We need to see to Mrs. Gunnarsson immediately." I stood straight and tall before him, almost his own height, and that may have decided him.

"Come along, then." Turning quickly, Gunnarsson led the way up the curving oak staircase. Even with a runner, his footsteps were heavy on the treads.

"Bring me a pitcher of hot water, a bowl for steeping, and a teacup," I told the servant, rushing to follow in Gunnarsson's wake.

The second floor of Lone Oak was as lovely as the first, with a real tapestry hanging in a sitting room at the end of the hallway. Mrs. Gunnarsson was still in her nightclothes, lying in her wide bed. She was weeping and trying to get up, but Jesse was pushing her back into the bed.

"But there's nowhere safe, child! I have to find a place to keep you safe! I won't lose you too!" was coming out between sobs.

"We're fine, Mother," Jesse kept repeating, holding her mother's hands reassuringly. "I'm fine, and Papa is fine. We're all fine. You have your sewing scissors right here, see? Cold iron at your hand."

I immediately opened my bag and dug out packets of chamomile, hawthorn, and hops. The young woman appeared with the things I'd asked for, the steam still rising from the teapot.

"Momma had already boiled water," the girl said swiftly, setting the tray carefully on a covered table. "I brought sugar, too, 'cus Miz Gunnarsson likes her tea sweet."

"Good! Thank you." I worked swiftly, because I was afraid Mrs. Gunnar would make herself sick with all that crying. It seemed like the herbs took forever to steep, but soon the right color and taste were reached. I was grateful the servant thought of sugar, because this was not a very pleasant concoction. But at her current level of exhaustion, it would settle Mrs. Gunnarsson fast.

When I finally had cool tea, I dissolved a bit of sugar

in hot water and added it to the infusion. Then I offered the teacup to Jesse.

"She won't let go," Jesse hissed under her breath, so I steeled myself and pushed the cup to Mrs. Gunnar's lips.

"You must drink this, madam," I said firmly. "It will help you feel better." The next time the woman opened her mouth, I purposely tipped some tea onto her tongue. The surprise didn't stop her sobs, but she stopped shrieking and actually took a sip of the tea. She grimaced, but her grip on Jesse loosened.

"If—it—doesn't—taste bad—it's—not—working," she whispered between gasps, and I nodded encouragement, grateful I wasn't going to have to hold her down and pour the tisane into her. I could do it, but I was quite aware of Mr. Gunnarsson hovering in the doorway.

The lady seemed susceptible to hops, or maybe it was because she'd not eaten. She was breathing deeper by the time she'd finished the tisane. Jesse reached to plump up her pillows.

"You must rest, Mother. It's the only way you'll grow stronger," she said gently, pushing her mother back under the comforter.

"Yes, sleep, Judith," her husband said in his booming voice. "I'll go out and see if I can get you a turkey for Sunday dinner." The woman smiled wanly at him, her eyelids drooping.

She's exhausted. I'd never seen this stuff work so fast. It was like she'd prayed for oblivion.

"Stay with your mistress, Matilda." Having dismissed both wife and servant from his thoughts, Gunnarsson settled his gaze on me. "Well, you do know some of the tricks of the trade, don't you? Will your mistress come up later?"

"I'll tell her you asked," I promised, not about to commit Marta to anything, not with who knew how many people out there bleeding.

"I'm going to go with Miss Sorensson back into the village, Papa," Jesse said suddenly. "Perhaps I can be a help to her."

Fingering the ruffles at his neck, Gunnarsson nodded absently. "Perhaps you can comfort some people, child. Very well. Be back for dinner, though. I don't want a slave watching your mother all day." And that was it—he turned and started back down the corridor.

I had absolutely frozen at his last words. Slave? Hadn't Papa said something about the kingdom across the sea outlawing slavery? But not our country . . . not yet. I felt myself growing warm, and then got a grip on my emotions. A fragment of something Marta had once told me drifted into the front of my mind, and I decided to heed the warning.

One battle at a time. I had some kind of demon to deal with—later I could think about slave smuggling. Matilda was safer here than out in the wilderness.

Jesse set her hand on my arm. "You don't mind if I come, do you?" She was fresh and delicate in sprigged muslin, as if she'd never worked a day in her life, but I suspected she was stronger than that.

"Not at all. Let's pack my things."

I left a mixture of crushed chamomile and hawthorn in one of Mrs. Gunnar's jewelry dishes, and a bit of hops in another. Jesse said that Matilda could be trusted to alternate teas, first with hops and then without. Since I didn't know about the lady's heart, I wasn't going to take chances with too much hops.

It wasn't until we were halfway down the wide mansion road that Jesse whispered, "Do you know what herbs to use to stop a baby coming?"

EIGHTEEN

A SOARING, MELODIOUS TRILL of birdsong floated through the air, but I was too stunned to pay heed to it. Have you ever had time freeze for you? You're going along, minding your own business, and then someone says something that sets your stomach sinking and your ears ringing. You think it's been hours that you've stood there, staring at the other person, when in reality it's only a moment in time.

That's how I felt when Jesse asked her question. Praise be to my parents for my good manners, because I didn't blink and I didn't slow down. Jesse had a very good reason to ask this question—and a good reason not to ask it under her own roof.

"I think we'd better go to the Donovan house and talk," I said slowly. At her intake of breath, I added without looking at her: "No one will be there right now. We can talk about whatever we want."

It wasn't until we had reached the cabin, which was bathed in the pale gold of sunrise, that I realized I'd heard *my* bird, the one no one else—except maybe Marta—could hear. *That was a far piece to travel, little bird. Someday will you finally tell me why?*

I decided that this was worth using some of our precious Darjeeling tea, so I filled the kettle with water and placed it on the hook over the coals. Then I tossed on a log and stirred up the fire.

"This old place isn't so bad," Jesse said softly, her eyes on the tight tongue-and-groove joints of the set-in window.

"It keeps the cold and rain out, and means no one is in the line of fire if that demon comes after us," was my response. I checked, but of course the teacups were clean, because we hadn't had time for a meal that morning. "Do you need sweetening?"

"No, thank you," was her simple response. "A little cream, if you have it."

I checked and found that Elizabeth had already brought some over. "You're in luck. Mrs. Tregellas has already supplied us with some. I hope you won't mind if I eat something. I didn't have breakfast."

"Neither did I," she admitted, so we got out cheese and bread and peach preserves and had ourselves a fine little spread.

"You needn't worry about your mother," I said after I'd poured the hot water into the teapot to steep. "That mix should help her quite a bit, if her first reaction is any indication."

Jesse didn't say anything for a moment, and then she sighed. "I'm glad, for her sake," she started, "but it's hard to really care anymore, if you can understand that." For the first time, she looked me in the eye. "After six years of fear, there's a . . . a numbing, here in our village. We can't feel anymore—and we'd do anything to feel something again . . . joy, pain, something *real*."

The fierceness in her voice removed any question of who needed to lose a child. Sometimes bluntness serves where manners fail. "Did you find what you were looking for in his arms?"

"I thought so," she whispered. "But he's been gone over a month, and I'm afraid he's found someone else. Or maybe that horrible thing . . ." Her eyes started to tear up, so I dug out my fresh handkerchief and passed it to her.

"You love him, and you think he loves you," I started for her.

"Not just because he says so," Jesse said quickly. "Because of how he treats me. There's always a light in his eyes when he looks at me. That's good, isn't it?"

"Sounds promising," I said guardedly. While I didn't want to give her any false hope, I also didn't want her to stop talking. As for a light in his eyes, I wasn't any judge of such things; Wylie had always avoided catching my gaze. "Let's get ourselves some tea."

Jesse put cream in each cup, and I poured. Then we added our own hot water until it was just like we wanted it.

"Why did you . . . go at it?" It was embarrassing to ask someone I hardly knew, but it was an important question.

"It happened one evening, when we were talking out in the gazebo and lost track of time," she whispered. "We were trapped all night. I was so scared, and the wailing was so loud . . . it just happened. And, after it had happened once, then . . ." She trailed off, and looked hopefully at me from under her delicate eyebrows.

"I see." My momma was right—bundling wasn't like water from a pump; you couldn't turn it on and off. Just as well I hadn't succumbed to Wylie's hints. "Why would you think he threw you over?"

Her gaze dropped. "It happened to my older sister." Swallowing carefully, Jesse went on, "My sister, Nan, was thrown over for a lowland girl, because my father won't let anyone in town court his daughters. He says the boys here aren't good enough for his family."

"Indeed." And did he expect them to remain spinsters in order to nurse him in his old age? Not very realistic when marriageable females were scarce—and valuable— in these parts.

"But . . . I got pregnant . . . at least, I've missed two moon times." She looked back up at me, her eyes filled with tears. "Papa threw my sister out when Davin asked to marry her. I'm afraid that Papa . . . he could even kill me if he finds out I'm carrying a baby!" Jesse was so pale I was afraid she'd pass out.

"Here." I reached for the honey and put a dollop in her tea. "I know you don't want sweetening, but you need it. Drink." The fact that she obeyed me told me a lot of things.

For whatever reason, Jesse was truly terrified of her papa's reaction. Now, I would hate to have to tell my parents such a thing—especially if the father had taken off. But though they'd be very disappointed in me, I don't think either of them would try to kill me.

Still . . . Mr. Gunnarsson owned slaves. He probably treated his children the same way. Dressed them pretty and wanted them not to speak until spoken to. A woman had no rights in this world, and nothing she didn't take for herself. That I already knew.

Maybe he *would* kill his daughter.

But losing this baby—if there was a baby; I didn't know, like I had with Momma—wasn't a solution. Although I knew the herbs and stuff, I didn't know the proportions, or how to decide how much to give her. And what with the power of those plants, I wasn't about to guess. I could end up killing her.

"Why do you think he's thrown you over?" I repeated. "Just because your sister's lover was faithless doesn't mean yours is."

Jesse twisted her hands in her lap. "He went to see his great-uncle about some things," she whispered. "Over a month ago. The old man lives alone, his children are all dead. Why is it taking so long?"

"Where?" When she told me, it was all I could do to

keep from laughing. Lord, that was six days' ride easy! She was talking a fortnight's travel, minimum.

"Miss Gunnarsson," I said gently, "you've been worried about a lot of things, and you're not thinking clearly. Your fellow— "

"Richard La Croix," she supplied.

"Mr. La Croix wouldn't ride six days to see kin and then not visit. If he's fond of his uncle, and his uncle of him, surely he'd stay at least a se'nnight, if not a fortnight." I decided to make a jump, and added, "Chances are he's on his way home right now."

The girl looked visibly happier. "I—I hadn't thought of that," she admitted. "Do you really think so?"

Then I had an idea. "You know . . . I think a practitioner lives over Arbor way, and no stranger visits without the practitioner knowing. I bet there's some way my cousin could contact that practitioner and ask if Mr. La Croix is still there."

Jesse became wild-eyed and rose to her feet. "No! We can't tell your teacher. She'd tell my parents!"

"No, she wouldn't," I said quickly, rising and taking her hand to keep her from bolting. Just that easily, I knew that Jesse was carrying her first son. The enormousness of what I'd just sensed momentarily overwhelmed me. Then I said, "I can tell you exactly what she'll say. She'll say that if you're old enough for God to give you a baby, then you're old enough to decide what is best for that life and for yours. But she'll want to talk about all the things you might do before we consider sending your first son back to the Lord. No practitioner does that lightly."

Jesse didn't say anything, but she didn't run out of the house, either. We stared at each other for a few moments, and then she sat down.

"She won't tell my parents?"

"No." If necessary, I'd argue Marta down to the

ground, but we were not going to tell the Gunnarssons
. . . not yet, anyway. I wasn't going to let this girl use cotton root or celery root to send a baby back to God.

And I wasn't going to let Mr. Gunnarsson kill his
daughter—not if I could prevent it.

As I had expected, there *was* a way for practitioners to
communicate over long distances—a more reliable way
than dreams or trying to send thoughts.

"We'll send a letter," Marta told us when she'd heard
Jesse's tale. "A practitioner's letter, that is. What's the
boy's full name? And his uncle's?"

Bewildered, Jesse dutifully gave Marta both names,
which my cousin noted with a burnt stick on the tiles of
the fireplace. Then Marta took out a sheet of paper and
wrote a brief letter to the wizard of Arbor. Later she told
me she'd asked if Richard La Croix had visited his uncle,
Old Richard, and if he was still there. Right then, however, she explained nothing.

She also decided to tell the other wizard that this
information might have something to do with the haunting of Twisted Pines. Which meant the other wizard
would probably find an answer for us.

"This will take longer than usual," Marta explained
briskly. "I don't have a circle of power set up for mes-
sages."

"Do you normally?" I asked.

"There is a permanent circle for communication in the
house at Wild Rose Run," was her answer. Then she
moved over to her carpetbag, dug in one of her undyed
cotton sacks, and pulled out what looked like a chunk of
chalk. Her left fingertips pressed to her necklace, Marta
proceeded to walk around the room, finally concentrating
on the west corner to one side of the fireplace.

Beginning in the east, she drew a continuous line, forming a small circle. There were two major differences from when I'd watched her do it before. This time she used the powdery substance to produce her circle, as opposed to the knife pulled through dirt—and this time she stood outside the circle instead of inside it.

"We are not calling upon any outside influences this time," Marta said simply. "The circle is not to protect from evil influences, but to contain the power as it builds. We'll use our own strength and the fire's to send the note—it's not traveling far."

Marta placed the note in the center of the circle. A few runes were next, engraved on the perimeter of the circle, and then her familiar cup came out of her carpetbag. After sprinkling some salt into the depression, Marta once again drew water from the empty cup, flinging the fluid over the circle, the note, and the three of us.

"I need your help, ladies," she finally said. Wrapping the cup in a lovely piece of fabric and placing it back into her carpetbag, Marta gestured for us to join hands with her around the circle. "All the two of you need to do is concentrate on the town of Arbor and the joy of receiving a letter. Don't drop hands until I tell you to let go."

"I have never been to Arbor," Jesse said timidly.

"Orchards," Marta murmured dreamily. "Orchards and hardwoods and corn. Think of corn shocks tied for the winter, and bare fruit trees, and a mass of dark clouds far off to the west, over a lake you cannot see. A lake larger than some seas." Marta's voice was almost a drone, and I slipped into the spell of her words. I didn't doubt that she'd suggested the image that came to mind, and probably slipped the picture into Jesse's thoughts, too.

By the power of the threefold goddess, I heard whispered in my mind. *This is to thy service, Lady*.

I suddenly felt tired, as if the day was past and not just

beginning. Looking down, I saw that the circle was empty.

Our thanks, Lady. Your blessing and your protection upon us.

And then the room was filled with brilliant light, like the flare of a midwinter bonfire. Only a moment—then it was gone. I smelled charring.

The circle was now burned into the floor.

Marta was frowning, so I dared to ask, "Was that supposed to happen?"

"No." Her tone was both puzzled and irritated, as if someone had dared to place a toe wrong. Then her expression changed suddenly, and she bowed her head.

Bright blessings of the Light, we thank thee for thy guardianship. Aloud, Marta said, "You can let go now, ladies. I suggest we go impose on Mrs. Tregellas for something to eat, and then check on your mother, Miss Gunnarsson."

"Mrs. Miller?" There hadn't been time before to ask— I had launched into Jesse's tale before the girl could lose her resolve.

"She'll be fine, if the thing doesn't come back. She's a strong lady. So are the McGyvers—they ran the thing off before it could do any harm, but I left a bit of chamomile and hops to help calm them."

"McGyver?" Jesse was suddenly pale once again.

"Your sister is fine, my dear," Marta said gently. "Why don't you go warn my cousin that we're invading her kitchen, and we'll join you as soon as we've cleaned up here. It will be a few hours before we have any reply. The practitioner there is probably working, and not necessarily near her circle."

I waited until Jesse had closed the door, her footsteps ringing sharply on the wooden porch and then scuffing dirt, before I said, "Something went wrong?"

Marta shook her head, still looking at the circle. "Oh, the message got through, all right. But I think we can be sure that *thing* knows we're here now. Our use of power attracted its attention." Lifting her head to face me, she added, "This is why protection of some sort, and observation, are so important. I noticed that the three of us could—barely—represent the Goddess in her three major aspects, and so I asked for her aid in transporting the letter—and for her protection. While we were moving the letter, something tried to come at us back through the path we'd blazed to Arbor. The Goddess protected us."

Awe and unease trickled slowly down my spine. A power great enough to call a goddess . . . The fathers were right, I was a lousy Catholic. The idea of a mother goddess seemed, well, complete to me.

"And if we'd just used the fire and our own will?" I decided to ask.

"We could have had a pitched battle trying to keep the thing in that circle."

Oh. "Do we need to reinforce the circle?"

Marta smiled. "Hardly. The Goddess did that—the circle is etched down to bedrock, and it's now the safest communication spot in the region. But unless the next occupant of the cottage is a practitioner, it will probably give them fits to look at it." Leaning over, she whispered, "It won't sand out."

I had an insane desire to giggle, and clamped down on the feeling. Didn't work.

We laughed together, and it felt good, like something we hadn't done in way too long. Then we went to replenish our energy.

The day was spent warding every sleeping area in Twisted Pines and the surrounding area. Marta used a type of ward that ties into the life force of every living thing for quite a bit in any direction. That means just what you think it does—if a house was attacked in the village, the people living on either side of the besieged family would lend their will to live to those beseiged.

Even the ground, sliding into winter sleep as it was, would give us strength.

I'd thought the town would be falling apart on us, or losing any faith they had in our abilities; but, curiously, they seemed heartened by the previous night. The old widow had died only because she'd been too frightened to fight back with her knife—Marta was pretty sure of that. Two others had been attacked and had survived. This gave folks hope that maybe we were getting somewhere.

Huh. As if we'd had time to reason things through. Constructing those wards took everything I'd eaten for the past three days, and every drop of water I had to spare. Usually my feet swell by end of day, but not that evening—I was skin and bones. At least Elizabeth knew where the food was going. I decided not to worry when I saw what the Gunnarssons had sent down: cheeses, venison, fresh bread, bacon, beans, cornmeal, and a sack of ground wheat.

I *think* Marta was joking when she said, "Cook it all up!" but we did eat well that night.

The Tregellases were full of questions, of course, and Marta was patient with them. I was glad of that, because my thoughts were whirling, and I couldn't keep hold of the conversation. A girl desperate enough to take any chance to keep her family from discovering what she'd done . . . 'Course, I don't think Jesse knew how dangerous those plants could be, nor that people who dosed themselves usually died from the infusion. But still, to take such a risk . . . Was there no one else she could have turned to? How about her sister?

No. Jesse belonged to her father until her twenty-first birthday—that was the law. And I'm not sure a bunch of self-righteous old men would have done a thing to him if he'd "happened" to hit his daughter so hard he broke her neck.

An entity that bore malice for living things, but seemed to stalk women . . . *married* women—or at least women who once were married. I wondered if any virgins had been threatened. . . .

Something about it all rang an echo within me, but I couldn't put my finger on it. So I concentrated on johnny-cakes and syrup, letting my mind float down into a swirl of trilling birds and flipping leaves of a book.

That evening some of my unruly thoughts came home to roost. We were winding up for the evening—I won't say things had quieted down, for that never really happened in Twisted Pines. The wind still sobbed, and the footsteps rang too loudly in the lane, but we pointedly ignored it. Marta had heated water for a last cup of peppermint tea, and I was banking the fire for the night.

A soft scratching sound captured my attention. Why this rasp cut through the noise that was increasing outside, I had no idea. It was coming from the door . . . or the threshold, to be specific. I paused, hunched over the green log I'd tossed in the fireplace, my fingers wrapped around the poker.

Marta had also frozen in place. She stood next to the table, motionless as an oak tree, as if consciously waiting for something. Then I saw that her hands, resting lightly on the worn pine surface, were luminescent.

Finally I gathered the nerve to look over my shoulder. A pale mist, like a ground fog, was seeping under the door!

"Marta—" I started hoarsely.

"I see it." The calm in her voice helped me. "Try to stay close to me."

Standing, the poker still clutched in my left hand, I took a step toward Marta. Only a step—what was materializing upon the floor drained my strength away. A tiny, near-human shape was slowly forming before us. Its skin nearly blue, as if deathly cold, the creature had shrunken limbs and chest, the ribs pushing at the skin. Wide eyes stared at Marta as if she was its hope of heaven. It was almost like a little child.

Almost. The thing had claws, not fingers, and fangs as sharp as needles. This was what had killed the widow—had shredded old Nate the peddler.

It was now strong enough to waltz through our ward.

I was as helpless as any of those women had been. What little I'd learned about the Wise Arts would not serve me now. Almost by instinct, I knew I needed to give Marta room, yet be where she could keep her eye on me. It was too late to try to double the ward around us—I just hoped Marta could hold her own against this deceptive demon.

Soundlessly I slid my foot across the sanded boards, moving toward the circle burnt into the floor. If the power of the ancient mother and her immortal son was strong there, it might give me extra protection . . . and not just from the creature. If cold iron failed us, Marta would have to resort to magic, and that could get dangerous fast.

The creature moved inexorably toward Marta, even as I glided into the circle. My suspicions were confirmed when Marta nodded once at me. This was a good place; I sent down a probe and anchored myself in bedrock. Since this was a demon capable of doing physical damage, I wasn't sure running would help. But I wouldn't let it touch my soul—I'd already decided that.

Suddenly the childlike thing shimmered, becoming translucent as morning mist. The creature whirled into a dust devil and threw itself at Marta.

There was a crackle of sparks when it hit her inner ward, like a log shifting in a fireplace. Slashing arms reached from the tiny tornado, the claws coming unnervingly close to Marta's face. She was muttering something under her breath, a continuous flow of sound that failed to shift into language for me. A pale, golden glow kept the thing at bay, although the ward shrank under the onslaught.

I was tingling all over, like you sometimes do right before a thunderstorm. Marta had said this circle was to contain power . . . iron did conduct heat . . .

Marta's inner ward had shrunk to her skin, outlining her dark image like a child dancing before a bonfire. I wasn't sure she could hold it off much longer, but if I was wrong about my guess . . .

Reaching out with the poker, I slashed at the whirling vapor, inches from Marta.

As the circle was again broken, power flooded through me, arcing through the poker, which suddenly burned cherry red. I could scarcely breathe for the heat within my body.

The responding screech must have been heard in Castle Rock. Howling, roaring like an enraged panther, the creature threw itself away from Marta and toward the fireplace. I got ready for flying sticks of wood, but the thing no longer wanted a fight. We'd moved the pot hook to one side to remove the kettle, and the boiling wind took full advantage of the fact. It rose up the chimney in a billow of steam and sparks, and landed shrieking on the chimney, pacing with heavy tread across the shingles.

"Will it set fire to the roof?" I asked quickly.

Marta was remote, her attention elsewhere . . . then she said, "No. The sparks swirled off and went out." For a moment her concentration was intense, focused upon her left hand—then her polished wooden rod appeared in her hand! Beginning to chant in Latin, she went first to the fireplace to push the pot hook back into position and hang the kettle once again. Then she went east, circling like the sun as she repeated portions of her spell at the major compass points. After the fourth recitation, I felt something snap around me, like someone's fingers against my ear. After a graceful bow to the east, Marta reverently laid her rod down in her bag.

Reaching for the teacups, she brought them over to the fireplace and sat down on the floor. "Is your hand all right? And your feet?" she asked conversationally.

I walked over to the fire and carefully laid the cooling poker down on the tiles. Now the time had come—and I was afraid to look. Charred skin didn't hurt at all, it was said. . . . Turning my hand, I saw lines of blisters running from my fingers to the palm. "Just blisters," I answered, lifting up one foot to check the soles of my shoes. Nothing.

"We'll need to keep a pot of water over the banked fire, just for the extra iron."

"And keep that pot hook in place!" I said fervently.

"I'm not sure the hook alone could have stopped it," Marta replied. "It's getting stronger." Fixing me with a firm eye, she said, "Are you ready to tell me why you did that?"

Swallowing slowly and kneeling, I lifted the kettle and poured water into the teapot warming on the tiles. "Your ward had shrunk so quickly, and then that little hesitation . . . I thought you were in trouble. I remembered you said that circle was to contain power—but what if I gave it a path outside the circle? I thought iron would conduct, and protect me—and hurt it. I was careful not to touch your ward." *In for a penny, in for a pound—* "And so far, the thing hasn't touched a virgin. It seemed like a good gamble."

Marta added peppermint leaves to the pot. "Agreed. I was about to start drawing on my taproot for power, which might have weakened the wards elsewhere. I was worried that there might be more than one of the thing."

I must have looked horrified, because she went on quickly, "Oh, I think it's alone, or it would have demanded help from others. But that was the hesitation you saw. Also, to throw it back with power might have caught you in the backlash."

"But you were warded against my backlash," I stated, and was rewarded by her nod.

"Still, you took a chance you didn't realize, woman," Marta said softly. "The power that rushed through you is the same thing that fuels the sun or moves the stars. You could have been fried, just as if by lightning stroke."

With a demon stomping on the roof, I sat cold and alone for a few moments, thinking about dying young and far from home. It's said that Death comes in its own face for a practitioner, the last time . . . some even say the practitioner can ask to go when life becomes too much of a burden. But I hadn't talked about it with Marta, and was glad I hadn't ended up with firsthand experience.

"But when you learned to ground yourself, you learned the lesson well. Your body responded like grounding through a fire. That's impressive channeling, my dear, and it was all instinctive, wasn't it?"

Since I didn't know what she was talking about, I just nodded. Smiling, Marta said, "You have grounding down solidly, Allie." Then her smile faded, and she reached to pour the tea. "It wanted me—it didn't even know you were there until the poker hit it. Everyone who's been attacked was either married or had been, including Old Nate. . . ."

"Did Nate leave children behind him?" I asked, sipping my peppermint tea. Immediately I could feel my stomach start to unwind, and the stomping demon seemed a lot farther away.

"I think I heard him mention a son once," Marta murmured, her eyes on the few flames left in the fireplace. "So you saw the resemblance, too. The question is, was it once a child, did it want to be a child, or does it hate children and those who bring them into the world?" Looking over at me, a frown furling her forehead, she added, "I hope no one has been conjuring demon lovers. A half-demon is a terrible thing to force back into the nether-world. We might have to toss its human parent after it to sever the link to this plane of existence."

Shuddering at the mere thought, I stopped drinking. That memory teased me once more, dangling before me on a printed page. I jumped up and went to my things, digging until I reached *Denizens of the Night*.

"Cousin Elizabeth first heard this thing six years ago," I started, sitting down and placing the book in my lap. "The thing has grown in volume and strength since then. Iron and water did deter it, but it takes more of each as the thing grows stronger. . . . And it ignores virgins . . ." I flipped pages, digging through my many days spent avidly reading the tome. I scarcely noticed when the light improved tenfold as Marta lit her candelabra and brought it near.

Finally I reached the page, which I was now convinced I'd daydreamed about at dinner. I touched a paragraph. "This one." There was a tremor in my voice when I spoke aloud, and no wonder.

There was no guaranteed way to get rid of an *utburd*.

Marta reviewed the little bit written about a very rare and dangerous ghost. Then I heard her whisper, "I'm afraid you may be right."

● ● ●

An *utburd* was a legacy of the demon-haunted Norse lands. Both the best and the worst of a culture traveled, and nightmares had followed our ancestors. The word was very old Norse, meaning literally "child carried outside." Back in the old country, when a sickly child was born into a family that already had too many mouths to feed, or to a woman with no husband to provide for the infant, it was often exposed.

Sun-Return had never had a child left outside, as far as I knew—we were usually a prosperous community, and the one drought we had had so far in my lifetime had been made up by a bumper crop the next year. But other places were not so lucky, so fruitful.

And justified though the parents might feel, sacrificing a child who would die anyway to the health of its siblings, the spirit of the child might not see it that way. Hence the danger of an *utburd* rising. They build strength for years following their exposure, waiting for vengeance against those who caused their deaths. Sometimes invisible, sometimes a black dog or a snowy owl, sometimes a phantom child . . . capable of becoming a wisp of pipe smoke or a whirlwind the size of a tornado.

But an *utburd* could rage on generations after its parents were buried, waylaying travelers and ripping them to shreds. Water and iron could deter it, with a stout heart, but how . . . ?

"What are we going to do?" I whispered in turn.

Marta was silent a long time. Then she said, "A haunt is often laid when what bothers them is revealed—in this case, finding the body and giving it a public burial."

I stared at her. "One tiny corpse on a mountaintop?"

"Somehow we have to find out who bore the child and abandoned it," Marta said firmly.

Then something occurred to me. "It can't be Jesse's baby; that hasn't been born yet. The widow?"

"I thought to ask," Marta replied. "All hers lived but one, who came early and died."

"Then that shouldn't be it," I muttered. "It's as if it blames the entire town for its death."

"Not so farfetched when public opinion rules a community. A sickly child can cast a pall over the marriage prospects of an entire family," Marta reminded me. "And there are houses here with very old, basic wards on them. It's possible the *utburd* didn't have the strength to penetrate those old defenses."

We sat and thought for a while, and then Marta said heavily, "There's no help for it. Tomorrow we must go to every single household and announce what haunts the town. We must ask people to come forward—privately, if necessary, we can deal with that—and tell us of exposed newborns and babies.

"A ghost is tied to its past, Allie, and haunts what it knows. That skeleton is somewhere in Twisted Pines."

We called a meeting for noon the next day. The Tregellas boys were pressed into service once again, and thoroughly enjoyed charging down the road pursuing their "mission." I was especially glad to hear their shouts, because it had been a subdued and white-faced group of people who had flung open their door when we knocked that morning.

"We thought it had got you," was all Gavin Tregellas could say. Our run-in with the demon had proven just as noisy as I'd feared, because people began creeping into Twisted Pines before the sun was high in the sky.

When the time came, a clanging bell called us to the town meeting house. It didn't look like much of a church to me—too Spartan. Our own church was surely the starkest Catholic mission for many miles, since we shared it with other folks, but at least it had a cross behind the pulpit. This single room had pews, but nothing else to imply the greater power.

I couldn't imagine either Father John or the Reverend Jonathan Robertson preaching here. Maybe Cousin Elizabeth was right—maybe God had forsaken Twisted Pines. . . .

Or maybe people just thought that was the case.

Marta didn't waste any time once the meeting was called to order. Mr. Gunnarsson was in charge, of course, as the wealthiest landholder, despite the fact that he hadn't a clue as to what was going on. He got up and laboriously thanked everyone for coming so promptly. Then he introduced Marta and said that she would have an announcement as soon as Mr. Elwood was finished with a prayer. To think that this town had once been so prosperous it had a full-time rector!

Well, this skinny fellow in black stood up, and I clamped down on my lower lip to keep from laughing. I'd heard people say of a man, "He should have been a cleric," when he was gangly or shy and awkward. But now I understood the phrase. Mr. Elwood was long-jawed and his ears stuck out like wings. He had a kind, sad face rising over that cleric's collar, but when he opened his mouth, I knew we were in trouble.

Mr. Elwood had lost his faith. How I could tell that simply by the sound of his voice, I can't tell you, but I knew it was the truth. The man was putting up a brave front, but I suspected the haunting of his town had done something to him. The quiver in his loud whisper announced that he expected the end of the world at any moment, and he wasn't sure he was ready to go.

Nerves made the minister run on for a time, but he finally wound down to the "Amen." Marta was on her feet before the fellow had closed his mouth.

"Thank you, Mr. Elwood," Marta said briskly. She turned from her seat in the front pew and faced the packed crowd. Mr. Gunnarsson's attempt to catch her eye was ignored, and *I* certainly wasn't going to stop her.

"We have gathered here today to give you a bit of good news," she went on. "We have discovered what is haunting Twisted Pines." A murmur broke out at this, but Marta went right on speaking. "Knowing what is causing the problem is the first step toward solving it. But I warn you—what is facing this community is very dangerous." She paused then, until silence had returned to the hall. "It cannot be laid by exorcism. It cannot be driven back to the netherworld, for this world is its home. And there is no guarantee that if it succeeds in taking its revenge, it will leave the town in peace. These things have been known to haunt a place for generations."

Marta glanced my way briefly, and then looked out over the audience. I understood her meaning. Earlier we had discussed telling the townspeople. Marta wanted me to watch one half of the room, to see if there were any changes of expression when she announced the demon's kind. Marta was now facing the other half of the gathering.

"Among the people of the Norse lands, this demon was known as an *utburd*. For those of you raised in a different tradition, I should explain that an *utburd* is the ghost of a newborn child that was left exposed to the elements and died, usually unnamed and without baptism."

The whispers began again. And among those whispers, I heard a tiny gasp. It was no more than an inhaling cut short, but I heard it. Pinning down its location, now—that would be something else. But it was from my side.

"An *utburd* returns in strength," Marta went on relentlessly. "It grows in power and in fury. What vigor it lacked in its brief life is made up tenfold in its afterlife. Last night it attacked me. I was able to turn it aside with my apprentice's help. Next time I may have to drive it away. I might have to blow the mountaintop off the face of the earth to do it."

Total silence. Off in the distance, I could hear a dog barking.

"I see two possible solutions to this problem," Marta finally said. "One is to abandon the town. The *utburd* will not leave the region of its birth. If you relocated the town a day's ride from here, my professional opinion is that the creature would not follow you. The provincial governor has funds at his disposal for relocation in case of Indian trouble. If I spoke to the practitioner on staff, chances are good you would each get some seed money to start over. But of course it would not be the value of the land you have cleared and worked."

"I, for one, have no intention of abandoning my home," Mr. Gunnarsson said abruptly, his big voice rumbling. "What is the other option?"

Without blinking an eye, Marta said, "I must know about every child born in this region in the past seven years. One of them has not been laid to rest sufficiently. If we can properly inter the body, there is a good chance the *utburd* will diminish and return to its sleep."

"Properly inter?" the rector asked.

"A proper casket, and rites, and a funeral," Marta said succinctly.

"Then you'll need to know the name of the family involved," came Tregellas's slow voice.

"*I'll* need to know," Marta agreed. "I don't know that it's necessary for anyone else to know. I will be in the east woods, gathering herbs, if anyone has any information for me." Fixing a flinty eye on the group, she added, "Generations of haunting, men and women of Twisted

Pines. If you wish to hear folks calling you Cloudcatcher once again before your great-grandchildren are born, then we must act quickly, before this creature destroys your town and kills every adult in it." Nodding toward me, Marta walked down the aisle and out the crowded doorway, confident that I'd follow.

Almost running to catch up, I asked, "Now what?"

"We wait," she said calmly. "And we plan. I think we'll need to prepare a great spell to ward the burial ground. One way or another, it will all end there. Let's get home and check for mail."

Marta must have felt the stir when the letter came our way, because sure enough, there was a folded piece of parchment lying in the center of the burnt circle. Before she'd even removed her hat, Marta took out her black-handled knife, her *athame,* whispered a spell in Latin at the east side of the circle, and made a slicing motion. Only then did she reach in and remove the letter.

Looking over at me, she said, "The knife cuts the web and lets the power that arrived with the letter drain off into the wards of the house."

"So each use of the circle strengthens the wards?" I asked.

Opening the letter, Marta murmured, "Not exactly. Each arrival returns the power that was used for the sending. Power cannot be created or destroyed, only changed in form. You can borrow it, but each act changes the balance of energy within the web of the world." Closing the parchment, she tossed it on the worn table. "He left five days ago. His great-uncle was ill, and then died. Boy stayed to bury the man properly. Told Eve that he was going home to fetch his bride."

Grinning, I said, "Hope it's Jesse."

"Probably," Marta agreed. "But we'll let him tell his own tale. He could arrive as soon as tonight, if he has a

good animal. If Miss Gunnarsson comes by, just tell her
he's on his way home."

Nodding my agreement, I bent over to stir up the fire.
The bright golden days of the harvest had turned to silver, and there was definitely a chill in the air. Soon we'd
be in wool all the time.

"So when do we ward the church and cemetery?" I
asked.

"Late this afternoon," Marta replied absently. "We'll
need some fresh greenery—I want to trace the circle in
protective plants." As if dazed, she slowly moved things
off the table, setting them carefully next to the circle.
"Let's get started, Allie."

The first family came forward before we had found either
mistletoe or holly. The man who approached us among
the protection of the pines was older than Gavin
Tregellas—or looked it. He removed his battered tri-
cornered hat and smoothed back thinning hair.
"Wizards? I've come to talk about lost children."

Interesting way to put it, I thought, but didn't say a
word. I was wearing my breeches and didn't want to attract
much attention. Marta ushered the man to a fallen log.

"You know that the mountain's a chancy place to live,
unless you have cows or goats like the Gunnarssons," he
said without preamble.

"Indeed it can be, Mr . . . ?" Marta prompted gently.

"Just call me Jeb, everyone does," was the brisk reply.
He twisted his hat in his hands a time or two, and then
said, "A couple of years back, we had a child born
wrong."

"Wrong," Marta repeated. "You mean breech?"

"No," he said quickly, shaking his head. "Twisted, his
spine all messed up. He didn't move around hardly at

all—no swinging his hands or anything. It was our third year of bad weather, and we were in hock for everything to the Gunnarssons."

Marta simply nodded her head. There was no judgment in her face, only sympathetic listening. Encouraged by her thoughtful face, the man continued, "We talked about it, Martha and I, and we decided we couldn't do it; we just couldn't take care of a child that might never walk when we were scarcely holding body and soul together. That was the year we ate johnnycake and molasses for an entire summer. Scarcely a bean to our name. Winter was coming up fast. So . . ." He shifted his feet and looked beyond us toward the village.

"You . . . left him unattended?" The man nodded unhappily. "And after he died?"

"I built a little oak box for him," Jeb said softly. "We lined it with the blanket Martha had made—she always makes at least one new thing for a baby—and dressed him in new clothes. Then we called the preacher to come say the right things, and we buried him in our plot behind the house. With the two we lost to the putrid fever." His voice husky, the man whispered, "We didn't mean to make trouble for the town, ma'am. We just knew that babe would break us, and we already had five to feed and clothe."

But no lack of respect . . . That new baby gown and blanket were a form of wealth, and they'd freely given it to the dead. I let my gaze flick Marta's way.

"I don't think your son is the one doing the haunting, Jeb," my aunt said gently. "You honored your dead, and that generally keeps an *utburd* from forming. Did you mark the grave?"

He nodded vigorously. "Little crosses for all three of them. Names and years—we named the twisted one Matthew, for my grandfather."

"Thank you for telling us about this, Jeb," Marta said seriously. "I don't think there'll be any reason for others to know of this."

"If we'd thought he had a chance—any chance at all—we wouldn't have done it," the man mumbled. "But he wasn't hardly moving. What kind of life would he have if he couldn't move at all?"

"That's not for me to say, Jeb. You'll have to talk to the Most High about it," Marta said simply. "I'd go home and pray for your children, both the ones with you and the three you've lost."

"Yes, wizard." He stood and nodded respectfully to both of us, and then walked off into the dense forest with scarcely a rustle of dry needles.

"If we're lucky, we won't have to disinter any bodies to verify stories," Marta murmured to me.

People gotta do what's needful to give their children the best chance they can. But I was glad I didn't have that decision on my conscience.

That little one was only the beginning. By midafternoon we'd heard from two other families about two other infants who didn't survive their first se'nnight. One babe simply came too soon and never got the hang of breathing. The other? Well, it sounded a bit like pneumonia, but we'd never really know.

None seemed like a good candidate for an *utburd*. And none of the families had been sitting on my side of the meeting house. Someone was holding back.

There was time yet . . . a few days, maybe, before Marta would give up and leave, advising the townsfolk to do the same. In the meantime, we'd found mistletoe and holly near the road into town, and we'd need some before nightfall.

• • •

Because an *utburd* is strongest after dark, we'd assumed that we were safe during daylight.

Assuming is a dangerous thing to do.

I was perched in an oak tree cutting mistletoe when the black dog appeared. It was as big as a goat, and its yellow eyes looked like living flame. The ghost dogs people spoke of were nothing next to it.

The creature didn't hesitate. It bounded toward Marta, who was trimming holly branches, and as it ran it belled, its voice echoing off the great trunks surrounding us. I promise you, the sound would have quailed the Gabriel Rachets.

We didn't need to summon Death; Death had come for us.

NINETEEN

MARTA'S HEAD SNAPPED UP and her hands rose in a defensive position. The huge knife was still in her right hand, for which I was grateful. This time I could see her personal ward take effect, lining her body like moonlight.

"Stay in the tree!" she yelled as the *utburd* knocked her into the brush.

My heart was flying like a windmill in a rainstorm, and I hung on so tightly the bark of the tree tore at my hands. Now I understood what people meant by "an agony of indecision." I could stay in the tree and maybe be overlooked, or I could jump into the melee and maybe be torn apart. Somehow I didn't think throwing mistletoe was going to help.

In the midst of all this, the sound of a Kentucky flintlock sizzled beneath the canopy of the forest. Acrid smoke rose to my nostrils, masking the scent of pine. Straining to see through the dense treetops, I spied a tall, slender human dressed in heavy wool breeches and a stained buckskin tunic running toward our small glade.

He was rushing to his death, and I might never know why. One deep breath, and then I started down the branches.

The *utburd* had staggered at the impact of the bullet, allowing Marta to roll out from under it. Now flames erupted from her body, driving the creature back several steps. Startled but undeterred, the *utburd* turned its shaggy head, the glowing eyes alighting on the newcomer.

A born woodsman, that one—he was ramming another bullet down the barrel of his rifle even as he ran. The gesture was useless. Another hit might knock the beast off its feet, but it wouldn't penetrate the body. Lead could not hurt an *utburd*.

I missed a handhold and fell several feet, catching myself on the lowest branch. No one—and nothing—noticed.

Something slowed the man's steps; the glowing eyes, perhaps, or a woman burning without being consumed. The creature favored the hunter with a long, purposeful stare, and then dissolved into smoke. A dust devil of wind swirled away, dissipating even as we watched.

Marta's fire petered away, leaving her unscathed by the flames. The young stranger stood his ground, facing her, uncertainty in every move he made.

"Now that was interesting," Marta said aloud. "What are you, that a demon runs from your presence?"

"Demon?" the man said weakly. "There is a demon in Twisted Pines?"

"I didn't call that meeting this morning for my health," Marta went on dryly. "Granted, it hasn't bothered anyone that we know of during the day, but I did mention the *utburd* was getting stronger."

"Utburd?" After a long silence, the stranger said, "The wailing, then . . . You are a practitioner, yes?" There was just a hint of accent to his voice, a strange framing of vowels.

Wincing at the pain, I dusted off my sore hands on my breeches and walked right up to him. He was younger than I'd thought, no more than twenty years, surely, and with a pretty face. Without much ado I set my left hand on his exposed wrist.

It startled him—he jumped like a spooked deer. Recognition grew in me, and I said the first thing that came to my head: "You're the father of the boy Jesse's carrying."

Dark eyes narrowing, the youth tilted his head, surveying first me in my breeches and then Marta, tall and impressive, her practitioner's necklace visible. "I am Richard La Croix," he said slowly. "I live with my father and older brother on a farm east of here. Much has happened since I left to see my mother's uncle, yes?"

"A great deal," Marta agreed. "If you'll let me get a few more sprigs of holly, we'll tell you all about it. I am Mistress Donaltsson, and this is Miss Sorensson," she added as she reached once again for the holly bush. "We are here to lay the *utburd* of Twisted Pines."

With the utmost respect, La Croix gave a slight bow. "I have returned to claim Jesse Gunnarsson as my bride. We have a stake for our future. My uncle has passed on, and he left everything to me, his namesake." Pulling himself up straight, La Croix added, "Let Gunnarsson keep his wealth—thanks to my uncle, we need none of it." With a nod, the youth indicated he would fetch his horse.

In the meantime, I stifled my sigh and crawled back into the oak. Not without rocky nerves . . . my heart was still racing like a sluice at a mill. *I* didn't know how to burn at will.

Not yet.

"This is not a good idea," I muttered, but neither Marta nor La Croix paid any attention to me. Since I wasn't sure anyone else was watching for signs of that black dog, I kept a sharp eye out for any odd movements. Nothing strange tickled my inner senses, but I wasn't taking chances.

I freely admit I'd hoped for a bath, after tumbling through a forest all afternoon. But once he'd heard our tale, Richard La Croix was hot to confront Gunnarsson, and he wanted us as witnesses. Although I commended his intentions, I did not think my appearance added to our strength. For some people, a woman in dirty breeches might overwhelm the senses.

And it was entirely too close to sundown. If the thing had the strength to attack during the day, then the night would be beyond imagining. . . .

The house on the hill dozed in the late afternoon light, deceptively peaceful. Strange that such a lovely home was so cold within. But when I caught sight of Gunnarsson's portrait, rising above the dining room fireplace, I knew that no fire built within these walls would ever warm the folks living at Lone Oak Farm. The Gunnarssons were frozen to the marrow, and I wasn't sure there was a cure for it.

It wasn't a time for thinking. I knocked the mud from my boots and followed Marta down the long corridor of the main house.

The young maid who escorted us into the wainscoted sitting room vanished into the shadows like a wisp of smoke, leaving us to face the family. Jesse kept her eyes resolutely upon the needlework in her lap, but her rosy cheeks betrayed her joy. In contrast was Mrs. Gunnarsson, dressed in vivid blue with a lace-trimmed scarf about her shoulders but pale and listless, her eyes like a wounded animal's. And of course the lord of the manor, elegant in his old coat with braid trim, irritation written over every inch of him.

Gunnarsson's gaze touched and dismissed me, passed over Richard La Croix as if he wasn't present, and settled upon Marta. "How can I help you, Mrs. Donaltsson?" he asked in his gravelly voice. There was a slight edge to the tone.

"By listening to Mr. La Croix, squire," was her grave response. "He has something of import to say."

"Mr. La Croix seems to have forgotten how to dress for a gentleman's sitting room," was all Gunnarsson said aloud, but hostility rimmed the words. Lord forgive me, I did *not* like the man.

Unlike Jesse, Richard La Croix did not blush. He looked more like white marble. Nodding briefly, La Croix drew himself up like a military man. "I return from my uncle Richard's funeral. His illness was swift, for which we may thank the Lord. He has honored me by making me his heir. Twenty-five hundred acres of rich valley soil, with a stream, orchards, and good bloodstock. A two-story framed house and outbuildings are part of the farm, and seven hundred pounds completes my inheritance."

"What has this windfall to do with me?" Gunnarsson said tersely.

You'd think the *utburd* was building within this house, the tension was so thick. I let my gaze slide over to the tall window casings, where I could see the light of a sun nearly touching the horizon.

"I have made no secret of my admiration for Miss Gunnarsson," La Croix went on.

"And your admiration for the wealth she will inherit upon my death," Gunnarsson almost spat out. He was keeping his body still, but his skin was growing mighty flushed, and his eyes had narrowed.

"Keep your wealth," the youth said with convincing disdain. "She is her own dowry. I will take her with none, and settle money upon her, if necessary."

Gunnarsson didn't answer at first—too angry to speak, I suspected—and I got real worried. Plus the sun was setting! Whatever was Marta thinking of, to have us come here so close to darkness?

"How sharper than a serpent's tooth," Gunnarsson

murmured, throwing a quick look at his daughter. "I feed and clothe her, raise her in luxury, make plans to send her East to spend time with her aunt—and I discover this." With two strides, he was standing before Jesse. "Tell me you know nothing of this!"

Jesse physically shrank into herself, trying to swallow with a throat I had no doubt had gone dry. "I must marry someone, Papa," she said timidly.

"An uneducated Frenchie? A Papist? Have you lost your mind? And I thought your sister was crazy! At least she chose a young man who worships the Lord in a civilized tongue!" The sitting room door opened behind us, but I had no intention of turning around. I knew better than to turn my back on a dangerous animal.

"In your aunt's house you could be presented to the cream of Eastern society! Do you think she has any interest in hosting the wife of a farmer?" Gunnarsson was past the point of polite discussion; this was rage, pure and simple.

"My aunt invited me, before the birth of Susannah prevented me from traveling," came a woman's voice. "The invitation still stands, with or without the children, once they can manage on their own."

This time I did hazard a glance. The dark-haired woman standing in the doorway did not have the lace shawl that was still popular among the women of Twisted Pines. Her clothing was closer to Jesse's empire-waisted muslin, although made of good wool. The indomitable gray irises marked her as Jesse's elusive older sister. Hovering in the background was a tall, blond man with a broad, high-cheekboned face and gentle eyes. This fellow did not slavishly follow the squire's lead in fashion, but his garments were certainly finer than La Croix's.

"You think your cow midwife will pay for the clothing you'd need for a sojourn among your grandmother's class?" This was shouted, and I winced away from the big man.

"I might," said the newcomer, though it sounded more like "Eye mite," the weighted words of an educated Scotsman.

"I told you never to set foot in this house again," Gunnarsson said, in his anger spacing the words carefully.

"I needed to speak to the practitioner," was Nan Gunnarsson McGyver's calm answer.

As she turned toward Marta, Gunnarsson stepped forward and seized her arm. "I will have no whore under my roof!"

A sinewy hand moved with the speed of a snake, clamping down on Gunnarsson's wrist and squeezing until the older man gasped soundlessly and released his daughter. "I'll have you keep your hands—and your thoughts—to yourself, sir," McGyver said softly. "You may speak as you please, but lay either hand or ill word upon my wife at your peril."

It was then that Mrs. Gunnarsson's whisper penetrated a deepening silence. "You were a fool to demand perfection in your children. You should have known they would rebel—they have your stubbornness, after all."

"Hush, woman," Gunnarsson muttered, still rubbing his wrist and glaring at McGyver.

A deep, harsh sob was her reply as she pressed a wisp of linen to her lips. "Your anger has led us all to this fate, and I hope God curses you for it, as I do!" The intensity of her words could have etched glass. Tears began trickling down her cheeks, and her body shook like a leaf in high wind. Jesse dropped her needlepoint and rushed to her side.

"It will be all right, Mother," she said soothingly, putting her arms around the woman. Outside, a gust of wind against the house put the lie to Jesse's words, and the sound of running footsteps hurried up the stone pathway.

"I did not know!" Mrs. Gunnarsson shrieked. "Or I would have fought for you!" The woman crumpled, folding over on herself, as Marta moved to help Jesse support her mother.

"Have your servant bring the tisane for her," Marta said in a tone that brooked no nonsense, and Gunnarsson pushed past his unwanted son-in-law and into the corridor.

I was trying to keep my pounding heart under control, and had crossed my arms over my chest to hold myself together. I'd never imagined . . . I mean, I knew there were families with stricter parents than my own. I knew that some folks yelled at their children. But this . . . this *hate* in the voices. I could almost see Mrs. Gunnarsson's words floating in the air, waiting for the squire to put one foot wrong.

Such a curse could follow a man to his death.

Still, all the anger had not kept me from hearing the words . . . or the spaces between the words. I turned slightly and looked at Nan McGyver. "Was your mother speaking of you or your sister?" It was only a guess, but I suspected it was a good one.

Pale but steady on her feet, Nan McGyver nodded once, as if conceding something to me. "It seems we think the same, Mother and I," she started slowly. "Six years ago Tom Whitman threw me over for a Marcotte girl down Fort Pontchartrain way. A tidy dowry, I've heard, and no bull of a father guarding girl or gold." This was clipped, but it was the tightness of old shame, not current anger. Her flinching was for the wail beyond the walls, not for her own words.

Then Nan looked away from me, her throat visibly

tightening. "But I was pregnant. I still had fading bruises from the last beating Papa had given me. . . . I didn't think I'd survive what would happen when he found out. Either way the child was dead. At least it would die at the hands of someone who loved it."

"You . . . lost it?" I asked carefully.

Her face smooth, Nan caught my gaze and held it. "Nature did not oblige, so I tried an old remedy I'd heard whispered about, a tea of mistletoe leaves—"

"Mistletoe!" I shrieked, all thoughts of Nan's father returning gone straight out of my head. "Lord and Lady of Light, woman, praise be you didn't use the berries. You'd be a corpse yourself."

"I nearly was," she whispered. "My heart pounded like a drum for days, and I bled so much Mother would not let the leech touch me. But the babe had come fast, out in the woods—in deep snow," she added softly. "I barely made it home. When I finally had the strength to return . . . to bury the remains, everything was gone."

Not surprising, in the midst of winter. Nature wasted nothing.

"That was it. I never even told Jesse why I'd been so ill," Nan added, looking over at her now-pale sister, who'd heard enough of the tale despite Mrs. Gunnarsson's weeping. "By summer Davin had asked me to marry him. I was so happy." She looked back at me. "I think God has forgiven my sin—has he not given me two healthy children? My father can keep his coin. I have found someone worth more than words can say."

I'd kept an eye on McGyver during Nan's little speech. He'd run the gauntlet of surprise, horror, and then a strange calm. When Nan finally found the courage to look over at him, he reached to take her hands. "Why didn't you tell me, lass? We could have raised it as our own."

Whatever Nan might have said to this magnificent

statement was overwhelmed by the sudden shrieking of the *utburd*. It was loud enough that I covered my ears. Gunnarson didn't notice—he was too busy shouting himself. Marta and Jesse were busy pouring a tisane into Mrs. Gunnarsson, and simply had to bear the sound. The little maid cowered, however, and Richard La Croix was clutching his rifle again, looking for a target.

"It won't do any good, Mr. La Croix," I said in his ear. "Lead can't stop it. You startled it once, but it'll be ready this time. I can't think why it didn't—"

And then I could. The *utburd* was almost certainly untimely born from that dose of mistletoe tea. La Croix and Jesse Gunnarsson could have been reliving that same story—except that Richard La Croix came back for his girl. I rather thought Richard would have Jesse in the end, even if he had to spirit her away by night. What I'd seen of Gunnarsson told me he wouldn't bother following; he'd simply disinherit the girl.

Which meant a tiny baby boy would be born to parents who wanted him. Could the *utburd* somehow respect that, consider them untouchable by its fury, even as it seemed uninterested in virgins?

Gunnarsson had thrown open the door to the hallway and was striding toward the massive entranceway. Most of his shouting was masked by the howling of the *utburd,* but I could pick out "whore of Babylon" and "cause of all our trials and sorrows" among the threats and obscenities.

The build of pressure within the house was neither my imagination nor my inner senses. Something pushed me to follow the squire, and as I stepped into the long corridor my ears popped. Suddenly a nausea of fear ran down my bones like water and pooled in my stomach. Could it be a twister? It was late in the year for one, but an *utburd* could change all the weather patterns.

The candles branching from the wall blew out in a swirl of smoke and sparks. A great gust struck me in the face, causing me to stumble. Wind? Where was the wind—

"Don't open the door!" I screamed at the man, heedless of his turning his strength on me, but it was too late. Now Gunnarsson was trying to keep the door from blowing out of his fierce grip.

"If the misbegotten thing wants the mother who killed it, then it's welcome to come and have her!" Gunnarsson shrieked.

Seizing one of the carved banisters of the staircase, I clung for dear life and turned away from the punishing gale. Marta had sternly warned every family not to open doors or windows between dusk and dawn, for fear of unbalancing the spells of protection. "Don't breach the wards!" I yelled, but he was clearly beyond hearing, maybe beyond reason. I had no idea what myth he'd spun to himself about his family, but the knowledge of a daughter not only marrying against his will but casting off a love child had pushed him beyond common sense.

Gunnarsson turned and braced himself in the door frame, a hulking figure reshaping wind and blocking rain. "If it doesn't kill her, I will!" he roared. "I'll bury my hard-earned gold before I leave it to such children! How do you invite a demon to take its lawful prey?"

"Not like this!" I pushed my shoulder through a set of posts to hold myself in place while I moved along the bottom of the handrail to the next banister. Gods and angels, where was Marta? There was no circle of protection, and Lone Oak was so far from the other houses I wasn't sure the wards would link properly.

Releasing one hand, Gunnarsson managed a single step onto the large columned porch. "Come, then, life out of time! The one who caused your death is here! Spare the rest of my foolish family, but unrepentant murder requires an eye for an eye!"

The sound had built to the roar of a thunderstorm, as if the mother of winds was rushing down the mountainside. Terror was fluttering wildly in my chest, but I didn't know what to do. There was no way I was going to get to that door before Gunnarsson walked right on out, and even if I did, how could I haul back such a big man?

Then nothing mattered anymore.

Gunnarsson gave a ragged gasp, as if he was choking or his heart had stabbed him. His hand dropped from the door frame, and he crumpled into a pile sprawled across the threshold.

I was only a couple of arms' lengths away, maybe three, and feeling wildly for something to anchor me on my way to the man, when a funnel of wind touched down on the porch.

Clasping the banisters with everything I had left, I hid my face against the wood and prayed to every God I'd ever known.

And the wind stopped blowing through the hallway.

I was so surprised I almost let go, but my body had better sense. Peeping over one shoulder, I saw Marta outlined in pale silver light, her hands raised as if in invocation. Her face was serene, her necklace wound down her left arm, her right hand offering a huge, glowing coal to the tempest beyond. I couldn't make out the chant over the noise outside, but it didn't matter. I knew better than to mimic something I didn't understand.

The door began to close. Slowly, even ponderously, the heavy oak and brass portal seemed to close in on itself. I looked to see if Gunnarsson had been pushed back inside by the wind, but there was no sign of him.

It was a moment hung in eternity—never before had time seemed *motionless*. Then I heard the fancy door

latch click and the bolt slide home. The *utburd* was outside, and we were in. We were safe . . . for the moment.

The glowing light vanished, followed by a dull thud.
Sudden exhaustion almost pulled me off the banisters. I
heard Marta whisper faintly, "Feed everyone," and I knew
that she'd collapsed. *Food* . . . she must have drawn on
the entire household.

Later, come the dawning, we'd bury what was left of
Gunnarsson.

Nan stopped before an oddly shaped rock, narrow and
curved from a wind-worn hole. Touching it lightly, she
said, "This is the place."

I sighed, but I managed to keep it to myself. *I can't do
this,* I thought wildly, looking around the dappled oak
glade. The depth of shadows in the first light of morning
was not comforting, and the cloud of our breath gave
everything a misty halo.

You can, came the faint tickle of Marta's thoughts.

But I don't know the ritual to create a circle! was my
indignant response. *I'm not an initiate!* Marta had been
much too tired for me to argue about the situation, but
that didn't mean I wouldn't speak my mind before getting
et by a demon.

*You are a virgin, and you have my necklace. For this
spell, in this time and place, you need nothing else.*
Marta's thoughts were as heavy as the linked chain
around my neck. She'd even given me the large piece of
coal she'd compressed in her hand the night before . . .
now a tiny, flawless diamond. I reached into my pocket to
touch this evidence of a great deed.

"I wish we could just look for the bones," I murmured
aloud.

"Think how tiny the bones of our fingers are," Nan

said slowly. "I can't imagine finding the bones of a newborn."

Or younger. But I didn't say that aloud. Nan was already dealing with her father's death, her mother's collapse, and the ghost she had brought upon her birthplace. She'd had six years to carry the guilt of this deed—I didn't need to bring up what was staring her in the face.

"The spell will make them glow," I reminded her. "It's still dark enough that we may get lucky and find everything here."

"Let's start, then," she whispered. "We may not have another night."

Nodding, I wound my fingers into the two necklaces I was wearing, the diamond clenched in my right hand. No point in using Marta's rod or knife—she'd made those tools, and they would respond only to her.

The spell was a specific request for light. There was only one real problem, as far as I saw things. Performing this without a circle meant asking the Goddess to handle those details for you.

Did I believe—truly believe—in a Mother Goddess?

Nan had retreated to give me room, taking our baskets with her. Back at Lone Oak, Jesse was sitting at her mother's bedside while she quilted the satin lining for a tiny casket. All I had to do was find those bones—without offending Nan with my rite. Marta had told me to be humble and sincere. . . .

I felt insignificant enough to be *very* humble.

Holy Mother of us all, I whispered within, *Lady of infinite mercy, She who opens and closes the Great Doors, who holds bunting, veil, and shroud in Her gentle hands, whose strength spans worlds and time*—I took a quick breath—*help me in my need. A soul is lost, and must be led back to this side of life. I cannot guard myself, save*

You stand at the doors. I cannot find this soul, save You point the way. I cannot solve this crisis, save by Your leave.

By that time I could feel myself shake with the intensity of my fear. Hoping Nan hadn't noticed that I'd started to sweat, I prayed for help from something—anything of the Light. *Lady who is the font of the cycles, answer my call. Goddess whom I do not know, yet will serve—as children are sacred to You, help this child.*

Would She know whether I meant the *utburd* or myself?

Did I know?

My answer began as the dull glow of a pipe, and broadened into flickering licks of flame, much like will o' the wisps. But these ghost candles did not scurry away when we came close; they were stationary.

In the shredded mulch of years past, bones peeped out from the litter of the forest floor. Tiny bones, as small as a bird's, as white as marble. Not split, any of them . . . too small for that, I guess. But they were definitely present, if wildly scattered.

It seemed it was not so important that I believed in the Goddess, as long as She believed in me. *Thank you, Lady,* I breathed into the stillness of my mind.

Perhaps it was my imagination, but while we searched I felt a great, brooding maternal presence hovering over the glade.

It was a comfort to me.

I confess I was a nervous wreck the entire day. It took us until well into the afternoon to find all the two hundred and more bones. To be honest, I was grateful to be looking for clean bone and not the bloody pieces of Gunnarsson. McGyver, La Croix, and the servants of

Lone Oak took care of that duty, for which I was profoundly grateful.

We had to finish before sunset. I don't know why I was so sure of this, but I could not shake the feeling that the *utburd* was not finished with us. Many might say that the true cause of its death was now dead—for I had no doubt Gunnarsson would have killed the baby, and Nan too, if he'd found out she was increasing—but Nan lived, and the *utburd*'s father still lived, if in another town.

The society that decreed its death had been soundly punished, stretched to the edge of sanity. Was it enough?

Marta slept the day away, looking like a fever victim given another chance at life. That had been a mighty spell, on the spur of the moment—I still didn't know just how she'd done it. I was grateful for Elizabeth's constant attention to Marta, waking her at intervals and forcing soup and bread upon her. Marta had told me how to ask the Mother for help—she expected me to take care of things.

Somehow, I would.

The sun was low in a cloudy sky when everything was in readiness. A fresh pine box, the sap still oozing from its knots, had been lined for Gunnarsson. It was the full six feet and some he'd been in life—we'd not deny him that dignity. But the six men who carried it were for tradition only; like the tiny casket next to it, there was little weight involved.

Every person in Twisted Pines turned out for the funeral. Two graves had already been dug, up on the highest hill of the cemetery, a balding meadow where cattle and goats often grazed. Folks honored the dead with their mourning clothes and their church finest, somber in the fading light.

There was terror there, too—barely veiled horror. Several women—and one man—had had to be dragged out of their homes, and were being held in place. No one had missed the implications of the previous night's attack. Either this funeral worked, or we were fresh out of ideas.

I couldn't blame them for their fear. I was frightened myself. Marta was barely strong enough to walk to the cemetery with us. She could have nothing to do with any power that was needed this night.

Maybe power wouldn't be needed.

No time for a wake, no time for mourning or tradition . . . the life of a town was at stake. As Marta and I walked up that last hill with the Tregellas family, I let my eyes settle on the Reverend Elwood, who stood at the head of the open graves.

He looked very dignified in his black robe, but his eyes were a bit wild. Nary a look did he spare for anyone around him. A poor excuse for a preacher, was Mr. Elwood, but Squire Gunnarsson had been his patron, and it was his place to give the service.

What could you say about a man who had abused his wife and daughters, about an unborn spirit that had killed?

Somebody actually got up the courage to sing a hymn, and the crowd slowly joined in. It was a very old tune, with several verses, and I hoped folks would last to the final stanza.

A soaring, trilling run of notes wove through the singing, almost echoing off the hillside. Looking around quickly in the velvet dusk of Frost, I didn't see a single bird. I prayed for that waxing moon to fight its way through the clouds.

As if someone had heard me, silver light poured out of the sky across the barren hill. At a chirp of glittering notes I turned completely around, forgetting all about the crowd.

The sight struck me speechless.

It wasn't a bird. Tall, taller than I was, which was saying something, and as white as fresh snowfall. Its rack of antlers claimed it was full-grown, and then some. Like a stag, yet I'd never seen a stag that big, with that type of rack. Soft, crooning sounds came from its throat, and I took a step forward.

A hand tightened on my forearm. *Let him come to you,* came Marta's mind-whisper.

Why was she so sure it was a he? I waited, part of me aware that the hymn went on. Did no one else see this creature?

It came within a few steps of us, its gaze fastened on my face. Although its eyes were as dark as any deer's, tiny flickers of light danced in them, like a fire seen from miles away. Without thinking, I held out my left palm to the great stag.

Keep your hand flat, like giving carrots to a horse, came Marta's thought. I did as she bade me.

The huge animal had whiskers, which tickled my hand as it inhaled my scent. Its own odor was born of wind, musk, and fresh-turned earth. Then it—oh, yes, definitely *he*—breathed on my palm, making it tingle, all the while holding my gaze. For a brief moment it was as if I was looking out those flickering eyes . . . and he was looking out of mine.

Suddenly he tossed his huge head, the tines of an antler just missing my face, and tore off toward the peak of the hill.

I turned toward my cousin, who was smiling.

Most are halfway through their apprenticeship before their Good Friend comes to them. You must need great power.

Good Friend?

Marta slipped an arm around me and turned me back toward the yawning graves. *Later. If we survive this night.*

The singers were finally winding down, finishing the last chorus of the hymn. A night breeze curled past us, full of secrets, waiting for what would come next.

As if the entire sky was waiting . . .

A stench was rising from around me . . . from the gathering. The fear was so thick I thought I'd start gagging. In that moment I recognized my dream. I had seen the bespectacled minister and the Gunnarsson girls, muted in their funeral best. This was the place—changed, maybe, from what things might have been along other paths, but the right place.

There was tingling in the air, the sharpness you sometimes smell after a thunderstorm. Magic often comes like that, overwhelming your senses.

But we weren't producing the magic. It was the *utburd,* and it was starting to build.

I realized the silence was growing, as alive as the magic tingling in my blood. Everyone was waiting for Mr. Elwood to speak, and it clearly was beyond him. Even the ritual couldn't shield him from what had happened in the past day. Did anyone else know the ritual?

Someone *had* to speak.

The White Wanderer sang out, its trill imperative, and I found myself stepping forward.

"Dearest Lord—" I was so tight it was a whisper; that would never do. This time the words came out. "Highest Lord, we, the people gathered here this evening, ask you to take up the souls of one Karl Gunnarsson—" *Now how did I know his Christian name?* "And his grandson . . . his grandson . . . "

"Sten," Nan Gunnarsson McGyver said clearly, naming

the lost spirit that was her son. Her sister Jesse made no sound, but beneath her veils Mrs. Gunnarsson pressed her fingers to her lips.

"Sten," I repeated obediently. "In life, these two were not what they appeared to be. In death, we all wish them the peace they never knew on earth." I swallowed then, and just let something flow out from the back of my skull. "We leave them in your hands, Highest God, for it is not for us to judge others. Help us to forgive, but not to forget, lest our nightmare be born again."

The moonlight that dusted us slowly faded, even as the tension stretched tight as rope. I felt as if a thunderstorm had poured itself inside of me, and was rumbling around, looking for a path to ground. The power didn't flow downward, though . . . it waited.

It was my turn to be terrified, because I didn't know what was happening, or how to stop it—or if I should stop it. My heart was doing its dance once again, and my breath was shorter. Any moment now I'd break out in a cold sweat.

Nan McGyver must have seen my wild expression, because she reached out and took my hand. "Are you—" she started to say. Then she gasped.

I was a waterfall, and the water was rushing out of me in a torrent, so quickly my throat felt parched and my nerves wrung out. When my head finally cleared, I realized that Nan McGyver was pregnant.

She hadn't been the day before. That didn't mean anything . . . folks sometimes get feisty after an emergency, and the previous night had surely been an emergency. But still . . . Nan had felt something, too, just now; that swift intake of breath . . .

An owl hooted, off in the dark woods below. No odd snowy owl, that one—it was a great horned owl, starting to build into his hunting cry. Wind sighed through the

trees and swirled past us, lifting strands of hair. Off in the
distance, I could hear the calling of geese, crying to their
neighbors, keeping order as they flew south.

They were such ordinary sounds, I could have wept.
For the first time, I believed the ghost of Twisted Pines
was finally . . . at rest?

Or dreaming, waiting to be born again?

"People of Cloudcatcher," Marta said softly, her voice
carrying to the edges of the crowd. "Go in peace, and
may the Lord bless you and keep you all."

The Gunnarssons stooped, the young women still sup-
porting their mother; each picked up a handful of cold
dirt and cast it upon the tiny coffin.

I didn't stay to see if they threw any on Gunnarsson's
grave.

It was one of those dreams that sort out the day, and I
was sunk deep within it. All that energy tossed around,
and without any limits—I was lucky I made it to my bed
without Mr. Tregellas carrying me.

Marta had prepared hot milk and some of her precious cocoa to help us sleep. It'd been good enough to
sip slowly, and so my dream-self was remembering
cocoa. I'd asked her about the White Wanderer, as I
called him to myself, and her reply had been characteris-
tically brief.

"Those who use the power properly often attract sympathetic spirits, who choose to stay close and aid our
efforts. Having a Good Friend of the sex opposite to your
own can mean control of great power."

"A familiar?" I'd asked, curling up before the fire. I'd
thought that practitioners didn't have familiars.

"No!" she'd said quickly. Then, calmer, she'd continued, "A witch cannot do *any* magic without a familiar. A

Good Friend merely enhances your perception, makes it easier to draw power—that sort of thing."

At the time I'd been too tired to pursue the topic, but my dreaming self wondered what the White Wanderer got out of the relationship. A creature who had dogged my steps for several years, although I was too tired to tell Marta that.

The business with Nan had seemed more important.

"There was this strange build of power, after I finished speaking," I had begun slowly.

"A big one," Marta had agreed.

"It felt like it was inside me, until Nan touched my hand. Then it drained away . . . but Nan gasped when she touched me." I had looked over at my teacher. "Nan's pregnant."

"Do you see a connection?" Gentle as a morning breeze.

"Maybe," I had whispered, turning my cup in my hands. "She wasn't pregnant yesterday."

The silence had gone on for a while, until Marta finally said, "We've no proof either way. Let it lie."

As I waited for the dream to change once again, Marta asked, "Are the sins of the fathers visited upon the children?"

That hadn't happened last night.

"I don't know. . . . Can we point fingers in this?" my dreaming self asked in turn. "Everyone just acted like no one was responsible. Well, that won't wash. If no one is responsible, then everyone is responsible. You can't turn your back on trouble like that. If you do, something in the life of the village begins to rot, deep inside—not to mention what the powers that be think of you."

"Wizards do not punish. Chastisement is left to the greater powers," the dream Marta murmured. "The town has had its punishment, I'd say—six long years of torment.

Nan has her penitence—her mother suffered many years of abuse. I doubt the woman will be able to live alone again."

"Nan will take care of her," I predicted. "She needs to do what she can to atone."

"Maybe her effort will be accepted." The dream Marta set her cup down on the tray. "I am always grateful it is not my place to judge."

Yes, indeed. And then I'd fallen into a dream I couldn't remember, with old friends I loved and new friends who proved their worth. . . .

"Are you awake, Allie?" came Marta's voice into my dream.

"I am now," I mumbled in reply, burying my face in the pillow. I heard the front door creak, and saw light streaming in. How late was it?

"Get yourself together, we've got company."

"Ummm." But I pulled myself upright and shivered in the cool, bright air. Marta had even set a jug of warm water next to my bed. "I think I'll dress by the fire. Winter's coming."

"I think you'll think twice, with menfolk here."

Oops. Thank heavens for the screen. I couldn't hear voices, so maybe they'd stepped outside. Still, I wasn't planning on taking a chance. I was just starting to have something worth looking at, up on top, and I wasn't in a hurry to share it with anyone.

Marta hadn't said anything about us leaving Twis—Cloudcatcher right away, so I pulled on my wool dress of golden honey and tied a ribbon around my waist. All that tingling last night had done me some good—I had color in my face, and my hair felt clean for the first time in days. I braided it French, high on the head and curving to one side, where it trailed over my right shoulder. Adding my necklace as a final accent, I felt ready for just about anyone.

Except for the folks I saw when I rounded the screen.

"Lord and Lady, darlin', don't you look just fine!" Cory boomed out, laughing at my astonishment. Sitting to his right was Shaw, who tried a smile but ended up staring.

"What are you doing here?" I gasped out.

Still laughing, Cory said, "Your letter, darlin'. You didn't think we'd get it and ignore it, did you?" At my astonished look, Cory glanced over at Marta, who was pouring us morning coffee—though the light told me it was past noon. "What have you been teaching her, Marta?"

"She's taught me a thing or two," Marta observed as she set the kettle back on the hob. "Remember Elizabeth's letter, Allie? How we reacted to it?"

Oh, yes. I nodded vigorously, feeling the fool.

"They had the same reaction to *your* letter. Been pushing their horses to get here before we were eaten by a demon." Marta gave the two an exasperated look of affection. "Sorry to disappoint you, but things are well in hand."

"We're not disappointed," Shaw said abruptly. "We were worried." He was still looking at me.

"We thank you for your worry. Cream?"

Both men nodded as I pulled over the other rocker and sat down in it. I gave Shaw a long look, to see if he was checking out how the necklace was holding up. Uh-uh . . . he was taking me in all of a piece. The thought made me blush. Whatever was he thinking about?

"So, my fellow wise-bards, what had so tainted the famous town of Cloudcatcher?" Cory asked as he reached for his cup of coffee and eyed the small cakes. Elizabeth had clearly outdone herself.

Marta looked over at me. It seemed I was being given the honor of starting our tale.

"The sins of the father," I said softly. Shaw nodded in response, as if my words made sense to him, and suddenly I was very glad that I'd awakened to find him on my hearth.

"Biblical justice?" Cory turned to Marta.

Marta gave me an especially warm look before she said, "It all started with a man who demanded perfection in his family. . . ."

That's the crux of it, I couldn't help but think, basking in the warmth of her gaze. All my father had ever asked of us was to love each other and take care of our neighbors. Family and friends were the most important things we were given, and he hadn't wanted us to lose sight of that.

At the root of all things, life is good. Not everyone is lucky enough to learn that from the cradle.

So I'll just have to do my best to prove it to others.

"Hungry?" I asked, and passed the plate of cakes to the people I loved.